Old Fritz And The New Era

by

L. Muhlbach

Double9 BOOKS

Old Fritz And The New Era

by L. Muhlbach

ISBN: 978-93-76396-35-1

Published by

DOUBLE 9 BOOKS
2/13-B, Ansari Road
Daryaganj, New Delhi – 110002
info@double9books.com
www.double9books.com
Tel. 011-40042856

ABOUT THE AUTHOR

Louise Muhlbach, the pen name of Clara Mundt (1814-1873), was a prolific German author renowned for her historical novels. Born on January 2, 1814, in Neubrandenburg, Mecklenburg-Schwerin, Germany, she married Theodore Mundt, a literary critic and author. This marriage significantly influenced her literary career, providing her with access to intellectual circles and literary discussions of the time. Muhlbach is best known for her novels that vividly depict 18th-century and 19th-century European history. She adeptly blended historical facts with fictionalized personal drama, making her works both engaging and accessible. Some of her most notable novels include "Joseph II and His Court," "Frederick the Great and His Court," "Marie Antoinette and Her Son," and "Old Fritz and the New Era." These novels often focused on significant historical figures and events, bringing them to life through vivid characterizations and intricate plots. Muhlbach's novels are characterized by rich historical detail, though she often took creative liberties with facts for dramatic effect. Her works reflect the intellectual currents of her time, particularly the influences of the Enlightenment and Romanticism. She emphasized themes of individualism, heroism, and the complexities of historical change.

CONTENTS

BOOK I
OLD FRITZ

CHAPTER I
THE LONELY KING

"Well, so let it be!" said the king, sighing, as he rose from his arm-chair; "I must go forth to the strife, and these old limbs must again submit to the fatigue of war. But what matters it? The life of princes is passed in the fulfilment of duties and responsibilities, and rarely is it gladdened with the sunny rays of joy and peace! Let us submit!

"Yes, let us submit!" repeated the king, thoughtfully, slowly pacing his cabinet back and forth, his hands folded upon his staff behind him, and his favorite dog, Alkmene, sleepily following him.

It was a melancholy picture to see this bowed-down old man; his thin, pale face shaded by a worn-out, three-cornered hat, his dirty uniform strewn with snuff; and his meagre legs encased in high-topped, unpolished boots; his only companion a greyhound, old and joyless as his master. Neither the bust of Voltaire, with its beaming, intelligent face, nor those of his friends, Lord-Marshal Keith and the Marquis d'Argens, could win an affectionate glance from the lonely old king. He whom Europe distinguished as the Great Frederick, whom his subjects called their "father and benefactor," whose name was worthy to shine among the brightest stars of heaven, his pale, thin lips just murmured, "Resignation!"

With downcast eyes he paced his cabinet, murmuring, "Let us submit!" He would not look up to those who were gazing down upon him from the walls—to those who were no more. The remembrance of them unnerved him, and filled his heart with grief. The experiences of life, and the ingratitude of men, had left many a scar upon this royal heart, but had never hardened it; it was still overflowing with tender sympathy and cherished memories. To Lord-Marshal Keith, Marquis d'Argens, and Voltaire, Frederick owed the happiest years of his life.

D'Argens, who passionately loved Frederick, had been dead five years; Lord-Marshal Keith one month; and Voltaire was dying! This intelligence the king had received that very morning, from his Paris correspondent, Grimm. It was this that filled his heart with mourning. The face, that smiled so full of intelligence, was perhaps distorted with agony, and those beaming eyes were now closing in death!

Voltaire was dying!

Frederick's thoughts were with the dead and dying—with the past! He recalled, when crown prince at Rheinsberg, how much he had admired, loved, and distinguished Voltaire; how he rejoiced, and how honored he felt, when, as a young king, Voltaire yielded to his request to live with him at Berlin. This intimacy, it is true, did not long continue; the king was forced to recognize, with bitter regret, that the MAN Voltaire was not worthy the love which he bestowed upon the POET. He renounced the MAN, but the poet was still his admiration; and all the perfidy, slander and malice of Voltaire, had never changed Frederick. The remembrance of it had long since faded from his noble heart—only the memory of the poet, of the author of so many hours of the purest enjoyment, remained.

Voltaire was dying!

This great and powerful spirit, who so long a time, in the natural body, had instructed, inspired, and refreshed mankind, would leave that body to rise—whither?

"Immortality, what art thou?" asked the king, aloud, and for the first time raising his eyes with an inquiring glance to the busts of his friends. "I have sought for thee, I have toiled for thee, my whole life long! Neither the researches of the learned, nor the subtleties of philosophy reveal thee to me. Is there any other immortality than fame? Any other eternal life than that which the memory of succeeding generations grants to the dead?" In this tone of thought Frederick recited, audibly, the conclusion of a poem, which he had addressed to D'Alembert:

"I have consecrated my days to philosophy, I admit all the innocent pleasures of life; And knowing that soon my course will finish, I enjoy the present with fear of the future. What is there to fear after death? If the body and the mind suffer the same fate, I shall return and mingle with nature; If a remnant of my intellectual fire escapes death, I will flee to the arms of my God." *[Footnote: Posthumous works, vol. vii., p.88.]*

"And may this soon be granted me!" continued the king; "then I shall be reunited to those loved ones—gone before. I must be content to tarry awhile in this earthly vale of sorrow, and finish the task assigned me by the Great Teacher; therefore, let us submit."

He sighed; pacing to and fro, his steps were arrested at a side-table, where lay a long black velvet box; it contained the flute that his beloved teacher, Quantz, had made for him. Frederick had always kept it in his cabinet as a memento of his lost friend; as this room he had devoted to a temple of Memory—of the past!

"Another of the joys, another of the stars of my life vanished!" murmured the king. "My charming concerts are at an end! Quantz, Brenda, and my glorious Graun are no more. While they are listening to the heavenly choir, I must be content with the miserable, idle chatter of men; the thunder of battle deafening my ears, to which that mad, ambitious Emperor of Austria hopes to force me!"

As the king thus soliloquized, he involuntarily drew from the box the beautiful ebony flute, exquisitely ornamented with silver. A smile played around his delicate mouth. He raised the flute to his lips, and a melancholy strain floated through the stillness—the king's requiem to the dead, his farewell to the dying!

No sound of the outer world penetrated that lonely room. The guard of honor, on duty upon the Sans-Souci terrace, halted suddenly, as the sad music fell upon his ear. The fresh spring breeze swept through the trees, and drove the laden-blossomed elder-bushes tapping against the windowpanes, as if to offer a May-greeting to the lonely king. The servant in waiting stole on tiptoe to the door of the anteroom, listening breathlessly at the key-hole to the moving melody.

Even Alkmene suddenly raised her head as if something unusual were taking place, fixed her great eyes upon her master, jumping upon his knee, and resting her fore-paws lovingly upon his breast.

Frederick neither observed nor felt the movement of his favorite; his thoughts were absent from the present—absent from the earth! They were wandering in the unknown future, with the spirits of those he longed to see again in the Elysian fields.

The wailing music of his flute expressed the lamentation of his soul, and his eyes filled with tears as he raised them to the bust of Voltaire, gazing at it with a look of pain until the melody was finished. Then abruptly turning, half unwillingly, half angrily, he returned the flute to the box, and stole away, covering his face with his hands, as if to hide his emotion from himself.

"Now we have finished with the dead, and the living claim our thoughts," sighed the king. "What an absurd thing is the human heart! It will never grow cold or old; always pretending to a spark of the fire which that shameful fellow Prometheus stole from the gods. What an absurdity! What have I, an old fellow, to do with the fire of Prometheus, when the fire of war will soon rage around me," At this instant the door gently opened. "What do you want, Muller? What do you poke your stupid face in here for?" said the king.

"Pardon me, your majesty," replied the footman, "the Baron von Arnim begs for an audience."

"Bid him enter," commanded the king, sinking back in his old, faded velvet arm-chair. Resting his chin upon his staff, he signed to the baron, who stood bowing upon the threshold, to approach. "Well, Arnim, what is the matter? What papers have you there?"

"Sire," answered Baron von Arnim, "the contract of the French actors, which needs renewing, I have to lay before your majesty; also a paper, received yesterday, from Madame Mara; still another from the singer Conciliani, and a petition from four persons from the opera."

"What stupid stuff!" growled the king, at the same time bestowing a caress upon Alkmene. "Commence with your report. Let us hear what those singers are now asking for."

"The singer Conciliani has addressed a heart-breaking letter to your majesty, and prays for an increase of salary—that it is impossible for him to live upon three thousand dollars."

"Ah! that is what is wanted?" cried the king, furious, and striking his staff upon the floor. "The fellow is mad; When he cannot live upon three thousand, he will not be able to live upon four. I want money for cannon. I cannot spend it for such nonsense. I am surprised, Von Arnim that you repeat such stuff to me."

"Your majesty, it is my duty that I—"

"What! Your duty is not to flatter them. I pay them to give me pleasure, not presumption. Remember, once for all, do not flatter them. Conciliani will get no increase of salary. If he persists, let him go to the mischief! This is my decision.—Proceed! What is Madame Mara begging for?"

"Madame Mara constantly refuses to sing the airs which your majesty commanded to be introduced into the opera of 'Coriolanus.' She has taken the liberty to address you in writing; here is the letter, if your majesty will have the grace to read it."

"By no means, sir, by no means!" cried the king; at the same instant catching the paper with his staff, he slung it like a shot arrow to the farthest corner of the room, to the great amusement of Alkmene, who, with a loud bark, sprang from her master's knee, and with a bound caught the strange bird, and tore it in pieces. "You are right, my pet," said the king, laughing, "you have written my answer with your nose to this arrogant person.

Director, say to Madame Mara that I pay her to sing, not to write. She must sing both airs, or she may find herself at Spandau for her obstinacy, where her husband is, for the same reason. She can reflect, and judge for herself."

The director could scarcely repress a sigh, foreboding the disagreeable scene that he would have to encounter with the proud and passionate singer. Timidly Von Arnim alluded to the four persons from the opera. "Who are these demoiselles, and what do they want?" asked the king.

"Sire," replied the Baron von Arnim, "they are the four persons who personate the role of court ladies and maids of honor to the queens and princesses. They beg your majesty to secure to them a fixed income."

"Indeed! Go to my writing-table and bring paper and pencil; I will dictate a reply to them," said the king. "Now write, Von Arnim: 'To the four court ladies and maids of honor of the opera: You are mistaken in addressing yourselves to me; the affair of your salaries concerns YOUR emperors and kings. To them you must address yourselves.—Adieu.'"

Von Arnim could scarcely repress a smile.

"Now we come to the last affair—the salaries and pensions of the French actors," said the king; "but first tell me the news in Berlin—what report has trumpeted forth in the last few days."

"Your majesty, the latest news in Berlin, which rumor brings home to every hearth-side and every heart is, that your majesty has declared war with Austria on account of the Bavarian succession. Every one rejoices, sire, that you will humble that proud and supercilious house of Austria, and enter the lists for Germany."

"Listen!" answered the king, sternly. "I did not ask you to blow the trumpet of praise, as if your honor, inspector of the theatres, thought yourself upon the stage, and would commence a comedy with the king of lamps. So it is known then that my soldiers will enter the great theatre of war, and that we are about to fight real battles."

"It is known, sire," replied Von Arnim, bowing.

"Then what I am about to communicate to you will not surprise you. The present juncture of affairs leads us to await very grave scenes—we can well dispense with comedy. I withdraw the salaries and pensions of the French actors—your own is included. After you have dismissed the French comedians, you will be entirely at leisure to pursue your love-intrigues.—Farewell!"

"Your majesty," cried the baron, amazed, "has your highness dismissed me?"

"Are you deaf, or have you some of the cotton in your ears which I presented to you at your recall from Copenhagen?" replied the king. *[Footnote: Baron von Arnim was ambassador to Copenhagen until 1754, when he begged for his recall, stating that the damp climate was injurious to his health. The king granted his request, and the baron returned to Berlin. At the first audience with the king, Frederick handed Baron von Arnim a carefully-packed box, saying, "I do not wish the government to lose so valuable a servant; in this box you will find something that will keep you warm." Arnim could scarcely await his return home, to open the box; it contained nothing but cotton. Some days afterward, however, the king increased Von Arnim's income a thousand dollars, and sent him ambassador to Dresden. Von Arnim was afterward director of the Royal Theatre until dismissed in the above manner.]*

"Sire, I have heard all, but I cannot believe it."

"Yes, yes," interrupted the king, "To believe is difficult; you, I presume, never belonged to the pious and believing. Your intrigues would not admit of it; but now you have the leisure to pursue them with a right good-will. You have only to discharge, as I have said, the entire French troupe, and the whole thing is done with.—Adieu, Arnim, may you be prospered!"

Baron von Arnim muttered some incomprehensible words, and retreated from the royal presence. The door had scarcely closed, when it was again opened without ceremony by a young man, wearing a gold-laced dress.

"Your majesty," said he, hastily, in an undertone, "your majesty, she has just gone to the Palace Park, just the same hour she went yesterday."

"Is she alone?" asked the king, rising.

"No, she is not alone; at a little distance the nurse follows with the princely infant!"

The king cast an angry glance at the saucy, laughing face of the young man, who at once assumed a devoted, earnest mien. "Has your majesty any further commands?" asked he, timidly.

"I command you to hold your tongue until you are spoken to!" replied the king, harshly. "You understand spying and hanging about, as you have good ears, a quick eye, and a keen scent. I therefore make use of you, because I need a spy; but, understand that a fellow who allows himself to be used as a spy, is, indeed, a useful subject, but generally a worthless one, and to whom it is becoming to be modest and humble. I am now going to Berlin; you will accompany me. Take off your finery, so that every one may not recognize at once the peacock by his feathers. Go to the taverns and listen to what they say about the war; whether the people are much dissatisfied about it. Keep your great ears wide open, and bring me this evening all the latest news. Go, now, tell my coachman to be ready; in half an hour I shall set off."

The young man slunk away to the door, but stood without opening it, his head down, and his under-lip hanging out.

"What is the matter?" asked the king, in a milder tone, "why do you not go, Kretzschmar?"

"I cannot go away if your majesty is angry with me," muttered the servant, insolently. "I do not wish to hear or see any thing more for you when your majesty abuses me, and considers me such a mean, base fellow. Your majesty first commanded me to listen, and spy, and now that I am obeying, I am despised and scolded for it. I will have nothing more to do with it, and I wish your majesty to leave me a simple footman rather than to accord me such a mean position."

"I did not mean so badly," said the king. "I mean well enough for you; but you must not permit yourself to be arrogant or disrespectful, otherwise you may go to Tophet! You are no common spy, you are listening about a little because you know I am fond of hearing what the people are saying, and what is going on in Berlin and Potsdam. But take care that they know nothing about it, otherwise they will be careful, and you will hear nothing. Now be off, and in order to see a cheerful face on you, I will make you a present." The king drew from his vest-pocket a purse, well filled with small coin, and gave it to the young man, who took it, though he still looked angry and insolent. "Do not let your under-lip hang down so, for I may step upon it," said the king. "Put the money in your pocket, and hurry off to tell old Pfund to harness quickly, or I shall not arrive in time at the park."

"There is no danger, your majesty, for the miss seems very fond of the promenade; she remained two hours in the park yesterday, always walking in the most quiet places, as if she were afraid to meet any one. She sat a whole hour on the iron seat by the Carp Pond, and then she went to the Philosopher's Walk, and skipped about like a young colt."

"You are a very cunning fellow, and know how to use your eyes well," said the king. "Now be off, and order the carriage."

CHAPTER II
WILHELMINE ENKE

The Palace Park was as quiet and deserted as usual. Not a voice, not a sound, disturbed the stillness of those silent walks. For this reason, undoubtedly, a young lady had sought it; at least her whole being expressed satisfaction and delight to wander unobserved through those quiet, shady alleys. She was of slight and elegant proportions, simply attired, without pretension, in a dark dress of some thin silk material. Her black silk mantle was thrown aside upon the stone seat near her, uncovering thus, in solitude, to the sun and birds, her lovely neck and arms, the beauty of which might rival the statues of the ancients. Her face was not of regular beauty, yet it possessed that expression of grace, spirit, and energy, which is oftener a more powerful and more enduring charm than regular beauty. Her large, expressive black eyes possessed a wonderful power, and her red, pouting lips wore a sweet smile; her fine Roman nose lent an air of decision, whilst her high-arched forehead led one to believe that daring, energetic thought lay hidden beneath those clusters of brown curls. She was not in the bloom of youth, but at twenty-five she appeared younger than many beauties at eighteen; and if her form no longer possessed the charm of girlhood, it was attractive from its suppleness and full, beautiful bust.

"Louisa, Louisa, where are you?" cried the young lady, stepping quickly forward toward a side-path, which led from the broad avenue, and at the end of which was a sunny grassplot.

"Here I am, miss; I am coming."

"Miss," murmured the young lady, "how dreadfully it sounds! The blush of shame rises to my face, for it sounds like bitter mockery and contempt, and brings my whole life before me. Yet, I must endure it—and I scarcely wish it were otherwise. Ah, there you are, Louisa, and there is my beautiful boy," she cried, with a glad voice, hastening toward the peasant-woman and bending fondly over her child. "How beautiful and how knowing he looks! It seems as if my little Alexander began to recognize me—he looks so earnest and sensible."

"He knows you, miss," said the nurse, courtesying, "and he knows, like other children, who loves him. Children and dogs know who love them.

The children cry, and the dogs hide themselves when people are around who dislike them."

"Nonsense, Louisa!" laughed the young lady, as she bent to kiss her child—"nonsense! did not my little boy cry when his father took him yesterday? And he loves his child most tenderly, as only a father can."

"Oh, there is another reason for that," said the nurse. "He has just passed his first stupid three months, and he begins to hear and see what passes around him, and it was the first man's face that he had seen. But only look, miss, what a beautiful little dog is coming up the path." It was indeed a lovely greyhound, of the small Italian race, which came bounding joyfully toward them, and as he saw the woman barked loudly.

"Be quiet, Alkmene, be quiet!" cried a loud, commanding voice.

"Oh, Heaven! it is the king!" whispered the young lady, turning pale, and, as if stunned, retreated a few steps.

"Yes, it is really the king," cried the nurse, "and he is coming directly from the grass-plot here."

"Let us go as quickly as possible, Louisa. Come, come," and she hastily threw her mantle around her, drawing the hood over her curly head. She had only proceeded a few steps, when a loud voice bade her to remain—to stand still. She stood as if rooted to the spot, leaning upon her nurse for support; her knees sank under her, and it seemed as if the whole world turned around with her. After the first tumult of anxiety and fear, succeeded an insolent determination, and, forcing herself to calmness, she said: "It is the turning-point of my life; the next few minutes will either crush me or assure my future; let me struggle for the future, then. I will face him who approaches me as my judge." Forcing herself to composure, slowly and with effort she turned toward the king, who, approaching by the side path, had entered the avenue, and now stood before her. But as she encountered the fiery glance of the king's eye, she quailed before it, casting down her own, covered with confusion.

"Who are you?" demanded the king, with stern authority, keeping his eagle eye fixed upon her. Silent and immovable she stood; only the quick, feverish breathing and the heaving bosom told the storm that was raging within.

"Who are you?" repeated the voice, with still more severity—"who permit themselves to use my park as a nursery? What child is that? and who are its parents? They should be of high position at court, who would dare to send their child and nurse to the royal park; and with what joy they must regard the offspring of their conjugal tenderness! Tell me to whom does this child belong?"

Sobbing convulsively, the lady sank, kneeling, with uplifted arms, imploring for mercy. "Sire, annihilate me with your anger, but do not crush me with your scorn!"

"What language do you permit yourself to hold?" asked the king.

"Sire, it is the language of an unhappy, despairing woman, who knows that she stands before that great monarch whose judgment she fears more than that of her God, who sees into her heart, and reads the tortures and reproaches of her conscience; who knows what she suffers, and knows, also, that she is free from self-interest, and every base desire. I believe that God will forgive what I fear your majesty will not."

"You speak presumptuously, and remind me of the theatre princesses who represent a grand scene with a pathetic exit. Let me inform you, I despise comedians—only high tragedy pleases me. Spare yourself the trouble to act before me, but answer me—who are you? Whose child is that?"

"Sire, only God and my king should hear my reply—I beg the favor to send away the nurse and child." The king assented, slightly nodding his head, at the same time bidding her not to kneel to him as to an image.

The lady rose and sought the nurse, who, from fright, had withdrawn into the shrubbery, and stood staring at the king with wide-open eyes. "Go home, Louisa, and put the child to sleep," said she, quickly.

The nurse obeyed promptly, and when alone, the king demanded again, "Who are you? and to whom does the child belong?"

"Your majesty, I am the daughter of your chapel musician Enke, and the child is the son of Prince Frederick William of Prussia," she replied, in a firm and defiant manner.

The king's eyes flashed as he glanced at the bold speaker. "You say so, but who vouches for the truth of it? You permit yourself to use a high name, to give your child an honorable father! What temerity! what presumption! What if I should not believe you, but send you to the house of correction, at Spandau, as a slanderer, as guilty of high-treason, as a sinner and an adulteress?"

"You could not do it, sire—you could not," cried Wilhelmine Enke, "for you would also send there the honor and the name of your successor to the throne."

"What do you mean?" cried the king, furiously.

"I mean, your majesty, that the prince has holy duties toward me. I am the mother of that child!"

"You acknowledge your shame, and you dare confess it to me, your king, that you are the favorite, the kept mistress of the Prince of Prussia, who has already a wife that has borne him children? You do not even seek to deny it, or to excuse yourself?"

"I would try to excuse myself, did I not feel that your majesty would not listen to me."

"What excuse could you offer?—there is none."

"Love is my excuse," cried Wilhelmine, eagerly. "Oh! my ruler and king, do not shake your noble head so unbelievingly; do not look at me so contemptuously. Oh, Father in heaven, I implore Thee to quicken my mind, that my thoughts may become words, and my lips utter that which is burning in my soul! In all these years of my poor, despised, obscure life, how often have I longed for this hour when I might stand before my king, when I might penitently clasp his knees and implore mercy for myself and my children—those poor, nameless beings, whose existence is my accusation, and yet who are the pride and joy of my life! Oh, sire, I will not accuse, to excuse myself; I will not cast the stone at others which they have cast at me. But it is scarcely charitable to judge and condemn a young girl fourteen years of age, who did but obey the command of her parents, and followed the man who was the first and only one that ever whispered the word of love in her ear."

"I have heard that your parents sold their child to shame. Is it true?" cried the king.

"Sire, my father was poor; the scanty income of a chapel musician scarcely sufficed to educate and support four children. The prince promised my father to educate me."

"Bah! The promises of a young man of twenty-five are made without reflection, and rarely ever fulfilled."

"Sire, to the Prince of Prussia I owe all that I know, and all that I am; his promise to my dying father was fully redeemed."

"Indeed, by whom were you taught, and what have you learned?"

"Your majesty, the prince wished, before all, that I should learn to speak French. Madame Girard was my French instructress, and taught me to play the guitar and spinet also."

"Oh, I presume you have learned to jabber a little French and drum a little music," said the king, shrugging his shoulders.

"I beg pardon, sire; I have a tolerable knowledge of history and of geography. I am familiar with the ancient and modern poets. I have read a good French translation of Homer, Horace, and Virgil, with a master. I have studied the history of Brandenburg, of Germany, and of America. We have read the immortal works of Voltaire, of Jean Jacques Rousseau, and of Shakespeare, with many of our modern poets. My instructor has read all these works aloud to me, and he was much pleased when I repeated parts of what he had read to me some days afterward."

"You appear to have had a very learned instructor," remarked the king, sneeringly. "What is his name?"

"His name, sire, is Prince Frederick William of Prussia. Yes, it is he who has taught me—he who has made me an intelligent woman. However young he was when he undertook the task, he has accomplished it with fidelity, firmness, and patience. He loved me, and would make me worthy of him, in heart and mind. I shall ever be grateful to him, and only death can extinguish the love and esteem with which he in spires me."

"Suppose I command you to leave the prince? Suppose I will no longer endure the scandal of this sinful relation?"

"I shall never willingly separate myself from my dear prince and master—from the father of my two children. Your majesty will be obliged to force me from him," answered Wilhelmine, defiantly.

"Oh, that will not be necessary, mademoiselle," cried the king. "There are ways enough. I will make known my wishes to the prince; I will command him to leave you, and have no further communication with you."

"Sire," she answered, gently, "I know that the prince is an obedient and respectful subject and servant to his king in all things, but this command he would not obey."

"He would not dare to brave my commands!"

"He would not brave them, sire. Oh, no; it would be simply impossible to obey them."

"What would hinder him?"

"Love, sire; the respect which he owes to me as the mother of his two children—who has consecrated her love, her honor to him, and of whom no one can say that she has injured the fidelity which she has sworn to the prince—to the man of her first and only love—even with a word or look."

"You mean to say, that I cannot separate you from the prince but by force?"

"Yes, your majesty," cried she, with conscious power, "that is exactly what I mean."

"You will find yourself deceived; you will be made to realize it," said the king, with a menacing tone. "You know nothing of the power that lies in a legitimate marriage, and what rivals legitimate children are, whom one dares acknowledge before God—before the world. Boast not of the love of the prince, but remember that an honorable solitude is the only situation becoming to you. Such connections bear their own curse and punishment with them. Hasten to avoid them. Lastly, I would add, never dare to mingle your impure hands in the affairs of state. I have been obliged to give the order to the state councillors in appointments and grants of office, not to regard the protection and recommendation of a certain high personage, as you are the real protectress and bestower of mercy. Take care, and never let it happen again. You will never venture to play the little Pompadour here, nor anything else but what your dishonor allows you; otherwise you will have to deal with me! You say that you have read Homer; then, doubtless, you remember the story of Penelope, who, from conjugal fidelity, spun and wove, undoing at night what she had woven by day. It is true, you bear little resemblance to this chaste dame, but you might emulate her in spinning and weaving; and if you are not in future retiring, I can easily make a modern Penelope of you, and have you instructed in spinning, for which you will have the best of opportunities in the house of correction at Spandau. Remember this, and never permit yourself to practise protection. I will keep the spinning-wheel and the wool ready for you; that you may count upon. Remember, also, that it is very disagreeable to me that you visit my park, as I like to breathe pure air. Direct your promenade elsewhere, and avoid meeting me in future."

"Your majesty, I—"

"Silence! I have heard sufficient. You have nothing more to say to me. Go, hide your head, that no one may recognize your shame, or the levity of the prince. Go—and, farewell forever!" He motioned impatiently to her to retire, fastening his eyes with a fiery, penetrating glance upon her pale, agitated face, her bowed, humble attitude, and still continued to regard her as she painfully dragged herself down the walk, as if her limbs were giving way under her. Long stood the king gazing after her, resting upon his staff; and as she disappeared at the end of the walk, he still stood there immovable. By degrees his face assumed a milder expression. "He who is free from sin, let him cast the first stone at her," said the king, softened, as he slowly turned down the path which would lead to his carriage, waiting outside the park.

Frederick was lost in thought, and addressed no conversation to the equerry, Von Schwerin, who sat opposite to him. But as they drove through the beautiful street Unten den Linden, at Berlin, Frederick glanced at the equerry, and found that he had fallen asleep, wearied with the long silence and the monotony of the drive. The king spoke to Alkmene, loud and earnestly, until Herr von Schwerin, awakened and startled, glanced at the king, frightened, and trying to discover whether his fearful crime against etiquette would draw upon him the royal censure. Frederick, however, appeared not to notice his fright, and spoke kindly to him: "Did you not tell me, Schwerin, that Count Schmettau would sell his country residence at Charlottenburg?"

"At your service, your majesty, he asked me to purchase it, or find him a purchaser."

"How much is it worth?"

"Sire, Count Schmettau demands eight thousand dollars for it. There is a beautiful park belonging to it, and the house is worthy the name of a castle, so large is it."

"Why do you not buy it, if the count offered it to you?"

The equerry assumed a sad mien, and answered, sighing: "Sire, I should be the happiest of men if I could buy that charming residence, and it would be a real blessing to me if I could enjoy in summer at times the fresh air. My finances unfortunately, do not allow such expenses, as I am not rich, and have a large family."

"Then you are right not to spend money unnecessarily," said the king, quietly. "You can have as much fresh air at Potsdam as can ever enter your mouth, and it costs neither you nor I any thing. Say to Count Schmettau that you have a purchaser for his residence at Charlottenburg."

"Oh, you are really too kind," cried the equerry, in an excitement of joy; "I do not know—"

Here the carriage entered the palace court, and the concluding words were inaudible. Herr von Schwerin alighted quickly to assist the king. "Say to Schmettau to present himself to my treasurer and cabinet councillor, Menkon, tomorrow morning at twelve o'clock, at Sans-Souci."

The king nodded kindly to the equerry, and passed into the Swiss saloon, and farther on into the private rooms which he was accustomed to occupy whenever he remained at the capital. The Swiss saloon was fast filling, not alone with the generals and staff-officers of the Berlin garrison, but with the officers of the regiments from the provinces, who presented themselves at the palace according to the order of the king. The most of them were old and worn out, body and mind. They all looked morose and sorrowful. The great news of the approaching war with Austria had spread through the military. The old laurel-crowned generals of the Seven Years' War were unwilling to go forth to earn new laurels, for which they had lost all ambition. Not one dared betray his secret thoughts to another, or utter a word of disapproval. The king's spies were everywhere, and none could trust himself to converse with his neighbor, as he might prove to be one of them. There reigned an anxious, oppressive silence; the generals and staff-officers exchanged the ordinary greetings. All eyes were turned toward the door through which the king would enter, bowed down, like his generals, with the cares of life, and the burden of old age. The king slowly entered. He was, indeed, an old man, like those he came amongst, and now saluted. An expression of imperishable youth lighted up his pale, sunken face, and his eyes flashed with as much daring and fire as thirty-eight years before, when he had assembled his young officers around him in this very hall, to announce to them that he would march against Austria. How many wars, how many battles, how many illusions, victories, and defeats had the king experienced in these thirty-eight years! How little the youthful, fiery king of that day resembled the weak old man of to-day; how little in common the young King Frederick had with "Alten Fritz." And now in this feeble body dwelt the same courageous spirit. In the course of these years King Frederick II had become Frederick the Great! And great he was to-day, this little old man—great in his intentions and achievements, never heeding his own debility and need of repose. All his thoughts and endeavors concentrated on the welfare of his people and his country—on the greatness and glory of Germany. Those eyes which now glanced over the circle of generals were still flashing as those of the hero-king whose look had disarmed the lurking assassin, and confounded the distinguished savant in the midst of his eloquence, so that he stammered and was silent. He was still Frederick the Great, who, leaning upon his staff, was surrounded by his generals, whom he called to fight for their fatherland, for Germany!

"Gentlemen," said the king, "I have called you together to announce to you that we must go forth to new wars, and, God willing, to new victories. The Emperor of Austria forces me to it, for, against all laws and customs, and against all rights of kingdoms, he thinks to bring German territory into the possession of the house of Hapsburg. Charles Theodore, prince-elector, having no children, has concluded a treaty with the Emperor Joseph, that at his death the electorate of Bavaria will fall to Austria. In consequence thereof an Austrian army has marched into Bavaria, and garrisoned the frontier.—The prince-elector, Duke Charles Theodore, was not authorized to proceed thus, for, though he had no children to succeed him, he had a lawful successor in his brother's son, Duke Charles von Zweibrucken. Electoral Saxony and Mecklenburg have well-founded pretensions, even if Zweibrucken were not existing. All these princes have addressed themselves to me, and requested me to represent them to the emperor and to the imperial government—to protect them in their injured rights. I have first tried kindness and persuasion to bring back Austria from her desire of aggrandizement, but in Vienna they have repulsed every means of peaceable arbitration. I, as one of the rulers of the empire (and as I have reaffirmed the Westphalian treaty through the Hubertsburger treaty), feel bound to preserve the privileges, the rights, the liberty of the German states. I have therefore well reflected, and decided to draw the sword—that what the diplomats have failed to arrange with the pen should be settled with the sword. These are my reasons, gentlemen, which make it my duty to assemble an army; therefore I have called you together." His fiery eyes flashed around the circle, peeling into the thin, withered faces of his generals, and encountering everywhere a grave, earnest mien.

The king repressed with an effort a sigh; then continued, with a mild voice: "My feeble old age does not allow me to travel as in my fiery youth. I shall use a post-carriage, and you, gentlemen, have the liberty to do the same. On the day of battle you will find me mounted; you will follow my example. Until then, farewell!" *[Footnote: The king's words.—See "Prussia, Frederick the Great," vol. iii.]*

"Long live the king!" cried General von Krokow; and all the generals who formerly joined in this cry of the Prussian warrior, now repeated it in weak, trembling tones. Frederick smiled a recognition, bowing on all sides, then turned slowly away, leaning upon his staff.

When once more alone, the youthful expression faded from his eyes, and the gloomy shadows of old age settled down upon his thoughtful brow. "They have all grown old and morose," said he, mildly, "they will not show any more heroism; the fire of ambition is quenched in their souls! A warm stove must warm their old limbs. Oh! it is a pitiful thing to grow old; and still they call themselves the images of God! Poor boasters, who, with a breath of the Almighty, are overturned and bent as a blade of grass in the sand!"

"Your majesty, may I come in?" asked a gentle, happy child's voice.

The king turned hastily toward the door, so softly opened, and there stood a charming little boy, in the uniform of a flag-bearer, with the cap upon his head, and a neat little sword by his side. "Yes, you may enter," nodded the king kindly to him. "You know I sent for you, my little flag-bearer."

CHAPTER III
FREDERICK WILLIAM

The little flag-bearer skipped into the room with graceful vivacity, and sprang, with a merry bound, up to the king, took his hand without ceremony, and pressed it to his lips. Then, raising up his head and shaking back his light-brown curls from his rosy cheeks, his bright-blue eyes sparkling, he looked him full in the face. "Your majesty, you say that you sent for me; but I must tell you that if you had not sent for me I would have come here alone, and begged so long at the door, that you would have let me come in!"

"And what if I would not have let you come in at all?" said the king, smiling.

The little flag-bearer reflected a moment, then answered with a confident air: "Your majesty, I would have forced open the door, thrown myself at your feet, and kissed your hand, saying, 'My king, my dear great-uncle, I must come in to thank you a thousand times for the flag-bearer's commission you have sent me, and for the beautiful uniform.' Then I would see if your majesty had the courage to send me away."

"Let me see, my prince—do you think my courage could fail me upon any occasion?"

"Yes, in bad things," zealously cried the prince, "and it would be bad if you would not let me thank you. I am so happy with the commission and the beautiful uniform which you so graciously sent to me! Tell me, your majesty, do I not look beautifully?" The boy straightened his elegant, slender form, and saluted the king, putting the two fingers of his right hand upon his cap.

"Yes, yes," said Frederick, "you look very nicely, my prince; but it is not enough that you look well—you must behave well. From a flag-bearer in my army I expect very different things than from any common child. Who wears my uniform must prove himself worthy of the honor."

"Your majesty," cried the prince, "I assure you, upon my word of honor, that I have no bad marks when I wear the uniform. Your majesty can ask my tutor. He came with me, and waits in the anteroom to speak with you. He will tell you that I have a good report."

"Very well, we will call him presently," said Frederick, smiling. "Now we will chat a little together. Tell me whether you are very industrious, and if you are learning anything of consequence?"

"Sire, I must learn, even if I had no inclination to; Herr Behnisch leaves me no peace. I have scarcely time to play. I am always learning to read, to write, to cipher, and to work."

"How about the geography and universal history?"

"Oh, your majesty, I wish there were no geography and history in the world, and then I should not have to study so cruelly hard, and I could play more. My mother sent me last week a new battledore and shuttlecock, but I can never learn to play with it. I no sooner begin, than Herr Behnisch calls me to study. To-day I was very cunning—oh, I was so sly! I put it in the great-pocket of my tutor's coat, and he brought it here without knowing it."

"That was very naughty," said the king, a little severely. The prince colored, and, a little frightened, said: "Sire, I could not bring it any other way. I beg pardon, the uniform is so tight, and then—then, I thought it would be dishonoring it to put a shuttlecock in the cartridge-box."

"That was a good thought, prince, and for that I will forgive you the trick upon your tutor. But what will you do with the ball here? Why did you bring it?"

"Oh, I wished to show it to your majesty, it is so beautiful, and then beg you to let me play a little."

"We will see, Fritz," said the king, much pleased. "If you deserve it, that shall be your reward. Tell me the truth, is your tutor satisfied with you?"

"Sire, Herr Behnisch is never really pleased, but he has not scolded me much lately, so I must have been pretty good. One day he wrote 'Bien' under my French exercise. Oh, I was so happy that I spent six groschen of the thaler my father gave me a little while since, and bought two pots of gilly-flowers, one for myself and one for my little brother Henry, that he should have a souvenir of my 'Bien!'"

"That was right," said the king, nodding approvingly. "When you are good, you must always let your friends and relations take part in it; keep the bad only for yourself."

"I will remember that, and I thank you for the kind instruction."

"The studies seem to go very well, but how is it with the behavior? They tell me that the prince is not always polite to his visitors; that he is sometimes very rude, even to the officers who pay their respects to him on his father's account, and on my account, not on his own, for what do they care for such a little snip as he? They go to honor Prince Frederick William of Prussia, though he is only a little flag-bearer. They tell me that you do not appreciate the honor, but that at Easter you behaved very badly."

"Sire, it is true; I cannot deny it—I did behave badly," sighed the little prince.

"What was the matter?" asked the king. "It was not from fear, I hope? I should be very angry at that. Tell me yourself, and tell me the truth."

"Your majesty can depend upon the whole truth. My tutor says that lying is despicable, and that a prince who will one day be a king should be too proud to tell a lie! I will tell you all about it. The officers came to see me at Easter, just as I had put the Easter eggs in the garden, for my little brother and some other boys whom I had invited to hunt for them. I had spent my last six groschen for the eggs, and I anticipated so much pleasure with the hide-and-seek for them. We had just begun, when the officers came."

"That was really unfortunate," said the king, sympathizingly.

"Yes, sire, very disagreeable, and I could not possibly feel kindly. While the officers were talking, I was always wishing they would go. But they stayed and stayed—and when Major von Werder began to make a long speech to me, and I thought there was no end to it, I became impatient and furious—and—"

"Why do you hesitate?" asked the king, looking tenderly at the frank, glowing face of the boy. "What happened?"

"Something dreadful, sire! I could not keep in any longer. The major kept on talking, and looked at me so sharply, I could not help making an abominable face. It is unfortunately true—I ran my tongue out at him—only just a little bit—and I drew it back in an instant; but it was done, and a dreadful scene followed. The major did not say any thing, my tutor was red as fire, and I was thunderstruck!"

"That was excessively rude, my little flag-bearer," cried the king.

The young prince was so ashamed, and was looking down so penitently, that he did not see the smile on Frederick's face, and the affectionate look with which he regarded the youthful sinner.

"Do you know that you deserve to be imprisoned fourteen days, and live on bread and water, for insubordination?"

"I know it now, sire. I beg pardon most humbly," said the prince, with quivering voice and with tears in his eyes. "I have been punished enough, without that. Herr Behnisch would not let me go to the garden again, and

I have never seen the eggs which I spent my last groschen for, nor the boys whom I had invited. I was made to stay in my room all Easter week, learn twenty Latin words every day, and write three pages of German words in good handwriting. It was a hard punishment, but I knew that I deserved it, and did not complain. I only thought that I would do better in future."

"If you thought so, and you have already been punished, we will say no more about it," said the king. "But tell me, how did you get on at Whitsuntide, when the officers paid you their respects again?"

"Your majesty," answered the prince, "it was a great deal better; I behaved tolerably well, except a very little rudeness, which was not so bad after all. *[Footnote: The little prince's own words.—See "Diary of Prince Frederick William," p. 18.]* Herr Behnisch did not punish me; he only said, another time, that I should do better, and not be so taciturn, but greet the gentlemen in a more friendly manner. I must tell you, sire, that when Herr Behnisch does not scold, it is a sure sign that I have behaved pretty well; and this time he did not."

"Fritz, I believe you," said the king, "and you shall have the reward that you asked for—stay here and play a little while. Go, now, and call your tutor; I have a few words to say to him."

The little prince sprang toward the door, but suddenly stopped, embarrassed.

"What is the matter?" asked the king. "Why do you not call your tutor?"

"Sire, I am very much troubled. Herr Behnisch will be very angry when you tell him about the shuttlecock. I beg you not to betray me!"

"Yes, but if you will play before me, you must get the plaything which you say is in his pocket."

"Sire, then I had rather not play," cried the prince.

"On the contrary," said the king, "your punishment shall be, to take the plaything as cleverly out of the pocket as you put it in. If you do it well, then I will say nothing about it; but, if your tutor discovers you, then you must submit to the storm. It lies in your own hands. Whilst I am conversing with the tutor, try your luck. Now call him in."

The prince obeyed thoughtfully, and the tutor entered. He stood near the door, and made the three prescribed bows; then he waited with a submissive air for further commands.

The king was sitting opposite the door, his hands folded upon his staff and his chin resting upon his hands, looking the tutor full in the face. Herr Behnisch bore it calmly; not a feature moved in his angular, wooden face. Near the tutor stood the little prince, his graceful, rosy, childlike face expressing eager expectation.

"Approach!" said the king.

Herr Behnisch stepped forward a little, and remained standing. The prince glided noiselessly after him, keeping his eyes fixed on the tails of the flesh-colored satin coat with which the tutor had adorned himself for this extraordinary occasion. The prince smiled as he saw the pocket open and the feathers of the shuttlecock peeping out. He stretched out his little hand and crooked his fingers to seize it.

"Come nearer! Herr Behnisch," said Frederick, who had observed the movement of the little prince, and who was amused at the thought of keeping him in suspense a little longer.

Herr Behnisch moved forward, and the prince, frightened, remained standing with outstretched hand. He menaced the king with a glance of his bright blue eyes. Frederick caught the look, smiled, and turned to the tutor.

"I believe it is three years since you commenced teaching the little prince?" said the king.

"At your service, your majesty, since 1775."

"A tolerably long time," said the king—"long enough to make a savant of a child of Nature. You have been faithful, and I am satisfied. The copybooks which you sent me according to my orders are satisfactory. I wished to acquaint you myself of my satisfaction, therefore I sent for you."

"Your majesty is very condescending," said the tutor, and his sharp, angular face brightened a little. "I am very happy in the gracious satisfaction of your royal highness. I wished also to make known to you personally my wishes in regard to the petition for the little prince's pocket-money; he should learn the use of money."

"Very well," said the king, nodding to the prince, who stood behind the tutor, holding up triumphantly the shuttle cock.

Yet, the most difficult feat remained to be accomplished. The battledoor was in the very depths of the pocket; only the point of the handle was visible.

"Your majesty," cried Herr Behnisch, who had taken the approving exclamation of "very well" to himself—"your majesty, I am very happy that you have the grace to approve of my petition for pocket-money."

"Yes, I think it well," said the king, "that the prince should learn not to throw money out of the window. I will send you, monthly, for the prince, two Fredericks d'or, and, before you hand it over to him, change it into small pieces, that there may be a great pile of it." *[Footnote: The king's own words—See "Confidential Letters."]*

Just at that moment the prince tried to seize the battle door. Herr Behnisch felt the movement, and was on the point of turning around, when Frederick stopped him, by saying, "I believe it is time to commence a regular course of instruction for the prince. At eight years of age the education of an heir to the throne must progress rapidly, and be regulated by fixed principles. I will write out my instructions, that you may always have them before you."

"It will be my most earnest endeavor to follow your majesty's commands to the letter," answered the tutor, who saw not the little prince, with beaming face, behind him, swinging the battledoor high in the air.

"I am about to enter upon a new war; no one knows if he will ever return from a campaign. I dare not spare my life, when the honor and fame of my house are at stake. Our life and death, however, are in God's hands. Before we risk our lives, we should put every thing in order, and leave nothing undone which it is our duty to do. I will write my instructions to-day, and send them to you. Promise me, upon your word of honor as a man, that you will act upon them, as long as you are tutor to Prince Frederick William, even if I should not return from the campaign."

"I promise it to your majesty," answered the tutor. "I will, in all things, according to the best of my ability, follow your majesty's instructions."

"I believe you; I take you to be an honorable man," said the king. "You will always be mindful of the great responsibility which rests upon you, as you have a prince to educate who will one day govern a kingdom, and upon whom the weal and woe of many millions are dependent. And when those millions of men one day bless the king whom you have educated, a part of the blessing will fall upon you; but when they curse him, so falls the curse likewise upon your guilty head, and you will feel the weight of it, though you may be in your grave! Be mindful of this, and act accordingly. Now you may depart. I will write the instructions immediately, so that you may receive them to-day."

Herr Behnisch bowed, backing out toward the door.

"One thing more," cried the king, motioning with his Staff to the tutor. "In order that you may ever remember our interview, I will present you with a souvenir."

He opened the drawer of his private writing-table, and took out a gold snuff-box, with his initials set in brilliants upon the cover; handing it to Herr Behnisch, he motioned him to retire, and thus spare him the expression of his gratitude.

"Your majesty," stammered Herr Behnisch, with tears in his eyes, "I—"

"You are an honest man, and so long as you remain so, you can count upon me. Adieu!—Now," said the king, as the door closed, "have you recovered the plaything?"

"Here it is, your majesty," shouted the prince, as he held up triumphantly the battledoor and shuttlecock high in the air.

"You deserve your reward, and you shall have it. You can stay with me and play with it here. Take care and not make too much noise, as I wish to write."

The king now seated himself, to draw up the instructions for Herr Behnisch. While he was thus occupied, the little prince tossed his shuttlecock, springing lightly after it on tiptoe to catch it; sometimes he missed it, and then he cast an imploring look at the king, as it fell upon the furniture; but he observed it not. He was absorbed in writing the instructions for the education of the future king, Frederick William III. The physical education of the prince was his first care. He dwelt upon the necessity of the frequent practice of dancing, fencing, and riding, to give suppleness, grace, and a good carriage—through severe training, to make him capable of enduring all hardships. The different branches of study next occupied the king. "It is not sufficient," he wrote, "that the prince should learn the dates of history, to repeat them like a parrot; but he must understand how to compare the events of ancient times with the modern, and discover the causes which produced revolutions, and show that, generally, in the world, virtue is rewarded and vice punished. Later, he can learn a short course of logic, free from all pedantry; then study the orations of Cicero and Demosthenes, and read the tragedies of Racine. When older, he should have some knowledge of the opinions of philosophers, and the different religious sects, without inspiring him with dislike for any one sect. Make it clear to him that we all worship God—only in different ways. It is not necessary that he should have too much respect for the priests who instruct him."

The shuttlecock fell, at this instant, upon the paper upon which the king was writing. Frederick was too much occupied to look up, but he threw it upon the floor, continuing to write:

"The great object will be to awaken a love of learning in the prince, to prevent any approach to pedantry, and not to make the course of instruction too severe at the commencement. We now come to the chief division of education, that which concerns the morals. Neither you nor all the power in the world would be sufficient to alter the character of a child. Education can do nothing further than moderate the violence of the passions. Treat my nephew as the son of a citizen, who has to make his own fortune. Say to him that, when he commits follies, and learns nothing, the whole world will despise him. Let him assume no mannerisms, but bring him up simply. The—"

It was the second time the shuttlecock fell upon the paper. The king looked up censuringly at the prince, who stood speechless with fright and anxiety. The king again threw it upon the floor, and wrote on:

"The prince must be polite toward every one; and if he is rude, he must immediately make an apology. Teach him that all men are equal—that high birth is a myth when not accompanied with merit. Let the prince speak with every one, that he may gain confidence. It is of no consequence if he talks nonsense; every one knows that he is a child. Take care in his education, above all things, that he is self-reliant, and not led by others; his follies, as well as his good qualities, should belong to himself. It is of very great importance to inspire him with a love for military life; and for this reason say to him, and let him hear others say it, that every man who is not a soldier is a miserable fellow, whether noble or not. He must see the soldiers exercise as often as possible; and it would be well to send for five or six cadets, and have them drill before him. Every thing depends upon cultivating a taste for these things. Inspire him with a love of our country, above all things. Let no one speak to him who is not truly patriotic."

Again the shuttlecock fell upon the paper. The little prince uttered a cry of horror, staring at the plaything. This time the king did not receive the interruption so calmly. He looked at the speechless boy as if very angry; then took it and put it in his pocket. Casting another angry glance at the prince, he continued:

"The officers who dine with the prince shall tease and annoy him, that he may become confident."

"Your majesty," said the prince, timidly and imploringly, "I beg pardon a thousand times for being so awkward. I am sorry, and I will be more careful in the future."

The king paid no attention to him, but continued to write: "When you understand him better, try to learn his chief passion to uproot it, but to moderate it." *[Footnote: This entire instruction is an exact translation of the original, which Frederick drew up in French, and which is included in his "Complete Works."]*

"My dear lord and king," began the prince again, "I beg you will have the goodness to give me my shuttlecock."

The king was silent, and with apparent indifference commenced reading over what he had written.

Prince Frederick William waited a long time, but, on receiving no answer, and understanding that his pleading was in vain, his face grew red with anger, and his eyes flashed. With an irritated, determined manner, he stepped close up to the king, his hands resting upon his hips. "Your majesty," cried he, with a menacing tone, "will you give me my ball or not?"

The king now looked up at the prince, who regarded him in an insolent, questioning manner. A smile, mild as the evening sunset, spread over the king's face; he laid his hand lovingly upon the curly head of the prince, saying: "They will never take away Silesia from you. Here is your shuttlecock." He drew it from his pocket, and gave it to the little prince, who seized his hand and pressed it to his lips.

CHAPTER IV
THE DRIVE TO BERLIN

Wilhelmine Enke passed the remainder of the day, after her meeting with the king, in anguish and tears. She recalled all that he had said to her, every word of which pierced her to the heart. Her little daughter of seven years tried in vain to win a smile from her mamma with her gentle caresses. In vain she begged her to sing to her and smile as she was wont to do. The mother, usually so kind and affectionate, would today free herself from her child, and sent her away with quivering lip, and tears in her eyes, to listen to her nurse's stories.

Once alone, Wilhelmine paced her room with rapid strides and folded arms, giving vent to her repressed anguish. She reviewed her life, with all its changing scenes. It was a sad, searching retrospection, but in it she found consolation and excuse for herself. She thought of her childhood; she saw the gloomy dwelling where she had lived with her parents, brothers, and sisters. She recalled the need and the want of those years—the sickly, complaining, but busy mother; the foolish, wicked father, who never ceased his constant exercise of the bugle, except to take repeated draughts of brandy, or scold the children. Then she saw in this joyless dwelling, in which she crouched with her little sisters, a young girl enter, and greet them smilingly. She wore a robe glittering with gold, with transparent wings upon her shoulders. This young girl was Wilhelmine's older sister, Sophie, who had just returned from the Italian opera, where she was employed. She still had on her fairy costume in which she had danced in the opera of "Armida," and had come, with a joyous face, to take leave of her parents, and tell them that a rich Russian count loved her, and wanted to marry her; that in the intervening time he had taken a beautiful apartment for her, where she would remove that very evening. She must bid them farewell, for her future husband was waiting for her in the carriage at the door.

Sophie laughed at her grumbling father, shook hands with her weeping mother, and bent to kiss the children. Wilhelmine, in unspeakable anguish, sprang after her, holding her fast, with both hands clinching the crackling wings. She implored her sister to take her with her, while the tears ran in streams down her cheeks. "You know that I love you," she cried, "and my only pleasure is to see you every day. Take me with you, and I will serve and obey you, and be your waiting-maid." Wilhelmine held the wings firmly with a convulsive grasp, and continued to weep and implore, until Sophie at last laughingly yielded.

"Well, come, if you will be my waiting-maid; no one combs hair as well as you, and your simple style of arranging it suits me better than any other. Come, come, it shall be arranged, you shall be my waiting-maid."

The pictures of memory changed, and Wilhelmine saw herself in the midst of splendor, as the poor little maid, unnoticed by her brilliant sister, the beloved of the Russian Count Matuschko. Joy and pleasure reigned in the beautifully gilded apartment where Sophie lived. She was the queen of the feasts and the balls. Many rich and fine gentlemen came there, and the beautiful Sophie, the dancer, the affianced of Count Matuschko, received their homage. No one observed the sad little waiting-maid, in her dark stuff dress, with her face bound up in black silk, as if she had the toothache. She wore the cast-off morning dresses of her sister, and, at her command, bound her face with the black silk, so that the admirers of her sister should not see, by a fugitive glance, or chance meeting, the budding beauty of the little maid.

Wilhelmine dared not enter the saloon when visitors were there; only when Sophie was alone, or her artistic hand was needed to arrange her sister's beautiful hair, was she permitted to stay with the future countess. Every rough touch was resented with harsh words, blows, and ill-treatment. The smiling fairy of the drawing-room, was the harsh, grim mistress for her sister, whose every mistake was punished with unrelenting severity. In fact, she was made a very slave; and now, after long years, the remembrance of it even cast a gloomy shadow over Wilhelmine's face, and her eyes flashed fire.

Another picture now rose up before her soul, which caused her face to brighten, as a beautiful beaming image presented itself, the image of her first and only love! She lived over again the day when it rose up like a sun before her wondering, admiring gaze, and yet it was a stormy day for her. Sophie was very angry with her, because in crimping her hair she had burnt her cheek, which turned the fairy into a fury. She threw the weak child upon the floor, and beat and stamped upon her.

Suddenly a loud, angry voice commanded her to cease, and a strong, manly arm raised the trembling, weeping girl, and with threatening tone bade Sophie be quiet. Prince Frederick William of Prussia took compassion on the poor child. The sister had not remarked him in her paroxysm of rage; had never heard him enter. He had been a witness to Wilhelmine's ill-treatment. He now defended her, blaming her sister for her cruelty to her, and declared his intention to be her future protector. How handsome he looked; how noble in his anger; how his eyes flashed as he gazed upon her, who knelt at his feet, and kissed them, looking up to him as her rescuer!

"Wilhelmine, come with me; I do not wish you to remain here," said he; "your sister will never forgive you that I have taken your part. Come, I will take you to your parents, and provide for you. You shall be as beautiful and accomplished a lady as your sister, but, Heaven grant, a more generous and noble-hearted one! Come!"

These words, spoken with a gentle, winning voice, had never died away in her heart. Twelve years had passed since then, and they still rang in her ear, in the tumult of the world as well as in the quiet of her lonely room. They had comforted her when the shame of her existence oppressed her; rejoiced her when, with the delight of youth and happiness, she had given herself up to pleasure. She had followed him quietly, devotedly, as a little dog follows his master. He had kept his word; he had had her instructed during three years, and then sent her to Paris, in order to give her the last polish, the tournure of the world, however much it had cost him to separate from her, or might embarrass him, with his scanty means, to afford the increase of expense. A year elapsed and Wilhelmine returned a pleasing lady, familiar with the tone of the great world, and at home in its manners and customs.

The prince had kept his word—that which he had promised her as he took her from her sister's house, to make her a fine, accomplished lady. And when he repeated to her now "Come," could she refuse him—him to whom she owed every thing, whom she loved as her benefactor, her teacher, her friend, and lover? She followed him, and concealed herself for him in the modest little dwelling at Potsdam. For him she lived in solitude, anxiously avoiding to show herself publicly, that the king should never know of her existence, and in his just anger sever the unlawful tie which bound her to the Prince of Prussia. *[Footnote: "Memoirs of the Countess Lichtenau," p. 80.]* Wilhelmine recalled the past seven years of her life, her two children, whom she had borne to the prince, and the joy that filled his heart as he became a father, although his lawful wife had also borne him children. She looked around her small, quiet dwelling, arranged in a modest manner, not as the favorite of the Prince of Prussia, but as an unpretending citizen's wife; she thought how oft with privations, with want even, she had had to combat; how oft the ornaments which the prince had sent her in the rare days of abundance had been taken to the pawnbrokers to provide the necessary wants of herself and children. Her eyes flashed with pride and joy at the thought which she dared to breathe to herself, that not for gold or riches, power or position, had she sold her love, her honor, and her good name.

"It was from pure affinity, from gratitude and affection, that I followed the husband of my heart, although he was a prince," she said.

Still the shame of her existence weighed upon her. The king had commanded her to hide her head so securely that no one might know her shame, or the levity of the prince.

"Go! and let me never see you again!"

Did not this mean that the king would remove her so far that there would not be a possible chance to appear again before him? Was there not hidden in these words a menace, a warning? Would not the king revenge on her the sad experiences of his youth? Perhaps he would punish her for what Doris Ritter had suffered! Doris Ritter! She, too, had loved a crown prince—she, too, had dared to raise her eyes to the future King of Prussia, for which she was cruelly punished, though chaste and pure, and hurled down to the abyss of shame for the crime of loving an heir to the throne. Beaten, insulted, and whipped through the streets, and then sent to the house of correction at Spandau! Oh, poor, unhappy Doris Ritter! Will the king atone to you—will he revenge the friend of his youth on the mistress of his successor? The old King Frederick, weary of life, thinks differently from the young crown prince. He can be as severe as his father, cruel and inexorable as he.

"Doris Ritter! Thy fate haunts me. On the morrow I also may be whipped through the streets, scorned, reviled by the rabble, and then sent to Spandau as a criminal. Did not the king threaten me with the house of correction, with the spinning-wheel, which he would have ready for me?"

At the thought of it a terrible anguish, a nameless despair, seized her. She felt that the spinning-wheel hung over her like the sword of Damocles, ready at the least occasion to fall upon her, and bind her to it. She felt that she could not endure such suspense and torture; she must escape; she must rescue herself from the king's anger.

"But whither, whither! I must fly from here, from his immediate proximity, where a motion of his finger is sufficient to seize me, to cause me to disappear before the prince could have any knowledge of it, before he could know of the danger which threatened me. I must away from Potsdam!"

The prince had arranged a little apartment in Berlin for the winter months, which she exchanged for Potsdam in the spring. This seemed to offer her more security for the moment, for she could fly at the least sign of danger, could even hide herself from the prince, if it were necessary to save him and herself. Away to Berlin, then! That was the only thought she was able to seize upon. Away with her children, before misfortune could reach them!

She sprang to the door, tore it open, rushing to the nurse, upon whose knees the baby slept, near whom her little daughter knelt. With trembling hands she took her boy and pressed him to her heart. "Louisa, we must leave here immediately; it is urgent necessity!" said she, with quivering lip. "Do not say a word about it to any one, but hasten; order quickly a wagon, bargain for the places, and say we must set off at once. The wagon must not be driven to the door, but we will meet it at the Berlin Gate. We will go on foot there, and get in. Quick, Louisa, not a word—it must be!"

The servant did not dare to oppose her mistress, or contradict the orders, but hastened to obey them.

"It is all the old king's fault," said Louisa to herself, as she hurried through the street. "Yes, the king has ordered mistress to Berlin. He looked so furious, the old bear! His eyes flashed so terribly, one might well fear him, and I thanked Heaven when mamselle sent me home from the park. It is coming to a bad end at last; I should have done better not to have taken the place at all. Oh, if we were only away from here; if I only could find a wagon to take us!"

Thanks to the nurse's fears and endeavors, the wagon was soon found, and scarcely an hour had passed before Wilhelmine Enke, her two children and nurse, were hidden under a plain linen-covered wagon, and on their way to Berlin.

The street was unusually animated, as the division of troops which the king had reviewed in Berlin, were marching out of the city to report themselves on the Bavarian frontier. Their first night's quarters were to be in Potsdam, and the last great parade was to take place there on the following morning, before the king commenced his journey. The driver had often to halt at the side of the street to let the troops pass, which with a full band of music, came marching on. At the head of one of the regiments, mounted upon a fiery steed, was a general in brilliant uniform, his breast covered with orders, which glittered in the sun. He was tall and rather corpulent, but appeared to advantage. His carriage was proud and imposing, his face was almost too youthful for a general, and his body too corpulent for the expressive and delicate features. As he passed by the poor, unpretending carriage, where Wilhelmine sat with her children, she heard distinctly his beautiful, sonorous voice, and merry laugh. "Oh Heaven, it is he!—it is he!" she murmured, drawing herself farther back into the wagon with her children. Just then, out of an opening in the linen cover, Louisa peeped, whispering, "Mamselle, it is the Prince of Prussia!"

"Be quiet—for mercy's sake be quiet, Louisa, that we may not be remarked!" said Wilhelmine, gently. "Take the child that he may not scream, for if the prince should hear him he will turn back. He knows the voice of his little son!"

"Yes, he knows the voice of his little son!" muttered the nurse, as she laid the child to her breast. "The little son must stop here on the street, in a miserable wagon, while his noble father rides past, so splendid and glittering with gold, not knowing that his little boy is so near him. Oh, a real trouble and a real heart-sorrow is this!"

"Indeed it is," said Wilhelmine, in her heart, "a real trouble and a real heart-sorrow. How all these men would present arms, and salute my children, if they had been born to a throne instead of obscurity! How they would bow and bend, if I were called Louisa of Hesse-Darmstadt, and the lawful wife of the prince! Did they not also bend and bow before the first wife, Elizabeth von Braunschweig, *[Footnote: The first wife of Prince Frederick William of Prussia was the Princess Elizabeth von Braunschweig, the niece of Frederick the Great. The crown prince was scarcely twenty-one years of age when betrothed to her. After four years they were separated, on account of the improper conduct of the princess, who was banished to Stettin. There she lived until her death in 1840, after seventy-one years of imprisonment. Never during these seventy-one years had the Princess 'Lisbeth', as she was called, dared to leave Stettin. There she was obliged to amuse herself. Her concerts and evening entertainments were celebrated. The second wife of the crown prince of Prussia was Louisa of Hesse-Darmstadt, the mother of Frederick William III. She died in 1805.]* although every one knew of her shameful conduct—knew of her intrigues with lackeys and common soldiers? Do they not now bow before her, although she is banished to Stettin for her infamous conduct, and lives there a prisoner? A fine imprisonment that! The whole town is her prison, and when she appears in public every one stands upon the street to salute the crown princess of Prussia. But when they see me they pass carelessly by, or they look at me with a contemptuous laugh, and fancy themselves miracles of virtue, and free from sin. My only crime is that my father was not a prince, and that I am of low birth. Am I to blame for that—to blame that the man whom I love, and who loves me, cannot marry me and make me his lawful wife?"

"Ho! gee, ho!" cried the driver to his horses. "Get up!" The troops had passed, the highway was now free, and uninterrupted rolled the heavy, creaking wagon into Berlin. Within all was quiet. The two children and nurse were asleep. The driver was half asleep, his head hung shaking about; only now and then he started to give his horses a crack, which the thin, wheezing animals did not heed in the least. Wilhelmine alone slept not; in her soul there was no quiet, no peace. She grumbled at fate, and at mankind. An unspeakable anxiety seized her for the immediate future, and fear of the king's anger. As the sun was setting they reached Berlin, and were entering the town, when the guard, in royal livery, sprang through the gate, calling, in a loud voice, to the wagon, "Halt—halt! Turn out of the way!" Then was heard the call of the sentinel, and the roll of the drums. An equipage, drawn by six black steeds, drove past. A pale, young wife, splendidly attired, leaned back in the carriage, and the little flag-bearer, Prince Frederick William, was by her side; on the seat opposite sat the second son, Prince Louis, and the lord steward. In this beautiful equipage drove the Princess of Prussia; at her side, in a miserable linen-covered wagon, crouching far in the corner, sat Wilhelmine Enke, the rival of the princess; near her, her two children, whose existence condemned her, and stamped her life with dishonor. Like a dream the brilliant apparition rushed past Wilhelmine, and it haunted her through the long streets, to the humble home where she sought a temporary refuge. And when finally alone, in her own room, where no one could spy into her face, nor understand her words, there broke forth from her soul a long-repressed wrong. She stood erect; a proud, insolent smile played around her mouth. "I am his wife, too; I alone am his beloved wife," said she, with a loud, triumphant voice, "and my children are his only truly-beloved children, for they are those of his love. How proudly she drove past me! How beautiful is her pale face, and how interesting her sad smile! She in sunlight, and I in shade! She knows that I am her rival, but she is not mine. No, the Princess of Prussia cannot rival Wilhelmine Enke. I have no fear of her. But the king I have to fear," cried she suddenly, shrinking with terror. In the meeting with the princess she had forgotten him, her anguish, her anxiety for the future. All were forgotten for the moment—to be recalled with renewed terror.

"Thank Heaven," she said, "I have escaped. For the moment I am safe! What will the prince do, when he finds that we have fled from Potsdam? Will he divine where we have gone? Will he come to seek me? If he still loves me—if I am really the happy rival of his wife and every other court lady—yes, then he will come. Then he will know where to find his Wilhelmine. But if it is true, what malicious people have repeated to me, with feigned sympathy, that the prince loves another—that he has withdrawn his love from me, is indifferent and cold—then he will not seek me; then I shall remain here alone!—alone, with my children, this long, fearful night! What, then, if I am alone? No, oh, no! I will not believe that I am forsaken. These are wicked thoughts which haunt me—only the agitation of this dreadful day, which imagination has overwrought. Rise up and be strong! Go to thy children," said she, "and read in their eyes that he can never leave thee!"

Forcing herself to composure, she sought her children; found Louisa humming and singing her little boy to sleep, and her daughter nodding, on a low stool at her feet.

"Come, my child, I will put you to sleep," said the mother, lifting her in her arms. "Your mother will make your bed softly. When you sleep and speak with the angels, intercede for us all."

With tender care she undressed her and bore her gently in her arms to her bed, and, kneeling before it, breathed a prayer over her sleeping child; then bent over the cradle of her son, blessing and kissing him. "Sleep my boy, sleep. I know not that I shall ever see thy beautiful eyes open again—whether I shall ever again press thee to my heart. Who can tell if they may not come this very night to remove me to prison—to punish me for you, my children, my beloved children!—Be calm, be calm! I shall remain here until morning, at least," added she.

She turned to the nurse, who, with anxious face and folded hands, stood at the farthest corner of the room. "Go, now, Louisa—go, and take something to eat. You must be hungry and tired. Buy at the next store what you need; but do not stop to talk with any one or repeat my name. Then return quickly, and take care of the children. Do not trouble yourself about me—I need nothing more."

"But you must eat something, mamselle; you must have some supper!"

Wilhelmine shook her head, refusing, and returned quickly to her own room.

CHAPTER V
THE OATH OF FIDELITY

Long after nightfall the nurse heard her mistress rapidly pacing her room, and talking aloud to herself. Soon, however, Sleep spread her soothing wings over Louisa, and she heard no more the rapid steps and loud talking of her mistress, nor the rolling of a carriage which stopped before the door, and the quick, vigorous steps of a man mounting the stairs. But Wilhelmine heard them. Breathless she stood, listening to the approaching footsteps, for she felt that they had to decide her future—the weal and woe of her children! Was it he, her beloved, the father of her children? or was it the king's bailiff who had followed her, and came to seize her?

Nearer they came; the bell was hastily, violently rung. Wilhelmine uttered a cry of delight. She recognized the voice, the commanding manner, and rushed through the anteroom to open the door. The prince encircled her in his arms, pressed her to his beating heart, and, lifting her up, bore her into the room.

"Why did you leave Potsdam, Wilhelmine? Tell me quickly, why did you do it?" asked the prince, tenderly kissing her, as he sat her upon the divan at his side. Overcome with her tears, she could not answer. "What mean these tears? Has any one dared to wound your feelings or injure you?"

"Yes, Frederick, and he who injures me hazards nothing—for it is the king! I met him in the park at Potsdam this morning. He has crushed me with his scorn and anger. He has threatened me with a fearful punishment—no less than the house of correction at Spandau! He has told me that the spinning-wheel is in readiness for me if I excite his further contempt."

A cry of fury escaped the prince. Springing up, he paced the room with rapid strides. Wilhelmine remained upon the divan, but her tears did not prevent her following the prince with a searching glance—to read his face, pale with rage. "I must bear it," he cried, beating his forehead. "I cannot protect those that I love!"

A ray of joy lighted up Wilhelmine's face as she listened, but it disappeared with the tears which flowed afresh. "I am a poor, unfortunate child," she sobbed, "whom every one despises, and fears not to injure, who has no one to counsel or protect her, and who is lost if God does not have compassion upon her."

The prince rushed to her, seizing both hands. "Wilhelmine, do not drive me mad with sorrow," he cried, trembling with excitement and anger. "Is it my fault that I cannot protect you against him? Have I not defended you from all the rest of the world? Have I ever allowed any one to treat you with contempt?"

"I have never given occasion for it, dearest. I have studiously avoided all men, to escape their contempt and scorn. Shame is hard to bear, fearfully hard. I felt it today, as his beautiful eyes flashed upon me with contempt, as his haughty language crushed me to the earth. This is the yoke, Frederick William, that I and my children must bear to our graves!"

"No, Wilhelmine, not as long as we live—only while he lives! Wait, only wait; let me rise from want and slavery; let the day come which makes me free—which exalts me: my first act will be to lift the yoke from you and our children, and woe to those—a thousand times woe to those who would hold it fast! Only be patient, Wilhelmine, submit, and bear with me the hard and distressing present. Tell me, my child, my loved one, why did you leave Potsdam so suddenly?"

"I was afraid, Frederick. A kind of madness seized me at the thought of the king's bailiffs carrying me off to Spandau; a nameless anxiety confused my mind, and I only realized that I must escape—that I must conceal myself. I felt in greater security here than at Potsdam for the night."

"And you fled without leaving me any sign or message to tell me whither you had gone! Oh, Wilhelmine, what if I had not divined your hiding-place, and had awaited at Potsdam in painful anxiety?"

"Then I should have fled from here at daybreak, leaving my children, and in some quiet, obscure retreat have concealed myself from every eye—even your own."

"Would you have hidden yourself from me?" cried the prince, encircling her in his arms, and pressing her to his heart.

"Yes, Frederick, when your heart did not prompt you where to find me, then it would have been a proof that you were indifferent to me. When I cannot lean upon your love, then there is no longer any protection or abiding-place for me in the world, and the grave will be my refuge."

"But you see my heart revealed you to me, and I am here," said the prince, smiling.

"Yes, Heaven be praised, you have come to me," she cried, exultingly, throwing her arms about his neck, and kissing him passionately. "You are here; I no longer dread the old king's anger, and his fearful words fall as spent arrows at my feet. You are here, king of my heart; now I have only one thing to dread."

"What is that, Wilhelmine?"

She bent close to his ear, and whispered: "I fear that you are untrue to me; that there is some ground for truth in those anonymous letters, which declare that you would discard me and my children also, for you love another—not one other, but many."

"Jealousy, again jealous!" the prince sighed.

"Oh, no," said she, tenderly, "I only repeat what is daily written me."

"Why do you read it?" cried the prince, vehemently. "Why do you quaff the poison which wicked, base men offer you? Why do you not throw such letters into the fire, as I do when they slander you to me?"

"Because you know, Frederick," she answered, proudly and earnestly—"you must know that that which they write against me is slander and falsehood. My life lies open before you; every year, every day, is like an unsullied page, upon which but one name stands inscribed—Frederick William—not Prince Frederick William. What does it benefit me that you are a prince? If you were not a prince, I should not be despised, my children would not be nameless, without fortune, and without justice. No, were you not a prince, I should not have felt ashamed and grief-stricken, with downcast eyes, before the lady who drove past in her splendid carriage, while I was humbly seated in a miserable wagon. No, were not my beloved a prince, he could have made me his wife, could have given me his name, and I should to-day be at his side with my children. Then, what benefit is it to me that you are a prince? I love you not that you are one, but notwithstanding it. And if I love you in spite of all this, you must know that my affection is ever-enduring and ever-faithful—that I can never forget you, never abandon you."

"And do you believe, Wilhelmine, that I could ever abandon or forsake you? Is it not the same with me?"

She shook her head, sadly answering: "No, Frederick, it is unfortunately not the same. You have loved me, and perhaps you love me still, but with that gentle warmth which does not hinder glowing flames to kindle near it, and with their passionate fire overpower the slight warmth."

"It may be so for the moment, I grant it," the prince answered, thoughtfully; "but the quick, blazing fire soon consumes itself, leaving only a heap of ashes; then one turns to the gentle warmth with inward comfort, and rejoices in its quiet happiness."

"You confess loving another?" said Wilhelmine, sorrowfully.

"No, I do not grant that," the prince cried; "but you are a sensible, clever woman, and you know my heart is easily excited. It is only the meteoric light of the ignis fatuus, soon extinguished. Let it dance and flicker, but remember that the only warmth which cheers and brightens my heart is your love and friendship. You are my first and only love, and you will be my last—that I swear to you, and upon it you can rely. Every thing is uncertain and wavering in life. They have ruined me, lacerated my heart, and there is nothing more in the world which I honor. Only sycophants and hypocrites surround me, who speculate upon my future greatness; or spies, who would make their fortune today, and therefore spy and hang about me, in order to be paid by the reigning king, and who slander me in order to be favorites of his. No one at court loves me, not even my wife. How should she? She is well aware that I married her only at the command of my royal uncle, and she accepted me almost with detestation, for they had related to her the unhappiness of my first marriage, and the happiness of my first love! She has learned the story of my first wife, Elizabeth von Braunschweig, and that of my only love, Wilhelmine Enke! She obeyed, like myself, the stern command of another, and we were married, as all princes and princesses are, and we have had children, as they do. We lead the life of a political marriage, but the heart is unwed. We bow before necessity and duty, and, believe me, those are the only household gods in the families of princes. Happy the man who, besides these stern divinities, possesses a little secret temple, in which he can erect an altar to true love and friendship, and where he can enjoy a hidden happiness. This I owe to you, Wilhelmine; you are the only one in whom I have confidence, for you have proved to me that you love me without self-interest and without ambition. You have said it, and it is true, you love me, notwithstanding I am a prince. I confess to you, there are many lovely women of the court who are your rivals, and who would try to separate us in order to attract me to themselves. They are beautiful and seductive, and I am young and passionate; and if these lovely women have no respect for my dignity as a married man, how then should I have it, who married for duty, not for love? But there is one whom I respect for disinterestedness and fidelity! Do you not know who alone is disinterested and faithful?—who has never seen in me the prince, the future king—only the beloved one, the man—one who has never wavered, never counted the cost?—that you are, Wilhelmine Enke, therefore we are inseparable, and you have not to fear that I can ever forsake you, even if I am sometimes entangled in the magic nets of other beautiful women. The chains which bind us together cannot be torn asunder, for a wonderful secret power has consecrated them with the magic of true love—of heart-felt friendship."

"Still they are chains, dearest," sighed Wilhelmine. "You have named them thus! The chains will at last oppress you, and you will forget the magic power which binds you, and will be free. No holy bond, no oath, no marriage tie—nothing but your love binds you to me. I rejoice in it, and so long as you do not forsake me, I am conscious that it is your own free choice and not force which retains you."

"I will give you an outward sign of our bond of union," cried the prince. "I will do it today, as a twofold danger hangs over us—the king menaces you, and war menaces me."

"Is it then true, do you go with the king to the field?" groaned Wilhelmine.

"Do you wish me to remain?" cried the prince, his eyes flashing. "Shall I here seek pleasure, with effeminate good nature, while the king, in spite of his age, exposes himself to all the fatigue of a campaign and the danger of battle? This war of the Bavarian succession is unfortunate, and no one knows whether the German empire will derive any important advantage from our sustaining by force of arms a little duchy. It is a question whether it would not be better to abolish the little principalities, in order to strengthen the greater German powers. The king will support Bavaria, because he envies Austria its possession, and, as he has decided upon war, it becomes his crown prince to yield to his decision without murmuring. Therefore, Wilhelmine, I will today witness to you the oath of fidelity. If God calls me to Him, if I fall in battle, this oath will be your legacy. I have nothing else to leave you, thanks to the parsimony of my noble uncle. I am a very poor crown prince, with many debts and little money, and not in a condition to reward your love and fidelity otherwise than with promises and hopes, and letters of credit for the future. Such a bill of exchange I will write for you—a legacy for my dear Wilhelmine. Give me pen and paper."

Wilhelmine hastened to her writing table and brought him paper with writing materials. "There, my Frederick," said she, "there is every thing necessary—only the ink, I fear, may be dried."

The prince shook his head, smiling. "Such a lover's oath as I will transcribe for you can be written with no common ink. See, here is my ink!"

The prince had suddenly made a slight incision in his arm, and, as the blood gushed out, he dipped his pen in it, and wrote; then handed it to Wilhelmine, saying: "Read it here, in the presence of God and ourselves."

Wilhelmine pressed it to her lips, and read, with a solemn voice: "'By my word of honor as a prince, I will never forsake you, and only death shall separate you from me.—Prince Frederick William of Prussia.'" *[Footnote: "Memoires of the Countess Lichtenau." p. 120.]*

"By my word of honor as a prince, I will never forsake you, and only death shall separate me from you," repeated the prince, as he bent over Wilhelmine, lifting her in his arms and placing her upon his knee. "Take the paper and guard it carefully," said he. "When I die, and you have closed my eyes, as I trust you will, give this paper to my son and successor, for it is my legacy to you, and I hope my son will honor it and recognize in you the wife of my heart, and care for you."

"Oh! speak not of dying, Frederick," cried Wilhelmine, embracing him tenderly; "may they condemn me, and imprison me as a criminal, when you are no more! What matters it to me what befalls me, when I no longer possess you, my beloved one, my master? Not on that account will I preserve the precious paper, but for the love which it has given me, and of which it will one day be a proof to my children. This paper is my justification and my excuse, my certificate and my declaration of honor. I thank you for it, for it is the most beautiful present that I have ever received."

"But will you make me no return, Wilhelmine? Will you not swear to me, as I have sworn to you?"

She took the knife from the table without answering, and pointing it to her left arm—

"Oh, not there!" cried the prince, as he sought to stay her hand. "Do not injure your beautiful arm, it would be a sacrilege."

Wilhelmine freed herself from him, as he sought to hold her fast, and in the mutual struggle the knife sank deep into her left hand, the blood gushing out. *[Footnote: The scar of this wound remained her whole life, as Wilhelmine relates in her memoirs.—See "Memoires of the Countess Lichtenau."]*

"Oh, what have you done?" cried the prince, terrified; "You are wounded!"

He seized her hand and drew the knife from the wound, screaming with terror as a clear stream of blood flowed over his own. "A physician! Send quickly for a physician," cried he. "Where are my servants?"

Wilhelmine closed his lips at this instant with a kiss, and forced herself to smile in spite of the pain which the wound caused her. "Dearest, it is nothing," she cried. "I have only prepared a great inkstand—let me write!"

She dipped her pen in the blood, which continued to flow, and wrote quickly a few lines, handing them to the prince.

"Read aloud what you have written. I will hear from your own mouth your oath. You shall write it upon my heart with your lips."

Wilhelmine read: "By my love, by the heads of my two children, I swear that I will never forsake you—that I will be faithful to you unto death, and will never separate myself from you; that my friendship and love will endure beyond the grave; that I will ever be contented and happy so long as I may call myself your Wilhelmine Enke."

"I accept your oath, dearest," said the prince, pressing her to his heart. "This paper is one of my choicest jewels, and I will never separate myself from it. We have now sealed our love and fidelity with our blood, and I hope that you will never doubt me again. Remember this hour!"

"I will," she earnestly promised, "and I swear to you never to torment and torture you again with my jealousy. I shall always know, and shall hold fast to it, that you will return to me."

A violent knocking on the house door interrupted the stillness of the night. A voice in loud, commanding tones called to the night-watch.

"Here I am!" answered the porter. "Who calls me? And what is the matter?"

"Open the door," commanded the voice again.

"It is our house," whispered Wilhelmine, who had softly opened the window. "It is so dark, I can only see a black shadow before the door."

"Do you belong to the house?" asked the night-watch. "I dare let no one in who does not belong there."

"Lift up your lantern, and look at my livery. It is at the king's order!"

Wilhelmine withdrew from the window, and hastened to the prince, who had retired to the back part of the room.

"It is Kretzschmar, the king's footman and spy," she whispered. "Hide yourself, that he does not discover you. Go there to the children."

"No, Wilhelmine, I will remain here. I—"

Wilhelmine pressed her hand upon his mouth, and forced him into the side-room, bolting the door.

"Now," said she, "I will meet my fate with courage; whatever may come, it shall find me firm and composed. My children are safe, for their father is with them."

She took the light, and hastened into the anteroom, which was resounding with the loud ringing.

"Who is there?" she cried. "Who rings so late at night?"

"In the name of the king, open!"

Wilhelmine shoved back the bolt, opening the door.

"Come in," she said, "and tell me who you are."

"I think you recognize me," said Kretzschmar, with an impudent smile. "You have often seen me at Potsdam in company with the king. I saw you this morning as the king did you the honor to speak with you, and I believe did not compliment you."

"Did his majesty send you here to say this to me?"

"No, not exactly that," answered he, smiling; "but, as you asked me, I was obliged to answer. I have come here with all speed as courier from Potsdam. I hope you will at least give me a good trinkgeld. I was commanded to deliver into your own hands this paper, for which I must have a receipt." He drew from his breast pocket a large sealed document, which he handed to Wilhelmine. "Here is the receipt all ready, with the pencil; you have only to sign your name, and the business is finished." He stretched himself with an air of the greatest ease upon the cane chair, near the door.

Wilhelmine colored with anger at the free conduct of the royal footman, and hastened to sign the receipt to rid herself of the messenger, and to read the letter.

"What will you give me for trinkgeld, Mamselle Enke?" asked the footman, as she gave him the receipt.

"Your own rudeness and insult," answered Wilhelmine proudly, as she turned, without saluting him, to the sitting-room.

Kretzschmar laughed aloud. "She will play the great and proud lady," said he. "She will get over that when in prison. The letter is without doubt an order of arrest, for when the king flashes and thunders as he did this morning, he usually strikes. I hope it will agree with you." He slowly left the anteroom, and descended the stairs to mount his horse, which he had bound to a tree.

Wilhelmine hastened in the mean time to the prince. "Here is the letter addressed to me," said she, handing him the sealed envelope. "I beg you to open it; courage fails me, everything trembles and swims before my eyes. Read it aloud—I will receive my sentence from your lips."

The prince exclaimed, breaking the seal: "It is the handwriting of the secret cabinet secretary, Menken, and the message comes immediately from the king's cabinet. Now, Wilhelmine, do not tremble; lean your head upon me, and let us read."

"'In the name of his majesty, Wilhelmine Enke is commanded, under penalty of severe punishment, not to leave her room or her dwelling, until the king shall permit her, and send some one to take her and all that belongs to her to her place of destination. She shall receive this order with patience and humility, and consider her apartment as a prison, which she shall not leave under severe penalty, nor allow any one to enter it. Whoever may be with her at the time of receiving the order, who do not belong there, shall speedily absent themselves, and if the same ride or drive to Potsdam, they shall immediately take a message to his royal highness the Prince of Prussia, and announce to him that his majesty expects him at Sans-Souci at ten o'clock tomorrow morning. The Minister von Herzberg will be in waiting to confer with the prince. The above is communicated to Wilhelmine Enke for her strict observance, and she will act accordingly.'"

A long silence followed the reading of this letter. Both looked down, thoughtfully recalling the contents.

"A prisoner," murmured Wilhelmine, "a prisoner in my own house."

"And for me the peremptory command to leave immediately for Potsdam, in order to be at Sans-Souci early in the morning. What can the king mean?"

"He will announce to you my imprisonment, my exile," sighed Wilhelmine.

The crown prince shook his head. "No," said he, "I do not believe it. If the king would send you to prison, he would not make such preparation; he would not commence with the house arrest, as if you were an officer, who had been guilty of some slight insubordination, but he would act with decision, as is his wont. He would at once have sent you to Spandau or some other prison, and left it to me to have taken further steps. No—the more I think it over, the more evident it is to me that the king is not really angry; he will only torment us a little, as it pleases his teasing spirit. The chief thing now is to obey, and give him no further occasion for anger. You must be very careful not to leave your apartment, or to allow any one to enter it. I shall start without delay for Potsdam. There are spies posted as well for you as myself; our steps are watched, and an exact account of them given. I must away quickly."

"Must you leave me a prisoner? Oh, how hard and cruel life is!"

"Yes, it is, indeed, Wilhelmine. But I must also humbly submit and obey. Is not life hard for me, and yet I am crown prince, the heir to the throne! I shall be reprimanded and scolded like a footman. I must obey as a slave, and am not permitted to act according to my will. I am only a mere peg in the great machine which he directs, and the—"

"Hush! for mercy's sake be quiet! What if some one should hear you? You know not if the spies may not be at the door."

"True," said the prince, bitterly. "I do not know! The nurse even, who suckles our child, may be a paid spy. The owner of this house may be in the king's service, and creep to the door to listen. Therefore it is necessary, above all things, that we act according to the king's commands. Farewell, Wilhelmine, I must set off at once. Kretzschmar is no doubt at the corner of the street to see whether I, as an obedient servant of his master, leave here. If I do it, he will take the news to Sans-Souci, and perhaps the king will be contented. Farewell, I go at once to the palace, to start from there for Potsdam."

"Farewell, my beloved one! May God in heaven and the king upon earth be merciful to us! I will force myself to composure and humility. What I suffer is for you! This shall be my consolation. If we never meet again, Frederick William, I know you will not forget how much I have loved you!"

CHAPTER VI
THE PARADE

Since early morning a gay, warlike life had reigned at Potsdam and the neighborhood of Sans-Souci. From every side splendid regiments approached, with proud and stately bearing, in glittering uniforms, to take in perfect order the places assigned to them. With flying banners, drums beating, and shrill blasts of trumpets, they came marching on to the great parade—the last, for the king was about to leave for the field. Thousands of spectators poured forth, notwithstanding the early hour, from Potsdam; and from Berlin even they came in crowds, to take a last look of the soldiers—of their king, who was still the hero at sixty-nine—the "Alto Fritz," whom they adored—though they felt the rigor of his government. It was a magnificent spectacle, indeed—this immense square, filled with regiments, their helmets, swords, and gold embroideries glittering in the May sun. Officers, mounted on richly caparisoned steeds, drew up in the centre, or galloped along the front of the lines, censuring with a thundering invective any deviation or irregularity. In the rear of the troops stood the equipages of the distinguished spectators on the one side, while on the other the people in compact masses swayed to and fro, gayly passing judgment upon the different regiments and their generals. The people—that means all those who were not rich enough to have a carriage, or sufficiently distinguished to claim a place upon the tribune reserved for noble ladies and gentlemen—here they stood, the educated and uneducated, shoemaker and tailor, savant and artist—a motley mixture! Two gentlemen of the high citizen class apparently were among the crowd. They were dressed in the favorite style, which, since the "Sorrows of Werther" had appeared, was the fashion—tight-fitting boots, reaching to the knee, with yellow tops; white breeches, over which fell the long-bodied green vest; a gray frock with long pointed tails and large metal buttons, well-powdered cue, tied with little ribbons, surmounted with a low, wide-brimmed hat. Only one of the gentlemen wore the gray frock, according to the faultless Werther costume, a young man of scarcely thirty years, of fine figure, and proud bearing; a face expressive and sympathetic, reminding one of the glorious portraits of men which antiquity has bequeathed to us. It seemed like the head of a god descended to earth, noble in every feature, full of grace and beauty; the slightly Roman nose well marked yet delicate; the broad, thoughtful brow; the cheeks flushed with the hue of youth and power; the well-defined chin and red lips, expressive of goodness, benevolence, roguery, and haughtiness; large, expressive eyes, flashing with the fire which the gods had enkindled. His companion was perhaps eight years younger, less well-proportioned, still of graceful appearance, in his youthful freshness, with frank, cheerful mien, clever, good-natured, sparkling eyes, and red, pouting lips, which never liked to cease chatting.

"See, Wolff! I beg," said the young man, "see that old waddling duck, Mollendorf. I know the old fellow, he is from Gotha; he imagines himself of the greatest importance, and thinks Prussia begets fame and honor from his grace. He trumpets forth his own glories at a dinner, and abuses his king. He makes Frederick the Great an insignificant little being, that he may look over him."

"Unimportant men always do that," answered the other. "They would make great men small, and think by placing themselves on high pedestals they become great. The clown striding through the crowd on his stilts may even look over an emperor. But fortunately there comes a time when the dear clown must come down from his stilts, and then it is clear to others, if not to himself, what little, earth-born snips the men of yesterday are."

"Only look, Wolff, there is just such a moment coming to that stiltsman Mollendorf. How the great man stoops, and how small he looks on his gray horse, for a greater springs past! Look at him well, Wolff—we shall dine with him, and he does not like to be stared at in the face."

"Is that, then, Prince Henry passing?" asked Wolff, with animation; "That little general, who just galloped into the circle with his suite, is that the king's brother?"

"Yes, that is just his misfortune that he is the king's brother," answered a deep, sonorous voice behind them.

Turning, they beheld a young, elegantly dressed man, in the light gray frock and gold-bordered, three-cornered hat, and a Spanish cane, with an ivory handle.

"What did you remark, sir?" asked Herr Wolff; his great, brown eyes flashing over the pale, intellectual face of the other, so that he was quite confused, yet, as if enchanted, could not turn away. "What did you remark, sir?" asked again Herr Wolff.

"I believe," stammered the other, "that I said it was the misfortune of the prince that he was the brother only, as he was worthy of being mentioned for himself; but I beg, sir, be a little indulgent, and do not pry into my very soul with your godlike eyes. It will craze me, and I shall run through the streets of Berlin, crying that the Apollo-Belvedere has arrived at Potsdam, and invite all the poets and authors to come and worship him."

"I believe you are right," cried the youngest of the two gentlemen, laughing. "I believe myself it is the Apollo-Belvedere."

"Be still, my dear sir, hush, and preserve our incognito," interrupted his companion.

"But I cannot help it, Wolff. Am I to blame that this clever fellow sees through your mask, and discovers the divine spark which hides itself under a gray Werther costume?"

"I pray, sir, grant my request, and respect our incognito," begged the other, gently but firmly.

"Well, well, you shall have your way," laughed the other, good-naturedly, and turning to the pale young man, who still kept his eyes fixed on Herr Wolff in a sort of ecstacy, he said: "Let the authors and poets stay in Berlin; we will persuade the disguised Apollo to meet them there, and read them a lecture, for among the Berlin poets and critics there are wicked heretics, who, if the Deity Himself wrote tragedies and verses, would find some fault to object to."

"Pray tell me, sir, do you think Prince Henry a great man?"

"Did not the king call him so in his 'History of the Seven Years' War?'" said the stranger. "Did he not publicly, in the presence of all his generals, say, 'that Prince Henry was the only general who had not made a mistake during the whole war?'"

"Do you believe the king will say that of the prince just riding in with his suite, after the present war?" asked the young man, with earnestness.

"You mean the Prince of Prussia," answered the other, shaking his head. "There are men who call this prince the 'hope of Prussia,' and regard him as a new Aurora in the clouded sky."

"And you, sir, do you regard him so?" cried Herr Wolff.

"Do you mean that the Prince of Prussia will usher in a brighter day for Germany?"

"No," answered the other. "I believe that day expires with Frederick the Great, and that a long night of darkness will succeed."

"Why do you think so?"

"Because it is the course of nature that darkness succeeds light. Look at the prince, gentlemen—the divine light of genius is not stamped upon his brow, as formerly, and care will be taken that it is soon extinguished altogether."

"Who will take care?"

"Those who are the enemies of light, civilization, and freedom."

"Who are they?" asked Herr Wolff.

The other smiled, and answered: "Sir, so far as I, in all humility, call myself a scholar, I also owe to the god Apollo obedience, and must answer him, though it may endanger me. I answer, then, the enemies of light and civilization are the disguised Jesuits."

"Oh, it is easy to perceive that you do not belong to them, or you would not thus characterize them, and—"

A mighty flourish of drums, and shrill blasts of horns and trumpets, drowned the youth's words, and made all further conversation impossible. The king, followed by a brilliant suite, had just arrived at the parade. The regiments greeted their sovereign with loud blasts of trumpets, and the people shouted their farewell. Frederick lifted lightly his hat, and rode along the ranks of the well-ordered troops. He listened to the shouts with calm, composed manner; the Jupiter-flashes from his great eyes seemed to be spent forever. Mounted upon Caesar, his favorite horse, he looked today more bent, his back more bowed with the burden of years; and it was plainly visible that the hand which held the staff crosswise over the horse's neck, holding at the same time the bridle, trembled from very weakness.

"That is Frederick," said Herr Wolff to himself. "That is the hero before whom Europe has trembled; the daring prince who caused the sun to rise upon his country, and awaken the spirits to cheerful life. Oh, how lamentable; how much to be regretted, that a hero, too, can grow feeble and old! Oh, cruel fate, that the noblest spirits embodied in this fragile humanity, and—"

Suddenly he ceased, and looked at the king amazed and with admiration. The old man had become the hero again. The bowed form was erect, the face beamed with energy and conscious power, the eyes flashed with bold daring, strong and sonorous was the voice. The king had turned to his generals, who were drawn up around him in a large circle, saying: "Gentlemen, I come to take leave of you. We shall meet again upon the battle-field, where laurels bloom for the brave. I hope that we may all return, crowned with fresh laurels. Tell my soldiers that I count upon them—that I know they will prove the glory of the Prussian troops anew, and that on the day of battle they will see me at their head.—Farewell!"

"Long live the king!" cried the generals and staff officers, in one voice. The people and the soldiers joined the shout, the ladies waved their handkerchiefs. Herr Wolff and his companions tore off their hats with enthusiasm, and swung them high in the air.

The great eyes of the king, who passed at this moment, rested upon Herr Wolff. "My heart quaked as if I were the pillar of Memnon, and had been touched by the sun's rays," sighed he, as he followed the king with his fiery glance.

"The ceremony is now finished," said the young man near him, "and we must leave, in order to be punctual to dinner at Prince Henry's."

"I wish the king had remained an hour longer," sighed Herr Wolff again. "As I looked at him, it seemed as if I were listening to a song from Homer, and all my faculties were in unison in delight and enthusiasm. Happy those who dare approach him, and remain near him!"

"Then, according to your opinion, his servants must be very fortunate," said the stranger, "and yet they say that he is not very kind to them."

"Because the servant is a little man," cried Herr Wolff, "and every one looks little to his belittling eyes."

"Yes, there are many others no more elevated than servants in the king's surroundings," said the other. The youth reminded him that they must leave.

"Only wait a moment, friend," begged Herr Wolff, as he turned to the stranger, saying, "I would like to continue our conversation of today. You live in Berlin. I will find you out if you will give me your name."

"I pray you to visit me; my name is Moritz. I live in Kloster Strasse, near the gray convent."

"Your name is Moritz?", asked Herr Wolff, earnestly. "Then you are the author of the 'Journey to England?'"

"Yes, the same, and my highest encomium is, that the work is not unknown to you, or the name of the author."

"All Germany knows it, and do you think I could possibly remain a stranger to it?"

"But your name, sir," said the stranger, with anxious curiosity. "Will you not give me your name?"

"I will tell you when we are in your own room," said Herr Wolff, smiling.

"The air is yet enchanted and intoxicated with the breath of the Great Frederick; it should not be desecrated with another name.—Farewell, we will meet in Berlin."

Not far from these gentlemen stood two others, wrapped in long military cloaks, both of striking and foreign appearance; the one, of slight delicate figure, of dark complexion, noble and handsome face, must be an Italian, as his very black hair and eyes betrayed; the other, tall, broad-shouldered, of Herculean stature, belonged to North Germany, as the blond hair, light blue eyes, and features indicated. A pleasing smile played around his thick, curled lips, and only when he glanced at his companion did it die away, and change to one of respectful devotion. At this instant the king passed. The Italian pressed the arm of his companion.

"The arch fiend himself," he murmured softly, "the demon of unbelief, to whom nothing is sacred, and nothing intimidates. The contemptuously smiling spirit of negation, which is called enlightenment, and is but darkness, to whom belief is superstition, and enlightening only deception. Woe to him!"

"Woe to him!" repeated the other.

The king was followed by his brilliant and select staff in motley confusion. First, Prince Henry, and then the Prince of Prussia. As the latter passed the two gentlemen, the Italian pressed the arm of his companion still harder. "Look at him attentively, my son," said he, "that is our future and our hope in this country."

The Hercules turned hastily, with a look of astonishment, to the Italian. "The Prince of Prussia?" asked he, with amazement.

The Italian nodded. "Do you doubt it?" he added, reproachfully. "Would you doubt your lord and master, because he reveals to you what you cannot seize with your clouded spirit?"

"No, no, master, I am only surprised that you hope for good from this lost-in-sin successor to the throne."

"Yes, you are poor, human children," sighed the Italian, compassionately smiling; "prompt to judge, mistaking light for darkness, and darkness for light. I have already remarked that to the celebrated and austere Minister Sully, as he complained to me of the levity and immorality of the French king, Henry IV. I told him that austere morals and moral laws suffered exceptions, and that those through whom the welfare of humanity should be furthered, had to transfer their heavenly bliss of love to the earthly sphere. Sully would contest the question with me, but I defeated him, while I repeated to him what the beautiful and unhappy Queen of Scotland, Mary Stuart, once said to me."

"Mary Stuart!" cried the other, vehemently.

"Yes, Mary Stuart," answered the Italian, earnestly. "Come, my son, let us go. We have seen what we wished to see, and that is sufficient. Give me thy arm, and let us depart."

They departed arm in arm, withdrawing from the crowd, and taking the broad walk which crossed to the park.

"You were about to relate to me the answer which Mary Stuart gave to you, sir," said the Hercules, timidly.

"True; I will now relate it to you," he answered, with sadness. "It was in Edinburgh I had surprised Mary (as I was admitted without ceremony), in her boudoir, as the handsome Rizzio sat at her feet, and sang love-songs to her. She was resting upon a gold-embroidered divan, and her figure appeared to great advantage in the heavenly blue, silver-embroidered gauze robe, which covered her beautiful limbs like a cloud. In her hair sparkled two diamonds, like two stars fallen from heaven, and more glowing still were her eyes, which tenderly rested upon Rizzio. Leaning upon her elbow, she inclined toward Rizzio, who, lute in hand, was looking up to her with a countenance expressive of the deepest love. It was a glorious picture, this young and charming couple, in their bliss of love; and never, in the course of this century, have I forgotten this exquisite picture—never have its bright tints faded from my memory. How often have I begged my friend, Antonio Vandyck, to make this picture eternal, with his immortal pencil. He promised to do it, but at the moment he was occupied with the portraits of Charles I. and his family—the grandson of Queen Mary. Later, as I was not with him, unfortunately, to save him, death seized him before he had fulfilled his promise. But her image is stamped upon my heart, and I see her now, as I saw her then, the beautiful queen, with the handsome singer at her feet. I had entered unawares, and stood a few moments at the door before they remarked me. As I approached, Rizzio suddenly ceased in the midst of a tender passage, and sprang to his feet. Mary signed to him, blushing, to withdraw. He glided noiselessly out, his lute under his arm, and I remained alone with the queen. I dared to chide her, gently, for her love affair with the handsome singer, and, above all, to exhort her to fidelity to her husband. Whereupon Mary answered me, with her accustomed smiling manner, 'There is but one fidelity which one must recognize, and that is to the god of gods—Love! Where he is not, I will not be. The god Hymen is a tedious, pedantic fellow, who burns to ashes all the fresh young love of the heart, and all the enthusiasm of the soul, with his intolerable tallow torch, for Love stands not at his side. I am faithful to the god Amor, therefore I can never be faithful to the god Hymen, as it would be unfaithful to Love!' That was the response of the beautiful Queen Mary. I could not contest the question, so I only looked at her and smiled. Suddenly, I felt a dagger, as it were, thrust at my heart, my spiritual eyes were opened, the lovely woman on the divan was fearfully changed. Instead of the gauze robe, sparkling with silver, a black cloth dress covered her emaciated limbs; instead of brilliants, sparkling in her hair, a mourning veil covered her whitened locks. The beauty and roundness of her neck had disappeared, and I saw around it a broad dark-red stripe. Her head moved, and fell at my feet dissevered. I saw it all, as distinctly as if it really happened, and seized with unspeakable pity I prostrated myself at her feet (who was unknowing of my vision), and besought her with all the anxiety and tenderness of friendship to leave Scotland, to fly from England, as there the death-tribunal awaited her. But Mary Stuart only laughed at my warning, and called me a melancholy fool, whom jealousy made prophetic. The more I begged and implored, the more wanton and gay the poor woman became. Then, as I saw all persuasion was vain, that no one could save her from her dreadful fate, I took a solemn oath that I would be at her side at the hour of her peril, and accompany her to the scaffold. Mary laughed aloud, and, with that mocking gayety so peculiarly her own, she accepted the oath, and reached me her white hand, sparkling with diamonds, to seal the vow with a kiss. I faithfully kept it. I had but just arrived in Rome when I received the account of her imprisonment. I presented myself immediately to the pope, the great Sixtus V., who then occupied the chair of St. Peter. Fortunately, he was my friend, and I had formerly been useful to him, in assisting him to carry out his great and liberal ideas for the welfare of humanity. As a return, I prayed the Holy Father to give me a consecrated hostie for the unhappy Queen Mary Stuart, and the permission to carry it to her in her prison. The Holy Father was incredulous of my sad presentiments, as Mary Stuart herself had been, but he granted me the request. I quitted Rome, and travelled with relays day and night. Reaching Boulogne, a Dover packet-boat had just raised anchor; I succeeded in boarding her, and arrived in London the next evening. The day following, the execution of the queen took place at Fotheringay. I was with her in her last hours, and from my hand she received the consecrated water of Pope Sixtus V. I had kept my oath. I accompanied her to the scaffold, and her head rolled at my feet, as I had seen it in my vision at Edinburgh. It was the 18th of April, 1587, and it seems to me as but yesterday. To the intuitive, seeing spirit, time and space disappear; eternity and immortality are to it omnipresent."

Given up to his souvenirs and visions, the Italian appeared not to know where he wandered, and turned unintentionally to the retired, lonely places in the park. His companion heeded not the way either, occupied with the strange account of the Italian. A dreadful feeling of awe and horror took possession of his soul, and, with devoted respect, he hung upon the words which fell from the lips of his companion.

"It was in the year 1587," said he, as the Italian ceased; "almost two hundred years since, and you were present?"

The Italian replied: "I was present. I have witnessed so many dreadful scenes, and been present at so many executions, that this sad spectacle was not an unusual one to me, and would not have remained fixed in my memory had I not loved, devotedly and fervently, the beautiful Queen Mary Stuart. For those who live in eternity, all horrors have ceased; time rushes past in centuries, which seem to them but a day."

"Teach me so to live, master; I thirst for knowledge," cried his companion, fervently.

"I know it, my son; I penetrate thy soul, and I know that thou thirstest. Therefore I am here to quench thy thirst, and feed thy hungry heart." He remained standing upon the grass-plot, which he had reached by lonely paths, and which was encircled by trees and bushes. Not a sound interrupted the peaceful morning stillness of the place, except the distant music of the departing regiments dying away on the air. "I will teach thee to live in eternity!" resumed the Italian, solemnly. "My predecessor the apostle, George Schrepfer, has initiated thee in temporal life, and the knowledge of the present. By the pistol-shot, which disclosed to him the invisible world, and removed him from our earthly eyes, has he to thee, his most faithful and believing disciple, given the great doctrine of the decay of all things earthly, and prepared thee for the doctrine of the imperishableness of the celestial. The original of humanity sends me, to make known to thee this holy doctrine. When I met thee in Dresden, at the side of the Countess Dorothea von Medem, thee, whom I had never seen, I recognized by the blue flame which trembled above thy head, and which was nothing else than the soul of thy teacher, Schrepfer, wrestling in anguish, which has remained with thee, and hopes for delivery from thee. I greeted thee, therefore, not as a stranger but as a friend. No one called thy name, and yet it was known to me. I took thee by the hand, greeting thee. Hans Rudolph von Bischofswerder, be welcome. The blue flame which glows upon thy brow, guides me to thee, and the pistol-shot under the oaks centuries old, at Rosenthal, near Leipsic, was the summons which my spirit received among the pyramids of Egypt, and which recalled me to Europe, to my own, and thou art one of them."*[Footnote: George Schrepfer, the founder of the Secret Free Mason Lodge (at the same time proprietor of a restaurant and a conjuror), invited his intimate disciples and believers in the year 1774, to whom Bischofswerder belonged, to meet him at Rosenthal, near Leipsic. He assembled them around him, beneath some old oaks, to take leave of them, as now he would render himself in the invisible realm, whence, as a spirit, he would distribute to some of his disciples gold, to others wisdom. He then commanded them to conceal their faces and pray. The praying ones suddenly heard a loud report, and, as they looked up Schrepfer fell dead. He had shot himself with a pistol.]*

"And as thou spakest, oh master, I recognized thee, and I called—' Thou art here, who hast been announced to me. Thou art the master, and my master Schrepfer was the prophet, who preceded thee and prophesied thee. Thou art the great Kophta—thou art Count Alexander Cagliostro!' As I uttered the name, the lights were extinguished, deep darkness and profound stillness reigned. The two countesses Dorothea von Medem and her sister, Eliza von der Necke, clung trembling to me, neither of them daring to break the silence even with a sigh. Suddenly the darkness disappeared, and, with trembling flashes of light, there stood written on the wall: 'Memento Domini Oagliostro et omnis mansuetudinis ejus.' We sank upon our knees, and implored thee to aid us. By degrees the strange, secret characters disappeared, and darkness and silence reigned. The stillness disquieted me at last, and I called for lights. As the servant entered, the two countesses lay fainting upon the floor, and thou hadst disappeared."

"Only to appear to thee at another time," said Cagliostro, "to receive thee with solemn ceremonies into the magic circle—to initiate thee in the secret wisdom of spirits, and prepare thee for the invisible lodge. Recall what I said to thee, three days since, in Dresden. Do you still remember it?"

"I recall it. Thou saidst: 'The secret service calls me to Mittau, with the Countess Medem, to raise hidden treasure, of which the spirit has given me knowledge, and decipher important magical characters on the walls of a cloister. Before I leave, I will lead thee upon the way which thou hast to follow in order to find the light, and let it illuminate the soul which is worthy. Follow me, and I will lead thee to the path of glory, power, and immortality.' These were thy words, master."

"I have now led thee hither," Cagliostro said to him, gently; "thy soul doubts and trembles, for thou art blind seeing eyes, and deaf with hearing ears."

"My soul doubts not, oh master—it comprehends not. I have followed thee, devotedly and believingly. Thou knowest it, master, for thou readest the souls of thy children, and seest their hidden thoughts. Thou hast said to me in Dresden, 'Renounce your service to the Duke of Courland.' I did it, and from equerry and lord chamberlain to the duke, became a simple, private gentleman. I have renounced my titles and dignities for thee, in happy trust in thee. My future lies in thy hands, and, anxious to learn the mysteries of immortality, as a grateful, trustful scholar, I would receive happiness and unhappiness at thy hand."

"Thou shalt receive not only happiness," said Cagliostro, solemnly, "but thou art one of the elect. The blue flame glows upon thy brow, it will illuminate thy soul, and lead thee to the path of glory, power, and might. To-day thou art a simple, private gentleman, as thou sayst, but to-morrow thou wilt become a distinguished lord, before whom hundreds will bow. Fame awaits thee—which thou hast longed for—as power awaits thee. Whom have I named to thee as our future and our hope in this land?"

"Prince Frederick William of Prussia," answered Herr von Bischofswerder, humbly.

"As I spake this name, thou trembledst, and calledst him 'one lost in sin.' Knowest thou, my son, from sin comes penitence, and from penitence elevation and purification. Thou art called and chosen to convert sinners, and lead back the earth-born child to heaven. Engrave these words upon thy memory, fill thy soul with them, as with glowing flames, repeat them in solitude the entire day, then heavenly spirits will arise and whisper the revelations of the future. Then, when thou art consecrated, I will introduce thee into the sacred halls of sublime wisdom. Thou shalt be received as a scholar in the temple hall, and it depends upon thee whether thou advancest to the altar which reaches to the invisible world of miracles."

"Oh, master," cried Bisehofswerder, with a countenance beaming with joy, and sinking upon his knees, "wilt thou favor me, and introduce me to the temple hall? Shall I be received in the sacred world of spirits?"

"Thou shalt, Hans Rudolph von Bischofswerder. The grand master of our order will bestow upon thee this happiness, and to-night shall the star of the future rise over thee. Hold thyself in readiness. At midnight, present thyself at the first portal of the royal palace in Berlin. A man will meet thee, and thou shalt ask, 'Who is our hope?' If he answers thee, 'The Prince of Prussia,' then he is the messenger which I shall have sent thee—follow him. Bow thy head in humility, shut thine eyes to all earthly things, turn thy thoughts inward, and lift them up to the great departed, which hovers over thy head, and speak with the blue flame which glows upon thy brow!"

Bischofswerder bowed still lower, covered his face with his hands, as if inwardly praying, and knelt. Cagliostro bent over him, laid his hand upon his head, breathing three times upon his blond hair.

"I have breathed upon thee with the breath of my spirit," said he. "Thy spirit receives power. Receive it in holy awe, in devotion, and remain immovable."

Bischofswerder continued motionless, with bowed head and concealed face. Cagliostro raised himself, his black eyes fixed upon his disciple, and noiselessly disappeared. Herr von Bischofswerder still remained kneeling. After some time he raised his head, shyly looking about, and, as he found himself alone, he rose. "He has soared away," he murmured, softly. "I shall see him again, and he will consecrate me—the consecration of immortals!"

CHAPTER VII
THE MIRACULOUS ELIXIR

The king withdrew from the parade slowly, followed by his generals, in the direction of Sans-Souci. The streets of Potsdam were lined with the people, shouting their farewell to the king, who received them with a smiling face. Arriving at the grand entrance, he turned to his suite, saying, "Gentlemen, we shall meet again in Bohemia; I must now take leave of you, and forego the pleasure of receiving you again to-day. A king about to leave for the field has necessary arrangements to make for the future. I have much to occupy me, as I set out early to-morrow morning. You, also, have duties to attend to. Farewell, gentlemen."

He raised his worn-out three-cornered hat, saluted his generals with a slight inclination of the head, and turned into the broad avenue which led to the park of Sans-Souci. No one followed him but two mounted footmen, who rode at a respectful distance, attentively regarding the king, of whom only the bowed back and hat were visible. Half way down the avenue his staff was raised above his hat, the sign the footmen awaited to dismount with the greyhounds, which rode before them upon the saddle. At the shrill barking of the animals, Frederick reined in his horse, and turned to look for them. They bounded forward, one upon each side of the king, who regarded them right and left, saying: "Well, Alkmene, well Diana, let us see who will be the lady of honor to-day."

Both dogs sprang with loud barking to the horse, as if understanding the words of their master. Alkmene, stronger, or more adroit, with one bound leaped to the saddle; while poor Diana landed upon the crouper, and, as if ashamed, with hanging head and tail, withdrew behind the horse. "Alkmene has won!" said Kretzschmar to his companion. "Yes, Alkmene is the court-lady to-day, and Diana the companion," he nodded. "She will be cross, and I do not blame her."

"Nor I," said Kretzschmar; "there is a great difference between the court-lady and the companion. The lady remains with the king all day; he plays with her, takes her to walk, gives her bonbons, and the choice morsels of chicken, and only when she has eaten sufficient, can the companion enter to eat the remainder." *[Footnote: This was the daily order of rank with the favorite dogs, for whose service two dog-lackeys, as they were called, were always in waiting. They took them to walk.]*

"One could almost envy the king's greyhounds!" sighed the second footman. "We get dogs' wages, and they the chicken and good treatment. It is a pity!"

"The worst of it is, the king forbids us to marry!" said Kretzschmar sadly. "All the others would leave him, but I pay no attention to old Fritz's snarling and scolding, for he pays for it afterward; first, it rains abusive words, then dollars, and if the stupid ass hits me over the head, he gives me at least a ducat for it. Why should not one endure scoldings when is well paid for it? I remain the fine handsome fellow that I am, if the old bear does call me an ass! His majesty might well be satisfied if he had my fine figure and good carriage."

"Yes, indeed, we are very different fellows from old Fritz!" said the second lackey, with a satisfied air. "A princess once thought me a handsome fellow! It is eleven years since, as I entered the guards on account of my delicate figure. I was guard of honor in the anteroom of the former crown princess of Prussia. It was my first experience. I did not know the ways of the lords and ladies. Suddenly, a charming and beautifully-dressed lady came into the anteroom, two other young ladies following her, joking and laughing, quite at their pleasure. All at once the elegantly-attired lady fixed her large black eyes upon me, so earnestly, that I grew quite red, and looked down. 'See that handsome boy,' she cried. 'I will bet that it is a girl dressed up!' She ran up to me, and began to stroke my cheek with her soft hand, and laughed. 'I am right. He has not the trace of a beard; it is a girl!' And before I knew it she kissed me, then again, and a third time even. I stood still as if enchanted, and, as I thought another kiss was coming, whack went a stout box on my ear. 'There is a punishment for you,' said she, 'that you may know enough to return a kiss when a handsome lady gives you when the king did not wish them with him; in summer, in an open wagon, the dogs upon the back-seat, and the footmen upon the forward seat, and whenever they reproved them, to bring them to order, they addressed them in the polite manner of one, and not stand like a libber,' and with that she boxed me again. The other two ladies laughed, which made me angry, and my ears were very warm. 'If that happens again,' said I, 'by thunder, she will find I do not wait to be punished!' I laid down the arms, and at once sprang after the lady, when—the folding-doors were thrown open, and two gentlemen, in splendid gold-embroidered dresses, entered. As they saw the little lady, they stood astonished, and made the three prescribed bows. I smelt the rat, and put on my sword quickly, and stood stiff as a puppet. The gentlemen said, that they must beg an interview with her royal highness, to deliver the king's commands. The princess went into an adjoining room.

One of the court-ladies stopped before me a moment, and said: 'If you ever dare to tell of this, you shall be put in the fortress. Remember it, and keep silent.' I did so, and kept it a secret until to-day."

"Did the princess ever punish you again?" asked Kretzchmar, with a bold, spying look.

"No, never," answered the lackey Schultz. "The princess was ordered to Stettin the next day, where she still lives as a prisoner for her gay pranks. I remembered her punishment, and when a lady has kissed me, I have bravely returned it."

The footmen had followed the king up the slowly ascending horse-path to the terrace, and now they sprang quickly forward. Kretzschmar swung himself from his saddle, threw Schultz the reins, and, as the king drew up at the side-door of the palace of Sans-Souci, he stood ready to assist him to dismount. The king had given strict orders that no one should notice his going or coming, and to-day, as usual, he entered without pomp or ceremony into his private room, followed by Kretzschmar alone. He sank back into his armchair, the blue damask covering of which was torn and bitten by the dogs, so that the horse-hair stood out from the holes.

"Now relate to me, Kretzschmar, how your expedition succeeded. Did you go to Berlin to see Mademoiselle Enke last night?"

"Yes, your majesty, I was there, and have brought you the writing."

"Was she alone?" asked the king, bending over to caress Alkmene, who lay at his feet.

"Well," answered Kretzschmar, grinning, "I do not know whether she was alone or not. I only know that, as I waited a little on the corner of the street, I saw a gentleman go out, wrapped in a cloak, a tall, broad-shouldered gentleman, whom I—"

"Whom you naturally did not recognize," said the king, interrupting him; "it was a dark night, and no moon, so that you could not see."

"At your service, your majesty, I could see no one; I would only add that the unknown may have been at Mademoiselle Enke's."

"And he may not have been," cried the king, harshly. "What else did you learn?"

"Nothing at all worth speaking about. Only one thing I must say, the lackey Schultz is a prattling fool, and speaks very disrespectfully."

"Did he talk with you?"

"Yes, your majesty, with me."

"Then he knows well that it would be welcome. What did he say?"

"He related to me a love-affair with the crown princess of Prussia eleven years since. He plumes himself upon the crown princess having stroked his beard."

"Be quiet!" commanded the king, harshly. "If Schultz was drunk, and talked in a crazy manner, how dare you repeat it to me? Let this happen again, and I will dismiss you my service. Remember it, you ass!"

"Pardon me, your majesty, I thought I must relate all that I hear of importance."

"That was not important, and not worth the trouble of talking about. If Schultz is such a drunken fellow I did not know it, and he is to be pitied. You can go now; I give you a day to make your farewells to your friends, and to console them with the hope of meeting you again. Put every thing in order that concerns you. If you have debts, pay them."

"I have no money to pay them, your majesty," sighed Kretzschmar.

The king stepped to the iron coffer, of which no one possessed the key but himself, and looking within said: "You cannot have much money to-day, as the drawer which contains the money for the gossips and spies is quite empty, and you have had a good share of it. Five guldens remain for you."

"Alas! your majesty, it is too little; twenty-five guldens would not pay my debts."

The king closed the drawer, saying: "Judas only received twenty shillings for betraying his Master. Twenty-five is quite enough for Kretzschmar for betraying his comrade."

Kretzschmar slunk away. The king fixed his great eyes upon him until the door closed. "Man is a miserable race; for gold he would sell his own brother—would sell his own soul, if there could be found a purchaser," he murmured. "Why do you growl, Alkmene, why trouble yourself, mademoiselle? I was not speaking of your honorable race; only of the pitiful race of men. Be quiet, my little dog, be quiet; I love you, and you are my dear little dog," he said, pressing her caressingly to his breast.

The footman Schultz appeared to announce the equerry Von Schwerin.

"Bid him enter," nodded the king.

Von Schwerin entered, with a smiling face. "Have you accomplished what I confided to you?"

With a profound bow Von Schwerin drew a roll of paper from his breast-pocket, and handed it to the king, saying, "I am so fortunate as to have accomplished your commands."

"Will Count Schmettau give up the villa at once?"

"Yes, your majesty, the new occupant could take possession to-day, with all the furniture and house arrangements, for seven thousand five hundred dollars. Here is the bill of sale, only the purchaser's name is wanting. I have obeyed your majesty's commands, and acted as if I were the purchaser."

"Schmettau is not such a stupid fellow as to believe that, for he knows that you cannot keep your money. You say the contract is ready, only the signature of the purchaser is wanting and the money?"

"Pardon me, your majesty, the name of the present possessor has not been inserted. I did not presume to write it without the unmistakable command of your majesty."

"Do you know the name?" asked the king.

"I do not, but the generosity of my most gracious king and master allows me to divine it, and my heart is filled to bursting with thankfulness and joy. My whole life will not be long enough to prove to you my gratitude."

"What for?" asked the king, staring at Von Schwerin, quite surprised; "you cannot suppose that I have purchased the villa for you?"

Herr von Schwerin smilingly nodded. "I think so, your majesty."

Frederick laughed aloud. "Schwerin, you are an uncommonly cunning fellow. You see the grass grow before the seed is sown. This time you deceived yourself—the grass has not grown. What good would it do you? You do not need grass, but thistles, and they do not grow at Charlottenburg. Take the contract to my minister Von Herzberg, whom you will find in the audience-room, and then walk a little upon the terrace to enjoy the fresh air. I promised you the privilege. First go to Von Herzberg, and say to him to send the Prince of Prussia to me immediately upon his arrival. Why do you wear so mournful a face all of a sudden? Can it be possible that my chief equerry has so lowered himself as to go among the mechanics, and build chateaux en Espagne? You know such houses are not suitable for our northern climate, and fall down. Now, do what I told you, and then go upon the terrace."

The equerry glided away with sorrowful mien to Von Herzberg, and communicated the king's commands to him.

"You have made a good purchase," said the minister, in a friendly manner. "His majesty will be very much pleased with the extraordinary zeal and the great dexterity with which you have arranged the matter. Count Schmettau has just been here, and he could not sufficiently commend your zeal and prudence, and the sympathy and interest which you showed in the smallest matters, as if the purchase were for yourself. The count wishes to reserve two oil paintings in the saloon, which are an heirloom from his father. We cannot but let the count retain them."

"Arrange it as you will," answered the equerry, fretfully; "I have nothing more to do with the affair—it lies in your hands."

"But where are you going in such haste?" said Herzberg, as the equerry bowed hastily, and strode through the room toward the door.

"His majesty commanded me to go upon the terrace," he replied, morosely.

Herr von Herzberg looked after him surprised. "Something must have occurred, otherwise he is very tractable. Ah! there comes the prince. I will go to meet him, and communicate to him the king's command—I will await your royal highness here until you have spoken with the king, if you will have the grace to seek me."

"I will return by all means, if you will have the kindness to wait for me," replied the prince, smiling, and hastened to the interview with his royal uncle.

Frederick was seated in his arm-chair, upon his lap Alkmene, when the crown prince entered. "Bon jour, mon neveu! pardon me," said he, with a friendly nod, "that I remain seated, and do not rise to greet the future King of Prussia."

"Sire, Heaven grant that many years pass before I succeed to the title which my great and unapproachable predecessor has borne with so much wisdom and fame, that one can well doubt the being able to emulate his example, and must content himself to live under the shadow of his intelligence and fame!"

Frederick slowly shook his head. "The people will not be satisfied, nor the coffers filled by fame. No one can live upon the great deeds of his ancestors; he must be self-sustaining, not seek for the laurels in the past, but upon the naked field of the future, which lies before him. Sow the seeds of future laurels; fame troubles me but little, and I advise you, my nephew, not to rely upon it. One must begin anew each day, and make fresh efforts for vigorous deeds."

The crown prince bowed, and seated himself upon the tabouret, which the king, with a slight wave of the hand, signified to him.

"I will endeavor, sire, to follow the elevated sentiments of your majesty, that I may not dishonor my great teacher."

"You express yourself too modestly, my nephew, and I know that you think otherwise; that your fiery spirit will never be contented to dishonor yourself or your ancestors. Fate is favorable to you, and offers the opportunity to confirm, what I judge you to be—a brave soldier, a skilful captain—in a word, a true Hohenzollern! I would make you a commander of a division of my army, and I shall follow every movement—every operation, with lively interest."

A ray of joy beamed upon the face of the prince; Frederick saw it with satisfaction, and his heart warmed toward his nephew. "He has at least courage," he said to himself; "he is no sybarite to quail before the rough life of war."

"Will your majesty so greatly favor me as to accord me an independent position in the campaign?"

"I offer you what belongs to you as a general and heir to the throne. On me it devolves to direct the plans and operations, and on you to detail them and direct the execution. I shall rejoice to see that you understand the profession of war practically as well as theoretically. Therefore, this war is so far welcome, that it will give my crown prince an opportunity to win his first laurels, and adorn the brow which, until now, has been crowned with myrtle."

"Your majesty, I—"

"Be silent—I do not reproach you, my nephew; I understand human nature, and the seductive arts of women. It is time that you seek other ornament—myrtle becomes a youthful brow, and the helmet adorns the man crowned with laurels."

"I have long desired it, and I am deeply grateful to your majesty for the opportunity to win it. This campaign is good fortune to me."

"War is never a good fortune," sighed the king—"for the people it is great misfortune. I would willingly have avoided it for their sake. But the arrogance and the passion for territorial aggrandizement of the young Emperor of Germany forces me to it. I dare not, and will not suffer Austria to enrich herself through foreign inheritance, ignoring the legitimate title of a German prince. Bavaria must remain an independent, free German principality, under a sovereign prince. It is inevitably necessary for the balance of power. I cannot yield, therefore, as a German prince, that Austria increase her power in an illegitimate manner, but I will cast my good sword in the scales, that the balance is heavier on the side upon which depends the existence of Germany, that she may not be tossed in the air by Austria's weight. These are my views and reasons for the war upon which I now enter with reluctance. When the greatness and equilibrium of Germany are at stake, no German prince should dare hesitate. Austria has already cost Germany much blood, and will cause her to shed still more. Believe it, my nephew, and guard yourself against Austria's ambition for territorial aggrandizement. You see, I am like all old people, always teaching youth, while we have much to learn ourselves. We are all pupils, and our deeds are ever imperfect."

"Your majesty cannot believe that of himself. The sage of Sans-Souci is the type, the master, and teacher of all Europe."

"My son," replied the king, "the great men of antiquity recognized it as the acme of wisdom, that they must be mindful that 'in the midst of life we are in death.' At the gay festivities and the luxurious feasts they were interrupted in the merry song and voluptuous dance, with the warning: 'Remember, O man, that thou must die!' Let us profit by their wisdom! I have startled you from the banquet of life, and I doubt not that many singers and dancers will be enraged that I should put an end to the feasts of roses and the merry dance in such an abominable manner. It would be an evil omen in our warlike undertaking, if the rosy lips of the beauties should breathe curses to follow us; therefore, we must try to conciliate them, and leave a good souvenir in their hearts. You smile, my prince, and you think it vain trouble for an old fellow; that I cannot win the favor of the ladies under any pretension; so you must undertake for me the reconciliation and the hush-money."

"I am prepared for any thing which your majesty imposes upon me; only I would defend myself against the interpretation which you give my smile—and—"

"Which was very near the truth," interrupted the king. "I have called you from the banquet of life, and I have interrupted the dancers, crowned with roses in the midst of their dance, which they would finish before you. I pray you, then, indemnify the enraged beauties, and let us go forth with a quiet conscience, that we in no respect are indebted to any one."

"Oh, sire, it will be impossible for me to go to the field with a quiet conscience upon this point."

"Permit me to extend to you the means to do so," replied the king, graciously smiling. "Take this little box; it contains a wonderful elixir, proof against all the infirmities and weaknesses of humanity, of one of the greatest philosophers of human nature. By the right use of it, tears of sorrow are changed to tears of joy, and a Megerea into a smiling angel, as by enchantment. Before going to the war, I pray you to prove the miraculous elixir upon one of the angry beauties. For, I repeat, we must put our house in order, and leave no debts behind us. The debts of gratitude must not be forgotten. Let us say 'Gesegnete Mahlzeit' when we have been well feasted."

The king handed the prince a little box, of beautiful workmanship, and smiled as he rather vehemently thanked him, and at the same time tried to open it.

"I remark with pleasure that you have a tolerably innocent heart, as you betray curiosity about the wonderful elixir. I supposed men, to say nothing of beautiful women, had long since instructed you that it was the only balsam for all the evils of life. My minister Herzberg will give you the key of the little box, and advise you as to the right use of the elixir. Farewell, with the hope of soon seeing you again, my nephew. I start for Silesia to-morrow, as I must travel slower than you young people. You will follow me in a few days. Again farewell!"

Extending his meagre white hand to the prince, he withdrew it quickly, as the latter was about to press it to his lips, and motioned to the door kindly.

CHAPTER VIII
THE GOLDEN RAIN

Prince Frederick William betook himself, with painful curiosity, to the audience-room, where the Minister von Herzberg awaited him.

"Your excellency," said he, "his majesty refers me to you, for the true explanation of the miraculous elixir contained in this little box, and about which I am naturally very curious, and beg of you the key to open it."

"Will your royal highness," said the minister, smiling, "have the grace to grant me a few moments' conversation, which may serve as an explanation, for his majesty has not in reality given me a key?"

"I pray you, my dear excellency, to explain it," cried the prince, impatiently.

"Pardon me if I probe the tenderest feelings of your heart, my prince. The command of the king imposes this duty upon me. He has known for a long time of your connection with a certain person, to whom you are more devoted than to your wife."

"Say, rather, his majesty has twice forced me to marry two unloved and unknown princesses, when he knew that I already loved this certain person. Twice I have married, because the command of his king is law to the crown prince of Prussia. For my love and my sympathy there is no law but that of my own heart, and this alone have I followed."

"His majesty does not reproach you. The philosopher of Sans-Souci understands human nature, and he feels indulgent toward your weakness. He is quite satisfied that you have chosen this person, as friend and favorite, to console yourself for an unhappy marriage. Her low birth is a guaranty that she will never mingle in politics, an act which would be visited with his majesty's highest displeasure. While his majesty permits you to continue this intimacy, and recognizes the existence of this woman, he wishes her to be provided for as becomes the mistress of a crown prince, and not as the grisette of a gentleman. She should have her own house, and the livery of her lord."

"As if it were my fault that this has not already been arranged!" cried the prince. "Am I not daily and hourly tormented with poverty, and scarcely know how to turn, between necessary expenses and urgent creditors? You know well yourself, your excellency, how stingy and parsimonious the king is to the crown prince. He scarcely affords me the means to support my family in a decent, to say nothing of a princely, manner. How dependent we all are, myself, my wife, and my children upon the king, whose economy increases, while our wants and expenses also increase every year! It is sufficiently sad that I cannot reward those who have proved to me during ten years their fidelity and love, but I must suffer them to live in dependence and want."

"His majesty understands that, and thinks that as your royal highness is to go to the field, and will be exposed, as a brave commander, to the uncertain fate of battle, that you should assure the future of all those who are dear to you, and arrange a certain competency for them. A good opportunity now offers to you. Count Schmettau will sell his villa at Charlottenburg, and it would be agreeable to his majesty that you should purchase it, and assign it to those dearest to you. In order to give you as little trouble as possible, his majesty has had the matter already arranged, through his equerry, Count Schmettau, and the purchase can be made this very hour. Here is the bill of sale; only the name of the present possessor is wanting, the signature of the purchaser, and the payment of seven thousand five hundred thalers."

"The names can be quickly written; but, your excellency," cried the prince, "where will the money come from?"

"I have just given your royal highness the key to the little box: have the goodness to press hard upon the rosette."

The prince touched the spring, the cover flew back—it contained only a strip of paper! Upon it was written, in the king's own handwriting, "Bill of exchange upon my treasurer. Pay to the order of the Prince of Prussia twenty thousand thalers." *[Footnote: "Memoirs of the Countess Lichtenau," vol.1]* The prince's face lighted up with joy. "Oh! the king has indeed given me a miraculous elixir, that compensates for all misfortunes, heals all infirmities, and is a balsam for all possible griefs. I will bring it into use immediately, and sign the bill of sale." He signed the paper, and filled with haste the deficiency in the contract. "It is done!" he cried, joyfully, "the proprietress, Wilhelmine Enke; purchaser, Frederick William of Prussia. Nothing remains to be done but to draw upon the king's treasury, and pay Count Schmettau."

"Your royal highness is spared even that trouble. Here are twenty rolls, and each roll contains one hundred double Fredericks d'or, and, when your highness commands it, I will reserve seven rolls and pay Count

Schmettau; then there remain thirteen for yourself. Here is the contract, which you will give in person to the possessor."

"First, I must go to the king," said the prince; "my heart urges me to express my gratitude to him, and my deep sense of his goodness and tenderness. I feel ashamed without being humbled, like a repentant son, who has doubted the generosity and goodness of his father, because he has sometimes severely reprimanded his faults. I must go at once to the king."

"He will not receive your royal highness," answered Herzberg, smiling. "You know our sovereign, who so fully deserves our admiration and love. His favor and goodness beam upon us all, and he desires neither thanks nor acknowledgment. He performs his noble, glorious deeds in a harsh manner, that he may relieve the recipients of his bounty from the burden of gratitude; and often when he is the most morose and harsh, is he at heart the most gracious and affectionate. You and yours have experienced it to-day. He appeared to be angry, and enveloped himself in the toga of a severe judge of morals; but, under this toga, there beat the kind, noble heart of a friend and father, who punishes with rigorous words, and forgives with generous, benevolent deeds."

"For this I must thank him—he must listen to me!" cried the prince.

"He will be angry if your royal highness forces him to receive thanks when he would avoid them. He has expressly commanded me to entreat you never to allude to the affair, and never to speak of it to others, as it would not be agreeable to his majesty to have the family affairs known to the world. You would best please his majesty by following exactly his wishes, and when you meet him never allude to it. As I have said, this is the express wish and command of the king."

"Which I must naturally follow," sighed the prince, "although I acknowledge that it is unpleasant to me to receive so much kindness from him without at least returning my most heart-felt thanks. Say to the king, that I am deeply, sensibly moved with his tender sympathy and generosity. And now I will hasten to Wilhelmine Enke; but, it occurs to me that it may not be possible; the king has made her a prisoner in her own house."

"Do not trouble yourself about that. If it is your royal highness's pleasure, drive at once to Charlottenburg. You will find the new possessor there and she will relate to you her interview with the mayor of Berlin."

"Oh! I shall drive at once to the villa. I am curious to learn what Von Kircheisen has told her."

"I imagined that you would be, and ordered your carriage here, as you could not well ride upon horseback with the heavy rolls of gold; and if it is your pleasure, I will order the footman to place the box, into which I have put them, in the carriage."

"No, no; I beg you to let me carry them," cried the prince, seizing the box with both hands. "It is truly heavy, but an agreeable burden, and if it lames my arm I shall bethink myself of the miraculous elixir, which will give me courage and strength. Farewell, your excellency; I shall hurry on to Charlottenburg!"

The prince hastened to his carriage, and ordered the coachman to drive at full speed to the villa. Thanks to this order, he reached it in about an hour. No one was there to receive him upon his arrival. The hall was empty, and the rooms were closed. The prince passed on to the opposite end, where there was a door open, and stood upon a balcony, with steps descending into the garden, which, with its flower-beds, grass-plots, shrubbery, and the tall trees, formed a lovely background. The birds were singing, the trees rustled, and variegated butterflies fluttered over the odorous flowers. Upon the turf, forming a beautiful group, was Wilhelmine playing with her daughter, and the nurse with the little boy upon her lap, who laughingly stretched out his arms toward his mother.

"Wilhelmine—Wilhelmine!" cried the prince.

With a cry of joy she answered, and flew toward the house. "You have come at last, my beloved lord," she cried, almost breathless, mounting the steps. "I beg you to tell me what all this means? I am dying of curiosity!"

"I also," said the prince, smiling. "Have the goodness to lead me to one of the rooms, that I may set down this box."

"What does that hobgoblin contain, that it prevents your embracing me?"

"Do not ask, but hasten to assist me to relieve myself of the burden." They entered the house, and Wilhelmine opened the wide folding-doors, which led into a very tastefully-furnished room. Frederick William set the box upon the marble table, and sank upon a divan with Wilhelmine in his arms. "First of all, tell me what Von Kircheisen said to you?"

"He commanded me, in the name of the king, to give up my dwelling at Berlin and at Potsdam, and to avoid showing myself in public at both places, that those who had the right to the love and fidelity of the Prince of Prussia should not be annoyed at the sight of me; that I should live retired, and leave the appointed residence as little as possible, for then the king would be inclined to ignore my existence, and take no further notice of me. But, if I attempted to play a role, his majesty would take good care that it should be forever played out."

"Those were harsh, cruel words," sighed Frederick William.

"Harsh, cruel words," repeated Wilhelmine, sorrowfully. "They pierced my soul, and I shrieked at last from agony. Herr von Kircheisen was quite frightened, and begged me to excuse him, that he must thus speak to me, but the king had commanded him to repeat his very words. The carriage was at the door, he said, ready to convey me to my future dwelling, for I must immediately leave Berlin, and the king be informed of my setting out. The coachman received the order, and here I am, without knowing what I am to do, or whether I shall remain here."

"Yes, Wilhelmine, you are to remain here; at last we have a home, and a resting-place for our love and our children. This house is yours—you are mistress here, and you must welcome me as your guest."

"This house is mine!" she cried, joyfully. "Did you give it to me? How generous, and how extravagant you are! Protect me with the gift of your love, as if you were Jupiter and I Danae!"

"A beautiful picture, and, that it may be a reality, I will play the role of Jupiter and open the box."

He took a roll of gold, and let it fall upon Wilhelmine's head, her beautiful shoulders, and her arms, like a shower of gold. She shrieked and laughed, and sought to gather up the pieces which rolled ringing around her upon the floor. The prince seized another roll, and another still, till she was flooded with the glistening pieces. Then another and another, until Wilhelmine, laughing, screamed for grace, and sprang up, the gold rolling around her like teasing goblins.

CHAPTER IX
GERMAN LITERATURE AND THE KING

The Minister Herzberg had, in the mean time, an interview with the king, informing him of the concluded purchase of the Schmettau villa, and of the emotion and gratitude of the crown prince at his royal munificence.

"That affair is arranged, then," said Frederick. "If Fate wills that the prince should not return from this campaign, then this certain person and the two poor worms are provided for, who are destined to wander through the world nameless and fatherless."

"Let us hope that fate will not deal so harshly with the prince, or bring such sorrow upon your majesty."

"My dear sir, Fate is a hard-hearted creature, the tears of mankind are of no more importance to her than the raindrops falling from the roof. She strides with gigantic power over men, crushing them all in dust—the great as well as the little—the king as well as the beggar. For my part I yield to Fate without a murmur. Politicians and warriors are mere puppets in the hands of Providence. We act without knowing why, for we are unknowingly the tools of an invisible hand. Often the result of our actions is the reverse of our hopes! Let all things take their course, as it best pleases God, and let us not think to master Fate. *[Footnote: The king's words.—"Posthumous Works," vol. x., p. 256.]* That is my creed, Herzberg, and if I do not return from this infamous campaign, you will know that I have yielded to Fate without murmuring. You understand my wishes in all things; the current affairs of government should go on regularly. If any thing extraordinary occurs, let me be informed at once. Is there any news, Herzberg?"

"Nothing worth recounting, sire, except that the young Duke of Weimar is in town."

"I know it; he has announced himself. I cannot speak with him. I have asked my brother Henry to arrange the conditions under which he will allow us to enlist men for my army in his duchy. I hope he will be reasonable, and not prevent it. That is no news that the Duke of Weimar has arrived!"

"Not only the duke has arrived, but he has brought his dear friend with him whom the people in Saxe-Weimar say makes the good and bad weather."

"Who is the weather-maker?"

"Your majesty, this weather-maker is the author of 'The Sorrows of Young Werther,' Johann Wolfgang Goethe, who for four years has aroused the hearts and excited the imaginations of all Germany. If I am not deceived, a great future opens for this poet, and he will be a star of the first magnitude in the sky of German literature. I believe it would be well worth the trouble for your majesty to see him."

"Do not trouble me with your German literature, and your stars of the first magnitude! We must acknowledge our poverty with humility; belles-lettres have never achieved success upon our soil. Moreover, this star of the first magnitude—this Herr Goethe—I remember him well; I wish to know nothing of him. He has quite turned the heads of all the love-sick fools with his 'Sorrows of Young Werther.' You cannot count that a merit. The youth of Germany were sufficiently enamoured, without the love-whining romances of Herr Goethe to pour oil on the fire."

"Pardon me, sire, that I should presume to differ from you; but this book which your majesty condemns has not only produced a furor in Germany, but throughout Europe—throughout the world even. That which public opinion sustains in such a marked manner cannot be wholly unworthy. 'Vox populi, vox dei,' is a true maxim in all ages."

"It is not true!" cried the king. "The old Roman maxim is not applicable to our effeminate, degraded people. Nowadays, whoever flatters the people and glorifies their weaknesses, is a good fellow, and he is extolled to the skies. Public opinion calls him a genius and a Messiah. Away with your nonsense! The 'Werther' of Herr Goethe has wrought no good; it has made the healthy sick, and has not restored invalids to health. Since its appearance a mad love-fever has seized all the young people, and silly sentimentalities and flirtations have become the fashion. These modern Werthers behave as if love were a tarantula, with the bite of which they must become mad, to be considered model young men. They groan and sigh, take moonlight walks, but they have no courage in their souls, and will never make good soldiers. This is the fault of Herr Werther, and his abominable lamentations. It is a miserable work, and not worth the trouble of talking about, for no earnest man will read it!"

"Pardon me, sire; your majesty has graciously permitted me to enter the lists as knight and champion of German literature, and sometimes to defend the German Muse, who stands unnoticed and unknown under the shadow of your throne; while the French lady, with her brilliant attire and painted cheeks, is always welcomed. I beg your majesty to believe that, although this romance may have done some harm, it has, on the other hand, done infinite service. A great and immortal merit cannot be denied to it."

"What merit?" demanded the king, slowly taking a pinch of snuff; "I am very curious to know what merit that crazy, love-sick book has."

"Sire, it has the great merit to have enriched the German literature with a work whose masterly language alone raises it above every thing heretofore produced by a German author. It has emancipated our country's literature from its clumsy, awkward childhood, and presented it as an ardent, inspired youth, ready for combat, upon the lips of whom the gods have placed the right word to express every feeling and every thought—a youth who is capable of probing the depths of the human heart."

"I wish all this might have remained in the depths," cried Frederick, annoyed. "You have defended the German Muse before; but you remember that I am incorrigible. You cannot persuade me that bungling is master-work. It is not the poverty of the mind, but the fault of the language, which is not capable of expressing with brevity and precision. For how could any one translate Tacitus into German without adding a mass of words and phrases? In French it is not necessary; one can express himself with brevity, and to the point."

"Sire, I shall permit myself to prove to you that the brevity of Tacitus can be imitated in the German language. I will translate a part of Tacitus, to give your majesty a proof."

"I will take you at your word! And I will answer you in a treatise upon German literature, its short-comings, and the means for its improvement. *[Footnote: This treatise appeared during the Bavarian war of succession, in the winter of 1779] Until then, a truce. I insist upon it—good German authors are entirely wanting to us Germans. They may appear a long time after I have joined Voltaire and Algarotti in the Elysian Fields."[Footnote: The king's words.—See "Posthumous Works," vol. II., p. 293.]*

"They are already here," cried Herzberg, zealously. "We have, for example, Lessing, who has written two dramas, of which every nation might be proud—'Minna von Barnhelm, and Emilia Calotti.'"

"I know nothing of them," said the king, with indifference. "I have never heard of your Lessing."

"Your majesty, this wonderful comedy, 'Minna von Barnhelm,' was written for your majesty's glorification."

"The more the reason why I should not read it! A German comedy! That must be fine stuff for the German theatre, the most miserable of all. In Germany, Melpomene has untutored admirers, some walking on stilts, others crawling in the mire, from the altars of the goddess. The Germans will ever be repulsed, as they are rebels to her laws, and understand not the art to move and interest the heart."

"But, sire, you have never deigned to become acquainted with 'Minna von Barnhelm' nor 'Emilia Calotti.'"

"Well, well, Herzberg, do not be so furious; you are a lover of German literature, and some allowance must be made for those who are in love. You will not persuade me to read your things which you call German comedies and tragedies. I will take good care; my teeth are not strong enough to grind such hard bits. Now do not be angry, Herzberg. The first leisure hours that I have in this campaign I shall employ on my treatise."

"And the first leisure hours that I have," growled the minister, "I shall employ to translate a portion of Tacitus into our beautiful German language, to send to your majesty."

"You are incorrigible," said Frederick, smiling. "We shall see, and until then let us keep the peace, Herzberg. When one is about to go to war, it is well to be at peace with one's conscience and with his friends; so let us be good friends."

"Your majesty, your graciousness and kindness make me truly ashamed," said the minister, feelingly. "I beg pardon a thousand times, if I have allowed myself to be carried away with unbecoming violence in my zeal for our poor neglected German literature."

"I approve of your zeal, and it pleases me that you are a faithful knight, sans peur et sans reproche. I do not ascribe its poverty to the German nation, who have as much spirit and genius as any nation, the mental development of which has been retarded by outward circumstances, which prevented her rising to an equality with her neighbors. We shall one day have classical writers, and every one will read them to cultivate himself. Our neighbors will learn German, and it will be spoken with pleasure at courts; and it can well happen that our language, when perfectly formed, will spread throughout Europe. We shall have our German classics also." *[Footnote: The king's words—see "Posthumous Works," vol. III.]*

The king smiled, well pleased, as he observed by stolen glances the noble, intelligent face of Herzberg brighten, and the gloomy clouds dispersed which had overshadowed it.

"Now, is it not true that you are again contented?" said the king, graciously.

"I am delighted with the prophecy for the German language, your majesty; and may I add something?"

"It will weigh on your heart if you do not tell it," said the king.

"I prophesy that this Goethe will one day belong to the classic authors, and therefore I would beg once more of your majesty to grant him a gracious look, and invite him to your presence. If you find no pleasure in 'The Sorrows of Werther,' Goethe has created other beautiful works. He is the author of the tragedy of 'Stella.'"

"That sentimental, immoral piece, which we forbid the representation of in Berlin, because it portrays a fellow who made love to two women at once, playing the double role of lover to his wife and his paramour, while he had a grown-up daughter! It is an immoral piece, which excites the tear-glands, and ends as 'Werther,' by the hero blowing his brains out. It is directed against all morals, and against marriage; therefore it was forbidden." *[Footnote: The tragedy of "Stella" was represented in Berlin with great applause, and denounced by the king as immoral, in the year 1776, and the further representation forbidden.—See Plumke, "History of the Berlin Theatres."]*

"But, sire, Herr Goethe has not only written 'Stella,' but 'Clavigo' also, which—"

"Which he has copied exactly from the 'Memoires de Beaumarchais,'" interrupted the king. "That is not a German, but a French production."

"Allow me to cite a genuine German production, which Johann Wolfgang Goethe has written. I mean the drama 'Gotz von Berlichingen.'"

"Stop!—it is sufficient. I do not wish to hear any thing more," cried the king, indignant, and rising. "It is bad enough that such pieces should appear upon the German stage as this 'Gotz von Berlichingen.' They are nothing less than abominable imitations of the bad English pieces of Shakespeare! The pit applauds them, and demands with enthusiasm these very disgusting platitudes. *[Footnote: The king's own words.—See "Posthumous Works," vol. iii.]* Do not be angry again, you must have patience with the old boy! I shall rejoice heartily if this Herr Goethe becomes a classic writer one day, as you say. I shall not live to witness it. I only see the embryo where you see the full-grown author. We will talk further about it when we meet in the Elysian Fields; then we will see, when you present this Herr Johann Wolfgang Goethe, as a German classic writer, to Homer, Horace, Virgil, and Corneille, if they do not turn their backs upon him. Now adieu, Herzberg! So soon as circumstances permit, I shall send for you to go to Silesia, and then you can give me your German translation of Tacitus."

The king nodded in a friendly manner to his minister, and slowly walked back and forth, while he took leave and withdrew. After a few moments he rang, and the summons was immediately answered by the footman Schultz.

The king fixed upon him one of those searching glances of his fiery eyes which confounded and confused the footman. He remained standing and embarrassed, with downcast look.

"What are you standing there for?" asked the king. "Did I not ring for you, and do you not know what you have to do?" Frederick continued to regard him, with flashing eyes, which increased the lackey's confusion.

He forgot entirely that the summons was for his majesty's lunch, and all that he had to do was to open the door to the adjoining room, where it stood already prepared.

Frederick waited a moment, but the footman still stood irresolute, when his majesty indicated to him to approach.

He approached, staggering under the puzzling glance of his master.

"Oh! I see what it is," said Frederick, shrugging his shoulders; "you are drunk again, as you often are, and—"

"Your majesty," cried Schultz, amazed, "I drunk!"

"Silence!—will you be bold enough to reason with me? I say that you are drunk, and I want no drunken footmen. They must be well-behaved, sober fellows, who keep their ears open and their mouths shut—who are neither drunkards nor gossips, and do not take for truth what they have experienced in their drunken fits. I do not want such fellows as you are at all; you are only fit food for cannon, and for that you shall serve. Go to General Alvensleben, and present yourself to enter the guards. You are lucky to go to the field at once; to-morrow you will set off. Say to the general that I sent you, and that you are to enter as a common soldier."

"But, your majesty, I do not know what I have done," cried Schultz, whiningly. "I really am not drunk. I—"

"Silence!" thundered the king. "Do as I command you! Go to General Alvensleben, and present yourself to enter the guards at once. Away with you! I do not need drunken, gossiping footmen in my service. Away with you!"

The footman slunk slowly away, his head hanging down, with difficulty restraining the tears which stood in large drops in his eyes.

The king followed him with his glance, which softened and grew gentler from sympathy. "I pity him, the poor fellow! but I must teach him a lesson. I want no gossips around me. He need only wear the uniform two weeks or so, that will bring him to reason. Then I will pardon him, and receive him into my service again. He is a good-natured fellow, and would not betray any one as Kretzschmar betrayed him."

The king stepped to the window to look at the gentleman who was eagerly engaged in conversation with the castellan of Sans-Souci. At this instant the footman entered with a sealed note for the king. "From his royal highness Prince Henry," said he.

"Who brought it?"

"The gentleman who speaks with the castellan upon the terrace. I wait your majesty's commands."

"Wait, then." The note ran thus: "Your majesty, my dearly-beloved brother: The bearer, Johann Wolfgang Goethe, one of the literati, and a poet, and at this time secretary of legation to the duchy of Saxe-Weimar, is a great favorite of the duke's, our nephew. I met him returning from the parade in company with the duke, who expressed to me the strong desire his secretary had to visit the celebrated house of the great philosopher of Sans-Souci, and see the room once occupied by Voltaire. I could not well refuse, and therefore address these few lines to your majesty before returning to Berlin with the duke, who will dine with me, accompanied by his secretary. I am your majesty's most humble servant and brother, HENRY."

"Tell the castellan that I grant him permission to show the house and park to the stranger; he shall take care not to come in my way, so that I shall be obliged to meet him. Tell this aside, that you may not be overheard. Hasten, for they have already been waiting some time."

The king walked again to the window, and, hidden by the curtain, peeped out. "So, this is Herr Goethe, is it? What assurance! There he stands, sketching the house. What wonderful eyes the man has! With what a proud, confident manner he looks around! What a brow! Truly he is a handsome fellow, and Herzberg may be right after all. That brow betokens thought, and from those eyes there flashes a divine light. But he looks overbearing and proud. Now, I am doubly pleased that I refused Herzberg to have any thing to do with him. Such presumptive geniuses must be rather kept back; then they feel their power, and strive to bring themselves forward. Yes! I believe that man has a future. He looks like the youthful god Apollo, who may have condescended to descend to earth! He shall not entrap me with his beautiful head. If he is the man who makes good and bad weather in Weimar, he shall learn that rain and sunshine at Sans-Souci do not depend upon him; that the sun and clouds here do not care whether Herr Goethe is in the world or not. For sunshine and storm we depend upon the Great Weather-Maker, to whom we must all bow; evil and good days in Prussia shall emanate from me, so long as I live. Sometimes I succeed in causing a little sunshine," continued the king. "I believe the Prince of Prussia has to-day felt the happy influence of the sun's rays; and while it is dull and lonely at Sans-Souei, may it be brighter and more cheerful at Charlottenburg! Eh bien! old boy," said the king, stopping, "you are playing the sentimental, and eulogizing your loneliness. Well, well, do not complain.—Oh, come to me, spirits of my friends, and hold converse with me! Voltaire, D'Argens, and my beloved Lord-Marshal Keith! Come to me, departed souls, with the memories of happier days, and hover with thy cheering, sunny influence over the wrinkled brow of old Fritz!"

While the lonely king implored the spirits of his friends, to brighten with their presence the quiet, gloomy apartment at Sans-Souci, the sun shone in full splendor at Charlottenburg—the sunshine beaming from the munificence of Frederick. Wilhelmine Enke had passed the whole day in admiring the beautiful and tasteful arrangement of the villa. Every piece of furniture, every ornament, she examined attentively—all filled her with delight. The prince, who accompanied her from room to room, listened to her outbursts of pleasure, rejoicing.

"I wish that I could often prepare such happiness for you, dearest, for my heart is twice gladdened to see your beaming face."

"Reflected from your own. You are my good genius upon earth. You have caused the poor, neglected child to become the rich and happy woman. To you I owe this home, this foot of earth, which I can call my own. Here blossom the flowers for me—here I am mistress, and those who enter must come as my guests, and honor me. All this I owe to you."

"Not to me," said the prince, smiling; "I only gave to you what was given to me! To the king belong your thanks. Harsh in words, but gentle in deeds, he has given you this refuge, freeing you from the slavery of poverty, from the sorrow of being homeless. But tell it not, Wilhelmine. The king would be angry if it were known that he not only tolerated but showed great generosity to you. It is a secret that I ought not even to disclose to you. I could not receive your thanks, for I have not deserved them. From the king comes your good fortune, not from me. The day will come when I can requite you, when the poor crown prince becomes the rich king. On that day the golden rain shall again shower upon you, never to cease, and, vying with the shower of gold, the brightest sunbeams play continually around you. As king, I will reward your fidelity and love, which you have proved to the poor crown prince, with splendor, power, and riches. Until then rejoice with the little that his grace has accorded you, and await the much that love will one day bring you. Farewell, Wilhelmine, the evening sets in, and I must forth to Potsdam. The king would never pardon me if I did not pass the last evening with my wife in the circle of my family. Farewell!"

He embraced her tenderly, and Wilhelmine accompanied the prince to the carriage, and returned to survey anew the beautiful rooms which were now her own possession. An unspeakable, unknown feeling was roused in her, and voices, which she had never heard, spoke to her from the depths of her heart. "You are no longer a despised, homeless creature," they whispered. "You have a home, a foot of earth to call your own. Make yourself a name, that you may be of consequence in the world. You are clever and beautiful, and with your prudence and beauty you can win a glorious future! Remember the Marquise de Pompadour, neglected and scorned as you, until a king loved her, and she became the wife of a king, and all France bowed down to her. Even the Empress Maria Theresa honored her with her notice, and called her cousin. I am also the favorite of a future king, and I will also become the queen of my king!"

Wilhelmine had remained standing in the midst of the great drawing-room, which she was passing through, listening to these seductive voices, to these strange pictures of the future. In her imagination she saw herself in this room surrounded with splendor and magnificence, and sparkling with gems. She saw around her elegantly-attired ladies and gentlemen, in brilliant uniforms, glittering with orders; saw every-where smiling faces, and respectful manners. She saw all eyes turned to her, and heard only flattering words, which resounded for her from every lip—for her, once so despised and scorned! "It shall be, yes, it shall be," cried she aloud. "I will be the queen of my king! I will become the Prussian Marquise de Pompadour; that I swear by the heads of my children, by—"

"Rather swear by thy own beautiful head, Wilhelmine," said a voice behind her. Startled, she turned, and beheld the tall figure of a man, wrapped in a long cloak, who stood in the open door.

"Who are you?" she cried, amazed. "How dare you enter here?"

The figure closed the door, without answering, and, slowly approaching Wilhelmine, fixed his black eyes upon her with a searching gaze. She tried to summon help, but the words died on her lips; her cheeks blanched with terror, and, as if rooted to the floor, she stood with outstretched arms imploring the approaching form. The figure smiled, but there was something commanding in its manner, and in the fiery eyes, which rested upon her. When quite near her, it raised its right hand with an impatient movement. Immediately her arms fell at her side, her cheeks glowed, and a bright smile lighted up her face. Then it lifted the three-cornered, gold-bordered hat which shaded its face, nodding to her.

"Do you recognize me, Wilhelmine?" he asked, in a sweet, melodious voice.

"Yes," she answered, her eyes still fixed upon him. "You are Cagliostro, the great ruler and magician."

"Where did we meet?"

"I remember; it was in Paris, at the house of the governor of the Bastile, M. Delaunay. You caused me to read in a glass the future—a bright, glorious future. I was surrounded with splendor and magnificence. I saw myself glittering with gems; a king knelt at my feet. I was encircled by richly-attired courtiers, who bowed before me, and honored me, whispering: 'We salute you, O beautiful countess; be gracious to us, exalted princess!' It sounded like heavenly music, and I shouted with delight."

"Was that all?" said Cagliostro, solemnly, "that the crystal showed you."

Shuddering, she murmured: "The splendor, glory, and power vanished, and all was changed to a fearful picture. I saw myself in a plain, dark dress, in a deserted, lonely room, with iron-barred windows, and a small iron door closed in the dreary white walls—it was a prison! And I heard whispered around me: 'Woe to you, fallen and dethroned one! You have wasted away the days of your splendor, submit in patience to the days of your shame and humiliation.' I could not endure to behold it, and screamed with terror, fainting."

"You demanded to see the future, and I showed it to you," said Cagliostro, earnestly. "Though I let the light shine into your soul, still it was dark within; you pursued the way of unbelief, and desired not to walk in the way of knowledge. I sent messengers twice to you to lead you in the right path, and you sent them laughing away. Recall what I told you in Paris. I will it!"

"I remember, master; you said that in the most important days of my life you would come to me, and extend to me a helping hand: if I seized it, the first picture would be fulfilled; if I refused it, the prison awaited me!"

"I have kept my word: to-day is an eventful day in your life; you have risen from want and degradation—you have mounted the first rounds of the ladder of your greatness and power. You are the mistress of this house." "How did you know it?" asked Wilhelmine, astonished. With a pitying smile he answered: "I know every thing that I will, and I see many things that I would willingly close my eyes upon. I see your future, and my soul pities you, unhappy one; you are lost if you do not seize the hand extended to you. You see not the abyss which opens before you, and you will fall bleeding and with broken limbs."

"Mercy, mercy!" she groaned—"stretch out your hand and protect me." Wilhelmine sank as if crushed to the earth. Cagliostro bent over her, and stroked her cold, pale face, breathing upon her the hot breath of his lips. "I will pity you—I will protect you. Rise, my daughter!" He assisted her to rise, and imprinted a passionate kiss upon her hand. "From this hour I count you as one of mine," he said; "you shall be received into the holy band of spirits! You shall be consecrated, and enter the Inner Temple. Are you prepared?" "I am, master," she humbly replied.

"To-morrow the Temple brothers will open the temple of bliss to you. You shall hear, see, and be silent." "I will see, hear, and be silent," she murmured.

"When evening sets in, send away your servants," commanded Cagliostro. "Let the doors stand open; they shall be guarded, that no one may enter but the summoned. Art thou prepared?"

"I am, master!"

"Withdraw now to your room, Wilhelmine, and elevate your thoughts in devotion and contrition, and await the future. Kneel, my daughter, kneel!" She sank upon her knees. "Bless me, master, bless me!" "I bless you!"

She felt a hot, burning sensation upon her forehead, and suddenly a bright light shone in the obscure room. Wilhelmine screamed, and covered her eyes. When she ventured to look up, only soft moonlight penetrated from the high window into the apartment, and she was alone. "To-morrow—to-morrow, at midnight!" she murmured, shuddering, and casting a timid look around.

BOOK II
ROSICRUCIANS AND POWERFUL GENIUSES

CHAPTER X
GOETHE IN BERLIN

"I wish I only knew whether it were a man, or whether the god Apollo has really appeared to me in human form," sighed Conrector Moritz, as he paced his room—a strange, gloomy apartment, quite in keeping with the singular occupant—gray walls, with Greek apothegms inscribed upon them in large letters—dirty windows, pasted over with strips of paper; high, open book-shelves, containing several hundred books, some neatly arranged, others thrown together in confusion. In the midst of a chaos of books and papers stood a colossal bust of the Apollo-Belvedere upon a table near the window, the whiteness and beauty of which were in singular contrast, to the dust and disorder which surrounded it.

At the back of the room was an open wardrobe, filled with gay-colored garments. A beautiful carpet of brilliant colors covered the middle of the dirty floor, and upon this paced to and fro the strange occupant of this strange room, Philip Charles Moritz, conrector of the college attached to the Gray Monastery. There was no trace of the bearing and demeanor which distinguished him at the parade at Potsdam yesterday—no trace of the young elegant, dressed in the latest fashion. To-day he wore a white garment, of no particular style, tied at the neck with a red ribbon (full sleeves, buttoned at the wrist with lace-cuffs); and, falling from the shoulders in scanty folds to just below the knees, it displayed his bare legs, and his feet shod with red sandals.

His hair was unpowdered, and not tied in a cue, according to the fashion, but hung in its natural brown color, flowing quite loosely, merely confined by a red ribbon wound in among his curls, and hanging down in short bows at each temple like the frontlet of the old Romans. Thus, in this singular costume, belonging half to old Adam, and half to the old Romans, Philip Moritz walked back and forth upon the carpet, ruminating upon the beaming beauty of the stranger whose acquaintance he had so recently made, and whom he could not banish from his thoughts. "What wicked demon induced me to go to Potsdam yesterday?" said he to himself. "I who hate mankind, and believe that they are all of vulgar, ordinary material, yield to the longing for society, and am driven again into the world."

A loud knocking at the door interrupted this soliloquy, and the door opened at the commanding "Come in!"

"It is he, it is Apollo," cried Moritz, joyfully. "Come in, sir, come in—I have awaited you with the most ardent desire."

Moritz rushed to the young gentleman, who had just closed the door, and whose beautiful, proud face lighted up with a smile at the singular apparition before him. "Pardon me, I disturb you, sir; you were about to make your toilet. Permit me to return after you have dressed."

"You are mistaken," cried Moritz, eagerly. "You find me in my usual home-dress—I like my ease and freedom, and I am of opinion that mankind will never be happy and contented until they return to their natural state, wearing no more clothing, but glorying in the beauty which bountiful Nature has bestowed upon her most loved and chosen subjects."

"Sir," cried the other, laughing, "then benevolent Nature should adapt her climate accordingly, and relieve her dear creatures from the inclination to take cold."

"You may be right," said Moritz, earnestly, "but we will not quarrel about it. Will you not keep your promise to reveal to me your name?"

"Tell me your own once more. Tell me if this youth, whom I see before me in this ideal dress, is the same modest young man whom I met at the parade yesterday, and who presented himself as Philip Moritz? Then please to inform me whether you are the Philip Moritz who wrote a spirited and cordial letter to Johann Wolfgang Goethe some years since about the tragedy of 'Stella,' the representation of which had been forbidden at that time?"

"Yes, I am the same Philip Moritz, who wrote to the poet Goethe to prove to him, with the most heart-felt sympathy, that we are not all such stupid fellows in Berlin as Nicolai, who pronounced the tragedy 'Stella' immoral; that it is only, as Goethe himself called it, 'a play for lovers.'"

"And will you not be kind enough to tell me what response the poet made to your amiable letter?"

"Proud and amiable at the same time, most gracefully he answered me, but not with words. He sent me his tragedy 'Stella' bound in rose-colored satin. *[Footnote: "Goethe in Berlin,"—Sketches from his life at the anniversary of his one hundredth birthday.]* See there! it is before the bust of Apollo on my writing-table, where it has lain for three years!"

"What did he write to you at the same time?"

"Nothing—why should he? Was not the book sufficient answer?"

"Did he write nothing? Permit me to say to you that Goethe behaved like a brute and an ass to you!"

"Sir," cried Moritz, angrily, "I forbid you to speak of my favorite in so unbecoming a manner in my room!"

"Sir," cried the other, "you dare not forbid me. I insist upon it that that man is sometimes a brute and an ass! I can penitently acknowledge it to you, dear Moritz, for I am Johann Wolfgang Goethe himself!"

"You, you are Goethe!" shouted Moritz, as he seized him with both hands, drawing him toward the window, and gazing at him with the greatest enthusiasm and delight. "Yes, yes," he shouted, "you are either Apollo or Goethe! The gods are not so stupid as to return to this miserable world, so you must be Goethe. No other man would dare to sport such a godlike face as you do, you favorite of the gods!"

He then loosed his hold upon the smiling poet, and sprang to the writing-table. "Listen, Apollo," he cried, with wild joy. "Goethe is here, thy dear son is here! Hurrah! long live Goethe!"

He took the rose-colored little book, and shouting tossed it to the ceiling, and sprang about like a mad bacchant, and finally threw himself upon the carpet, rolling over and over like a frolicksome, good-natured child upon its nurse's lap.

Goethe laughed aloud. "What are you doing, dear Moritz? What does this mean?" he asked.

Moritz stopped a moment, looking up to Goethe with a face beaming with joy. "I cannot better express my happiness. Language is too feeble—too poor!"

"If that is the case, then I will join you," said Goethe, throwing himself upon the carpet, rolling and tumbling about. *[Footnote: This scene which I relate, and which Teichman also mentions in his "Leaves of Memory of Goethe in Berlin," has been often related to me by Ludwig Tieck exactly in this manner. Teichman believes it was the poet Burman. But I remember distinctly that Ludwig Tieck told me that it was the eccentric savant, Philip Moritz, with whom Goethe made the acquaintance in this original manner.—The Authoress.]*

All at once Moritz jumped up without saying a word, rushed to the wardrobe, dressed himself in modest attire in a few moments, and presented himself to Goethe, who rose from the carpet quite astounded at the sudden metamorphosis. Then he seized his three-cornered hat to go out, when Goethe held him fast.

"You are not going into the street, sir! You forget that your hair is flying about as if unloosed by a divine madness."

"Sir, people are quite accustomed to see me in a strange costume, and the most of them think me crazy."

"You are aware that insane people believe that they only are sane, and that reasonable people are insane. You will grant me that it is much more like a crazy person to strew his hair with flour, and tie it up in that ridiculous cue, than to wear it as God made it, uncombed and unparted, as I do my beautiful hair, and for which they call me crazy! But, for Heaven's sake, where are you going?" asked Goethe, struggling to retain him.

"I am going to trumpet through every street in Berlin that the author of 'Werther,' of 'Clavigo,' of 'Gotz von Berlichingen,' of 'Stella,' of the most beautiful poems, is in my humble apartment. I will call in all the little poets and savants of Berlin; I will drag Mammler, Nicolai, Engel, Spaulding, Gedicke, Plumicke, Karschin, and Burman here. They shall all come to see Wolfgang Goethe, and adore him. The insignificant poets shall pay homage to thee, the true poet, the favorite of Apollo."

"My dear Moritz, if you leave me for that, I will run away, and you will trouble yourself in vain."

"Impossible; you will be my prisoner until I return. I shall lock you in, and you cannot escape by the window, as I fortunately live on the third story."

"But I shall not wait to be looked in," answered Goethe, slightly annoyed. "I came to see you, and if you run away I shall go also, and I advise you not to try to prevent me." His voice resounded through the apartment, growing louder as he spoke, his cheeks flushed, and his high, commanding brow contracted.

"Jupiter Tonans!" cried Moritz, regarding him, "you are truly Jupiter Tonans in person, and I bow before you and obey your command. I shall remain to worship you, and gaze at you."

"And it may be possible to speak in a reasonable manner to me," said Goethe, coaxingly. "Away with sentimentality and odors of incense! We are no sybarites, to feed on sweet-meats and cakes; but we are men who have a noble aim in view, attained only by a thorny path. Our eyes must remain fixed upon the goal, and nothing must divert them from it."

"What is the aim that we should strive for?" asked Moritz, his whole being suddenly changing, and his manner expressing the greatest depression and sadness.

Goethe smiled. "How can you ask, as if you did not know it yourself. Self-knowledge should be our first aim! The ancient philosophers were wise to have inscribed over the entrances to their temples, 'Know thyself,' in order to remind all approaching, to examine themselves before they entered the halls of the gods. Is not the human heart equally a temple? only the demons and the gods strive together therein, unfortunately. To drive the former out, and give place to the latter, should be our aim; and when once purified, and room is given for good deeds and great achievements, we shall not rest satisfied simply to conquer, but rise with gladness to build altars upon those places which we have freed from the demons; for that, we must steadily keep in view truth and reality, and not hide them with a black veil, or array them in party-colored rags. Our ideas must be clear about the consequences of things, that we may not be like those foolish men who drink wine every evening and complain of headache every morning, resorting to preventives."

Did Goethe know the struggles and dissensions which rent the heart of the young man to whom he spoke? Had his searching eyes read the secrets which were hidden in that darkened soul? He regarded him as he spoke with so much commiseration that Moritz's heart softened under the genial influence of sympathy and kindness. A convulsive trembling seized him, his cheeks were burning red, and his features expressed the struggle within. Suddenly he burst into tears. "I am very, very wretched," he sighed, with a voice suffocated by weeping, and sank upon a chair, sobbing aloud, and covering his face with his hands.

Goethe approached him, and laid his hand gently upon his shoulder. "Why are you so miserable? Is there any human being who can help you?" he kindly inquired.

"Yes," sobbed Moritz; "there are those who could, but they will not, and I am lost. I stand upon the brink of a precipice, with Insanity staring at me, grinning and showing her teeth. I know it, but cannot retreat. I wear the mask of madness to conceal my careworn face. Your divine eyes could not be deceived. You have not mistaken the caricature for the true face. You have penetrated beneath the gay tatters, and have seen the misery which sought to hide itself there."

"I saw it, and I bewailed it, as a friend pities a friend whom he would willingly aid if he only knew how to do it."

"No one can help me," sighed Moritz, shaking his head mournfully. "I am lost, irremediably lost!"

"No one is lost who will save himself. He who is wrecked by a storm and tossed upon the raging sea, ought to be upon the watch for a plank by which he can save himself. He must keep his eyes open, and not let his arms hang idly; for if he allows himself to be swallowed up he becomes a self-murderer, who, like Erostratus, destroyed the holy temple, and gained eternal fame through eternal shame."

"What are you saying?" cried Moritz, "you, the author of 'Werther,' of that immortal work which has drunk the tears of the whole world, and has become the Holy Testament for unhappy souls!"

"Rather say for lovers," replied Goethe, "and add also those troubled spirits who think themselves poetical when they whine and howl; who cry over misfortune if Fate denies them the toy which their vanity, their ambition, or their amorousness, had chosen. Do not burden me with what I am not guilty of; do not say that wine is a poison, because it is not good for the sick. It is intended for well people; it animates and inspires them to fresh vigor. Now please to consider yourself well, and not ill."

"I am ill, indeed I am ill," sighed Moritz. "Oh! continue to regard me with those eyes, which shine like stars into my benighted soul. I feel like one who has long wandered through the desert, his feet burnt with the sand, his hair scorched with the sun, and, exhausted with hunger and thirst, feels death approaching. Suddenly he discovers a green oasis, and a being with outstretched arms calling to him with a soft, angel-like voice: 'Come, save thyself in my arms; feel that thou art not alone in the desert, for I am with thee, and will sustain thee!'"

"And I say it to you from the bottom of my heart," said Goethe, affectionately. "Yes, here is one, who is only too happy to aid you, who can sympathize with every sorrow, because he has himself felt it in his own breast, who may even say of himself, like Ovid: 'Nothing human is strange to me.' If I can aid you, say so, and I will willingly do it."

"No, you cannot," murmured Moritz.

"At least confide your grief to me; that is an alleviation."

"Oh, how kind and generous you are!" Moritz said, pressing the hand of his new-made friend to his bosom. "How much good it does me to listen to you, and look at your beautiful face! I believed myself steeled against every thing that could happen to mortals; that the fool which I would be had killed within me the higher man. I was almost proud to have succeeded in deceiving men; that they mistook my grotesque mask for my real face; that they point the finger at me, and laugh, saying to each other: 'That is a fool, an original, whom Nature herself has chosen as a kind of court fool to society.' No one has understood the cry of distress of my soul. Those who laughed at the comical fellow by day, little dreamed of the anguish and misery in which he sighed away the night."

"You not only wrong yourself, but you wrong mankind," said Goethe, kindly. "In the world, and in literature, you bear an honored name; every one of education is familiar with your excellent work on 'Prosody of the German Language'—has read also your spirited Journey to England. You have no right to ask that one should separate the kernel from the shell in hastily passing by. If you surround yourself with a wall bedaubed with caricatures, you cannot expect that people will look behind what seems an entrance to a puppet-show, to find holy temples, blooming gardens, or a church-yard filled with graves."

"That is just what I resemble," said Moritz, with a melancholy air. "From the depths of my soul it seems so. Nothing but buried hopes, murdered ideals, and wishes trodden under foot. From childhood I have exerted myself against circumstances; I have striven my whole life—a pledge of my being against unpropitious Fate. Although the son of a poor tradesman, Nature had given me a thirst for knowledge, a love for science and art. On account of it I passed for a stupid idler in the family, who would not contribute to his own support. Occupation with books was accounted idleness and laziness by my father. I was driven to work with blows and ill-treatment; and, that I might the sooner equal my father as a good shoemaker, I was bound to the stool near his own. During the long, fearful days I was forced to sit and draw the pitched, offensive thread through the leather, and when my arms were lame, and sank weary at my side, then I was invigorated to renewed exertion with blows. Finally, with the courage of despair, I fled from this life of torture. Unacquainted with the world, and inexperienced, I hoped for the sympathy of men, but in vain. No one would relieve or assist me! Days and weeks long I have wandered around in the forest adjoining our little village, and lived like the animals, upon roots and herbs. Yet I was happy! I had taken with me in my flight two books which I had received as prizes, in the happy days that my father permitted me to go to the Latin school. The decision of the teacher that I was created for a scholar, so terrified my father, that he took me from the school, to turn the embryo savant, who would be good for nothing, into a shoemaker, who might earn his bread. My two darling books remained to me. In the forest solitude I read Ovid and Virgil until I had memorized them, and recited them aloud, in pathetic tones, for my own amusement. To-day I recall those weeks in the forest stillness as the happiest, purest, and most beautiful of my life."

"And they undoubtedly are," said Goethe, kindly. "The return to Nature is the return to one's self. Who will be an able, vigorous man and remain so, must, above all things, live in and with Nature."

"But oh! this happy life did not long continue," sighed Moritz. "My father discovered my retreat, and came with sheriffs and bailiffs to seize me like a criminal—like a wild animal. With my hands bound, I was brought back in broad day, amid the jeers of street boys. Permit me to pass in silence the degradation, the torture which followed. I became a burden to myself, and longed for death. The ill-treatment of my father finally revived my courage to run away the second time. I went to a large town near by, and decided to earn my living rather than return to my father. To fulfil the prophecy of my teacher was my ambition. The privations that I endured, the life I led, I will not recount to you. I performed the most menial service, and worked months like a beast of burden. For want of a shelter, I slept in deserted yards and tumble-down houses. Upon a piece of bread and a drink of water I lived, saving, with miserly greediness, the money which I earned as messenger or day-laborer. At the end of a year, I had earned sufficient to buy an old suit of clothes at a second-hand clothing-store, and present myself to the director of the Gymnasium, imploring him to receive me as pupil. Bitterly weeping, I opened my heart to him, and disclosed the torture of my sad life as a child, and begged him to give me the opportunity to educate myself. He repulsed me with scorn, and threatened to give me over to the police, as a runaway, as a vagabond, and beggar. 'I am no beggar!' I cried, vehemently, 'I will be under obligation to no one. I have money to pay for two years in advance, and during this time I shall be able to earn sufficient to pay for the succeeding two years.' This softened the anger of the crabbed director; he was friendly and kind, and promised me his assistance."

"Poor boy!" sighed Goethe. "So young, and yet forced to learn that there is a power to which not only kings and princes, but mind must bow; to which science and art have submitted, as to their Maecenas! This power opened the doors of the Gymnasium to you."

"It was even thus. The director took pity upon me, and permitted me to enter upon my studies at once; he did more, he assured my future. Oh, he was a humane and kind man! When he learned that I possessed nothing but the little sum to which the drops of blood of a year's toil still clung, then—"

"He returned it to you," interrupted Goethe, kindly.

"No, he offered me board, lodging, and clothing, during my course at the Gymnasium."

"That was well," cried Goethe. "Tell me the name of this honorable man, that I may meet him and extend to him my hand."

A troubled smile spread over Philip's face. "Permit me for the time being to conceal the name," he replied. "I received the generous proposal gratefully, and asked, deeply moved, if there were no services which I could return for so much kindness and generosity. It proved that there were, and the director made them known to me. He was unmarried, hence the necessity of men's service. I should be society for him—be a companion, in fact; I should do what every grateful son would do for his father—help him dress, keep his room in order, and prepare his breakfast."

"That meant that you should be his servant!" cried Goethe, indignant.

"Only in the morning," replied Moritz, smiling. "Evenings and nights I should have the honor to be his amanuensis; I should look over the studies of the scholars, and correct their exercises; and when I had made sufficient progress, it should be my duty to give two hours to different classes, and I should read aloud or play cards with the director on leisure evenings. Besides, I was obliged to promise never to leave the house without his permission; never to speak to, or hold intercourse with, any one outside the hours of instruction. All these conditions were written down, and signed by both parties, as if a business contract."

"A transaction by which a human soul was bargained for!" thundered Goethe. "Reveal to me, now, the name of this trader of souls, that I may expose him to public shame!"

"He died a year since," replied Moritz, softened. "God summoned him to judgment. When the physician announced to him that the cancer was incurable, when he felt death approaching, he sent for me, and begged my forgiveness, with tears and deep contrition. I forgave him, so let me cease to recall the life I passed with him. By the sweat of my brow I was compelled to serve him; for seven long years I was his slave. I sold myself for the sake of knowledge, I was consoled by progress. I was the servant, companion, jester, and slave of my tyrant, but I was also the disciple, the priest of learning. In my own room my chains fell off. In the lonely night-watches I communed with the great, the immortal spirits of Horace, Virgil, and even the proud Caesar, and the divine Homer. Those solitary but happy hours of the night are never to be forgotten, never to be portrayed; they refreshed me for the trials of the day, and enabled me to endure them! At the close of seven years I was prepared to enter the university, and the bargain between my master and myself was also at an end. Freed from my tyrant, I bent my steps toward Frankfort University, to feel my liberty enchained anew. For seven years I had been the slave of the director; now I became the slave of poverty, forced to labor to live! Oh, I cannot recall those scenes! Suffice it to say, that during one year I had no fixed abode, never tasted warm food. But it is passed—I have conquered! After years of struggle, of exertion, of silent misery, only relieved by my stolen hours of blissful study, I gained my reward. I was free! My examination passed, I was honored with the degrees of Doctor of Philosophy and Master of Arts.

After many intervening events, I was appointed conrector of the college attached to the Gray Monastery, which position now supports me."

"God be praised, I breathe freely!" answered Goethe, with one of those sunny smiles which, in a moment of joyful excitement, lighted up his face. "I feel like one shipwrecked, who has, at last, reached a safe harbor. I rejoice in your rescue as if it were my own. Now you are safe. You have reached the port, and in the quiet happiness of your own library you will win new laurels. Why, then, still dispirited and unhappy? The past, with its sorrows and humiliations, is forgotten, the present is satisfactory, and the future is full of hope for you."

"Full of misery is the present," cried Philip, angrily, "and filled with despair I glance at the future. You do not see it with your divine eyes, you do not perceive it, poet with the sympathetic soul. You, too, thought that Philip Moritz had only a head for the sciences, and forgot that he had a heart to love. I tell you that he has a warm, affectionate heart, torn with grief and all the tortures of jealousy; that disappointed happiness maddens him. I was not created to be happy, and my whole being longs for happiness. Oh! I would willingly give my life for one day by the side of the one I love."

"Do not trifle," said Goethe, angrily. "He who has striven and struggled as you have, dare not offer, for any woman, however beautiful and seductive, to yield his life, which has been destined to a higher aim than mere success in love. Perhaps you think that God has infused a ray of His intelligence into the mind of man, created him immortal, and breathed upon him with His world-creating breath only, to make him happy, and find that happiness in love! No! my friend, God has given to man like faculties with Himself, and inspired him, that he might be a worthy representative of Him upon the earth; that he should prove, in his life, that he is not only the blossom, but the fruit also, of God's creation. Love is to man the perfume of his existence. She may intoxicate him for a while, may inspire him to poetical effusions, to great deeds, even; but he should hesitate to let her become his mistress, to let her be the tyrant of his existence. If she would enchain him, he must tear himself away, even if he tear out his own heart. Man possesses that which is more ennobling than mere feeling; he has intellect—soul."

"Ah!" cried Moritz, "it is easy to see that you have never loved madly, despairingly. You have never seen the woman whom you adore, and who perhaps reciprocates your passion, forced to marry another."

A shadow flitted over Goethe's brow, and the flashing brilliancy of his eyes was changed to gloomy sadness. Gently, but quickly, he laid his hand upon Moritz's shoulder, saying: "In this hour, when two souls are revealed to each other, will I acknowledge to you that which I have never spoken of. I, too, love a woman, who loves me, and yet can never be mine, for she is married to another. I love this sweet woman as I have never loved a mortal being. For years my existence has belonged to her, she has been the centre of all my thoughts. It would seem to me as if the earth were without a sun, heaven without a God, if she should vanish from life. I even bless the torture which her prudery, her alternate coldness and friendliness cause me, as it comes from her, from the highest bliss of feeling. This passion has swept through my soul, as if uniting in itself all my youthful loves, till, like a torrent, ever renewing itself, ever moving onward, it has become the highway of my future. Upon this stream floats the bark laden with all my happiness, fame, and poetry. The palaces which my fancy creates rise upon its shore. Every zephyr, however slight, makes me tremble. Every cloud which overshadows the brow of my beloved, sweeps like a tempest over my own. I live upon her smile. A kind word falling from her lips makes me happy for days; and when she turns away from me with coldness and indifference, I feel like one driven about as Orestes by the Furies."

"You really are in love!" cried Moritz. "I will take back what I have said. You, the chosen of the gods, know all the human heart can suffer, even unhappy love."

Almost angry, and with hesitation, Goethe answered him: "I do not call this passion of mine an unhappy one, for in the very perception of it lies happiness. We are only wretched when we lose self-control. To this point Love shall never lead me. She yields me the highest delight, but she shall never bring me to self-destruction. Grief for her may, like a destructive whirlwind, crush every blossom of my heart; but she shall never destroy me. The man, the poet, must stand higher than the lover; for where the latter is about to yield to despair, the former will rise, and, with the defiance of Prometheus, challenge the gods to recognize the godlike similitude, that man can rise superior to sorrow, never despairing, never cursing Fate if all the rosy dreams of youth are not realities, but with upturned gaze stride over the waste places of life, consoling himself with the thought that only magnanimous souls can suffer and conquer magnanimously. Vanquished grief brings us nearer to the immortal, and gradually bears us from this vale of sorrow up to the brighter heights, nearer to God—the earth with her petty confusion lying like a worthless tool at our feet!"

"It is heavenly to be able to say that, and divine to perceive it," cried Moritz, bursting into tears. "The miseries of life chain me to the dust, and do not permit me to mount to the heights which a hero like Goethe reaches victorious. It is indeed sublime to conquer one's self, and be willing to resign the happiness which flees us. But see how weak I am—I cannot do it! I can never give up the one I love. It seems as if I could move heaven and earth to conquer at last, and that I must die if I do not succeed—die like Werther."

Goethe's eyes flashed with anger, and with heightened color he exclaimed: "You all repeat the same litany—do not make me answerable for all your weaknesses, and blame poor Werther for the creations of your own imagination. I, who am the author of Werther, am free from this abominable sentimentality. Why cannot others be, who only read what I have conceived? But pardon my violence," he continued, with a milder voice and gentler manner. "Never did an author create a work which brought him at the same time so great fame and bitter reproach as this work has brought to me. 'The Sorrows of Young Werther' have indeed been transformed into the sorrows of young Goethe, and I even fear that old Goethe will have to suffer for it. I have spoken to you as a friend to a friend: cherish my words, take them to heart, and arise from the dust; shake off the self-strewn ashes from your head. Enter again as a brave champion the combat of life—summon to your aid cunning, power, prudence, and audacity, to conquer your love. Whether you succeed or not, then you aim at the greatest of battles—that of mind over matter—then remember my farewell words. From the power which binds all men he frees himself who conquers himself.—Farewell! If ever you need the encouragement of a friend, if ever a sympathizing soul is necessary to you, come to Weimar; sympathy and appreciation shall never fail you there."

"Oh! I will surely go," answered Moritz, deeply moved, and pressing heartily Goethe's offered hand.

"One thing more I have to say to you: Live much with Nature; accustom yourself to regard the sparrow, the flower, or the stone, as worthy of your attention as the wonderful phoenix or the monuments of the ancients with their illegible inscriptions. To walk with Nature is balsam for a weary soul; gently touched by her soft hands, the recovery is most rapid. I have experienced it, and do experience it daily. Now, once more, farewell; in the true sense of the word fare-thee-well! I wish that I could help you in other ways than by mere kind words. It pains me indeed that I can render you no other aid or hope. You alone can do what none other can do for you.—Farewell!"

He turned, and motioning to Moritz not to follow him, almost flew down the stairs into the street. Drawing a long breath, he stood leaning against the door, gazing at the crowd—at the busy passers-by—some merrily chatting with their companions, others with earnest mien and in busy haste. No one seemed to care for him, no one looked at him. If by chance they glanced at him, Johann Wolfgang Goethe was of no more consequence to them than any other honest citizen in a neighboring doorway.

Without perhaps acknowledging it to himself, Goethe was a little vexed that no one observed him; that the weather-maker from Weimar, who was accustomed to be greeted there, and everywhere, indeed, with smiles and bows, should here in Berlin be only an ordinary mortal—a stranger among strangers. "I would not live here," said he, as he walked slowly down the street. "What are men in great cities but grains of sand, now blown together and then asunder? There is no individuality, one is only a unit in the mass! But it is well occasionally to look into such a kaleidoscope, and admire the play of colors, which I have done, and with a glad heart I will now fly home to all my friends—to you, beloved one—to you, Charlotte!"

CHAPTER XI
THE INNER AND THE MIDDLE TEMPLE

Wilhelmine Enke had passed the day in great anxiety and excitement, and not even the distraction of her new possession had been able to calm the beating of her heart or allay her fears. Prince Frederick William had arrived early in the morning, to bid her farewell, as he was to march in the course of the day with his regiments from Potsdam. With the tenderest assurances of love he took leave of Wilhelmine, and with tears kissed his two children, pressing them to his heart. As he was about to enter his carriage he returned to the house to embrace his weeping mistress, and reassure her of his fidelity, and make her promise him again and again that she would remain true to him, and never love another.

It was not alone the farewell to her beloved prince which caused Wilhelmine such anxiety and made her so restless. Like a dark cloud the remembrance of Cagliostro's mysterious appearance arose in her mind, overshadowing her every hour more and more, filling her soul with terror. In vain did she seek refuge near her children, trying to cheer and forget herself in their innocent amusement—one moment running about the garden with them, then returning to the house to reexamine it. Her thoughts would revert to Cagliostro, and the solemnities which were to take place at her house that night. The thought terrified her that at nightfall she was obliged to send away all her servants, and not even be permitted to lock herself in the lonely, deserted house. For the great magician had commanded her to let the doors of her house stand open; he would place sentinels at every entrance, and none but the elect would be allowed to enter. Wilhelmine had not the courage to resist this command. As evening approached, she sent the cook, with other servants, to her apartment at Berlin, ordering them to pack her furniture and other effects, and send them by a hired wagon to Charlottenburg the following morning. An hour previous to this she had sent the nurse and two children to Potsdam with a similar commission, ordering them to return early the next day. Alone she now awaited with feverish anxiety Cagliostro's appearance. Again and again she wandered through the silent, deserted rooms frightened at the sound of her own footsteps, and peering into each room as if an assassin or robber were lurking there. She had many enemies—many there were who cursed her, and, alas! none loved her—she was friendless, save the prince, who was far away. The tears which the princess had shed on her account weighed like a heavy burden upon her heart, burning into her very soul in this hour of lonely, sad retrospection. She tried in vain to excuse herself, in the fact that she had loved the prince before his marriage; that she had sacrificed herself to him through affection, and that she was not entitled to become his wife, as she was not born under the canopy of a throne.

From the depths of her conscience there again rose the tearful, sad face of the princess, accusing her as an adulteress—as a sinner before God and man! Terrified, she cried: "I have truly loved him, and I do still love him; this is my excuse and my justification. She is not to be pitied who can walk openly by the side of her husband, enjoying the respect and sympathy of all to whom homage is paid, and who, one day, will be queen! I am the only one, I alone! I stand in the shade, despised and scorned, avoided and shunned by every one. Those who recognize me, do so with a mocking smile, and when I pass by they contemptuously shrug their shoulders and say to one another, 'That was Enke, the mistress of the Prince of Prussia!' All this shall be changed," she cried aloud; "I will not always be despised and degraded! I will be revenged on my crushed and scorned youth! I will have rank and name, honor and position, that I will—yes, that I will, indeed!"

Wilhelmine wandered on through the silent rooms, all brilliantly illuminated, a precaution she had taken before dismissing her servants. The bright light was a consolation to her, and, at least, she could not be attacked by surprise, but see her enemy, and escape. "I was a fool," she murmured, "to grant Cagliostro this reception to-night. I know that he is a charlatan! There are no prophets or wizards! Yet, well I remember, though a stranger to me, in Paris, how truthfully he brought before me my past life; with what marvellous exactness he revealed to me secrets known only to my Maker and myself. Cagliostro must be a wizard, then, or a prophet; he has wonderful power over me also, and reads my most secret thoughts. He will assist me to rise from my shame and degradation to an honored position. I shall become a rich and influential woman! I will confide in him, never doubting him—for he is my master and savior! Away with fear! He has said that the house should be guarded, and it will be! Onward then, Wilhelmine, without fear!"

She hastened to the large drawing-room, in order to see the effect of the numerous wax-lights in the superb chandeliers of rock crystal. The great folding-doors resisted all her efforts to open them. "Who is there?" cried a loud, threatening voice. Trembling and with beating heart Wilhelmine leaned against the door, giddy with fear, when a second demand, "Who is there? The watchword! No one can pass without the countersign!"

roused her, and she stole back on tiptoe to her room. "He has kept his word, the doors are guarded!" she whispered. "I will go and await him in my sitting-room." She stepped quickly forward, when suddenly she thought she heard footsteps stealing behind her; turning, she beheld two men wrapped in black cloaks, with black masks, stealthily creeping after her. Wilhelmine shrieked with terror, tore open the door, rushed across the next room into her own boudoir. As she entered a glance revealed to her that the two masks approached nearer and nearer. She bolted the door quickly, sinking to the floor with fright and exhaustion. "What are they going to do? Will they force open the door and murder me? How foolish, how fearfully foolish to have sent away all my servants. Now I understand it: Cagliostro is not only an impostor—a charlatan, but he is a thief and an assassin. I have been caught in the trap set for me, like a credulous fool! He and his associates will rob me and plunder my beautiful villa, but just given to me, and, when they have secured all, murder me to escape betrayal." With deep contrition, weeping and trembling, Wilhelmine accused herself of her credulity and folly. For the first time in her life she was dismayed and cowardly, for it was the first time that she had had to tremble for her possessions. It was something so new, so unaccustomed to her to possess any thing, that it made her anxious, and she feared, as in the fairy tale, that it would dissolve into nothing. By degrees her presence of mind and equanimity were restored. The stillness was unbroken—and no one forced the door, to murder the mistress of this costly possession. Gathering courage, she rose softly and stole to the window. The moon shone brightly and clearly. The house stood sideways to the street, and separated from it, first by thick shrubbery, and then a trellised lawn. Whoever would enter, directly turned into a path leading from the street into the shrubbery. Just upon this walk, Wilhelmine perceived masked men approaching, one by one, as in a procession—slowly, silently moving on, until they neared the gate of the trellised square, where two tall, dark forms were stationed to demand the countersign, which being given, they passed over the lawn into the house.

"I will take courage; he has told me the truth, the house is well guarded," murmured Wilhelmine. "None but the summoned can enter; I belong to the number, and when it is time Cagliostro will come and fetch me. Until then, let me await quietly the result," said she, as she stretched herself comfortably upon the sofa, laughing at her former cowardice and terror. "No one can enter this room unless I open the door, and fortunately there is but one exit. The wizard himself could not gain admittance unless the walls should open or the bolt drive hack for him. Hark! it strikes eleven, one tedious hour longer to wait. I must try to rest a little." She laid her head upon the cushion, closing her eyes. The calm and the quiet were refreshing after the excitement of the day. Gradually her thoughts became confused—

dim pictures floated past her mental vision, her breathing became shorter, and she slept. The stillness was unbroken, save the clock striking the quarters of every hour. Scarcely had the last quarter to midnight sounded, when the window was softly opened, and a dark form descended into the room. He listened a moment, looking at the sleeping one, who moved not; then extinguished the light, creeping toward the door. Wilhelmine slept on. Suddenly it seemed to her as if sunbeams blinded her, and she started up from a profound sleep. It was indeed no dream. A white form stood before her of dazzling brilliancy, as if formed of sun-rays.

"Rise and follow me!" cried a commanding voice. "The Great Kophta commands you. Mask yourself, and, as your life is dear to you, do not raise it for one instant!" Wilhelmine took the mask, upon which flickered a little blue flame, and held it close to her face. "Pray in spirit, then follow me." Wilhelmine followed without opposition the bright form which moved before her through the dark rooms. She felt as if under the influence of a charm; her heart beat violently, her feet trembled, but still she felt no more wavering or fear; a joyous confidence filled her whole being. With her eyes bent upon the moving form of light, she went onward in the obscurity, and entered the great drawing-room, where profound darkness and silence reigned. A slight murmur, as of those in prayer, fell on her car, and it seemed as if numberless black shadows were moving about. "Kneel and pray," whispered a voice near her. Her conductor had disappeared, and the gloom of night surrounded her. Wilhelmine knelt as she was bidden, but she could not pray; breathless expectation and eager curiosity banished all devotion and composure. Occasionally was heard, amid the silence and darkness, a deep sigh, a suppressed groan, or a shriek, which died away in the murmuring of prayer. Suddenly a strange music broke the stillness—sharp, piercing tones, resonant as bells, and increasing in power, sometimes as rich and full as the peals of an organ, then gentle and soft as the murmuring wind, or a sorrow-laden sigh. Then, human voices joined the music, swelling it to a wonderful and harmonious choir—to an inspired song of aspiration, Of fervent expectation, and imploring the coming of him who would bring glory and peace, filling the hearts of believers with godliness. The chorus of the Invisibles had not ceased, when a strange blue light began to glimmer at the farther end of the room; then it shot like a flash through the dark space. As their dazzled eyes were again raised, they saw in a kind of halo, in the midst of golden clouds, a tall, dazzling figure, in a long, flowing robe, sparkling with silver. The lovely bust, the beautiful arms and shoulders, were covered with a transparent golden tissue, over which fell the long, curly hair to the waist. A glittering band, sparkling like stars, was wound through the hair, which surrounded a feminine face of surpassing beauty. Perpetual youth glowed upon her full, rosy cheeks; bright intelligence beamed from the clear, lofty brow; peace, joy, and happiness, were revealed in the smile of the red lips; love and passion flashed from the large, brilliant eyes. The choir of the Invisibles now sang in jubilant tones: "The eternal Virgin, the everlasting, holy, and pure being, greets the erring, blesses those that seek, causing them to find, and partake with joy."

The heavenly woman raised her lovely arms, extending them as if for a tender embrace. A captivating smile lighted up her features; a fiery glance from her beautiful eyes seemed to greet every one, separately, to announce to them joy and hope. While they regarded her entranced with delight, the golden cloud grew denser, and covered the virgin with her luminous veil. It then gradually disappeared, with the golden splendor. The chorus of the Invisibles ceased, and the music died away in gentle murmurs. Upon the spot where the beaming apparition was visible, there now stood a tall priest, in a long, flowing black robe; a pale-blue light surrounded him, and rendered the dark outline distinctly visible by the clear background. Snow-white hair and a black mask made him unrecognizable to every one.

Extending his arms, as if blessing them, the masked one cried: "My beloved, the unknown fathers of our Holy Order of Rosicrucians send me to you, and command me to salute you with the greeting of life. I am to announce to you that the time of revelation approaches, and that the sublime mysteries of earth and Nature will soon be revealed to you. As the rose is unfolded in her glowing red, which has so long slept in her lap of green leaves, you represent the green leaves, and Nature is the rose. She will disclose herself to you with all her secrets. In her calyx you will find the elixir of life and the secret of gold, if you walk in the path of duty; if you exercise unconditional obedience to the Invisible Fathers; if you submit yourselves in blind confidence to their wisdom; if you swear to abstain from every self-inquiry, and to distrust your own understanding." *[Footnote: So run the very words in the laws of the Rosicrucians.—See "New General German Library," vol. lvi., p. 10.]*

"We swear it!" cried solemn voices on all sides.

"Swear, blindly, silent obedience to all that the Invisible Fathers shall announce to you through their directors, or shall order you under the holy sign of the Rosicrucians by word or writing."

"We swear it!" again resounded in solemn chorus.

"Shame, disgrace, perdition, and destruction, be your curse," thundered the priest, "if you deviate in thought even from your oath; if you seek to ponder and reflect; if you measure by your own limited reason the dispositions and operations of the sublime fathers, to whom Nature has revealed herself, and to whom all the secrets of heaven and earth are disclosed. Eternal destruction, and all the tortures of hell and purgatory, be the portion of the doubting! Damned and proscribed be the traitor to the holy order! Listen, ye spirits of the deep, and ye spirits of darkness, withdraw from here in terror, ere the anger of the Invisible Fathers fall upon you like destroying lightning! Open, ye doors, that the wicked may flee, and only the good remain!"

With a wave of the hand the great folding-doors now opened, and a flood of light from the adjoining apartment revealed the drawingroom to be filled with the dark forms of men enveloped in black cloaks, hoods drawn over the heads, and black masks covering the faces—all kneeling close together and exactly resembling one another. No one moved, the doors closed again, darkness reigning. The priest was no longer visible, though continuing to speak: "Only the good and obedient are now assembled here, and to them I announce that life is to us, and death awaits beyond the door to seize the traitor who would disclose the holy secrets of the order. Be faithful, my brothers, and never forget that there is no place on the earth where the traitor is secure from the avenging sword of the Invisible Fathers. None but the good and obedient being here assembled, I now announce to you that the time of revelation approaches, and that it will come when you are all zealously endeavoring to extend the holy order, and augment the number of brothers. For the extension of the order is nothing less than universal happiness. It emanates alone from the Invisible Fathers, who link heaven to earth and who will open again the lost way to Paradise. The supreme chiefs of our holy order are the rulers of all Nature, reposing in God the Father. *[Footnote: The wording of the laws of the Order of the Rosicrucians.—See "New General German Library," vol. M., p. 10.]* They are the favorites of God, whom the Trinity thinks worthy of his highest confidence and revelation. If you will take part in the revelations of God, and witness the disclosing of the hidden treasures of Nature, swear that you will be obedient to the holy order, and that you will strive to gain new members.

"We swear it," resounded in an inspired chorus through the room. "We swear unconditional obedience to the Invisible Fathers. We swear to strive with all our means for the extension of the holy order.

"Unbelief, free-thinking, and self-knowledge are of the devil, who steals abroad, to turn men from God. The pride of reason seeks to misguide men, and lead them away from God and the secrets of Nature. The devil has chosen his disciples, who teach sinful knowledge and arrogant free-thinking, and who are united in Berlin in the Order of the Illuminati. The Invisible Fathers command you to fight this shameful order in word, deed, and writing. If any of you are acquainted with one of the members, you shall regard him as your most deadly enemy, and shall hate and pursue him as you hate sin and as you pursue crime. You shall flee his intercourse as you would that of the devil, otherwise you will be damned, and the

Invisible Fathers never will forgive you, and the secrets of Nature will be withheld from you. Swear therefore hate, persecution, and eternal enmity, to the Order of the Illuminati. This I command you in the name of the Invisible Fathers."

"We swear it! We swear hate, persecution, and eternal enmity, to the Order of the Illuminati!"

"Every one who belongs to the order is damned and cursed; and if it were your brother or your father, so shall you curse and damn him!"

"We swear it!"

"Then I bring you the blessing of the Invisible rulers and fathers, who announce to you, through me, that every lost one which you gain for the Order of the Rosicrucians, and consequently lead back to God and Nature, is a step toward entering the holy sanctuary of revelation, where the elixir of life and the tincture of gold awaits you. Every cursed member of the Illuminati becomes one of the blessed when you lead him from the path of vice in penitence and contrition, and gain him to the Order of the Rosicrucians; and he who can prove that he has gained twelve new members for our holy order mounts a round higher in the ladder of knowledge, and rises to a new degree. At the sixth grade he passes from the Inner to the Middle Temple, where all the secrets of the universe and of Nature are disclosed. Be mindful of this, and recruit. Until we meet again, let the watchword be, 'Curses and persecution for the devil's offspring, the Illuminati!'"

"Curses and persecution for the devil's offspring, the Illuminati, we swear!"

"Now depart! Pay your tribute at the door, which you owe, and receive in return the new sign of the order, which will serve to make the brothers known to each other. Only the directors and the members of the sixth grade shall knock again at this door after paying tribute, and, receiving the new word of life, the guard will let them enter. Depart! I dismiss you in the name of the Holy Father and the Trinity!"

"Take this cloak, and cover yourself, that no one can recognize you," whispered a person near Wilhelmine, and threw a soft covering over her. "Will you now depart, or seek further in the way of knowledge?"

"I will seek further," answered Wilhelmine, firmly.

"You wish to enter the sixth grade, and learn the secrets of Nature?"

"I do!"

"Then I will give you the watchword of the order. But woe unto you if you reveal it! Swear that you will never betray it!"

"I swear it!"

"Then, listen!"

Wilhelmine felt a hot breath upon her cheek, and a voice whispered in her ear the significant words: "Now depart; pay your tribute, you cannot tarry here. Go, and return with the chosen!"

A hand seized her arm and conducted her to the door. Almost blinded by the bright light, she entered the adjoining apartment, where it seemed as if she saw through a veil muffled figures go forward to the centre, and deposit money in a marble basin which stood upon a kind of altar; naphtha burned in silver basins upon each end of it, and a muffled figure stood near.

Wilhelmine advanced to the altar, and with quick decision drew a diamond ring from her finger, and begged permission to deposit it instead of money.

The muffled figure bowed, and handed to her the new watchword—a picture of a Madonna, with the sign of the Rosicrucians underneath. Then she returned, and awaited at the door, with a little gathering, which must consequently belong to the sixth grade. Gradually the others had withdrawn; the naphtha-flames upon the altar were extinguished, and the wax-lights of the centre lustres had grown dim, and gradually extinguished themselves. Soon the doors were opened, and a bright light, as of the sun's rays, filled the hall. Three blasts of trumpets sounded, and a choir of immortal voices sang, "Enter, ye blessed ones! Enter, ye elect!"

They entered, whispering the sign to the guards, who stood with drawn swords, and passed on to the throne upon which stood a couch, surrounded with blooming flowers and covered with a cloud of silvery gauze. They soon discovered a secret something was hidden under the cloud, though they knew not whether it were child, woman, or man. They knelt upon the lower step of the throne, with folded hands and bowed heads, praying in a low voice. A solemn stillness reigned, the prayers died away on the lips, and the hearts scarcely beat for anxiety and expectation. Suddenly a voice, which seemed to come from the silver cloud, so distant and lofty, and rolling like majestic thunder, cried, "He comes, the chosen one! The Great Kophta comes!"

The folding-doors flew open, and the Great Kophta entered. Wilhelmine recognized in the majestic figure, enveloped in a flowing, silver-embroidered satin robe, with a band of brilliants around his brow, the handsome face of Cagliostro, beaming as if in an ecstasy. He saluted the brothers with a gentle voice, and bade them approach and touch his hand. As Wilhelmine did so, a thrill ran through her whole being, and she sank overpowered at his feet. He bowed and breathed upon her. "You are chosen, ye heavenly brothers," he said, in a sweet, melodious voice; "the secrets of heaven and earth are disclosed to you. I receive you in the Holy Order of the Favorites of God, which I founded with Enoch and Elias when we dwelt in the promised land. From them I received the Word of Life, and they sent me to the ancient sages of Egypt, who revealed to me in the pyramids the secret sciences which subject the earth and all her treasures to our command. He who devotes himself to me with fidelity will receive eternal life and the secret of immortality."

"We believe in thee, blessed one of God," murmured the kneeling ones; "we know that we receive life and salvation from thee. Bend to us, and give us of the breath of immortality!"

He bowed and breathed upon them, and they broke forth in words of thankfulness and delight.

Only Wilhelmine kept silent; she only failed to feel the magical influence, and he bowed again to her, fixing his great fiery eyes upon her. "Thou art called, thou art chosen," he said. "Mount to the tabernacle, and lift the veil."

She did as commanded, and beheld the figure of a wonderful woman stretched upon the couch as in deep sleep, clothed in transparent robes. "Lay your hand upon her brow, and direct in your thoughts a question to the prophetess of the order, and she will answer you!" Upon the lofty, white brow of the sleeping one, she laid her hand; immediately a smile flitted over her beautiful face, and she nodded. "Yes," said she, "you must believe. You dare not doubt. He is the elect, the holy Magus!" Wilhelmine trembled, for the answer was suited to the question. "Demand a second question of the prophetess," commanded Cagliostro. Again she laid her hand upon the brow of the sleeping one, and again she smiled and nodded with her beautiful head. "Fear not," she replied; "he will always love you, and will never reject you, only you must not lead him astray from the right course—but guide him to the temple of faith and knowledge. When you cease to do it, you are lost. Shame upon earth and damnation will be your portion." The answer was exact—for Wilhelmine had prayed to know if the prince would always love and never reject her. "Still a third question," cried Cagliostro. In silence Wilhelmine asked, and the prophetess answered aloud: "You will be countess, you will become a princess, you will possess millions, you will have the whole world at your feet, if you call to your aid the Invisible Fathers, and implore the power and miraculous blessing of the Great Kophta." Wilhelmine, deeply moved, sank overpowered upon her knees, and cried aloud: "I call upon the Invisible Fathers for aid and assistance; I implore the power and miraculous blessing of the Great Kophta." Suddenly, amid the rolling of thunder and intense darkness, Wilhelmine felt herself lifted up—borne away, as loud prayers were uttered around her. Then she felt herself lowered again and with the freedom of motion. "Fly! fly from the revenge of the immortals, if you still doubt, still mistrust!" cried a fearful voice above her. "Behold how the immortals revenge themselves." Immediately a light began to dawn before her, a form rose from the darkness like her own. She beheld herself kneeling, imploring, her face deluged with tears, and before her a tall, erect, muffled figure, with a glittering sword in his uplifted arm, which sank gradually lower and lower until it pierced her bosom and the blood gushed forth. Wilhelmine shrieked and fainted. She witnessed no more miracles, beard no more prophecies and revelations which the magi made to the elect. She beheld not the appearance of the blessed spirits, which at the importunity of the brothers flitted through the apartment. She heard not Cagliostro take leave of Baron von Bischofswerder, when all had withdrawn, saying, "I have now exalted you to be chief director of the holy order. You will at once receive orders from the Invisible Fathers, announced to you in writing, and you will follow them faithfully."

"I will follow them faithfully," humbly answered Bischofswerder.

"You will be rewarded by the knowledge of life and of money; you shall discover the philosopher's stone, and the secret of gold shall be revealed to you, when you perform what the Invisible Fathers demand."

"I will do every thing," cried Bischofswerder, fervently; "only make known to me their commands."

"They desire, at the present, that you seek to be the confidant of the Prince of Prussia. Gain his affection, then govern him, making yourself indispensable to him. Surround him with servants and confidants that you can rely upon. Inspire him with devotion to the holy order. Become, now, the friend of the prince, that you may, one day, rule the king. You are the chief of the order in Prussia; the more members you gain the more secrets will be revealed to you. The holy fathers send me afar, but I shall return: if you have been active and faithful, I will make known to you a great secret and bring you the elixir of life."

"When will you return, master?" asked Bisehofswerder, enthusiastically.

Cagliostro smiled. "Before the crown prince of Prussia becomes king. Ask no further. Be faithful!"

CHAPTER XII
THE JESUIT GENERAL

No one remained in the drawing-room but Cagliostro and the beautiful woman who still lay quietly on the couch, upon the throne. Cagliostro approached her, and, raising the veil, regarded her a moment, with an expression of the most passionate tenderness: "We are alone, Lorenza," said he. She opened her great eyes, and looked around the dimly-lighted room; then, fixing them upon Cagliostro, who stood before her in his brilliant costume of magician, she burst into a merry laugh, so loud and so irresistible, that Cagliostro was seized involuntarily, and joined her.

"Oh! was it not heavenly, was it not a glorious comedy, and did I not play divinely, Joseph? Was I not bewitching as the goddess of Nature?"

"You looked truly like a goddess, Lorenza, and there is nothing more beautiful than you, in heaven or upon earth. But come, my enchantress, it is time to break up, as we are to set off early to-morrow morning."

"Have we now much money? Was the tribute richly paid?"

"Yes, we have a hundred louis d'ors and a diamond ring from the mistress of this house."

"Give it to me," cried Lorenza.

"Not the ring, Lorenza, but the diamond, so soon as I have a false stone set in the ring—which I must keep as a ring in the chain which will bind this woman to our cause."

"Was I not astonishingly like her? Was it not almost unmistakable?"

"Yes, wonderfully deceptive. I shuddered myself as I saw the dagger pointed at your bosom."

"And the blood, how it gushed forth, Joseph!" Lorenza burst into a merry laugh again, and Cagliostro joined her, but suddenly stopped, and, listening, turned toward the door, which he had closed after Bischofswerder departed. It seemed as if he heard a noise—a peculiar knocking. Four times it was repeated, and Cagliostro waved his hand to Lorenza not to speak. Again were heard the four peculiar rhythmical sounds. "Be quiet, for Heaven's sake be quiet, Lorenza! Let me cover you with the veil; it is a messenger from the Invisibles." Cagliostro flew to the door, unbolted it, and stood humbly near the entrance. A masked figure, enveloped in a cloak, opened it, and entered, rebolting it.

Slowly turning toward Cagliostro, he harshly demanded, "Whose servant are you?"

"The servant of the Invisible Rulers and Fathers," he humbly answered.

"Who are the Invisible Fathers?"

"The four ambassadors of the great general of the exiles."

"Call him by that name which he bore before a heretic pope in Rome, a weak empress, a free-thinking emperor in Germany, a lost-in-sin French emperor, and a heretic Spanish minister, condemned him to banishment and destruction."

"General of the Jesuits," he answered respectfully, bowing lower.

"Do you know the sign by which he may be recognized?"

"Yes, by a ring with the likeness of the founder of the order, the holy Ignatius Loyola."

"Then look, and recognize me," cried the mask, extending his hand to Cagliostro.

"The General," he murmured, frightened, gazing at the ring upon the small, white hand of the other. "The holy founder of the order himself!" He seized his hand and pressed it to his lips, sinking upon his knees. The mask remained standing before the magician, as lowly as he might bow himself, who was still arrayed in his brilliant costume with the band upon his brow sparkling like diamonds.

With a cold, reserved manner he answered, "I am he, and am come here to give you my commands by word of mouth."

"Command me; I am thy humble servant, and but a weak tool in thy hands."

"It is my will that you should become a powerful tool in my hands. Rise, for I will speak to the man who must stand erect in the storm. Rise!" The proud commander was now an humble, obedient servant. He rose slowly, standing with bowed head.

"When and where did we last meet?" demanded the mask.

"In 1773, at Rome."

"In the year of curse and blasphemy," said the mask, in a harsh voice. "The year in which the infamous Pope Clement XVI. condemned the holy order, and hurled his famous bull, Dominus redemptor noster. The holy order, condemned and disbanded by his infamous mouth, were changed into holy martyrs, without country, without possessions or rights, as persecuted fugitives, wandering around the world, to the wicked a scorn, to the pious a lamentable example of virtue and constancy. Exiled and persecuted, you fled to a house of one of our order, and there we for the first time met. The daughter of this man was your beloved. Tell me why did you conceal yourself after flying from Palermo? I will see if the elevated one ungratefully forgets the days of his degradation."

"They accused me in Palermo of falsifying documents by which rightful owners were deprived of their lawful possessions. They threw me into subterranean dungeons, and I was near dying, when the Invisible Protectors rescued me."

"Was the accusation well founded? Had you committed the crime you were accused of?"

"Yes," answered Cagliostro, in a low voice, "I was guilty."

"For whom, by whose authority?"

"For the pious fathers, who commanded me, and whose pretensions to the possessions of the Duc Costa Rica were clearly proved by those documents."

"You then learned the power and the gratitude of our order. From underground prisons they freed you, and procured a way of escape to Rome, to find a safe asylum in the house of a believer. But just at that time condemnation burst upon us, and from a powerful order we were changed into a persecuted one. The forger Joseph Balsamo sought the brazier Feliciano, who gave him money, letters of recommendation, and instructed him how to serve the order, and procure an agreeable life for himself. Is it not so?"

"It is so," answered Cagliostro, softly. "It was the order of the General which united you in marriage to your beloved Lorenza Feliciana, who initiated you in the secret sciences and the secrets of Nature, that you might employ them for the well-being of humanity."

"It is so, master."

"You implored also, as you were about to separate, to see the face of your benefactor, to engrave it upon your heart. Would you now be able to recognize it?"

"I could in an instant, among thousands."

The General slowly raised the mask; a pale, emaciated face was visible, with great black eyes in sunken sockets, thin bloodless lips, and a high, bony brow. "Do you recognize me?"

"No!" sadly answered Cagliostro, "it is not the same face."

"You see, my son, man changes, but knowledge not. I am another, and yet the same, for the outward human form is only the vessel of the eternal band into which everlasting truth and the holy doctrines are poured. If the vessel breaks, it is replaced by another, and an inexhaustible spring. Thought and holy knowledge flow into the renewed vessel. I am a new vessel, but the same spirit which formerly spoke to you. I know your past life, and for what purpose you are in the world. As the General then spoke to you, so speak I now. The unholy have put the holy under a ban—they have persecuted and condemned us. The Holy Order of the Fathers of Jesus is lifeless before the world, but not before God. Jesuits do not die, for they bear eternal life in them, and there will a day come when they will burst forth from darkness into light. Go, my son, and help prepare the day, help smooth the way, that we may walk therein. Have you obeyed?"

"I have consecrated my whole life to it, your eminence. I have wandered around the world, and everywhere striven to disseminate the doctrine of the Invisible Fathers, and win disciples and adherents to the order. The Brothers of the Egyptian Masons, the Brothers of the Rosicrucians, are the disciples which I have won, and you know well there are many mighty and illustrious men among them."

"I know it, and I am satisfied you are an active and useful tool. This I came to tell you, that I might stimulate and advise you. Great deeds you shall perform, great achievements the holy Ignatius Loyola announces by my mouth. The world lies in sin, and the devil strides victorious over it, since the holy order has been proscribed and persecuted by the wicked. The devil is arrogant progress and boasting reason. They who listen to him think themselves wise when they are fools, and speak of their enlightenment while they still wander in the dark. To combat this reason, to oppose this intelligence, is the task of our order, which will never die. For God Sent it forth to the world to fight the devil of progress, who is the ruler of darkness. I have observed you, I have followed you, and I am satisfied. But I await still greater things from you."

"What shall it be? Speak, O master; command, and I obey!"

"You shall strive throughout Europe for the restitution of the holy order. You shall subject to it all minds; make the rich, the powerful, the eminent and great, serviceable to it. Into the Orders of the Rosicrucians and Egyptian Masons you shall gather all the stray and isolated sheep into a flock, to await with longing the coming of the shepherd, and prepare a place for him. To the holy Church you shall consecrate the band of brothers, the only blessed Church, which is the lofty abode of the father of our order. To us belongs the world; you shall assist to reconquer it. Unbelievers shall be fought with every weapon. Every deception, slander, persecution, and murder, are holy if used for the benefit of the holy order. You shall shrink from nothing which is useful and beneficial for the sublime goal. The murder of a prince is no sin, but a just punishment, when it is necessary to remove a mighty enemy. If you create revolutions, cause nations to tear each other to pieces in grim civil war, these revolutions will be sanctified, the civil wars blessed, if they serve to strengthen the power of our order, and gain victory at last against the opponents. Only through our order can happiness reenter the world, and mankind be rescued. If the Holy Fathers do not sit in the council of princes, if they are not the conscience of the powerful, and steer the machine of state, the world goes to destruction, and mankind is lost. You shall help, my son, to turn aside the evil, and prepare happiness for earth. You have already done much, but much more is required. Go and work miracles; belief in them sanctifies the mind. Our fathers will sustain you everywhere, for you well know they are always present, though it is imagined they are not. The infamous Ganganelli has stripped them of their uniform, but not annihilated them, as we are, and ever shall be. I have sent out nine thousand brothers in Europe for the benefit of the order, and you will recognize them by the watchword. They will serve you as you will serve them. If danger menaces you, our brothers will know it, and rescue you. You will be unassailable, so long as you work for the order, and win disciples for it. Prussia is our important station as you rightly judged, and I extol you for your foresight. You prepare the future, for here it will be! When the royal mocker of religion dies, then comes a new kingdom, and the Rosicrucians will rise to power. Vices as well as virtues must serve us; therefore Dischofswerder and Wilhelmine Enke are useful means for holy purposes. That you have recognized it I praise you. Continue, my son, as you have begun, and you shall become powerful upon the earth. Not a hair of your head shall be touched so long as you are faithful to the Invisible Fathers. But so soon as you turn traitor to the holy cause you are lost, and our anger will crush you!"

"Never will I turn traitor," cried Cagliostro, holding up his hands as if taking an oath.

"I hope not. Our enemies shall be your enemies, and our friends your friends. If one of the brothers orders you in my name, 'Kill this man or that woman,' so kill them! Swear it!"

Shuddering, Cagliostro repeated, "I swear it!"

"As soon as one of the brothers orders you, in my name, 'Rescue this man or that woman,' so do every thing; even risk and sacrifice your life to rescue him."

"I swear it."

"You stand in the holy temple of the order, but also under its avenging sword. Be mindful of it in all your acts. The world is open to you, and our influence will be with you everywhere. You shall win the hearts of the great and the mighty to us, and place the Order of the Rosicrucians on the steps of the throne. The Great Kophta shall lead believers to us."

"The Great Kophta will perform all that you command, as he is only the humble servant of his general," said Cagliostro, kissing the hand extended to him.

"Do not kiss the hand, it is only that of an inferior mortal: kiss the ring, for it is the imperishable sign of our immortal saint."

"I kiss the ring of the immortal Ignatius Loyola, and swear eternal fidelity, constant obedience, and firm love, until death."

"Rise! for the time has come for us to separate. I have provided for the journeys the necessary means. Here are letters of recommendation to Warsaw and Mittau, others to Paris and London; but, the most important of all, letters of credit upon well-known bankers to the value of five hundred thousand dollars—all valid, though delivered years hence."

"A half million!" cried Cagliostro, almost terrified.

"Does a half million astonish you?" repeated the General, and his gray, fleshless face was distorted into a smile. "The Great Kophta must travel and live like a prince, that he may dazzle the eyes of the brothers, and subjugate the minds of the powerful. We give you the money, but remember you are always under the watchful eye of the order, and there is no spot on earth where you can hide yourself from our vengeance with the trust confided in you. You shall spend it to buy souls and win thrones, for hearts and consciences are sold; money will buy every thing. Take your letters of credit; you shall live as a great lord, and the Great Kophta shall be equal with princes."

He handed Cagliostro five sealed letters, saying: "They are made out for five years; only one for each year, as the number indicates. Number one is for this year, and number five is only valid at the expiration of five years. The order is mindful of your security, and thus five years of your life are freed from earthly care. You shall work in spirit, and you shall enchant the world, that it may be saved through the only saving Church, and the Holy Order."

He bowed a farewell, making the sign of the cross upon Cagliostro, and bent his steps to the throne, raising the veil which enveloped Lorenza. She looked up to him with glowing cheeks and sparkling eyes, smiling. By this she would express her thanks for the princely gift to her husband, and swear to the General her delight, her fidelity, and love. He regarded her as coldly and calmly as a physician a patient.

"Yes, holy father, I have heard all," she said, with a sweet, flute-like voice. "My heart is filled with gratitude and emotion."

"Prove it by assisting your husband to attain the goal for which we send him forth. I have already said that vice must serve virtue, Lorenza. Beauty is a power, and if it serves holy purposes, so is it sanctified. Employ your beauty to win adherents to the order, and extend the power of the Rosicrucians in every land, and among all nations."

"I swear that this shall be my holiest endeavor," cried Lorenza, rising.

The General pressed her back upon the pillow, saying: "Remain, for there is no one here for you to enchant. I bring you pardon for your sins, and an indulgence for every sin which you will commit, if you swear to serve faithfully the holy Church and the pious fathers of Jesus."

"I swear," solemnly cried Lorenza.

"Here is the letter of indulgence from Pius VI. himself, made out in your name for you. Take it, and perform your duty." He laid down the parchment provided with the papal seal upon her shoulder, and drawing the veil over her made the sign of the cross, saying, "I bless you, and give you absolution for your sins."

"Bless me also, lord and master," cried Cagliostro, kneeling upon the lowest step to the throne.

"I bless you in the name of Loyola. Remain upon your knees, and follow me not." He extended his hands over him, and blessed him, then slowly withdrew.

The first beams of the morning sun shone through the great window-panes, lighting up with its golden rays Cagliostro's kneeling form. He remained with his head bowed until the General had passed out. "He is gone; Heaven be praised, he is gone!"

"Yes, he is gone," repeated Lorenza, springing from the couch. "Is it true, has he given you half a million?"

Cagliostro held up with triumphant air the letters. "See, these addresses are upon the first banking-houses in Rome, Paris, London, and Berlin!"

"Do you believe that they are genuine?"

"I am convinced of it."

"Then we have attained our aim; we are rich and powerful."

"No," answered Cagliostro, mournfully, "we are poorer than ever. This money makes us slaves, makes us dependent tools. Did you not hear him say, 'You are admitted into the Temple, but the avenging sword of the order everywhere hangs over you.'"

CHAPTER XIII
A PENSIONED GENERAL

"Wife," cried the General von Werrig, limping around the room, leaning upon his crutch, "here is the answer from our most gracious lord and king. The courier arrived to-day from the war department, and sent it to me by an express."

"What is the king's answer?" asked the general's wife, a pale, gaunt woman, with a pock-marked face, harsh, severe features, dull gray eyes, which never beamed with emotion, and thin, bloodless lips, upon which a smile never played. "What is the king's answer?" she repeated, in a rough voice, as her husband, puffing and blowing from the effort of walking, sank down upon a chair, and dried his fat, ruby face with a red cotton pocket-handkerchief.

"I have not read it," panted the old man. "I thought I would leave the honor to you, as you, my very learned wife, wrote the letter to his majesty."

His wife was not in the least astonished at this thoughtful conduct of her husband. She impetuously seized the sealed document, and, retiring to the window-niche, slowly unfolded it, whilst the old general fixed his little gray eyes upon her emotionless face. His own was bloated and red, expressing the greatest anxiety and expectation. Perfect stillness reigned for some minutes, only the regular strokes of the pendulum were heard from the clock on the wall; and, as the hands pointed to the expiration of the hour, a cuckoo sprang out of the tree painted over the dial, and eleven times her hoarse, croaking voice was heard.

"It gets every day more out of tune," growled the general, as he looked up to the old, yellow dial, and ran his eye over the cords which supported the weights. Then glancing around the room, he saw everywhere age, decay, and indigence. There was an old divan, with a patched, faded covering of silk, and a grandfather's arm-chair near it, the cushion of which the general knew, by the long years of experience, to be hard as a stone. A round table stood near the divan, covered with a shabby woollen cover, to hide the much-thumbed, dull polish. A few cane-chairs against the wall, an old black-oak wardrobe near the door, and the sewing-table of Madame von Werrig in the window-niche, completed the furniture of the room. At the window hung faded woollen curtains, and on the green painted walls some pictures and portraits, conspicuous among them a beautiful portrait of the king, painted on copper, which represented Frederick in his youthful beauty. It was a morose, sullen-looking room, arranged most certainly by its feminine occupant, and harmonized exactly with her fretful face and angular figure, void of charms. At last the general broke the silence with submissive voice: "I pray you, Clotilda, tell me what the king wrote."

She folded the paper, joy beaming in her eyes. "Granted! every thing granted!"

The general jumped up to embrace his wife with youthful activity, in spite of the gout. "You are a capital wife," he cried, at the same time giving her a loud, smacking kiss upon her cold, gray cheek. "It was the brightest, cleverest act of my life marrying you, Clotilda."

"I might well say the reverse, Emerentius," she replied, complainingly. "It surely was not sensible for me, a young lady from such a genteel family, and so spoiled, to marry an officer whom the king ennobled upon the battle-field, and who possessed nothing but his captain's pay—a fickle man, and a gambler, too."

"Yes, Clotilda, love usurped reason," soothingly replied the general; "love is your excuse."

"Nonsense!" cried Madame von Werrig. "Love is never an excuse; it is folly."

"Well, let us suppose, then, that you did not marry for love, only from pure reason, because you found that it was quite time to espouse some one; and that, in spite of your many ancestors and genteel family, no other chance was offered you, unfortunately no one but this captain, whom the king ennobled upon the battle-field of Leuthen on account of his bravery, and who was a very handsome, agreeable officer, expecting still further promotion. And you were not deceived. I was major, when the Hubertsburger treaty put an end to a gay war-life. You will remember I was advanced during peace; his majesty did not forget that I cut a way for him through the enemy, and he made me lieutenant-colonel and colonel, when I was obliged to resign on account of this infamous gout, and then I received the title of general."

"Without 'excellency,'" replied his wife, dryly. "I have not even this pleasure to be called 'excellency.' It would have been a slight compensation for my sad, miserable existence, and vexed many of the female friends of my youth if they had been obliged to call me 'excellency.' But my marriage brought me only cares, not even a title."

"Do not forget a lovely daughter, Clotilda. Our Marie is beautiful, wise, and good, and through her you will yet have tranquil happiness. For you say the king has granted all we wish."

"Every thing!" repeated the wife, with emphasis. "We have at last finished with want and care, and can count upon an independent, quiet old age, for God has been gracious, and forced you, from the gout, to give up gambling, and we are freed from the misery which has so often threatened us from your unhappy passion."

"At the beginning, I played from passion; afterward, I only played to win back what I had lost."

"And in that manner played away all we possessed, and played upon your word of honor, so that for years the half of our pension went to pay your gambling-debts. Heaven be thanked, the king did not know it, or we would have experienced still worse!"

"I pray you, beloved Clotilda, do not fret yourself needlessly about the past; it is all over, and, as you say, I am unfortunately a prisoner in the house from the gout, which shields me from the temptation."

"I did not say unfortunately; I said 'Heaven be praised, the gout had put an end to your fickle life.'"

"Then, thank Heaven, my dear; we will not quarrel about it. It is past, and, as the king has granted all, we shall have a pleasant life now."

"We will soon receive from our son-in-law a yearly pension, which will be paid to me, and I shall spend it."

The general sighed. "In that case I fear that I shall not get much of it."

"At any rate, more than I have ever received from your pension."

"There is but one thing wanting," replied the general, evasively, "Marie's consent."

Madame von Werrig gave a short, gruff laugh, which did not in the least brighten her sullen face. "We will not ask her consent, but command it."

The general remarked, timidly, shrugging his shoulders, "Marie had a very decided character, and—"

"What do you hesitate to speak out for? What—and—"

"I think she still loves the Conrector Moritz."

A second laugh, somewhat menacing, sounded like a challenge. "The schoolmaster!" she cried, contemptuously.

"Let her dare to tell me again she loves the schoolmaster; she the daughter of a general, and a native-born countess of the empire!"

"My dear, it was your fault—the only fault you ever committed, perhaps. How could you let such a young, handsome, and agreeable man come to the house as teacher to our daughter?"

"How could I suppose my daughter was so degenerated as to love a common schoolmaster, and wish to marry him?"

"It is truly unheard of, and it would make any one angry, my dear wife, for she insists upon loving him."

"She will not insist, she will do what she is commanded to do—my word for it! But why talk about it? It is better to decide the matter at once."

So Frau von Werrig rose with a determined manner, and rang the small brass bell which was upon the sofa-table. But a few seconds elapsed before a little, crooked servant appeared at the side-door, with her dirty apron put aside by tucking the corner in her belt. "Go to my daughter, and tell her to come down immediately!"

The servant, instead of hastening to obey the order, remained standing upon the threshold. "I dare not go," said she, in a hoarse, croaking voice. "Fraulein told me not to disturb her to-day, for she has still two bouquets of flowers to arrange, and two lessons to give, and she is so busy that she is not at home to visitors. She torments herself from morning till night."

"I order you to tell Fraulein to come down at once; we have something important to tell her. No contradiction! go, Trude!"

The servant understood the cold, commanding tone of the mother, and dared not disobey.

"It is nothing good that they have to tell her," grumbled Trude, as she hurried up the stairs which led from the first story into the little, low room in the attic, under the sloping roof. Here and there a few tiles could be lifted, which lighted the garret sufficiently to show the door at the end. "May I come in, my dear Fraulein? it is Trude."

"The door is open," cried a sweet voice, and Trude entered. It is a most charming little room, just that of a young girl. The bed has a snow-white covering, and white curtains, suspended from a hook in the wall around it. The same curtains at the low gable-windows, whose depth, so to speak, made a light anteroom to the real gloomy one in the background. In this little anteroom the young girl had placed all that was necessary for her pleasure and use. There were the most beautiful, sweet-scented flowers upon the window-stool; in a pretty metal cage was a light-colored canary. There were also pretty engravings, and upon the table stood a vase filled with superb artificial flowers, and before it sat the possessor of this room, the daughter of General and Frau von Werrig, surrounded with her work-tools, paper, and colored materials—a young girl, scarcely twenty, of a proud, dignified appearance, but simply and gracefully dressed. According to the fashion of the day, her hair was slightly powdered, and raised high above her broad, clear brow with a blue rosette, and ends at the side. The nobly-formed and beautiful face was slightly flushed, and around the month was an expression of courageous energy. As old Trude entered, the young girl raised her eyes from the rose-bud which she was just finishing, and looked at her. What beautiful black eyes they were as they sparkled underneath the delicately-arched, black eyebrows!

"Now, old one," said she, kindly, "what do you wish? Did you forget that I wanted to work undisturbed to-day?"

"Didn't forget it, my Fraulein, but—"

"But you have forgotten that up here, in my attic-room, I am not your Fraulein, but your Marie, whom you have taken care of and watched over when a child, and whose best and truest friend you have been. Come, give me your hand, and tell me what you have to say."

Old Trude shuffled hurriedly along in her leather slippers. Her old, homely face looked almost attractive, with its expression of glowing tenderness, as she regarded the beautiful, smiling face before her, and laid her hard brown hand in the little white one extended to her. "Marie," she said, softly and anxiously, "you must go down at once to your mother and father. They have something very important to tell you."

"Something very important!" repeated Marie, laying aside her work. "Do you know what it is?"

"Nothing good, I fear," sighed the old woman. "A soldier has been here from the war department and brought a letter for the general, and he told me that it was sent from the king's cabinet at Breslau."

"Oh, Heaven! what does it mean?" cried Marie, frightened, and springing up. "Something is going to happen, I know. I have noticed certain expressions which escaped my father; the proud, threatening manner of my mother; but above all the bold importunity of that man, whom I despise as one detests vice, stupidity, and ennui. They will not believe that I hate him, that I rather—"

"Marie, are you not coming?" called the mother, with a commanding voice.

"I must obey," she said, drawing a long breath, and hastening to the door, followed by Trude, who pulled her back and held her fast upon the very first step. "You have forbidden me to speak of him, but I must."

Marie stood as if rooted to the spot, her face flushed, and in breathless expectation looking back to old Trude.

"Speak, Trude," she softly murmured.

"Marie, I saw him to-day, an hour ago!"

"Where, Trude, where did you see him?"

"Over on the corner of Frederick Street, by the baker's. He stood waiting for me, as he knows I always go there. He had been there two hours, and feared that I was not coming."

"What did he say? Quick! what did he say?"

"He said that he was coming to see you to-day at twelve o'clock; that he would rather die than live in this way."

"To-day? and you have just told me of it!"

"I did not mean to say any thing at all about it; I thought it would be better, and then you would not have to dissemble. But now, if any harm comes to you, you know he is coming, and will stand by you!"

"He will stand by me—yes, he will—"

"Marie!" cried her mother, and her dry, gaunt figure appeared at the foot of the stairs. Marie flew down to the sitting-room of her parents, following her mother, who took her place in the niche at the open window without speaking to her.

CHAPTER XIV
THE KING'S LETTER

"Marie," said the general's wife, after seating herself upon the hard cushion of the divan, near which sat the general in his arm-chair, busily stroking his painful right leg—"Marie, take a chair, and sit near us."

Marie noiselessly brought a cane-chair, and seated herself by the table, opposite her parents.

"We have just received a communication from the king's cabinet," said the mother, solemnly. "It is necessary that you should know the contents, and I will read it aloud to you. I expressly forbid you, however, to interrupt me while I am reading, in your impetuous manner, with your remarks, which are always of the most obstinate and disagreeable kind. You understand, do you, Marie?"

"Perfectly, mother; I will listen without interrupting you, according to your command."

"This communication is naturally addressed to your father, as I wrote to the king in his name."

"I did not know that you had written to his majesty at all, dear mother."

The mother cast a furious glance at the gentle, decided face of her daughter. "You already forget my command and your promise to listen without interrupting me. I did, indeed, write to his majesty, but it is not necessary to tell you what I, or rather your father, solicited, as you will hear it in the answer from our most gracious king. It runs thus: 'My faithful subject: I have received your petition, and I was glad to learn by this occasion that you are well, and that you now lead a steady, reasonable life. Formerly you gave good cause of complaint; for it is well known to me that you led a dissolute life, and your family suffered want and misfortune from your abominable chance-games. You know that I have twice paid your debts; that at the second time I gave you my royal word of assurance that I would never pay a groschen for you again. If you gave yourself up to the vice, and made gambling-debts, I would send you to the fortress at Spandau, and deprive you of your pension. Nevertheless you played again, and commenced your vicious life anew. Notwithstanding which, I did not send you to prison as I threatened, and as you deserved, because I remembered that you had been a brave soldier, and did me a good service at the battle of Leuthen. For this reason I now also grant your request, that, as you have no son, your name and coat-of-arms may descend to your son-in-law. The name of Werrig-Leuthen is well worthy to be preserved, and be an example to succeeding generations. I give my permission for Ludwig Ebenstreit, banker, to marry your daughter and only child, and—'"

Marie uttered a cry of horror, and sprang from her seat. "Mother!—"

"Be still! I commanded you not to interrupt me, but listen, with becoming respect, to the end, to the words' of his majesty." And, with a louder voice, occasionally casting a severe, commanding glance at her daughter, she read on: "'And call himself in future Ludwig Werrig von Leuthen. I wish that he should honor the new name, and prove himself a true nobleman. Ludwig Ebenstreit must give up, or sell, without delay, his banking business, as I cannot permit a nobleman to continue the business of citizen, and remain a merchant. A nobleman must either be a soldier or a landed proprietor; and if your future son-in-law will not be either, he can live upon his income, which must indeed be ample. But I command him to spend it in the country, not go to foreign countries to spend what he has gained in the country. If he should do it, it will not be well with him, and he shall be brought back by force. You may communicate this to him, and he can judge for himself. I will have the letters of nobility made out for him, for which he shall pay the sum of one hundred louis d'ors to the 'Invalids' at Berlin. It depends upon him whether as a true nobleman he will not give my poor 'Invalids' a greater sum. The marriage shall not take place until the letters of nobility have been published in the Berlin journals, for I do not wish the daughter of a general, and a countess, to marry beneath her. You can prepare every thing for the wedding, and let them be married as soon as publication has been made. I will give the bride a thousand thalers for a dowry, that she may not go to her rich husband penniless; the money will be paid to your daughter from the government treasury at her receipt. As ever I remain your well-disposed king, FREDERICK.'

"And here on the margin," continued the general's wife, looking over to her husband with malicious pleasure, "the king has written a few lines in his own hand: 'I have given orders that the money shall be paid to your daughter in person, with her receipt for the same, for I know you, and know that you do not play, not because you have not the money, but the gout. If you had the cash and not the gout, you would play your daughter's dowry to the devil, and that I do not wish, for a noble maiden should not marry a rich husband as poor as a church mouse. FREDERICK.'"

A profound stillness prevailed when the reading was finished. The general busied himself, as usual, rubbing his gouty leg with the palm of his hand. Marie sat with her hands pressed upon her bosom, as if she would force back the sighs and sobs which would break forth. Her great, black eyes were turned to her mother with an expression of painful terror, and she searched with a deathly anxiety for a trace of sympathy and mercy upon her cold, immovable face.

Her mother slowly folded the letter, and laid it upon the table. "You know all now, Marie—that, as it becomes parents, we have disposed of your future and your hand. You will submit to their wishes without murmuring or opposition, as it becomes an obedient, well-brought-up daughter, and receive the husband we have chosen for you. He will come today to hear your consent, and you from this day forth are the betrothed of the future Herr von Werrig. Of course from this very hour you will cease the highly improper and ungenteel business which you have pursued. You must not make any more flowers, or give any more lessons. The time of such degradation and humiliation is past, and my daughter can no longer be a school-mistress. You have only to write the receipt to-day, and I will go with you to the treasury to get the money."

"I will not write the receipt," said Marie, gently but firmly. Her mother, in the act of rising, sank back upon the divan; and the general, apparently quite occupied with his leg, stopped rubbing, and raised his red, bloated face to his daughter in astonishment. "Did I understand rightly your words, that you would not write the receipt?"

"Yes, mother, I said so; I cannot and will not write it," replied Marie, gently.

"And why cannot you, and will you not write it?" said her mother, scornfully.

"Because I have no right to the money, and cannot take it, mother, as I will never be the wife of the man you intend me to marry."

The general sprang with a savage curse from his arm-chair, and would have rushed to his daughter, but his wife pushed him back into his seat, and approached Marie, who rose, regarding her mother with a firm, sad expression. "Why can you not be the wife of the man we have chosen for you? Answer me, WHY you cannot?"

"You know, mother," she replied, and gradually her voice assumed a more decided tone, her cheeks reddened, and an inspired expression beamed from her eyes, and pervaded her whole being—"you know, mother, that I can never be the wife of Herr Ebenstreit, for I do not love him. I despise and abominate him, because he is a man without honor; he knows that I do not love him, and yet he insists upon marrying me. If it were not so, if I did not despise and abominate him, I would not receive his suit and marry him."

"Why not?" cried the general, shaking his fist at his daughter.

"Why not?" cried the mother, with a cold, icy glance, void of pity or anger.

Marie encountered these looks with beaming eyes. "Because I am betrothed to another," and the words came like a cry of joy from her heart—"because I am engaged to my beloved Moritz!"

"Shameless, obstinate creature, have we not forbidden it?" cried her father.

"Stop!" interrupted his wife, with a commanding wave of her hand, which silenced the obedient husband immediately. "It belongs to me to question her, for I am her mother, and my daughter owes me submission and obedience above all things.—Answer me, Marie, did you not know that we had forbidden you to speak to this man, or have any communication with him? Did you not know that I, your mother, had menaced you with a curse if you married this man, or even spoke to the miserable, pitiable creature?"

"Mother," cried Marie, vehemently, "he is not a poor, miserable creature. You may hate him, but you dare not outrage the noble, the good, and just man!"

"He is a good-for-nothing fellow," cried her father; "he has tried to win a minor behind the parents' back. He is a shameful, good-for-nothing seducer."

"He is dishonorable," cried the general's wife—"a dishonorable man, who has misused our confidence. We confided to him our daughter to teach, and paid him for it. He improved the opportunity to make a declaration of love, and stole the time from us to infatuate the heart of our daughter with flattery, and from his pupil win a bride."

"Oh, unworthy, shameful slander!" cried Marie, her eyes flashing with anger. "You well know that it is a vile scandal, that Moritz was no paid teacher. If he had been—if he had felt obliged to yield to the sad necessity of being paid for his valuable time, because he was poor, and forced to live by his intellect, he was a free man, and had the right to love whom he chose. He loves me, and I have accepted his love as the most precious, most beautiful, and most glorious gift of my life. Ah! do not look so angry with me, father; I cannot say otherwise. I cannot crush or deny the inmost life of my life.—Oh, mother, forgive me that I cannot change it! You know that otherwise I have been a most obedient daughter to you in all things, although you have never taught me the happiness of possessing a loving mother; though neither of you could ever forgive your only child for not being a son, who could inherit your name, and win a brilliant position, yet I have always loved you tenderly and truly, and never complained that the unwelcome daughter received neither love nor tenderness, only indifference and coldness from her parents."

"Beautiful, very beautiful!" replied the mother, contemptuously. "Now you wish to blame us that you are a heartless and thankless daughter.—We have not understood her heart, and it is our fault that her love has flown somewhere else.

"This is the language of romance. I have, indeed, read it in the romances of Herr Moritz, and my daughter has only repeated what she learned as a docile pupil from her schoolmaster. Very fine, to pay Herr Moritz to form our daughter into the heroine of a romance! She ought to have learned the languages, but has learned only the language of romances."

"You are very severe and very cruel, mother," said Marie, sadly. "I would not complain, only excuse myself, and implore pity and indulgence, and defend myself from the reproach of having been a cold, unloving daughter. Oh! God knows how I have longed for your love; that I would willingly prove that I would joyfully do every thing to embellish your life and make you happy. It gave me such pleasure to earn something for you with my dear flowers and lessons, and afford you a little gratification!"

"Ah! now, she will reproach us with having toiled for us and sacrificed herself. Husband, thank yourself for the victim who worked for you, who gave her youth for us that she might strew our life with roses."

"I have had enough of this talking and whining," cried the general, furiously beating the table with his fist. "My daughter shall not be a heroine of romance, but an obedient child, who submits to the will of her parents. You shall marry the man that we have chosen for you; the king has given his consent, and it shall take place. I command you! That is sufficient! I will hear no more about it; the thing is done with. Herr

Ebenstreit is coming this afternoon to make you a proposal of marriage with our consent, and you must, accept him. I command you to do it!"

"I cannot obey you! Oh, do not force me to rebel against God's holy laws! Have pity upon me! I have obeyed you until now, and yielded to your wishes, although I thought it would break my heart sometimes. You have forbidden Moritz the house, and turned him out of doors like a servant, with scorn and contempt, and he has silently borne it on my account. You have forbidden me to write or receive letters from him, or ever to meet him. My mother would curse me if I disobeyed her, and I submitted. I have given up every thing, sacrificed every wish, and renounced my love. But you cannot expect more from me, or dare ask it. I can forego happiness, but you cannot ask me to consent to be buried alive!"

"And what if we should wish it?" asked her mother. "If we should demand our daughter to give up a romantic, foolish love, to become the wife of a young man who loves her, and who loves us, and who is rich enough to assure us a comfortable old age, free from care?"

"Marie," cried the general, in a begging and almost imploring tone, "Marie, prove to us now that you are really a good and grateful child—we have had so much care and want in our life, so many sorrowful days! It lies in your hands to make our declining days joyous and bright, and free us from want. We have often grumbled against God, that He did not give us a son; now make us to rejoice that He has given us a daughter, who will bring us a son and inherit our name through her children, and who will give us what we have never known—prosperity and riches. I beg you, my dear, good child, grant your parents the few last years of their life freedom from care!"

"And I, Marie," said her mother, in a softened and tender tone, which Marie had never heard from her—"I beg you also, be a good daughter, pity your mother! I have always led a joyless, unhappy life. I lived unmarried, a native-born countess, with proud relations, who made me feel bitterly my dependence; when married my existence was only trouble, privations, care, and sorrow. I beg you, Marie, teach me to know happiness, for which I have so longed in vain; give me independence and prosperity, which I have always desired, and never known. I pray, Marie, make us happy in bringing us a rich, genteel, and good son-in-law, Herr Ebenstreit."

Marie, who met the scorn and threats of her mother with firmness and a proud demeanor, trembled as she heard these severe and merciless lips, always so cold and harsh, now begging and imploring. At first she was quite frightened, and then terrified, and covered her face with her hands, her head sinking upon her breast as her mother spoke.

"Speak, my daughter," cried the general, as his wife was silent. "Speak, my dear Marie. Say the word, and we shall be all happy, and there will be no happier family found in Berlin, or the world even. Say that you will marry Ebenstreit, and we will love and bless you so long as we live. Do say yes, dear Marie!"

Her hands fell from her face, and stretching them out toward her parents, she looked at them in despair.

There was a fearful pause. "I cannot, it is impossible!" she shrieked. "I cannot marry this man, for I do not love him. I love another, whom I can never forget, whom I shall love forever. I love—"

"Herr Conrector Moritz!" announced Trude, hastily bursting open the door, and looking in with a triumphant smile.

CHAPTER XV
HATE AND LOVE

"Herr Conrector Moritz wishes to pay his respects," called out Trude again.

"We do not wish to receive him," cried Frau von Werrig.

"He dare not presume to enter!" shrieked the general.

Marie cried, "Moritz! Oh! my beloved Moritz," rushing with outstretched arms toward her lover, who just appeared at the door. "God has sent you to sustain me in this fearful hour."

Old Trude peeped through the half-closed door, well satisfied to see her dear young lady folded in Moritz's arms, and her head leaning upon his shoulder. "Yes," she murmured, closing softly the door, "Marie is right, God himself sent her lover in this hour, and I would not let her wicked, hard-hearted parents send him away."

Quick as thought she turned the key, fastening the door, and betook herself to the farthest room, carefully closing every door between them. "Now we will see for once whether they will show him the door, and pitch him out. No, they will be obliged to listen to him. Old Trude wishes it, for it will make her dear Marie happy. It is all the same to me if the old German tries to scratch my eyes out for it; I will take good care to keep out of his way. I must go and listen once."

She put her ear to the keyhole, and then her eye, to see how the quarrellers looked.

At first the general and his wife were quite alarmed, and almost speechless as they witnessed the joyful meeting of the lovers. The father sprang up suddenly, with clinched fist, but instead of bitter invectives only a fearful shriek of pain was heard, as he sank groaning and whimpering into his armchair. The gout had again seized its victim. Anger had excited the general's blood, and had also brought on the pain in his leg again. His wife took no notice of his cries and groans, for it was quite as agreeable to her to be the only speaker, and have her moaning husband a kind of assenting chorus. "Leave each other!" she commanded, as she approached the lovers, flourishing her long shrivelled arms about. "Leave each other, and leave my house!"

Laying her hand on Marie's arm, which was thrown around her lover's neck, she endeavored to tear her away, and draw her daughter toward herself. But Marie clung only the more firmly, and Moritz pressed her more fervently to his heart. They heeded not and heard not the outburst of anger which the mother gave way to. They read in each other's eyes the bliss, the joy of meeting again, and the assurance of constant, imperishable love.

"You are pale and thin, my beloved!"

"Sorrow for you is consuming me, Marie, but, thank Heaven, you are unchanged, and beautiful as ever!"

"Hope and love have consoled and strengthened me, Philip."

"Enough! I forbid you to speak another word to each other," and with the power which rage lends, the mother tore Marie away. "Herr Moritz, will you tell me by what right you force yourself into our house, and surprise us like a street-thief in our peaceful dwelling? But no! you need not tell me, I will not listen to you. Those who permit themselves to enter our room unasked and unwelcomed—I will have nothing to say to them. Leave! there is the door! Out with you, off the threshold!"

With calm demeanor, Moritz now approached Fran von Werrig, demanding her pardon, saying: "You see, madame, that I am not so unwelcome here, therefore you will be obliged to let me remain."

"Yes, that she will," sneered Trude, outside the door. "It will be difficult for her to send him off so long as I am unwilling."

"No, I will not permit it. We have nothing to do with each other. Out of my sight!—Away!"

"Away!" cried the general. "Oh, the gout, the maddening pains! I cannot throw the bold fellow out of the house! I must lie here, and writhe like a worm! I cannot be master of my house. Oh, oh! what pain!"

"Stay, Philip," whispered Marie, as she again leaned toward Moritz. "They wish to sell me and force me to a hated marriage. Do not yield! save me!"

"You are mine, Marie; you have sworn to me eternal constancy, and no one can compel you to marry if you do not wish to."

"We are her parents; we can, and we will compel her," triumphantly cried Frau von Werrig. "The king has given his consent, and if it is necessary we will drag her to the altar by force!"

"Do it, mother, and I will say no before all the world."

"We will take care that no one hears you but the priest, and he will not listen, as he knows that the king has commanded you to say yes!"

"But God will hear her, Frau von Werrig, and He will take vengeance on the cruel, heartless mother."

"I will await this vengeance," she sneered. "It does not concern you, and you need not trouble yourself about it. Leave the house!"

"I came here to speak with you, and I will not go away until you have listened to me."

"Then I will leave, for I will not hear you, and I command you to follow me, Marie!"

She seized Marie with irresistible force, and drew her toward the side door, which was fast. Then hurried toward the entrance, dragging her daughter after her, but shook it in vain; that door was fastened also.

"Oh! I could kiss myself," murmured Trude, as she patted her old, wrinkled cheeks. "I was as cunning and wise as Solomon. There, shriek for Trude, order her to open it. Trude is not there, and she has no ears for you!"

"This is a plot—a shameful plot!" cried Frau von Werrig, stamping her feet. "That good-for-nothing creature, Trude, is in it. She has locked the doors, and the schoolmaster paid her for it."

Trude shook her fist at her mistress behind the door. "Wait! that good-for-nothing creature will punish you! You shall have something to be angry about with me every day."

"I swear to you that I do not know who locked the doors," replied Moritz, calmly. "But whoever did it, I thank them from the depths of my soul, for it forces you to listen to me, and may love give my words the power to soften your heart. General and Frau von Werrig, I conjure you to have compassion upon us. Is it possible that you are deaf to the cry of grief of your own child?"

Suddenly assuming a contemptuous calm, Frau von Werrig sank back upon the divan with great dignity. "As I am obliged to listen to you, through a shameful deception, let it be so. Try to make ears in my heart, which you say is deaf. Let me listen to your wonderful eloquence!"

"Oh, Philip!" said Marie, clasping his arms, "you see it will all be in vain."

"Let me hope to succeed in awakening a spark of loving mercy, as Moses caused the fountain to gush from the rock.—A year since you turned me insultingly from your door, Frau von Werrig, and you forbade me with scorn and contempt to ever cross your threshold. In the rebellious pride of my heart I swore never to do it again, never to speak to those who had so injured me. The holy, pure love which binds me to this dear girl has released me from my oath. We have tried to live separated from each other a long year, an inconsolable, unhappy year! We hoped to renounce each other, although we could not forget. Marie, as an obedient daughter, obeyed your commands, and returned the ring, which I gave her in a moment of affection and holy trust. I released her from the oath of constancy, and made her free! But it is in vain! During this year I have striven with sorrow as a man, helpless in a desert, who writhes in the folds of the poisonous serpent. I should have gone mad if a consoling word from a great and noble mind had not roused me from my desolation, and if love had not shed a ray of light into my benighted soul. I listened no longer to sickening pride and humbled sense of honor. Love commanded me to come here, and I came to ask you, Marie, in the presence of your parents, if you will be my wife; if you will accept my poor, insignificant name, and be contented by my side to lead a quiet, modest existence. I can only earn sufficient to assure us a peaceful life. I have no splendor, no treasures to offer you, but only my love, my heart, my life, my whole thought and being. Will you accept it, Marie?"

"I do accept it, Moritz, as the greatest happiness of my life. I desire only your love, and I can return only my love to you! Here is my hand, Philip, it belongs to you alone! Let us kneel in humility before my parents, and implore their blessing.—Oh, my father and mother, have pity upon us! See this dear man, to whom my whole heart belongs. I desire only to live and toil with him. There are no riches, no treasures, to compare with his love!"

"General and Frau von Werrig, grant me the wife of my heart!" cried Philip Moritz, deeply moved. "It is true, I am not worthy of her, I have no name, no position, to offer her, but I swear to strive to gain it for her. I will win by my talents and knowledge a distinguished name, and perhaps one day you will concede to my fame that I am a noble man, though not a nobleman. Will you separate two hearts which belong to each other? Take me for your son-in-law, and I swear to be devoted and faithful, to love and honor you for your daughter's sake. I can say no more—words cannot express all that I feel. Love causes me to kneel before you, love makes me humble as a child. I implore you to give me your daughter in marriage."

"I also implore you," cried Marie, sinking down beside Moritz, "give to me this man, whom I love and honor, for my husband."

It was a beautiful and impressive scene—these two young beings pleading for happiness; their eyes flashing with the inspiration of feeling, conscious that they were one in affection, and ready to combat the whole world for each other. But Frau von Werrig was immovable, and the general was too much occupied with his gouty, throbbing leg even to cast a look upon the beautiful group of youth, love, manly determination, and tender resignation.

Outside the door, Trude knelt imploringly, with folded hands, while the tears ran down her old cheeks in big drops. "O God, I well know that they have no pity; have mercy Thou, and cause my dear Marie to be happy! Suffer not that that hard-hearted woman should sell her, and marry her to that bad man my Marie despises. I well know that I am a poor creature, and not worthy that Thou shouldst listen to me, O Lord! But I love that young girl as if she were my own child, and I would give my heart's blood for her. Oh, my God! I implore Thee to let my Marie be happy!" Then she continued, as she rose from her knees. "Now, I have spoken, and I commit every thing to God, and He will do what is best. She has been obliged to listen to him, and if it cannot be otherwise, he must go."

Carefully old Trude unlocked both doors, and then stopped to listen.

Trude was right, there was no mercy in Frau von Werrig's heart. "Have you finished? Have you any thing more to say?" she asked, in her most unsympathizing manner.

"Nothing more with our lips, but our hearts still implore you."

"I do not understand this language, sir, and you have not succeeded in giving me hearing, or ears to hear with. In this useless strife I will say a last word, which I hope will be for life. You shall never be the husband of my daughter! You can never be united."

Marie and Moritz sprang from their knees, laying their hands in each other's, and looked what words could not have better expressed—"We are inseparable, nothing can disunite us but death!"

"I desire you not to interrupt me," commanded Frau von Werrig; "I have listened to you, and now you shall listen to me. I promise you to speak with more brevity than you have. I will not trouble you with useless phrases and tedious lamentations. I will speak to the point. Marie is the daughter of General Werrig von Leuthen, whose name would become extinct if the grace and favor of the king had not prevented it, by permitting the husband whom we have chosen for our daughter to take our name, and therewith become our son. You may think, in your arrogance of commoner, and the pride you take in having won the love of the daughter of General von Leuthen, that you could be this husband and son-in-law. But two things fail you: first, the necessary fortune; and, secondly, the king's consent, and that of her father. If you were rich, it might be possible that we should be touched by the tender amorousness of our daughter, and conquer our aversion to you for her sake. You are of low birth, and take a subordinate position in society. It would be extremely laughable for the schoolmaster Moritz to change suddenly into a Herr von Werrig Leuthen. Our son-in-law must be a rich man, in order to be able to give his new title consideration; and, fortunately, the wooer of my daughter's hand possesses this qualification, and therefore we have given our consent. The king has approved our choice, and permits the rich banker Ludwig Ebenstreit to become our son-in-law, and take our name. The king has in this communication, which lies upon the table, and which Marie has heard read, given his assurance to ennoble Ebenstreit upon two conditions: first, that the banker should give up his business, and live upon his income; and, secondly, that the marriage should not take place until the papers of nobility are made out and published, so that the daughter of General von Werrig should not make a misalliance. You know all now, and you will at last understand that there is but one thing for you to do—conquer your foolish presumption, and beg to be excused for your unheard-of boldness in forcing yourself into our house, and then withdraw quickly. If my ear does not deceive me, your accomplice has opened the doors. I think I heard rightly, if my heart has no ears, my head possesses better. We have finished. I would again enjoin upon you the duty of begging for pardon, and then I close this unrefreshing scene with the same words with which it opened—there is the door—go out!"

"Yes, there is the door—go out of it! I want to be quiet—go! My daughter is the betrothed of the rich banker Herr Ebenstreit; she will be his wife as soon as the papers are made out and published.—Go!" cried the general.

The young couple still stood there, hand in hand, looking at the general, until now their eyes met, beaming with tenderest affection for each other. "Is it true, Marie? Speak, my beloved, is it true, will you be the wife of this rich man whom your parents have chosen for you?"

"No, Philip," she calmly and firmly replied. "No, I will not, for I do not love him, I love only you; and here, in the presence of God and my parents, I swear to you that I will be constant to death! They can prevent my becoming your wife, but they cannot force me to wed another. I swear, then, that if I cannot be yours, I will never marry!"

"I receive your oath, and God has heard it also!" said Moritz, solemnly.

"I have also heard it, and I tell you," said Frau von Werrig, "that this romantic heroine will become a perjurer, for I will find means to make her break her silly oath."

"We will, perhaps, find means to delay the marriage," said Moritz proudly, "or, much more, prevent the marriage ceremony."

"I am very curious to know the means," said Frau von Werrig. "From this hour Marie is the betrothed of Herr Ebenstreit, and the wedding will take place so soon—"

"So soon as the title of nobility is published. That is it, is the clause to be filled; and therefore I tell you, beloved, wait and hope! This woman is without pity and without mercy; but God is in heaven, and Frederick the Great on the earth. Wait and hope. Be firm in hope, and constant in love. Do not lose courage, and let them force you to compliance by threats and anger. I have only you to confide in and to love in the world, and you are my hope, my goal, and the happiness of my life. If you forsake me, I lose my good angel, and am a lost, miserable man, whom it would be better to hurl into the deepest abyss than let him suffer the torments of hated existence. The knowledge of your love gives me strength and courage; it will inspire me to fight like a hero, to win the dear, beloved wife, to whom I would yield my life in order to receive it anew from her purified and sanctified. The knowledge that I had lost you, would ruin me."

Laying both hands upon his shoulder, Marie looked at him with eyes beaming with affection, renewing her vow that she would never love or marry another. "We will be courageous in hope, and brave in constancy. Listen to me, my beloved; listen, my mother—I betrothed myself to this dear man! You can prevent my becoming his wife now, but in four years I am of age, and then I shall be my own mistress. Then, my dear Philip, I will be your wife. Let us wait and hope!"

"Yes, Marie, we will wait and hope.—Farewell! Do not forget that there is a great God in heaven, and a great king upon earth.—Farewell!"

He pressed the hand clasped in his own passionately to his tips, and felt from the pressure of her delicate fingers a renewed vow of constancy. Buoyed with this hope in the sad hour of parting, they were happy and joyful. Marie accompanied him to the door—still hand in hand.

"Presume not to go a step farther," commanded her mother, and Marie, obedient to her wishes, remained near the door, bowed to Moritz, and never ceased to regard him, with love beaming in her eyes, until the door closed. Outside stood old Trude, to tell him that she would be at the baker's at seven o'clock every morning, and wait for his commissions, "and may be I shall have something to bring you," she said. "So do come!"

"I will, my good Trude; you are the only person who is friendly to us. Watch over my angel, console her with your affection, and when they are too hard upon her, come to me."

"I surely will, but listen—they are already quarrelling with my good angel. I will go in, to serve as a lightning-rod for dear Marie. I often do it, and it pleases me when the lightning strikes, and dashes my hard old head to the ground, but does not hurt me at all—Farewell, Herr Moritz, the lightning-rod must go in."

Trude entered suddenly and noiselessly the sitting-room, and interrupted the angry reproaches which Frau von Werrig hurled against Marie in a furious stream of words. The countess's rage turned against Trude, who stared as if to challenge her. "What do you want? How dare you enter uncalled?"

"I thought you were calling deaf old Trude, or why did you scream so?" replied Trude, tartly.

"Perhaps it was the general. Ah! there lies the poor, dear old man, groaning and crying, and nobody has any pity for him."

"Ah! Trude, it is good luck that you are here," whined the general. "No one troubles himself about me. Quick, bring warm covering for my leg, the pain is fearful!"

"Poor, dear father, I will take care of you, I will nurse you," said Marie, hastening to him. Her mother pushed her back violently. "Not a step farther; you have no right to go near him, you are his murderess. On your head will fall the guilt, if these dreadful scenes should cause his death."

"No, no, the general will not die quite yet," said Trude busying herself about his arm-chair. "But, Fraulein, you have got something else to do than stay here. They have already sent for the flowers twice, and the French lady is waiting up-stairs to parlez-vous."

Marie looked her friendly thanks, and quietly and quickly left the room.

"Now, bold woman, I have a last word to say to you. Who locked the door when that creature came?" "I, madame," answered Trude, who was just bringing a great cushion from the back-room to cover the general's feet.

"You acknowledge that you locked the door intentionally?"

"Now, my dear, good Frau von Werrig, one does not lock a door by mistake. I did not want Herr Moritz to run away with fright, before you had given him your mind, and set his head straight. He would certainly have escaped, and only heard the half of your beautiful talk, for he had no idea what a miserable fellow he is. So I locked both doors, and he was obliged to listen to you, and has gone away contrite and repentant. There, there, my poor, dear general, is your foot high enough? Shall I not bring the foot-warmer?"

"You shall not bring any thing, nor do any thing more. You are a hypocrite, who connives with Moritz. Leave my house this very hour! You are dismissed my service. Go pack up your things and be off!" cried Frau von Werrig.

"Oh, do not go, Trude, for mercy's sake, for then I have no one to help me," cried the general.

"I cannot do otherwise, she has given me my dismissal." Trude approached Frau von Werrig respectfully, saying, "So I must pack up and go away at once?"

"Immediately, you deceitful creature!"

"Immediately! but Frau von Werrig will be so good as to give me my wages."

"Yes," she answered in a slower and more subdued voice. "That shall be done presently."

"It will not be so very difficult to reckon them, I have been here twenty years; just as many years as Marie is old, for I came as child's nurse, and have helped her learn to talk and walk, and played mother to the dear child a bit. Then I obtained my wages, for they were good times; but the pension-time came, and we had no cook or servant but me. 'The rats run away if the ship springs a leak,' but the old mole Trude stayed. Mankind is in the world to work, I said, and why should not I be the cook and waiting-maid too, that my little Marie should not want any thing? So I became maid-of-all-work and have stayed here ever since. Then, you told me you would double my wages, and give me twenty thalers a year, and four thalers at Christmas. Is it not so, Frau von Werrig?"

"I believe that was the agreement."

"I am quite certain about it," cried the general, who began to understand the drift of Trude. "Yes, Trude was to have twenty thalers a year, and we are owing her many years' wages. You know, wife, I have always kept an account-book for the debts, and only a few days ago—Oh! oh! the pain! Trude, help me cover up the foot warmer!—we reckoned it up a few days ago, and we owe Trude one hundred and thirty thalers."

"One hundred and thirty thalers," repeated Trude, clapping her hands, astonished. "Is it true? oh, that is splendid. I shall be rich, and get a husband yet. I pray you give it to me, Frau von Werrig, right away."

"Not so quickly," said she, proudly. "We will reckon together how much you have saved—because—"

"Oh!" interrupted Trude, "how good you are to make me keep so much; you are my savings bank, where I can deposit my money."

"Because," she continued, with emphasis, without noticing the interruption, "our future son-in-law will pay your wages, the rich banker,

Herr Ebenstreit. Yes, the wealthy lover of our daughter. At the moment I have not so much cash in the house."

"Your grace will allow me to stay until Herr Ebenstreit is married, and, in your name, pays me my wages?"

"Yes, Trude, I will allow you to stay," she replied, very graciously. "You will be cunning, Trude, if you try to persuade Marie to accept the rich suitor, for when she does I will give you two hundred thalers."

"I will do all I can to get it. Can I remain here until Marie is married?"

"Yes, you have my permission for that."

"I thank you, Frau von Werrig. Now, general, I will bring you some warm coverings right away."

CHAPTER XVI
CHARLES AUGUSTUS AND GOETHE

"Now tell me, Wolf," asked Duke Charles Augustus, stretching himself comfortably on the sofa, puffing clouds of smoke from his pipe—"are you not weary of dawdling about in this infamously superb pile of stones, called Berlin? Shall we any longer elegantly scrape to the right and to the left, with abominable sweet speeches and mere flattering phraseology, in this monster of dust and stone, of sand and sun, parades and gaiters? Have you not enough of blustering generals, of affected women? and of running about the streets like one possessed to see here a miserable church, or there a magnificent palace? Are you not weary of crawling about as one of the many, while at home you stride about as the only one of the many? And weary also of seeing your friend and pupil Carl August put off with fair promises and hollow speeches like an insignificant, miserable mortal, without being able to answer with thundering invectives. Ah! breath fails me. I feel as if I could load a pistol with myself, and with a loud report shoot over to dear Weimar. Wolf, do talk, I beg you, I am tired out; answer me."

"I reply, I shoot, my dear Carl," cried Goethe, laughing. "I was out of breath myself from that long speech. Was it original with my dear prince, or did he memorize it from Klinger's great 'Sturm-und-Drang' tragedy? It reminded me of it."

"Do you mean to accuse me of plagiarism, wicked fellow? I grant that you are right, my cunning Wolf, it was a lapsus. I did think of Klinger, and I sympathized with his youthful hero Wild, who declared that, among the sweetest pleasures, he would like to be stretched over a drum, or exist in a pistol-barrel, the hand ready to blow him into the air."

Goethe shoved aside the breakfast-table, straightened his delicate form, with his noble head proudly erect, and one foot in advance, extended his right arm, giving one loud hurrah! "Now, for once, a tumult and noise, that thought may turn about like a weathercock. This savage noise has already wrought its own benefit. I begin to feel a little better. Rage and expand, mad heart, quicken yourself in hurly-burly-burly-burly!" *[Footnote: From Klinger's tragedy "Sturm und Drang."]*

"Bravo! bravo!" laughed the duke. "Is that Klinger, or who is it that refreshes himself in hurly-burly?"

"It is I who am every thing," replied Goethe, striding and swaggering up and down. "I was an assistant, in order to be something—lived upon the Alps, tended the goats, lay under the vault of heaven day and night, refreshed by the cool pastures, and burned with the inward fire. No peace, no rest anywhere. See, I swell with power and health! I cannot waste myself away. I would take part in the campaign here; then can my soul expand, and if they do me the service to shoot me down, well and good!" *[Footnote: From Klinger's tragedy "Sturm und Drang."]*

"Bravo! Wild, bravo!" cried the duke. "Hei! that thundered and rolled, and struck fire! It does me good to hear such vigorous words from an able rare genius in the midst of this miserable, starched elegance. The powerful Germans are healthy fellows. Something of the Promethean fire blazes forth in them. They were forced to come, those jolly, uproarious boys, after the affected cue period; they were the full, luxurious plants, and my Wolfgang, the favorite of my heart, my poet and teacher, is the divine blossom of this plant. Let them prevail, these 'Sturmer und Dranger,' for they are the fathers and brothers of my Wolfgang. Do me the sole pleasure not to refine yourself too much, but let this divine fire burst forth in volcanic flames, and leave the thundering crater uncovered. Sometimes when I see you so simpering, so modest and ceremonious, I ask myself, with anxiety, if it is the same Wolfgang Goethe, who used to drink 'Smollis' with me at merry bacchanals out of death-skulls?—the same with whom I used to practise whip-cracking upon the market-place hours long, to the terror of the good citizens?—the same who used to dance so nimbly the two-steps, and was inexhaustible in mad pranks. Now tell me, Herr Wolfgang, are you yourself, or are you another?"

"I am myself, and not myself," answered Goethe, smiling. "There still remains a good portion of folly in me, and it must sometimes thunder and flash, but I hope the atmosphere of my soul will become clearer, and over the crater a more lovely garden will spread out, in which beautiful, fragrant flowers will bloom, useful and profitable for my friends and myself. Sometimes I long for this as for the promised land; then again it foams and thunders in me like fermenting must, which, defying all covers and hoops, would froth up to heaven in an immense source of mad excitement!"

"Let it froth and foam, and spring the covers, and burst the old casks," cried the duke; "I delight in it, and every infernal noise you make, the prouder I am to recognize that from this foaming must will clear itself a marvellous wine, a delicious beverage for gods and men, with which the world will yet refresh itself, when we are long gone to the kingdom of shades—to the something or nothing. You know, Wolf, I love you, and I am proud that I have you! It is true that I possess only a little duchy, but it is large enough to lead an agreeable and comfortable existence—large enough for a little earthly duke, and the great king of intellects, Johann Wolfgang Goethe. Let us return to our dear home, for I acknowledge to you I sigh for Weimar. I long for the dear little place, where every one knows me and greets me, and even for my dogs and horses."

"And I," said Goethe, "I really mourn for my Tusculum, which I owe to the generous, kind duke; for the balcony of my little cottage, where, canopied by the blue, starry vault of heaven, I dream away the lonely May nights."

"Is there nothing else you sigh for but the summer-house at Weimar?"

"No!" cried Goethe, and an indescribable expression of rapture and delight was manifest in his whole manner.

"No, why should I deny it, how could I? It would be treason to the Highest and most Glorious. No, I long for my muse, my mistress, my—"

"Beloved!" interrupted the duke. "I pray you not to be so prudish, so reserved. Have the courage to snap your fingers at this infamously deceitful moral code, and proud and distinguished as you are, elevate yourself above what these miserable earthworms call morality. For the eagle there is a different law than for the pigeon. If the eagle soars aloft through the ether to his eyry, bearing a lamb in his powerful claws, has he not a right to it—the right of superiority and power by God's grace? Has he not as much right to the lamb as the pigeon to the pea which she finds in the dust? If the pigeon by chance sees the eagle with his lamb, she cries, 'Zeter! mordio!' with the pea in her own bill, as if she were in a position to judge the eagle."

"A beautiful picture," cried Goethe, joyfully—"a picture that would inspire me to indite a poem."

"Write one, and call it for a souvenir 'The Eagle and the Dove.' Make it a reality, my eagle youth, bear off the white lamb to your eyry, and let the world, with its affected morality, say what it likes. How can you bear to see the one you love at the side of another man? Tell me, confess to me, is not the beautiful Charlotte von Stein your beloved?"

"Not in the sense you mean, duke, not in the vulgar sense of the word. I love her, I adore her, with a pure and holy sentiment. I would not that Charlotte should have cause to blush before her children on my account. She would be desecrated to me if I, in my inmost soul, could imagine the blush of shame upon her cheek, or that her eye could brighten at other than great, beautiful, and noble acts. I adore her, and to me she is the ideal of the purest and sweetest womanhood. I rejoice that she is as she is, like clear mountain crystal—transparent and so brightly pure, that one could mirror himself therein. She stands above all other women, and to her belong all my thoughts, and would, even if I were wedded to another. To me she is the most beautiful of the beautiful, the purest of the pure, the most graceful of the graceful, and all my thoughts are in perfect harmony with hers. Now, duke, if it is agreeable to you, knowing my feelings, to call Charlotte von Stein my beloved, she is so in the most elevated sense of the word."

"Ah! you poets, you poets," sighed the duke, smiling.

"A streak of madness in you all, though I will grant that it is divine."

"Say rather that Whit-Sunday comes to us every day, and the divine Spirit descends daily upon us poets, and causes us to speak in unknown tongues."

"I will say that you are the god Apollo descended from heaven, and with gods one may not dare to dispute. They act differently in their sphere than we mortals upon earth. I will be contented if our ways cross from time to time, and we can once in a while walk on together a good piece the way of life in friendship and harmony. If it would please my Wolf, I propose to turn toward beloved Weimar, the dear place, half village, half city. For my part I am finished here, my business with General von Mollendorf is accomplished. As I told you previously, I have had made known to the king my refusal to allow recruiting in my duchy. I could not consent for the present. In short, I have spoken as my secretary Wolfgang Goethe has recorded.*[Footnote: This memorial upon recruiting is found. "Correspondence of the Grand Duke Carl August and Goethe," part, i., p. 4.]* General Mollendorf has waived his demand for the present—and to-day we have had the concluding conference, and if it is agreeable to my secretary, we might set off this afternoon and pass a day at Dessau, and then on to Weimar."

"Oh, gladly will I do it; it seems as if a star from heaven had twinkled to me to follow it, for at Weimar is centred all my happiness! I prefer a lowly cabin there to all the splendor and palaces of a city."

"Then you agree with me, that this magnificently vile Berlin does not enchain you in her magic net?"

"No, she holds me not, though it has been pleasant to take a peep into it (like a child into a curiosity-box). I have seen 'Old Fritz.' His character, his gold, and his silver, his marbles, his apes and parrots, and even his town curtains please me. It is pleasant to be at the seat of war at the very moment that it threatens to break forth. It has gratified me to witness the splendor of the royal city, the life, order, and abundance, that would be nothing if thousands of men were not ready to be sacrificed; the medley of men, carriages, horses, artillery, and all the arrangements. All are mere pins in the great clock-work, only puppets whose motion is received from the great cylinder, Fredericus Rex, who indicates to each one the melody they must play, according to one of the thousand pins in the rotary beam."*[Footnote: Goethe's own words.—See Goethe's "Correspondence with Frau von Stein," part i., p. 168. Riemer, "Communications about Goethe," part ii., p. 60.]*

"You are right to compare the great man to the chief cylinder in the machine of state," nodded the duke "He rules and sets all in motion, and cares not whether the rabble are suited or not. It has enraged me sometimes to hear the fellows curse him, and yet I acted as if I heard them not. Let us return to Weimar—mankind seems better there, Wolf."

"At any rate, more regardful of us than they are here, duke. The greater the world the uglier the farce; no obscenities and fooleries of the buffoon are more disgusting than the characters of the great, mediocre and insignificant, all mingled together. I prayed this morning for courage to hold out to the end, and to hasten the consummation. I am grateful for the benefit of the journey—but I pray the gods not to conduct themselves toward us as their image-man, for I should swear to them eternal hatred."*[Footnote: Goethe's own words.—See Goethe's "Correspondence with Frau von Stein," part i., p. 169.]*

"Then you are ready to depart, Wolf?"

"Almost, dear Carl, or, if you will it, quite ready. A few visits I would make, that the people shall not be too severe upon me and cry out against my pride and arrogance."

"Because they themselves are proud and supercilious, they are bold enough to suppose Wolfgang Goethe is like them. I hope you will not visit the very learned Herr Nicolai, the insipid prosaist, the puffed-up rationalist, who believes that his knowledge permits him to penetrate every thing, and who is a veritable ass."

"No, I am not going to Nicolai, Rammler, or Engel, or, as they should be named, the wise authors of Berlin. I shall visit the artist Chodowiecki, good Karschin, occasional poetess, and the philosopher Mendelssohn. Then, if it pleases you, we will set out this afternoon, shaking the sand of Berlin from our feet."

"I shall prepare whilst you make your visits. Will you take my carriage? You know there is one from the royal stables always at my service, which stands at the door."

"Beware! they would shriek if I should drive to their doors in a royal carriage. They would accuse me of throwing aside the poet, and being only secretary of legation. I will go on foot; it amuses me to push my way through the crowd, and listen to the Berlin jargon."

CHAPTER XVII
GOETHE'S VISITS

Taking leave of his ducal friend, Goethe betook himself the street, to commence his visits. Going first to Chodowiecki, the renowned delineator and engraver, whose fame had already spread throughout Germany. When Goethe entered, the artist was busy in his atelier, working upon the figures of the characters in the "Mimic," the latest work of Professor Engel. "Master," said he, smilingly, extending him his hand, "I have come to thank you for many beautiful, happy hours which I owe to you. You paint with the chisel and poetize with the brush. An artist by God's grace."

"If the poet Goethe says that, there must be something in it," replied Chodowiecki, with a radiant face. "I have to thank you for the most beautiful and best hours of my life, and I am proud and delighted to have been able in the least to return the pleasure. The only blissful tears among many bitter ones that I have wept, were shed over the 'Sorrows of Werther.' 'Gotz von Berlichingen' so inspired me that he appeared to me in my dreams, and left me no peace until I rose in the night to draw Gotz, as he sat talking with brother Martin on the bench in the forest. Wait, I will show you the drawing; you must see it."

Goethe examined it attentively, and expressed his pleasure at the correctness and dramatical conception of the design, and did not remark, or perhaps would not, that the artist was busily occupied with crayon and paper. "How wonderfully you have reproduced my 'German Knight,'" cried Goethe, after a long observation of it. "The middle ages entire, proud and full of strength, are mirrored in this figure, and if I had not written 'Gotz von Berlichingen,' I would have been inspired to it, perhaps, from this drawing. Oh! you artists are to be envied. We need many thousand words to express what a few lines represent, and a stroke suffices to change a smiling face into a weeping one. How feeble is language, and how mighty the pencil! I wish I had the talent to be a painter!"

"And I," cried Chodowiecki, "would throw all my pencils, brushes, and chisels to the devil, or sell him my soul, if I could cope with the genius and intellect of the poet, Wolfgang Goethe. What a man! What a profile the gods have given him! There! look—have you ever seen a man with such a face?" He handed Goethe the drawing, which proved to be a speaking profile-portrait of himself, dashed off with a few strokes full of genius.

Goethe looked at it with the air of a critic. "It is true," said he, perfectly serious, "there are not many such profiles, but I am not of your opinion that the gods fashioned it. Those sharp features look as if the joiner had cut them out of oak, and they lead me to infer a very disagreeable character. I naturally do not know who the picture represents, but I must tell you, master, that this man could never please me, although I could swear it is a speaking likeness. This sharp, bowed nose has something impudent, self-sufficient in it. The brow is indeed high, which betokens thought, but the retreating lines prove that the thoughts only commence, and then lose themselves in a maze. The mouth, with its pouting lips, has an insupportable expression of stupid good-nature and sentimentality; and the well-defined, protruding chin might belong to the robber-captain Cartouche. The great wide-open eyes, with their affected passionate glances, prove what a puffed-up dandy the man must be, who perhaps imagines all the women in love with his face. No, no, I am still of the opinion that the original could never please me, and if the physiognomist Lavater should see it, he would say: 'That is the portrait of a puffed-up, quaint, powerful genius, who imagines himself something important, and who is nothing! The likeness of a bombastic fellow, with an empty head behind the pretentious brow, and meaningless phrases on the thick lips.'"

"If Lavater says so, he is a fool and an ass," cried Chodowiecki, furiously, "and he can hide himself in the remotest corner of the earth. Lichtenberg of Gottingen is quite right when he says that this empty-headed Lavater has made himself ridiculous throughout Germany with his wonderful physiognomy of dogs' tails and his profiles of unknown pigtails. If Lavater is really so narrow-minded as not to be able to distinguish a crow from an eagle, it is his own affair; but he shall never presume to look at this portrait, and you, too, are not worthy, you scorner, that I should get angry with you. The likeness is so beautiful that Jupiter himself would be satisfied to have it imputed to him. It is so like, that you need not pretend you do not know that it represents Wolfgang Goethe. As you insult it, and regard it with scorn and contempt, I will destroy it."

"For mercy's sake do not tear it," cried Goethe, springing toward Chodowiecki, and holding him fast with a firm grasp. "My dear good man, do not tear it; it would be like splitting my own head."

"Ah, ah!" shouted Chodowiecki, "you acknowledge the likeness?"

"I do acknowledge it, with joy."

"And will you admit that it is the head of a noble, talented poet, a favorite of the Muses? Say yes, or I will tear it, and you will have terrible pains in your head your life long!"

"Yes, yes! all that you wish. I am capable of saying the most flattering things of myself to save this beautiful design. Give it to me, you curious fellow!"

"No," said Chodowiecki, earnestly, "I will not give it to you. Such a portrait is not made to be put in a dusty portfolio, or framed for the boudoir of your lady-love. All Germany, all the world should enjoy it, and centuries later the German women will still see Wolfgang Goethe as he looked in his twenty-ninth year, and hang an engraving on the wall in their parlor, and sighing and palpitating acknowledge—'There never was but one such godlike youth, and there never will be another. I wish that I had known him; I wish he had loved me!' So will they speak centuries later, for I will perpetuate this drawing in a steel engraving of my most beautiful artistic work." *[Footnote: This engraving from the artist Chodowiecki still exists, and the author of this work possesses a beautiful copy, which Ottille von Goethe sent her. It is a bust in profile, the most beautiful of his youth.]*

"You are a splendid fellow, and I must embrace you, and rejoice to be immortalized by you, for this portrait pleases me exceedingly. I might well be proud that this head with the rare profile is a counterpart of my own. Now we are good friends. Before I say farewell, let me see the work at which I just disturbed you upon entering."

Goethe was about to raise the cloth, when Chodowiecki waved him back. "Do not look at it," said he, quickly; "I dislike to appear as a mechanic before you, as I wish that you should honor only the artist. We poor toilers are badly off, as the old proverb is ever proving true with us, 'Art goes for bread.' We must be mechanics the chief part of our lives, in order to have a few hours free, in which we are allowed to be artists. I have to illustrate the most miserable works with my engravings, to buy the time to pursue works of art."

"That is the interest, friend, which you pay the world for the great capital which the gods confided to you. Believe me, the artist Chodowiecki would have but a morsel to eat if the mechanic Chodowiecki did not serve him a tempting meal, paying the bill. Do not be vexed about it; man must have a trade to support him, as art is never remunerated. *[Footnote: Goethe's words—See G. H. Lewes's "Goethe's Life and Writings," vol. 1., p. 459.]* I hope the mechanic will be well paid, that the artist may create beautiful and rare works for us. This is my farewell visit to-day, friend. If you will hear a welcome from me very soon, come to Weimar, and see how one honors the artists there, and how well appreciated Chodowiecki is."

Goethe embraced and kissed the artist, who regarded him, his face radiant with joy, and would not be prevented from accompanying him to the house door, as if he were a prince or a king. "Now to Madame Karschin," said Goethe to himself, as he hastened through the streets in that direction. "The good woman has welcomed me with so many pretty verses that I must make my acknowledgments, in spite of my decision to keep the Berlin authors at a distance."

From Wilhelm Street, where Chodowiecki lived, to the tilt-yard, was not far, and Goethe soon reached the old, antiquated house where the poetess lived. After many questionings and inquiries at the lower stories and more splendid apartments of the house, he found the abode of the poetess, and climbed up the steep stairs to the slanting attic-room. The dim light of a small window permitted Goethe to read upon a gray piece of paper, pasted upon the door, 'Anna Louisa Karsch, German poetess.' He knocked modestly at the door at first, then louder, and as the voices within never ceased for a moment their animated conversation, he opened it, and entered the obscure room.

"I will do it, sir," said the little woman sitting in the window-niche near a table to a young man standing near her. "I will do it, though I must tell you album writing is very common. But you must promise me to return here, and let me see what Herr Rammler writes, and tell me what he says about me. These are my conditions."

"Frau Karschin, I promise you, upon the word of honor of a German youth, who can never lower himself to break his word."

"Very well! then I will write."

There was perfect silence. The youth watched the little, dry hand which guided the pen, with a devotional mien, and Goethe with eager curiosity, who, unobserved, stood like a suppliant at the door of the obscure little room, the shabby furniture of which betrayed the narrow circumstances of the German poetess. It harmonized with the occupant, a little, bony, meagre figure, wearing a tight-fitting blue-flowered chintz dress. Upon the gray hair, which, parted in the middle, encircled the low forehead, was a cap, which had lost its whiteness and was, therefore, more in harmony with the ruff about her yellow, thin neck.

Her sharp, angular features were redeemed by large, dark eyes, flashing with marvellous brilliancy from under the thick, gray eyebrows, and with quick, penetrating glances she sometimes turned them to the ceiling thoughtfully as she wrote. "There, sir, is my poem," said she, laying down the pen. "Listen:

'Govern your will;
If it hinders duty,
It fetters virtue;
Then envy beguiles
Into fault-finding.'"

"Oh, how beautiful, cried the young man, enraptured. "I thank you a thousand times for those glorious words, and they shall henceforth be the guiding star of my existence."

"Go to Professor Rammler, and: then return and show me what he writes, for I am convinced—. Oh, Heavens! there is a stranger," she cried, as she discovered Goethe, who had remained standing by the door.

"Yes, a stranger," said Goethe, smiling, and approaching, as the happy possessor of the album withdrew—"a stranger would not leave Berlin without visiting the German poetess."

"And without verses in your album; is it not so? I have become the fashion, and if I could only live by immortalizing myself in your albums, I should be free from care. Now I have divined it—you wish an autograph?"

"No! only a good word, and a friendly shake of the hand, for I possess a poem and a letter which the good Frau Karschin sent me at Weimar some six months since, written by herself."

"Is it Goethe?" she cried, clasping her hands in astonishment. "The poet Johann Wolfgang Goethe, the renowned author of the work which—"

"Cost you many tears," broke in Goethe, laughing. "I beg you spare me these phrases, which follow me upon my journey as the Furies Orestes. I know that 'Werther' has become the favorite of the reading public; he has opened all the tear-ducts and made all lovers of moonlight as soft as a swaddling-cloth. I could punish myself for having written 'Werther.'"

Frau Karschin laughed aloud. "That is glorious! You please me! You are a famous poet and a genius, for only geniuses can revise and ridicule themselves. Welcome, Germany's greatest poet, welcome to the attic of the poetess! There is the good word which you would have, and here is the hand. Did you think it worth while to visit poor Karschin? I am rejoiced at it, for I see that they accused you unjustly of arrogance and pride!"

"Do they accuse me of it?" asked Goethe, smiling. "Can the Berlin poets and authors never forgive me that I live at a court, and am honored with the favor of a prince?"

"They would willingly forgive you if they had the power to push you one side, and take your place. They are angry with you, because they envy you and are not accustomed to be esteemed. Our prince and ruler, as great a hero and king as he otherwise is, cares little for German poetry, and for all he would care, the Berlin authors might starve, one and all; he would trouble himself no more about them than the flies dancing in the sunlight."

"The great king is still the same, then? He will never know anything of German literature?"

"No! he declares that it is the language of barbarians and bear-catchers; scolds about us, and despises us, and yet knows as little of us as the man in the moon. He adores his Voltaire. Old Fritz knows the French poet by heart, but Lessing he knows nothing of. He abuses 'Goetz von Berlichingen,' and 'Werther's Sorrows.'"

"Oh! I know it all—I know the king's adjutant-general, von Siedlitz. I often dine with him, and read aloud my poems to him, when he relates to me what the king says to enrage me. You must know when I am angry I speak in verse. I accustomed myself to it during my unhappy marriage with the tailor Karsch. When he scolded, I answered in verse, and tried to turn my thoughts to other things, and to make the most difficult rhymes. As he was always scolding and quarrelling, I always spoke in rhyme."

"And in this way you led a very poetical marriage?" smiled Goethe.

"Yes, indeed, poetical," she said, and her large brilliant eyes were dimmed. "If it is true that tears are the baptism of poets, then I was baptized daily for twelve years, and ought to be an extraordinary poetess."

"That you are, indeed," said Goethe, "who would dispute it? You have given evidence of great poetical talent, and I read your heroic poem upon the Great Frederick with real delight."

"Do you know what he did?" she asked, bitterly. "I turned to him, begging for assistance; for who should a poet turn to, but his God and his king? Moreover, he had promised it to me personally."

"You have spoken with him, then, yourself?" asked Goethe.

"Yes, eight years ago; General von Siedlitz procured me an audience. The king was very gracious, and among other things, asked me about my life; and as I explained to him my poverty and want, he most kindly promised to help me." *[Footnote: This interview which Frau Karschin had with the king is found in "Anecdotes and Traits of Character of Frederick the Great." vol. ii., p. 72.]*

"And did he not fulfil his promise?"

"No, had it been given to the least of the French writers he would have kept it, but to a German poet it was not worth while. What is a native poet to the great German king? A phantom that he knows not, and believes not. As great as he is, the king showed himself very small to me. I sang him as a poetess and he bestowed a pittance upon me as one would to a beggar in tatters by the wayside."

"Is it really true, upon your supplication—"

"Sent me two thalers! Yes, that is indeed true, and I see by your smile that you know it, and know also that I returned it to him. I had rather die with hunger than take a beggar's penny. But let me relate to you what happened two weeks since. I had borne patiently the affair of the two thalers, and forgotten it. I am more comfortable now; the booksellers pay me for my songs and poems very well, and a number of patrons and friends, at whose head is the Prince of Prussia, give me a small pension, from which I can at least live—though poorly. One of my patrons sent me a strip of land on the Spree not far from the Hercules Bridge, where I would gladly build me a little house, at last to have a sure abiding-place where I could retire—that would be a refuge against all the troubles and sorrows of life. As I thought it over, the old confidence and imperishable love for the great king rose again within me, and as I esteemed him I always hoped for the fulfilment of his promise. I applied to him again, and begged him to do for me what he had granted to so many cobblers and tailors, as the king gives building-money to help those who will build. All the houses of the Gensdarmen-markt are built by royal aid, and sometimes the king designs the facades, as he did for the butcher Kuhn's great house; and sent him a design to ornament the frieze of ninety-nine, sheeps' heads, only ninety-nine, for he said the butcher himself was the one hundredth. The butcher remonstrated, but he was obliged to keep them, if he would have the building-money."

"Really," cried Goethe, laughing, "the king is an ingenious and extraordinary man in every thing, and no one is like him."

"No one is like him, and no one would have treated me as he did. I addressed to him a poem, begging him with true inspiration and emotion to let a German poetess find favor in his sight—and that he would be for me a Maecenas, if I were not a Horace. My heart bled with sorrow, that I must so beg and pray, and my tears wet the paper upon which I indited my begging, rhyming petition. How much money do you think the great king sent me for my house? Think of the smallest sum."

"If it was small, yet for building-money he would send you at least two hundred thalers."

The poetess burst into a scornful laugh. "He sent me three thalers! The great Frederick sent me three thalers to build a house!"

"What did you do? Did you take them?"

"Yes," she answered, proudly, "and I will leave them as a legacy to my daughter, as an historical souvenir for succeeding generations, who will relate the benevolence of the German king for the German poetess. I sent the king a receipt—I will read it to you.

"'His majesty commanded, Instead of building-money, To send me three thalers. The order was exactly, Promptly fulfilled. I am indebted for thanks, But for three thalers can No joiner in Berlin My coffin make. Otherwise to-morrow I would order Such a house without horror Where worms feast, And, feasting, quarrel Over the lean, care-worn Old woman's remains That the king let sigh away.'" *[Footnote: See "Life and Poems of Louisa Karschin," edited by her daughter.]*

"Why do you not laugh?" said Frau Karschin, raising her flashing eyes to Goethe, who sat looking down earnestly and quietly before her.

"I cannot," he gently answered. "Your poem makes me sad; it recalls the keen sorrow of a poet's existence, the oft-repeated struggle between Ideality and Reality. The blessed of the gods must humble themselves; though they may raise their heads to heaven, their feet must still rest upon earth; and to find their way upon it, and walk humbly therein, they must again lower their inspired heads."

"Oh, that makes me feel better," cried Karschin, with tears in her eyes; "that is balsam for my wounds. You are a great poet, Goethe, I feel it to be so. You are a great man, for your heart is good and filled with pity. How unjustly they call you cold and proud! Only be a little more yielding, and call upon the Berlin poets and writers. You can imagine that the news of your arrival ran like wild-fire through the town. Nicolai, Rammler, Engel, Mendelssohn, and all the other distinguished gentlemen have stayed at home like badgers in their kennels, watching for you, so as not to miss your visit. At last they became desperate, and scolded furiously over your arrogance and pride in thinking yourself better than they. Why have you not called upon them?"

There was a loud knocking at the door, and the young man with his album entered, almost breathless. "Here I am," said he, "I came directly from Professor Rammler here, as I promised you."

"You saw him, then? Has he written something for you?"

"Yes, I saw him, and he granted my request."

"And abused me, did he not, with his nose turned up? You must know, Goethe, that Professor Rammler despises my poems, because I am not so learned in Greek and Roman mythology as he is. Now tell me, my young friend, what did he say about me?"

"I promised you, upon my word of honor, to tell you every thing, but I hope you will release me from the promise." sighed the young man.

"No, that I will not. Much more, upon the strength of your word of honor, I desire it. You promised, word for word, to relate it to me."

"If it must be, then, let it be. I went at once to Professor Rammler's. He asked me immediately if I had not been here."

"Just as I asked you," laughed Karschin.

"I affirmed it, saying that you showed me his house. Upon which he asked, 'Did she say any thing against me? She is accustomed to do it before strangers, like all old women.' He then turned over my album, and as he saw the lines you wrote he reddened, and striking the book—'I see it, she knew she had said something about me. She tells every stranger that I think she is censorious. What she has written is aimed at me.' Upon that he wrote some lines opposite yours, shut the book, and handed it to me. I have not even had the time to read them."

"Read them now, quickly."

"'He who slanders and listens to slander, let him be punished. She may be hung by the tongue, and he by the ears.'" *[Footnote: This scene took place literally, and may be found in "Celebrated German Authors," vol. II., p. 340.]*

"That is shameful—that is mean!" said Frau Karschin, while Goethe re-read the cutting epigram. "That is just like Rammler; his tongue is like a two-edged sword for every one but himself, and he fans his own glories, and does not know that he is a fool. Frederick the Great himself called him so. One of his generals called his attention to him, upon which Frederick turned his horse, riding directly up to him, asking, 'Is this the distinguished Rammler?' 'Yes, your majesty, I am he,' the little professor proudly bowed. 'You are a fool!' called out Frederick, very loud, and rode away, as all around the 'Great Rammler' laughed and sneered. There are many such stories. Shall I tell you how Lessing teased him?"

"No, dear woman, tell me nothing more. I perceive your Berlin writers and poets are a malicious, contentious set of people. I may well fear you, and shall be glad to escape unharmed. Think kindly of me, and have pity upon me; if the others are too severe, raise your dear hand and hold back the scourge that it may not fall upon poor Wolfgang Goethe. Adieu, dear Frau Karschin."

Goethe bowed, and hastened down into the street. "With the authors and poets of Berlin I wish nothing more to do, but with the philosophers I may be more fortunate, and with them find the wisdom and forbearance which fail the poets."

Goethe bent his steps to Spandauer Street, in which the merchant and philosopher Moses Mendelssohn lived; hastened up the stairs, and knocked, which was answered by an old servant, to whom Goethe announced himself. The servant disappeared, and the poet stood in the little, narrow corridor, smilingly looking to the study-door, and waiting for the "gates of wisdom" to open and let the worldling enter the temple of philosophy.

The crooked little man, the great philosopher, Moses, son of Mendelssohn, stood behind the door, turning over in his mind whether he would receive Goethe or not. "Why should I? The proud secretary of legation has already been in Berlin eight days, and wishes to prove to me that he cares little for Berlin philosophers. My noble friend, the great Lessing, cannot abide 'Gotz von Berlichingen;' and Nicolai, Rammler, and Engel are the bitter opponents, the very antipodes of the rare genius and secretary of legation from Weimar. If he wishes to see me, why did he come so late, so—"

"Herr Goethe is waiting—shall he enter?" asked the servant.

The philosopher raised his head. "No," cried he, loudly. "No! tell him you were mistaken. I am not at home."

The old servant looked quite frightened at his master—the first time he had heard an untruth from him. "What shall I say, sir?"

"Say no," cried Moses, very excited and ill-humored. "Say that I am not at home—that I am out."

With a determined, defiant manner the philosopher seated himself to work upon his new book, "Jerusalem," saying to himself, "I am right to send him away; he waited too long, is too late." *[Footnote: From Ludwig Tieck I learned this anecdote, and he assured me that Moses Mendelssohn told it to him.—See "Goethe in Berlin, Leaves of Memory," p. 6.—The Authoress.]*

CHAPTER XVIII
FAREWELL TO BERLIN

"What is the matter, my dear Wolf?" cried the duke, as Goethe returned from his visits. "What mean those shadows upon your brow? Have the cursed beaux-esprits in Berlin annoyed and tortured you?"

"No, duke, I—" and suddenly stopping, he burst into a loud ringing laugh, and sprang about the room, bounding up and down, shouting, "Hurrah! hurrah! Long live the philosophers, vivat the philosophers!"

"They shall live—live—live,'' shouted the duke!

"Vivat the philosophers! hurrah! To the May-sports upon the Blockberg they ride upon a little ass with golden horns—with Pharisaical mien, praying with their eyes, 'I thank Thee, O Lord, that I am a philosopher, that I am not as the world's children, vain, proud, and arrogant.' Hey, good Carl Augustus, today a great revelation has been made known to me by a philosopher. Wisdom flowed from his mouth. All the spiders in their gray, self-woven nets, whispered and sang in his corridor, 'We weave at the fountain of life, we spin the web of time.' The little mice crept out from the corners, whispering, Hallelujah! Here lives the great philosopher Moses, who has devoured wisdom, and is unknowing of earthly vanities. Oh! the mice and the spiders waltz together upon the threshold of the great philosopher. Hey, ha! a waltz we will dance!"

Goethe caught the duke with both arms around the waist, and tore around in a giddy whirl, both laughing, both shrieking. Wolfshund, the duke's dog, asleep in the corner, sprang up howling and barking at their wild bounds and goat-like springs, and joined the dancers. As Goethe felt the ribbon which confined his cue give way, he shook wildly his curly, powdered hair and it fell in mad confusion. Both he and the duke now sank exhausted to the floor, panting and laughing.

"Heaven be praised, Wolf," said the duke, "the must has once more fermented, and sprung a few of the hoops of dignity?"

"Yes," answered Goethe, who suddenly assumed a grave, serious mien, "the must has fermented, and I trust a fine wine will clear itself from it."

"Can you not set off, Wolf?" asked the duke, springing up. "Have you had sufficient of the Berliners?"

"I have done with them," replied Goethe, "not only with the Berliners, but it may be with all the rest of humanity. I feel, my duke, that the bloom of confidence, candor, and self-sacrificing love fades daily; only for you, and the friend whom I love, is there still attraction and flagrancy. Oh! you dear ones, be charitable, and do not consent that they fade for you. Let the goodness which I read in your eyes, my dear Carl, and the sunny rays of friendship strengthen the poor little blossom, that it does not entirely fade and wither away!" With passionate earnestness he threw his arms around the duke, pressing him to his bosom.

"Oh! Wolf, my dear Wolf, you have a child's heart and a poet's soul. Are you faint-hearted and dispirited? Do you not know that you are the sun which brings forth the flowers for us, and shines for us all? Let no clouds overshadow you, Wolf! Let your fresh, youthful vigor, and divine brilliancy, penetrate them. In the thick, sandy atmosphere of Berlin I confess the sun itself loses its force and brightness! Come! let us be off. Our steeds stamp with impatience." The duke drew his friend from the room and joyfully they sprang down the stairs to the carriage, the great dog following, howling and barking after them. "Forward, then, forward! Blow, postilion, blow! A gay little air! Let it peal through the streets, a farewell song! Blow, postilion, blow! and I will moisten your throat at the gates with the thin, white stuff, which you have the boldness to call beer." The postilion laughed for joy, and the German song resounded in quivering tones—"Three riders rode out of the gate." He blew so long and loudly, that the dog set up a mournful howl, and amid the peals of the postilion, and the distressed cry of Wolfshund, they drove through the long, hot streets of Berlin, through the Leipsic Gate, and the suburbs with their small, low houses. The wagon-wheels sank to the spokes in the loose, yellow sand of the hill they soon mounted, and, arriving at the top of which, the postilion stopped to let his horses take breath, and turned to remind his aristocratic passengers that this was their last view of the city.

"And will be seen no more," repeated the duke. "Come, let us take a farewell look at Berlin, Wolf!" and away they sprang without waiting for the footman to descend, and waded through the sand to a rising in the fallow fields. There they stood, arm in arm, and viewed the town with its towers and chimneys, houses, barracks, and palaces stretched at their feet. A thick, gray, cloud of vapor and smoke hovered over it, and veiled the horizon in dust and fog. "Farewell, Berlin, you city of arrogance and conceit!" cried the duke, joyfully. "I shake your dust from my feet, and strew the sand of your fields over every souvenir of you in memory," and suiting the action to his words, he tossed a handful of it in the air.

"Farewell, Muses and Graces of sand and dust!" cried Goethe, as his fiery eye flashed far out over the fog-enveloped roofs. "Farewell, Berlin, void of nature and without verdure! the abode of poetic art, but not of poesy. You Babylon of wisdom and philosophy, I have seen you with your painted cheeks and coquettish smile, your voluptuous form and seductive charms. You shall never ensnare me with your deceitful beauty, and suck the marrow from my bones, or the consciousness of pure humanity from my soul. Beautiful may you be to enslaved intellects, but to the free, they turn their backs to you and thrice strew ashes on your head. Farewell, Berlin, may I never see you again!" *[Goethe, in fact, never visited Berlin again, though he was often invited there, particularly when the new theatre was opened, with a poetic prologue written by himself. They inaugurated the festivity with Goethe's "Iphigenia," the first representation, and Prince Radzwill urgently invited the poet, through Count Bruhl, to visit Berlin at this time, and reside in his palace. But Goethe refused; he was seventy-two years old (1826), and excused himself on account of his age.]* Goethe stooped and threw a handful of sand in the air.

The postilion, tired of standing in the burning sun, blew loudly the air of the soldier's song: "Now, adieu, Louisa, wipe your face, every ball does not hit." Mournfully the melody sounded in the stillness, like accusing spirits who wept the insult of the prince and the poet.

"Now, on to our dear Weimar, Wolf!" The carriage rolled down the sandy hill, and Berlin disappeared to the travellers, lost in dreamy thought. Slowly they advanced, in spite of relays and fresh horses at every station. Night spread out her starry mantle over the world, and the sleepers who rested from the burdens and cares of the day. Goethe alone was wakeful and vigilant. With his beautiful eyes, as brilliant as fallen stars, uplifted to heaven, to God, his manly bosom heaving with noble thoughts and glorious aspirations, he reviewed the past, and recalled with joy that he had accomplished much and well. He peered into the future, and promised himself to do more and better. "Yes, I will," whispered he softly, pointing to the stars; "so high as possible shall the pyramid of my being rise. To that I will constantly bend my thoughts, never forgetting it, for I dare not tarry; with the years already on my head, fate may arrest my steps, and the tower of Babylon remain unfinished. At least they must acknowledge the edifice was boldly designed, and if I live, God willing, it shall rise."

BOOK III
STORM AND PRESSURE

CHAPTER XIX
THE KING AND THE AUSTRIAN DIPLOMAT

Frederick commenced the campaign against the house of Hapsburg with all the energy and bold courage of former days. The diplomats had once more been permitted to seek the arts of negotiation, and, these having failed, the king advanced rapidly, and entered Bohemia with his advance-guard. The imperial army, informed of the approach of the enemy, retired hurriedly to their intrenchments at Koeniggratz, beyond the Elbe, without a decisive battle. In the skirmishes at the outposts the Prussians had been victorious. On the opposite shore of the Elbe, at Welsdorf, the king took up his headquarters. Why did he not pursue his bold run of victory? Why did he not surprise the imperial army, which he knew was scattered, and not in a position to resist the strength of the Prussian forces? Moreover, the second column of the Prussian army, under the command of Prince Henry, had also entered Bohemia, and fortified a camp near Rimburg, having united with the Saxon allies, which caused the imperialists under Field-Marshal Loudon to seek protection beyond the Iser, near Muenchengratz and Yung-bunzlau. Why did the king then stop in the midst of his victorious career? He had advanced to the field with his fresh, youthful fire, a shining example to all. He was always mounted, shunning no danger, but taking part in the hardships and fatigue incident to the changing life of war; even showing himself personally active at the discovery of foraging-parties. Why did he suddenly hesitate and lie inactive in camp? Why did he not summon his generals and staff-officers to his quarters, instead of his Minister von Herzberg? Every one asked himself the question, and every one answered it differently.—Some said, "Because the Empress of Russia had raised objections to this war of German brothers;" others, that "the King of the French had offered to settle the quarrel as intermediator." A third said, the "empress-queen, Maria Theresa, was terrified at the rapid advance of the Prussians, and had immediately commenced negotiations for peace."

While the wise politicians of Germany and all Europe read and pondered, Frederick tarried quietly in his peasant-house, in which he had taken up his quarters, and which had been arranged very comfortably with carpets, camp-stools, and curtains. He sat in his cabinet upon the high, leather-covered arm-chair, which had been brought for him from the neighboring parsonage. Alkmene lay upon his knee, and Diana at his feet. His countenance was pale, and betrayed fatigue, but his eye beamed with undimmed brilliancy, and around his mouth played an ironical smile. "Well, so matters stand; therefore, I have summoned you to Welsdorf," said Frederick to his minister, Von Herzberg. "The empress-queen is, above all things, a most tender mother. She is fearfully anxious, now that the dear young Emperor Joseph has left for the army, and will be exposed to the dangers of war. My good friends in Vienna inform me that my entrance into Bohemia created a sensation at the brilliant capital, and had so much alarmed the empress-queen, that she was seriously thinking of negotiating for peace. As I learned this from a reliable source, I halted and encamped, that the empress should know where to find me, and sent to summon you immediately. I had not been here three days, when the empress's ambassador, Baron von Thugut, appeared to make offers, and consult about an armistice of two weeks. I made known my conditions, and promised the empress, through her negotiator, that I would so calculate my movements that her majesty would have nothing to fear for her blood and her cherished emperor. *[Footnote: The king's words.—See "Prussia, Frederick the Great," vol. iv., p. 102.]* Voila, mon cher ministre, you know all now. If the Austrian diplomat comes a second time, you can negotiate with him."

"Is your majesty also inclined to peace?" asked Herzberg.

The king shrugged his shoulders. "When it can be arranged with honor, yes," said he. "I will acknowledge, Herzberg, to you, the campaign is hard for me. The old fellow of sixty-eight feels the burden of life, and would gladly rest quietly, and enjoy the last few years as philosopher and writer instead of soldier."

"Your majesty has yet many years to live, God willing," cried Herzberg. "It would be a great misfortune to Prussia if she could not yet owe to her great king a long and happy reign."

"Hem!" replied the king, "there are in Prussia very many who think otherwise, and wish me to the devil. But I have no intention of seeking monsieur so soon, for there are sufficient devilish deeds to endure in this earthly vale of sorrow to prepare for one a very decent purgatory, and give him hereafter well-founded hopes of heaven. Therefore I count upon remaining here below a while, and to knead with you this leaven of life that may yield to my subjects an eatable bread. You must help me, Herzberg, when I am the baker, to provide the flour for my people; you must be the associate to knead the bread. In order that the flour should not fail, and the bread give out, it may be necessary, if possible, to make peace."

"Will your majesty be so gracious as to inform me what steps I may take, and upon what conditions?"

"Take this paper," said the king, extending a written document to Herzberg. "I have therein expressed my wishes, and you can act accordingly. I am prepared for peace upon any terms which can be made with honor, and which do not frustrate the aim I have in view. You well know that this is the security of Germany against Austria's ambitious love of territorial aggrandizement! I cannot and I will not suffer that the house of Habsburg should strive for unjust possession in Germany, and appropriate Bavaria to herself while a lawful heir exists. I well know that I play the role of Don Quixote, and am about to fight for the rights of Germany as the Chevalier de la Mancha fought for his Dulcinea del Toboso. Mais, que voulez-vous, it is necessary for my fame and repose that I enter the arena once more against Austria to prove to her that I exist. I take this step on account of the prestige I have gained in the German empire, and which I should lose if I had not faced Austria in this Bavarian contest. And besides, it is agreeable to me to accustom my successor to the thunder of cannon, and witness his bearing on the field of battle."

"He will certainly do honor to the heroic race of Hohenzollern," answered Herzberg, bowing.

A sudden flash from the king's fiery eyes met the calm pale face of Herzberg. "Mere words and flattery, which prove that you are not satisfied, Herzberg! Nay, nay, do not deny it; you do not like that I should tarry and treat, and set the pen in motion instead of the sword. You are a man of deeds, and if you had had your way, I should have already won a decisive battle, and be on the road to Vienna to besiege the empress in her citadel, and dictate an humiliating peace to her."

"Your majesty, I can assure you—"

"Well, well, do not quarrel!" interrupted the king; "do you suppose I cannot read your honest and obstinate face? Do you suppose I did not mean what I said? Acknowledge that I am right! confess it, I command you!"

"If your majesty commands it, then I will acknowledge it. Yes, I did wish that your majesty had not empowered Baron von Thugut to return for further negotiations. It would have been well if your majesty had marched victorious to Vienna, to let the proud Hapsburgers see for once that Frederick of Prussia does not stand behind them, but at their side; that he has created a new order of things; that the old, mouldy, rotten statutes of the imperial sovereignty have fallen in the dust before Frederick the Great; that Germany must be newly mapped out, in order to give room near the old man Austria for young Prussia. Yes, your majesty, I could have wished that you had even been less generous, less noble toward the supercilious, insolent enemy, and have accepted no conditions but those of 'equality for Prussia with Austria in the German empire!'"

> *"My dear sir, I am truly astonished at the vigor with which you express yourself; I am very glad to find you so enthusiastic," said Frederick, nodding to his minister; "but listen—I will confide to you that which I do not wish you to repeat: I am no longer, to my regret, what you so flatteringly call me, 'Frederick the Great,' but only 'Old Fritz.' Do you understand me? the latter is a deplorable, worn-out soldier, who no longer feels power or vigor. The lines of Boileau often recur to me on mounting my horse:*
>
> *'Unfortunate one, leave thy steed growing old in peace, For fear, that, panting and suddenly out of breath, In falling, he may not leave his master upon the arena!'*

It is the misery of life that man will grow old, and that the body, when worn and weary, will even subdue the spirit, and force her to fold her wings and suffer. I did not realize that it had gone so far with me, and I imagined that the winged soul could raise the old, decayed body. Therefore I risked, in spite of my lazy old age, to undertake this war, for I recognized it as a holy duty to enter into it, for the honor and justice of our country, and prove to the Emperor of Germany that he could not manage and rule at his will in the German empire. I long not for the honor of new laurels, but I should be satisfied, as father of my subjects, to gain a civil crown.

"There you have my creed. I have as sincerely confessed to you as my respectable cousin, the empress-queen, to her confessor; only I did not fall upon my knees to you, and you do not as the said confessor, betray me to the Holy Father at Rome."

"Your majesty well knows that every word which you have the grace to confide to me, is engraved upon my inmost soul, and that no power upon earth could force me to reveal it."

"I know that you are a true and zealous servant of your king and country," said Frederick. "Once more I say to you, other than an honorable peace I will not make; and if empress-queen does not accept the abandonment of Bavaria as the basis of peace, then I must conquer my aversion to war, and the sword must arrange what the pen has failed to do. And now, passons ladessus! Until Thugut arrives, let us speak of other things. I have been tolerably industrious, and have improved the leisure of camp-life as much as possible. I have written a panegyric upon Voltaire, and when it is revised and corrected you shall arrange an anniversary in memoriam, at the Berlin Academy, and read my eulogy."

"All Germany and all Europe will be surprised at the magnanimity of the royal mind which could occupy itself in the camp with the muse, and erect an imperishable monument to the man who witnessed such ingratitude and baseness to his benefactor and protector."

"Vous allez trop vite, mon cher; vraiment, trop vite," cried Frederick, ardently. "It is true Voltaire was a miserable fellow, but he was a great poet. He returned meanness and ingratitude to me for the many kindnesses I showed to him, for I treated him more like a friend than a king. Voltaire was my benefactor, in so far that I owed to him the most agreeable and elevating hours of my youth, In memory of these hours I have written this eulogy. It is not worthy of particular mention, and the Academie Francaise will doubtless severely criticise my knowledge of their language. But it is impossible to write well, one moment in camp and another on the march. If it is unworthy of him whom it was intended to celebrate, I have at least availed myself of the freedom of the pen, and will cause to be publicly read in Berlin what one dares not whisper in Paris." *[Footnote: The king's own words.—"Posthumous Works," vol. xv., p. 109. This eulogy upon Voltaire, which the king wrote in camp, Herzberg read, in the November following, before the Academy.]*

"I shall be most happy to be the instrument to make known this generous expression of your majesty's good-will," remarked Herzberg, bowing.

Frederick smiled, adding: "But with the other work which I have commenced, you are not quite satisfied. You are such an enthusiastic German, that you presume to assert that the intolerable German jargon is a beautiful and expressive language!"

"And I abide by this decision, your majesty," zealously cried Herzberg. "The German language is euphonious, and prolific in ideas, and it is well capable of rivalling in brevity and clearness those of the ancients."

"That you have already asserted, and I have contested it, and again I contest it to-day. Do not trouble me with your German language. It will only deserve notice when great poets, distinguished orators, and admirable historians, have given it their attention and corrected it, freeing it from such disgusting and effeminate phrases as now disfigure it, and cause one to use a mass of words to express a few ideas. At present it is only an accumulation of different dialects, which every division of the German empire thinks to speak the best, and of which twenty thousand can scarcely understand what the other twenty thousand are saying!" *[Footnote: The king's own words.—See "Posthumous Works," vol. xv.]*

"Sire," cried Herzberg, with vehemence, "should a German king thus speak of his native tongue, at the same time that he takes the field to vindicate the honor of Germany, and submits to all the miseries and hardships of war? Your majesty cannot be in earnest, to despise our beautiful language."

"I do not despise it; I only say that it must be reformed, and shorn of its excrescences. Until then we must use the French, which is to-day the language of the world, and in which one can render all the master-works of the Greeks and the Latins, with the same versatility, delicacy, and subtlety, as the original. You pretend that one can well read Tacitus in a German translation, but I do not think the language capable of rendering the Latin authors with the same brevity as the French."

"Sire, to my joy, I can give you proof to the contrary. A Berlin savant, Conrector Moritz, at my request, has translated a few chapters of the fourteenth book of the 'Annals of Tacitus,' word for word, most faithfully into German. He has written it in two columns, the translation at the side of the original. I have taken the liberty to bring this work with me and you will see how exactly, and with what brevity, Latin authors can be rendered into German, and that there are young learned men who have seized the spirit of our language and know how to use it with grace and skill."

"Indeed, give it to me," cried the king, zealously. "I am truly curious to admire the German linguist's work who has so boldly undertaken to translate Tacitus."

"Sire," said Herzberg, raising his eyes knowingly, with a mild, imploring expression to the king's face—"sire, I join a request with this translation."

"What is it? I am very curious about a petition from you, it is so seldom that you proffer one."

"Your majesty, my request concerns the translator of this very chapter of Tacitus. He is Conrector Moritz, attached to the Gray Cloister in Berlin—an unusually gifted young man, who has undoubtedly a brilliant future before him. He has already written many eminent works. The Director Gedicke recommended him to me as a most distinguished, scholarly person, and I have learned to know and appreciate the young man by this means."

"I see it," nodded the king. "You speak of him with great enthusiasm, and as what you so warmly recommend is generally able and well qualified, I begin to be interested in this Herr Moritz. When I return to Berlin—and Heaven grant that it may be soon!—I will at once empower you to present this luminary. Are you satisfied?"

"Sire, dare I ask still more? I would beg your majesty to grant this young man an audience at once."

"How, at once! Is this phoenix here, who so interests my Minister Herzberg? Where is he from, and what does he wish?"

"He is from Berlin; I met him making the journey on foot. He sat upon a stone, by the wayside, eating a piece of bread, with a glowing face, and so absorbed talking to himself in Latin that he heard not the creaking of my carriage through the sand. I recognized him immediately, and called him by name. He turned, perfectly unembarrassed and not at all ashamed to have been discovered in such an humble and poor position."

"That is to say, he is a good comedian," said the king. "He knew that you would drive past there, and placed himself expressly to call your attention to him."

"I beg pardon, sire; Conrector Moritz could not have known that I would take this journey. You will recollect that the courier arrived at midnight with your majesty's commands, and two hours later I was on the road, and have since travelled day and night. As I met the young man only five miles from this place, he must have set out many days before I thought of leaving Berlin."

"It is true," said the king, "it was a false suspicion. You invited him into your carriage, did you not?"

"I did very naturally, sire, as he told me he was going to beg an audience of your majesty. At first he refused decidedly, as he wished to travel on foot, like the pilgrims to the pope at Rome."

"An original, a truly original genius," cried the king.

"He is so indeed, and is so called by all his friends."

"Has he any friends?" asked the king, with an incredulous smile.

"Yes, sire, many warm and sympathizing friends, who are much attached to him, and, on account of his distinguished and brilliant qualities, are willing to indulge his peculiarities."

"Herzberg, you are charmed, and speak of this man as a young girl in love!"

"Sire, if I were a young girl, I should certainly fall in love with this Moritz, for he is handsome."

"Diable! I begin to fear this subject. You say he is handsome, learned, wise, and good, although he belongs to the airy, puffed-up Berliners. Did you let Herr Moritz wander on in his pilgrimage?"

"No, sire, I persuaded him at last to accept a seat in my carriage, by explaining to him that your majesty might soon leave Welsdorf, and he would run the risk of not arriving in season. Upon no condition would he get inside, but climbed up behind, for, said he, with a firm, decided manner, 'I go to the king as a beggar, not as a distinguished gentleman.'"

"Indeed it is an original," the king murmured to himself. "Do you know what the man wants?" he asked aloud.

"No, your majesty; he said that his business concerned the happiness of two human beings, and that he could only open his heart to his God and his king."

"Where is your protege?"

"He stands outside, and it is my humble request that your majesty will grant him an audience, and permit me to call him."

"It is granted, and—"

Just at that moment the door opened, and the footman announced that the private secretary of his highness Prince von Galitzin had arrived, and most respectfully begged an audience.

"It is he—it is the baron," said the king. "Tell your protege he must wait, and come again. Bid the Prince von Galitzin enter."

As the Minister von Herzberg withdrew, the Baron von Thugut appeared, the extraordinary and secret ambassador of the Empress Maria Theresa.

"Well, Herr Baron, you are already returned," said the king, as he scarcely nodded to the profoundly respectful bows of the ambassador. "I infer, therefore, that your instructions are not from the empress, but from the co-regent, the Emperor Joseph, who has betaken himself to the Austrian camp."

"Sire," answered Thugut, laconically, "I have driven day and night, and have received my instructions directly from the empress."

The king slowly shook his head, and an imperceptible smile played around his lips.

"Does the young emperor approve of these instructions?"

"Sire, his majesty, the emperor, is only the co-regent," answered Thugut, hastily. "It is not therefore necessary, that my sovereign should make her decisions dependent upon her son's concordance."

"The empress will negotiate for peace," said the king to himself, "but the emperor desires to win laurels in the war, and will try to cut off the negotiations of his mother by a coup de main. One must be on his guard!"

Just then the door opened and Herzberg returned.

"You perceive I expected you, Baron von Thugut," said the king, "and I ordered here my minister of state, Herr von Herzberg. This is the Baron von Thugut, my dear minister, the ambassador of the empress-queen, who carries in his pocket peace or war, as it may be."

"Sire, I must protest against being so important a personage, as peace and war alone depend upon your majesty. It alone depends upon the lofty King of Prussia whether he will give peace and tranquillity to Germany, or suffer the guilt of permitting the bloody scourge of civil war again to tear in pieces the unhappy German nation."

"That sounds very sentimental," cried the king, smiling. "The Baron von Thugut will appeal to my heart, when we have only to do with the head. Austria wishes to be the head of Germany, and as such would devour one German state after another, as a very palatable morsel. But if you will be the head, Monsieur le Baron, you cannot represent the stomach also, for, as I have been told, it only exists in those soft animals of the sea whose head is in their stomach, and which think and digest at the same time. Austria does not belong to this class, but has rather a very hard and impenetrable shell. We cannot let her devour as stomach what as the head she has chosen as booty. That the electorate of Bavaria is not to be devoured, is the necessary and fundamental preliminary upon which the temple of peace may be erected. If you, or rather the empress-queen, agree to it, the negotiations can be concluded by you two gentlemen. But if you think to erect a temple of peace upon any other basis, your propositions will be in vain. I have not taken the field to make conquests, but to protect the rights of a German prince, and not suffer others to appropriate a German state. I know, as you have said, that war is a bloody scourge for the nation; but, sir, we will not look at it in a sentimental light, and talk of civil war, when Austria herself compels us to take the field. Or, perhaps, you imagine to prove to my good Pomeranians, Markers, and my other German states, that the Croatians, Pandurians, Hungarians, Wallachians, Italians, and Polanders, are our German brothers, which imperial Austria opposes to us. I think this brotherhood may be traced to our common ancestor, Adam, and in this sense all wars are indeed civil wars. In any case war is a scourge for man, and I am convinced that the empress-queen would just as willingly spare her Croatians, Pandurians, Wallachians, and Galicians, as I all my German subjects collectively."

"Also your majesty's Polish subjects, as may be expected," added Baron von Thugut.

"My Polish subjects are the minimum portion, and are about in proportion to the German population as in imperial Austria the German is to the foreign. But enough of this; if I do not recognize this as a civil war, it is indeed a great misfortune. I would do every thing to avoid it—every thing compatible with the honor and glory of my house, as well as that of Germany in general. Therefore let us know the Views of the empress-queen!"

"Sire," answered Von Thugut, as he slowly untied and unfolded the documents, "I beg permission to read aloud to your majesty the acts relative to these points."

"No, baron," answered the king quickly, "the more minute details give to my minister; I wish only the contents in brief."

"At your majesty's command. The empress-queen declares herself ready to renounce the concluded treaty of inheritance to the succession of Bavaria at the death of Elector Charles Theodore; also to give up the district seized, if Prussia will promise to resign the succession of the Margraves of Anspach and Baireuth, and let them remain independent principalities, governed by self-dependent sovereigns."

"That means, that Austria, who will unjustly aggrandize herself by Bavaria, will deprive Prussia of a lawful inheritance!" cried the king, his eyes flashing anger. "I will not heed the after-cause, but I wish to satisfactorily understand the first part of the proposition, that Austria will cede her pretensions to Bavaria."

"Sire, upon conditions only which are sufficient for the honor, the wishes, and necessities of my lofty mistress."

"You hear, my dear Herzberg," said the king, smiling, and turning to his minister, "c'est tout comme chez nous. It will now be your task to find out these conditions, which too closely affect the honor of one or the other. For this purpose you will find the adjacent Cloister Braunau more convenient than my poor cabin. At the conferences of diplomats much time is consumed, while we military people have little time to spare. I shall move on with my army."

"How, then! will your majesty break up here?" cried Thugut, with evident surprise.

The king smiled. "Yes, I shall advance, as my remaining might be construed equal to a retreat. The arts of diplomacy may drag on until the imperialists have assembled all their foreign subjects to the so-called civil war. Then hasten the negotiations, Baron von Thugut, for every day of diplomatic peace is one day more of foraging war, and I know not that you count the Bohemians in the German brotherhood, to whom the calamity of war is ruinous. You have now to deal with the Baron von Thugut, my dear

Herzberg, and I hope the baron will accept some diplomatic campaigns with you in Cloister Braunau."

"Sire, I accept, and if your majesty will dismiss me, I will go at once to the cloister," answered Baron von Thugut, whose manner had become graver and more serious since the king's announcement of the intended advance.

"You are at liberty to withdraw. The good and hospitable monks have already been apprised of your arrival by an express courier, and have doubtless a good supper and a soft bed awaiting you."

"Had your majesty the grace to be convinced of my return?" asked Thugut.

"I was convinced of the tender heart of the empress-queen, and that she would graciously try once more, in her Christian mercy, to convert such an old barbarian and heretic as I am. Go now to the cloister, and when I pass by in the morning, with my army, I will not fail to have them play a pious air for the edification of the diplomats—such as, 'My soul, like the young deer, cries unto Thee,' or, 'Oh, master, I am thy old dog,' or some such heavenly song to excite the diplomats to pious thoughts, and therewith I commend you to God's care, Baron von Thugut."

The king charged Herr von Herzberg to play the role of grand-chamberlain, and accompany the ambassador to his carriage, smiling, and slightly nodding a farewell.

The baron was on the point of leaving, when the king called to him.

"Had your majesty the grace to call me?" asked Thugut, hastily turning.

"Yes!" answered Frederick, smiling, and pointing to the string which had served to bind the baron's papers. "You have forgotten something, my lord, and I do not like to enrich myself with others' property." *[Footnote: Historical. The king's words.—See Hormayr.]*

Baron von Thugut took this last well-aimed stab of his royal opponent somewhat embarrassed, and hastened to pick up the string, and withdraw.

CHAPTER XX
THE KING AND THE LOVER

The king smiled, glancing at the retreating figure of the baron, and approached the window to peep through the little green glass panes to see him as he passed by.

"A sly fox," said he, smiling, "but I will prove to him that we understand fox-hunting, and are not deceived by cunning feints."

"Will your majesty really break up to-day?" asked Von Herzberg, upon returning.

"Yes, my dear minister. That is to say, I do not wish to, but I must, in order to give the negotiations for peace a war-like character. The enemy asks for delay to finish their preparations for war—not peace. The negotiations for the latter emanate from the empress, but the conditions concerning Anspach come from the emperor. It is the Eris-apple, which he casts upon the table, by which his imperial mother and I would gladly smoke the pipe of peace. It is incumbent upon you, Herzberg, to negotiate for peace, while I pick up the apple and balance it a little upon the point of my sword. I shall leave early to-morrow, but I would speak with you before I set out. You must be weary with the journey, so rest awhile now, then dine with me, and afterward go to the conference."

"Sire, will you not receive my protege, Conrector Moritz?"

"Did you not say that he begged for a secret audience?"

"Yes, sire, he has for this purpose travelled the long distance from Berlin, and I assure your majesty, upon my word of honor, that I have not the least suspicion what his petition may be."

"Eh bien, say to your protege that I grant him the sought-for interview on your account, Herzberg. You are such a curious fellow—you are always petitioning for others instead of yourself, and the benefits which you ought to receive go to them. Let Moritz enter, and then try to sleep a little, that you may be wide awake to confer with Baron von Thugut."

Minister von Herzberg withdrew, and immediately the pale, earnest face of Conrector Philip Moritz appeared in the royal presence.

The king regarded him with a prolonged and searching glance, the noble, resolute face of whom was pallid with deep grief, but from whose eyes there beamed courageous energy. "Are you the translator of the chapters from Tacitus, which my Minister Herzberg handed me?" asked the king, after a pause.

"Yes, sire," gently answered Moritz.

"I am told that it is ably done," continued his majesty, still attentively observing him. "You will acknowledge that it is exceedingly difficult to render the concise style of Tacitus into the prolix, long-winded German?"

"Pardon me, sire," replied Moritz, whose youthful impetuosity could with difficulty be diverted from the real object of his pilgrimage. "Our language is by no means long-winded, and there is no difficulty in translating Latin authors into German, which equals any living tongue in beauty and sonorousness, and surpasses them all in depth of thought, power, and poesy."

"Diable!" cried the king, smiling; "you speak like an incarnate German philologist, who confounds the sound of words with profound thought. You will acknowledge that until now our language has not been much known."

"Sire," answered Moritz, "Martin Luther, in his translation of the Bible three hundred years since, employed hundreds of beautiful, expressive formations."

"He is not only a learned man," said the king to himself, "but he seems an honorable one; and now, as I have proved his scholarly attainments, I must indulge his impatience." The king's penetrating glance softened, and his features changed their severe expression. "The Minister von Herzberg informed me that he found you by the roadside, and that you would journey hither on foot."

"It is true, sire."

"Why did you travel in that manner?"

"Sire, I desired, as the poor, heavily-laden pilgrims of the middle ages, to make the pilgrimage to the Holy Father at Rome, who was the king of kings. Every step in advance seemed to them to lighten their burden and enhance their happiness. Your majesty is in our day what the pope was held to be in the middle ages, therefore I have wandered as a pilgrim to my king, who has the power to bind and to loose, and from whom I must not only implore personal happiness, but that also of a good and amiable young girl."

"Ah! it concerns a love-affair. As I now look at you, I can understand that. You are young and passionate, and the maidens have eyes. How can I help you in such an adventure?"

"Sire, by not granting a title to a certain person, or if it must be granted, annul the conditions attendant upon it."

"I do not understand you," answered the king, harshly. "Speak not in riddles. What do you mean?"

"General Werrig von Leuthen has addressed himself to you, sire, praying for the consent of your majesty to the marriage of his daughter with the banker Ebenstreit. Your majesty has consented, and added that Herr Ebenstreit shall take the name of his future father-in-law, and the marriage shall take place as soon as the title of nobility has been made out."

The king nodded. "For which the new-made nobleman has to pay a hundred louis d'ors to the Invalids at Berlin. But what is that to you? And what connection has Herr Ebenstreit's title to do with Conrector Moritz?"

Moritz's face brightened, and, deeply moved, he answered: "Sire, I love the daughter of General von Leuthen, and she returns my love. By not ennobling Ebenstreit, it lies in your power, most gracious majesty, to make two persons the most blessed of God's creatures, who desire nothing more than to wander hand in hand through life, loving and trusting each other."

"Is that all?" asked the king, with a searching glance.

Moritz quailed beneath it, and cast down his eyes. "No!" he replied. "As I now stand in the presence of your majesty, I am sensible of the boldness of my undertaking, and words fail me to express what is burning in my soul. Oh! sire, I only know that we love each other, and that this love is the first sunbeam which has fallen upon my gloomy and thorny path of life, and awakened in my lonely heart all the bloom of feeling. You smile, and your great spirit may well mock the poor human being who thinks of personal happiness, when for an idea merely thousands are killed upon the field of battle. My life, sire, has been a great combat, in which I have striven with all the demons escaped from Pandora's box. I have grown up amid privations and need. I have lived and suffered, until God recompensed my joyless, toiling, hungered existence by this reciprocated love, which is a beautiful ornament to my life, and is life itself, and to renounce it would be to renounce life. I am young, sire, and I long for the unknown paradise of earthly happiness, which I have never entered until now, and which I can only attain led by the hand of my beloved. I yearn just once, as other privileged men, to bask in the sunshine of happiness a long, beautiful summer day, and then at the golden sunset to sink upon my knees and cry, 'I thank Thee, O God, that in Thy goodness I have recognized Thy sublimity, and that Thou hast revealed thy glory to me.' All this appears of little importance to your majesty, for the heart of a king is not like that of other men, and the personal happiness of individuals appears a matter of little account to him who thinks and works for the good of an entire nation. But the fly, sire, which is sunning itself upon the plumes of the helmet of a victorious king, has its right to happiness, for God created it with the same care and love that He created the noblest of His creatures—man! and it would be cruel to kill it without necessity. Sire, I do not extol myself. I know that in your eyes I am no more than the fly upon your helmet, but I only implore you to grant me my life, for God has given it to me."

"You mean by this that I shall forbid General von Leuthen to marry his daughter to the rich man who seeks her, and to which marriage, understand me well, I have already given my consent."

"Sire, I only know that this union drives not only me to despair, but one of the noblest and best of God's creatures. Fraulein von Leuthen does not love the bridegroom forced upon her; she detests him, and she has good reason to, for the banker Ebenstreit is a cold-hearted, purse-proud man, enfeebled by a voluptuous, vicious life, and seeks nothing nobler and more elevated in the young girl to whom he has offered his hand, than the title and noble name which she can procure for him. Your majesty, I implore not for myself, but for the daughter of a man who once had the good fortune to save your life in battle! Have pity upon her, and do not sacrifice her to an inconsolably hopeless life by the side of an unloved and detested husband!"

The king slowly shook his head. "You forget that the general to whom I am indebted for this favor has begged my consent to this marriage, and that I have granted it."

"Sire, I conjure you to recall it! Upon my knees I implore you not to grant it! Do not make two people unhappy, who only beg of your majesty the permission to love and live with each other!" Moritz threw himself at the king's feet, praying with clasped hands, his face flushed with deep emotion, and his eyes dimmed with tears.

"Rise!" commanded Frederick, "rise, do not kneel to me as to a God. I am a feeble mortal, subject to the same ills which threaten you and the whole human race. Rise, and answer me one question—are you rich?"

"No," answered Moritz, proudly raising his head; "no, I am poor."

"Do you know that Fraulein von Leuthen is poor? Her father is worse off than Job, for he is in debt."

"If General von Leuthen's daughter were rich, or even moderately well off, I never would have presumed to address your majesty on the subject, for fear that you might misconstrue my intentions, and suppose that my love was inspired by self-interest. Fortunately, Marie possesses nothing but her noble, beautiful self. She leads a joyless existence under the severe discipline of her cold-hearted parents; and therefore I can truthfully say, that with me she will lose nothing, but gain what she has never known—a tranquil, happy life, protected by my love."

"How much salary do you receive as teacher?"

"Majesty, as conrector of the college attached to the Gray Monastery, three hundred and fifty dollars."

"Do you expect to live upon that yourself, and support a family besides?"

"Sire, I shall earn money in other ways, as I have already done. I shall write books. The publishers tell me that I am a favorite author, and they pay me well."

"If on the morrow you should fall ill, your income would vanish, and your family and you would starve together. No! no! you are an idealist, you dream how life should be, and not as it is in truth! I have listened to you, thinking that you would present some forcible argument upon which to found your pretensions, but I hear only the ravings of a lover, who believes the world turns upon the axis of his happiness. Let me tell you that love is an ephemera, which merrily sports in the sunlight a few short hours, and dies at sunset. Should a king forfeit his word for such a short-lived bliss? Should he reward a man to whom he is indebted by depriving him of a rich son-in-law, who is agreeable to him, and substituting a poor one, from whom he can never hope to receive a comfortable maintenance? You young people are all alike. You think only of yourselves, and it is a matter of little consequence to you if the aged pine away and die, provided you build up happiness on their graves! I ask you, who have talked so much about your own wishes, and those of your beloved, where is it written that man must be happy, that there is a necessity to make him so? Do you suppose that I have ever been happy—who have a long, active life in retrospection? Mankind have taken good care that I should not sip this nectar of the gods, and have taught me early to renounce it. Life is not consumed in pleasure, but in toil, and I believe its only happiness consists in the fact that at last, when weary and worn, we will sink into the grave—to an eternal rest! Every human being must work according to his abilities, and in the position which Fate has assigned to him. To maintain this position, his honor is at stake—the best and most sacred gift confided to man. You will not desert it—not despair in life because your dream of bliss is not realized."

"Sire," answered Moritz, with a cry of anguish, "it is no dream, but a reality!"

"Happiness is only ideal," said the king, slowly shaking his head. "What we sigh for to-day, we curse on the morrow as a misfortune. Let this serve as a lesson to you. Toil on—you are a scholar; woo Science for your bride. Her charms will never fade. In youth as in old age she will attract you by her beauty and constancy—that which you cannot hope for from women."

"Sire," asked Moritz, in deep dejection, "will you not grant the petition of my heart? Will you condemn this poor, innocent young girl who prays your majesty through me, to a long, joyless existence, to a daily-renewing sorrow?"

The king shrugged his shoulders. "I have already said that happiness is imaginary; I might have added unhappiness also. General von Leuthen's daughter will accustom herself to the misfortune of being a rich man's wife, and finally will drive with a smiling face in her four-in-hand gilded carriage!"

"Sire, I swear to you that you mistake this dear, noble-hearted young girl, you—"

"Enough!" interrupted the king. "I have given my consent to General von Leuthen, and I cannot recall it. Moreover, the marriage of the daughter of my general with you would be a misalliance—ridiculous. In the republic of intellect and science, you may have a very high position, but in my earthly kingdom you hold too modest a one to presume to raise your eyes to a noble young lady. I regret that I can offer you no other consolation than to listen to reason, and be resigned. As we cannot bring down the moon to earth, we must content ourselves with a lamp to light up our small earthly abode. If this ever should fail you, then come to me and I will assist you. I cannot, to be sure, give you the moon, for that belongs as little to me as the bride of the rich Herr Ebenstreit von Leuthen. One cannot give away that which one does not possess. Farewell! return to Berlin, and resign yourself bravely to your fate. Accustom yourself to the thought that in fourteen days Fraulein von Leuthen will become the wife of your wealthy rival. The wedding ceremony awaits only the papers of nobility, for which my order has already been forwarded to Berlin. I moreover propose to you not to return to the college at once, but travel for two weeks. I will be responsible for your absence, and provide you with the necessary means. Now tell me whether you accept my proposal?"

"Thanks to your majesty, I cannot," answered Moritz, with calm dignity. "There is but one balm which my king could grant me. Money is not a plaster to soothe and heal a wounded heart. Sire, I beg you to dismiss me, for I will return at once to Berlin."

"I hope that you have not the foolish idea to return on foot," said the king. "My courier will leave in an hour, and there are two places in the coupe, accept one of them."

"Sire," said Moritz, gloomily, "I—" suddenly the words died on his lips, and his eyes beamed with an unnatural fire, which paled under the observing glance of the king. "I thank you," said Moritz, gasping, "I will accept it."

The king nodded. "Au revoir, in Berlin! When I return after the campaign I will send for you. You will then have learned to forget your so-called misfortune, and smile at your pilgrimage!"

"I cannot think so, sire."

"I am convinced of it. Farewell."

Moritz answered the royal salutation with a mute bow, and withdrew with drooping head and sorrowful heart. The king continued to regard him with an expression of deep sadness. "Ah!" he sighed, "how enviable are those who can still believe in love's illusion, and who have not awakened from their dream of bliss by sad experience or age! How long since I have banished these dreams—how long I—"

The king ceased, his head sank back upon his chair, his large, fiery eyes, peering into the distance, as if he would re-people it with the memories of youth, with the delusions from which he had so long awakened. Those lovely, charming forms flitted before him one by one which had then captivated him: the beautiful Frau von Wrechem, his first love, and to whom he had vowed eternal constancy; another sweet, innocent face that suffered shame and degradation for him—"oh! Doris, Doris, dream of my youth, fly past!"—and now the face with the large eyes and energetic features, which turned so tenderly to him, that of his sister Frederika, who from affection to the crown prince had sacrificed herself to an unloved husband in order to reconcile the son with the father, and preserve for him the inheritance to the throne; still another calm and gentle face, with the expression of sorrowful resignation in the deep-blue eyes, that of his wife, who had so passionately loved him, and had faded away at his side unloved! All past—past. A new face arose, the pretty Leontine von Morien, the tourbillon of the princely court at Rheinsberg, who pined away in sighs. Now passed the sweetest and loveliest of all. The king's eyes, which stared into empty space, now beamed with glad recognition. The heart which had grown old and sobered beat with feverish rapidity, and the compressed lips whispered, sighing, "Barbarina!" She stood before him in her bewitching beauty, with the charming smile upon her ruby lips, and passionate love beaming from her flashing eyes. "Oh, Barbarina!" The king rose, a cold chill crept over him. He looked around so strangely in the desolate, darkened room, as if he could still see this form which greeted him with the sad smile and tearful glance. No one was there. He was quite alone. Only the feeble echo of far-distant days repeated the device of his youth—of his life:

"Soffri e taci! Resignation alone has remained true to me. But no—there is still another friend, my flute. Come, you faithful companion of my life! You have witnessed my sorrows, and from you I have nothing to conceal!" He tenderly regarded it, for it was long since he had taken it from its case. The sorrows and cares of life, the suffering from the gout which raged in his teeth, and sad, sobering old age, had caused him to lay it aside, but with the habit of affection he carried it everywhere. Frederick felt himself grow young again with the souvenirs of former days, and essayed to recall the echo of tenderer feelings upon his flute. The music of his heart was hushed, the melodious tones of former days would not return. The king laid it aside with an impatient movement. "Nothing is lasting in life," he murmured. A flourish of trumpets, a peal of drums announced that the regiment was passing which would parade before the king. What are they playing, which rouses the lonely king with bright memories and shouts of victory? It is the march which his majesty composed after the brilliant victory of Hohenfriedberg. The king raised his eyes gratefully to heaven, repeating aloud: "There is something lasting in life. Love ceases and music dies away, but the good we have accomplished remains. The most glorious of earthly rewards is granted to those who have achieved great deeds—the mortal becomes immortal—the gods ceding to him that which is more elevating than love or happiness—fame. Ye trumpets of Hohenfriedberg, ye will still quiver when I am gone, and relate to succeeding generations about 'Old Fritz.' Such tales are well worthy to live and suffer for! I am coming, ye trumpets of fame." With youthful activity and beaming face the king went out to receive his generals, who saluted him with silent reverence, and his soldiers, who greeted their beloved commander and king with an exultant shout.

CHAPTER XXI
IN WEIMAR

"There lies dear Weimar, encircled in its wreath of green. Do you not see it, Wolf? I will refresh my heart with its view; so halt, postilion, halt," cried the duke. "It is more beautiful to me than stately, proud Berlin. Though a poor, gray nest, I could press it to my heart, with all its untidy little houses, and tedious old pedants. Let us walk down the hill, Wolf."

"Most willingly," cried Goethe, stretching forth his arms to the little town, nestled in the peaceful valley, "be welcome, you lovely paradise, with your angels and serpents; we press on toward you with all our heart and soul, as to the seven-sealed book, filled with mysteries, and we would draw glorious revelations from your hidden contents."

"And grant, ye gods, that the inspired one may at last break the seal which a cruel friend has placed upon her lips, that he may not drink the kiss of love glowing beneath," said the duke, smiling. "Do you not see the gray roof yonder, with its background of tall trees, that—"

"The house where dwells my beloved, my dearest friend, my sister, and the mistress of my heart," interrupted Goethe. "She is all this, for she is my all in all. The fountains of bliss and love which here and there I have drawn from, refreshing my heart and occupying my mind, flow toward her, united in one broad, silvery stream, with heaven and earth mirrored therein, and revealing wonderful secrets in its rushing waves."

"Ah, Wolf!" cried the duke, "you are a happy, enviable creature, free and unfettered, sending your love where it pleases you. My dear Wolf, I advise you never to marry, for—"

Goethe hastily closed the duke's mouth with his hand. "Hush! not a word against the noble Duchess Louisa, my master and friend. She is an example of refined, womanly dignity; and you, Charles, are to be envied the love of so estimable a wife and sweet mother for your children."

"Indeed I am," cried the duke, enthusiastically. "I could not have found a more high-minded, lovely wife, or a more excellent, virtuous mother for my descendants. But you know, Wolf, that your Charles has still another heart, very susceptible and tender, which seeks for an affinity to call its own, and vent itself in the pleasures of youth, in glorious flirtations, melancholy signs, and blissful longings. You cannot expect me at twenty-two to play the grandfather, and have no eyes or heart for other captivating women, though I love my young wife most affectionately, and bless Fate that I am bound with silken cords to Hymen's cart—though I am forever bound, and you, Wolf, are happily free!"

"Because grim Fate refuses to unite me to my beloved. Oh, Charlotte, if you were free, how blessed would I be, enchained by you! Not to 'Hymen's cart,' as the fortunate mocker says, but to the chariot of Venus, drawn by doves, enthroned upon which you would bear me to heaven!"

"Do not blaspheme, Wolf," cried the duke; "rather kneel and thank the gods that you are not fettered and your wings clipped. They wish to preserve to you love's delusion, because you are a favorite, and deny you the object adored. Beware of the institution which the French actress, Sophie Arnould, has so wittily called the 'consecration of adultery.' You will agree with me that we have many such little sacraments in our dear Weimar, and I must laugh when I reflect for what purpose those amiable beauties have married, as not one of them love their husbands, but they all possess a friend besides."

"The human heart is a strange thing," said Goethe, as they descended the hill, arm in arm, "and above all a woman's heart! It is a sacred riddle, which God has given Himself to solve, and that only a God could unravel!"

At this instant a flash of lightning, followed by heavy-rolling thunder, was heard.

"Hear, Wolf—only hear!" laughed Charles—"God in heaven responds, and confirms your statement."

"Or punishes me for my bold speech," cried Goethe, as the hailstones rattled around him hitting his face with their sharp points. "Heaven is whipping me with rods."

"And our carriage has descended with a quick trot into the valley," said the duke. "I will call it." He sprang into the middle of the road, making a speaking-trumpet of his hands, and shouted in a full, powerful voice, "Oho, postilion! here, postilion!"

The continued rolling of the thunder, the whistling wind, and rattling hail, made all attempts inaudible. The two gentlemen sought shelter under the thick crowns of the oak-trees by the wayside, which formed an impenetrable roof to the flood of rain.

"I know nothing more sublime than a thunder-storm," said Goethe, looking up as if inspired; "when the thunder rolls in such awful majesty and wrath, it seems as if I heard Prometheus in angry dispute with the gods. In the dark clouds I see the Titan, enveloped in mist, overspreading the heavens, and raising his giant-arm to hurl his mighty wrath." At this instant a flash of lightning, followed by a deafening peal reverberated in one prolonged echo through the hills.

"Do you not hear him, Charles?" cried Goethe, delighted—"hear all the voices of earth united in the grumbling thunder of his wrath? See, there he stands, yonder in heaven—his form dark as midnight. I hear it—he calls—Overshadow the heavens, O Jupiter, With thy vaporous clouds! Cut off the oak and mountain-tops As a boy plucks the thistle. Leave me earth and my cabin Which thou hast not built, And my hearth-side, The glow of which thou enviest me! I know naught so miserable As you gods—you—"

Again the mighty peal silenced Goethe, who looked to heaven with defiance flashing from his eyes and his clinched hand upraised, as if he were Prometheus himself menacing the gods.

"Proceed, Wolf," cried the duke, as the echo died away. "How can you, yourself a god, be so excited with the anger of like beings? Proceed!"

The uplifted arm of the poet sank at his side, and the fiery glance was softened. "No human word is capable of expressing what Prometheus just spoke in thunder," said Goethe, musingly, "and I humbly feel how weak and insignificant we are, and how great we think ourselves, while our voice is like the humming beetle in comparison to this voice from the clouds."

"Be not desponding, Wolf, your own will ring throughout Europe; every ear will listen and every heart will comprehend, and centuries later it will delight with its freshness and beauty. The storm passes and dies away, but the poet lives in his heavenly melodies through all time. You must finish 'Prometheus' for me, Wolf. I cannot permit you to leave it as a fragment. I will have it in black and white, to refresh myself in its beauty bright. A spark of your divine talent is infused into my soul, and I begin to rhyme. Ah, Wolf, all that is elevated within me I owe to you, and I bless Fate for according you to me."

"And I also, dear Charles," said Goethe, feelingly. "For, fostered and protected by your noble mind and nature, my inmost thoughts develop and blossom. We give and receive daily from each other, and so mingle the roots of our being that, God willing, we will become two beautiful trees, like the oak which now arches over us. But see, the rain is fast ceasing, and the sun looks out by the clinched hand of Prometheus. We can now travel on to the loved spot."

"Oh, Wolf, are you in love? None but a lover could say the rain has ceased, when it pours down so that we should be drenched before we could arrive at Weimar. But hark! I hear a carriage in the distance; we may be favored with a shelter."

The duke stepped out from under the trees, and looked along the highway with his sharp hunter's eye. "A vehicle approaches, but no chance for us, as it appears to be a farm-wagon, crowded with men and women."

"Indeed it does," said Goethe, joining him; "a very merry company they are too, singing gayly. Now, grant the rain rain has ceased—"

"Charlotte von Stein is at Weimar," interrupted the duke. "Give me your arm, and we will walk on."

They advanced briskly arm in arm. A stranger meeting them would have supposed that they were brothers, so much alike were they in form, manners, and dress, for the duke as well as Goethe wore the Werther costume.

As they descended, the carriage came nearer and nearer. The duke's keen eye had not been deceived. It was a farm-wagon, filled with a frolicsome party, sitting on bags of straw for cushions. They were chatting and laughing absorbed in fun, and did not observe the two foot-passengers, who turned aside from them. A sudden cry of surprise hushed the conversation; a form rose, half man and half woman, enveloped in a man's coat of green baize, crowned with a neat little hat of a woman. "Oh, it is Charles!" cried the form, and at the same instant the duke sprang to the wagon. "Is it possible, my dear mother?"

"The Duchess Amelia!" cried Goethe, astonished.

"Yes," laughed the duchess, greeting them with an affectionate look. "The proverb proves itself—'Like mother, like son.' On the highway mother and son have met. You should have done the honors in a stately equipage."

"May I be permitted to ask where you come from?" asked the duke. "And the dress, of what order do you wear?"

"We walked to Ziefurt, and intended to walk back. Thusnelda is so delicate and weak, that she complained of her fairy feet paining her," answered the duchess, laughing.

"Ah, duchess, must I always be the butt?" cried the lady behind the duchess, crouching between the straw-sacks. "Must I permit you to follow in my footsteps, while I—"

"Hush, Goechhausen—hush, sweet Philomel," interrupted the duke, "or the Delphic riddle of this costume will be apparent."

"It is easily explained," said the duchess. "No other conveyance was to be had, and my good Wieland gave me his green overcoat to protect me from the pouring rain." *[Footnote: True anecdote.—See Lewes' "Goethe's Life and Writings," vol. 1., p. 406.]*

"And from to-day forth it will be a precious palladium," cried the little man with a mild, happy face on the straw by the duchess.

"And there is Knebel too," shouted the duke to the gentleman who just then pulled the wet hood of his cloak over his powdered hair.

"Our treasurer Bertuch, Count Werther, and Baron von Einsiedel also."

"Does not your highness ask after our bewitching countess?" asked Goechhausen, in her fine, sharp voice. "The countess is quite ill—is she not, Count Werther?"

"I believe so, they say so," answered the count, rather absent-minded. "I have not seen her for some days."

"What is the matter?" asked the duke, as Goethe was engaged in a lively conversation with the duchess. "Is the dear countess dangerously ill?"

"Oh, no," answered Goechhausen, "not very ill, only in love with genius, a malady which has attacked us all more or less since that mad fellow Wolfgang Goethe has raged in Weimar, and made it a place of torment to honorable people. Oh, Goethe—oh, Wolf! with what lamb-like innocence we wandered in comfortable sheep's clothing until you came and fleeced us, and infected us with your 'Sturm und Dranger' malady, and made us fall in love with your works!"

"Goechhausen, hold your malicious tongue, and do not hide your own joy beneath jest and mockery," cried the duchess. "Acknowledge that you are rejoiced to see your favorite, and that you will hasten to write to Madam Aja, 'Our dear duke has returned, and my angel, my idol, Wolfgang, also.' I assure you, Goethe, Thusnelda loves you, and was exceedingly melancholy during your absence. If asked the cause of her sadness, she wept like—"

"Like a crocodile," said the duke. "Oh, I know those tears of Fraulein Goechhausen; I could relate stories of her crocodile nature. Mother, how can you have such a monster in your society? Why not make the cornes, that the little devils may fly away?"

"Very good," cried the little, crooked lady. "I see your highness has not changed by this journey. Where have you been, dear duke? Oh, I remember; you flew over the Rhine, and have flown home again quite unchanged."

All laughed, the duke louder than any one. "Goechhausen, you are a glorious creature, and the Arminius is to be envied who appropriates this Thusnelda. Oh, I see the charming youth before me, who has the courage to make this German wife his own!"

"I will scratch his eyes out?" cried Goechhausen, "and then the Countess Werther can play Antigone, and lead him around as Oedipus. Why shut your eyes, Einsiedel? I do not scratch quite yet."

"I was not thinking of that," said the baron, astonished.

"You never think that every one knows; but did you not do it so soon as you understood the Countess Werther should lead blind Oedipus as Antigone?"

Before the count could answer, the court lady turned again to the duke. "What did your highness bring me? I hope you have not forgotten that you promised me a handsome present."

"No, I have not forgotten it; I have brought my Thusnelda a souvenir—such a gift!"

"What is it, your highness?"

"A surprise which, if Thusnelda is clever, she must think about all night.—But, Goethe, is it not time to leave the ladies?"

"Wait, I command you both," said the Duchess Amelia, extending her hand to her son, who pressed it to his lips most affectionately. "I have given out invitations for a soiree, for this evening. My daughter-in-law, the Duchess Louisa, has accepted, duke, and Frau von Stein also, Goethe. I hope to see you at Belvedere, gentlemen. The poet Gleim is in town, and will read his late 'Muse Almanach.' May I not expect both of you?"

They joyfully consented, gazing after the merry society as it drove away. "This is a good bite for the poisonous tongues of the honorable," cried the duke. "My mother in a farm-wagon, with Wieland's green overcoat on, and the reigning duke, with his Goethe, entering his capital on foot like a journeyman mechanic, after a long journey!"

"I wish we were there, my dearest friend," sighed Goethe.

"Oh, love makes you impatient! Come on, then. But listen, we must play Gochhausen a trick; I have promised her a surprise. Will you help me, Wolf?"

"With pleasure, duke."

"I have thought of something very droll, and your servant Philip must help us; he is a clever fellow, and can keep his own counsel."

"He is silent as the grave, duke."

"That is necessary for such a gentleman as the women all run after. Let us skip down the mountain, and then forward where our hearts incline us. This afternoon I will go for you and bring you to Belvedere, and then we can talk over the surprise." They ran down the declivity into the suburb, to the terror of the good people, who looked after them, saying that the young duke had returned with his mad protege. The "mad favorite" seemed more crazy than ever to-day, for after a brief farewell to the duke, he bounded through the streets across the English park, to the loved house, the roof of which he had so longingly greeted from the hillside. The door stood open, as is customary in small towns, and the servant in the vestibule came to meet him, and respectfully announced that her master had gone to his estate at Hochberg, but that Frau von Stein was most probably in the pavilion, in the garden, as she had gone thither with her guitar. "Is she alone?" asked Goethe. The servant answered in the affirmative, and through the court hastened the lover—not through the principal entrance, as he would surprise her, and read in her sweet face whether she thought of him. Softly he opened the little garden gate, and approached the pavilion by a side-alley. Do his feet touch the ground, or float over it? He knew not; he heard music, accompanied by a sweet, melodious voice. It was Charlotte's. Goethe's face beamed with delight and happiness. He gazed at her unseen, not alone with his eyes, but heart and soul went forth to her. She sat sideways to the door; upon a table lay her notes, and the guitar rested upon her arm. She sang, in a rich, sweet voice, Reinhardt's beautiful melody:

"I'd rather fight my way through sorrows Than bear so many joys in life; All this affinity of heart to heart, How strangely it causes us to suffer!"

She ceased, as if overpowered with her own thoughts, the guitar sank upon her lap, and her fingers glided over the chords, so that the tones died away imperceptibly. Her deep-blue eyes gazed pensively in the distance, and the sweet lips repeated softly, "How strangely it causes us to suffer!" Near the garden entrance, through which the odor of sweet flowers and the song of birds was wafted with every gentle zephyr, stood Goethe, looking at the woman whom he had so passionately loved for three years, so absorbingly, that to her were consecrated all his thoughts.

He could contain himself no longer; he rushed forward and threw himself at her feet. "Oh, Charlotte, I love you, only you, and once more I am by your side!"

A shriek! was it a cry of surprise or delight? Who let the guitar fall to the floor, he or she? Who embraced the other in affectionate haste, he or she? Who pressed the lips so lovingly to the other lips, he or she? And who said, "I love you? What bliss to again repose in your affection, I would fain die now. In this moment a whole life has been consecrated, for love has revealed to us our other self."

She sat upon the tabouret, and Goethe still knelt before her, clasping her feet and pressing them to his bosom. His eyes beamed with inexpressible delight as he regarded the face, usually so calm and indifferent—today glowing as sunrise.

"Oh, tell me, Charlotte, have you thought of me? But rather speak to me with your eyes, and may they be more than the cruel lips which refuse to confess. Oh, shade not those loved orbs, which are my stars shining upon me, whithersoever I wander. They are my light, my spring-time, and my love. They will never cease to beam upon me, as light and love never grow old. Let me read eternal youth in those eyes, and the secrets which rest as pearls in the depths of your heart. Only tell me, is the pearl of love to be found there, and is it mine?"

"It would be a misfortune if it were there," she whispered, with a sweet smile. "Pearls are the result of a malady, and my heart would be ill if the pearl of love were found there. No, no, rise, Wolf, dear Wolf, we have given away at the first moment of meeting; let us now be reasonable, and speak in a dignified manner with each other, as it becomes a married woman and her friend."

"Friend?" repeated Goethe, impetuously; "forever must I listen to this hated, hypocritical word, which, like a priest's robe, shall cover the sacred glow in my heart? I have told you, Charlotte, that I am not your friend, and I never shall be. There is not the least spark of this still, calm fire of the earthly moderation in me, by which one could cook his potatoes, or his daily vegetables, but by which one could never prepare food for the gods, or that which could refresh a poet's heart or quicken his soul. No, in me burns the fire which Prometheus stole from the gods, originating in heaven and glowing upon earth. This heavenly and earthly love unites in one flame. Again, I say, Charlotte, banish this hypocritical word 'friendship!' It is only love which I feel for you, let this sentiment enter at every avenue of your heart, and do not feign ignorance of it, sweet hypocrite. Surprise has torn away the mask! The passionate kiss, which still burns upon my lips, was not given by a friend or sister; but overcome by joy, the truth has been acknowledged!"

"Do you wish that the kiss of meeting should be that of parting also?" said Charlotte, sadly, as she raised her blue eyes with a languishing look to the handsome, ardent face of the man who stood before her. "Do you wish to separate forever? I must recall to you our last conversation: 'Only when you are resolved to moderate this impetuous manner, and curb this overflow of feeling, which reason and custom imposes upon us, shall I be able to receive you and enjoy your society.'"

"Yes, with these unmeaning phrases you banished me. Cruel and hard-hearted were you to the last. Oh, Charlotte! you know what I suffered at our last walk, with your reasoning remonstrances and cold-hearted reproaches;

they pierced my heart like poisoned arrows. If the duke and duchess had not been walking before us, I should have wept myself weary. My whole being cried within me: 'Oh! cruel and inexorable woman, to beg of me, who so unutterably loves her, to call her friend and sister!' I repeated the words daily during my absence, and sought to clothe your beloved image with meaning. They disfigured you, and the angel whom I adore was no longer recognizable. I cannot call you friend or sister."

"Then I can be nothing to you, dear Wolfgang," sighed Charlotte. "In this hour of meeting we will part, and to avoid a chance encounter even, I will go to my husband at Kochberg, and remain there the whole summer."

Goethe seized her, holding her fast in his strong arms, staring her in the face with a fierce, angry look. "Are you in earnest? Would you really do it?"

"Goethe, I beg you to loosen your hold; you hurt my arms."

"Do you not also hurt me? With your cold indifference do you not pierce my heart with red-hot daggers, and then smile and rejoice at my torture, which is a proof to you of my unbounded love? While you only play with me, and attach me to your triumphal car, to display to the world that you have succeeded in taming the lion, and have changed him into a good-natured domestic animal. Go! you do not deserve that I should love you, cold-hearted, cruel woman!"

He threw her arms from him, with tears in his eyes. Charlotte von Stein regarded him with anger and indifference.

"Farewell, secretary of legation. It seems to please you to insult and offend a poor woman, who has no other protection than her honor and virtue. Farewell! I will not expose myself to such offences; therefore I will retire."

She turned slowly toward the door, but Goethe bounded forward like a tiger, interrupted her path, falling upon his knees, imploring pity and begging for pardon. "Oh, Charlotte, I will be gentle as a child, I will be reserved, I know that I am a sinner! It is warring against one's own heart to seek comfort in offending what is dearest to it in a moment of ill-humor. But I have again become a child, with all my thoughts, scarcely recognizable for the moment, quite lost to myself, as I consent to the conditions of others with this fire raging within me. Oh, beloved Charlotte, forgive me! I submit to all that you wish." *[Footnote: Goethe's words.—See "Letters to Charlotte von Stein," roll., p. 358.]*

"Will you be satisfied to love me as your friend and sister?"

"I will be," he sighed. "Only in the future you must endeavor to persuade yourself into such a sisterly way that you will be indulgent to my rudeness, otherwise I shall have to avoid you when I need you most. Oh,

Charlotte, it seems terrible to me that I should mar through anguish the best hours of my life, the blissful moments of meeting with you, for whom I would pluck every hair from my head if it would make you happy. And yet to be so blind, so hardened! Have pity upon me. Again I promise you that I will be reasonable. Do not banish me from your presence. Extend to me your hand, and promise me that you will be my friend and sister!" *[Footnote: Goethe's words.—See "Letters to Charlotte von Stein," roll., p. 358.]*

"Then here is my hand," said she, with a charming smile.

"I will be your friend and sister, and—"

"What now, my Charlotte? do finish—what is it?"

She laid her hand gently upon his shoulder, and her words fell on his ear like soft music. "When my dear friend and much-beloved brother has conducted himself very prudently for two or three happy weeks, I will send him a ringlet of my hair, which he has so long begged for, and a kiss with it."

Goethe spoke not, but pressed her blushing face to his bosom, and laid his hand gently upon her head. A smile of delight—of perfect happiness—played around his lips.

CHAPTER XXII
THE READING

This happy smile still beamed upon Goethe's face as he walked with the duke late in the evening toward Belvedere to soiree of the Duchess Amelia, who was inspired with a love for the fine arts, and particularly literature. The two gentlemen had busily occupied themselves in preparing them for the lady of honor, Fraulein von Gochhausen, and, although aided by Goethe's servant, Philip, and workmen, it was late when they arrived.

As they entered, the ladies and gentlemen were seated in a large circle around the centre-table. At one end sat the Duchesses Amelia and Louisa, the mother and wife of Charles Augustus and near the former her friend and favorite the poet Wieland, once the tutor of her son the duke. Near the poet sat an elderly gentleman of cheerful, good-natured mien, who, with the exception of Wieland, was the only one who did not present himself, like the duke and Goethe, in Werther costume. He wore a white, silver-embroidered coat, with a dark-blue satin vest, and breeches of the same, shoes with buckles, and bosom and wrist ruffles of lace.

This gentleman, with the bright, sparkling eyes, and pleasant face, was the poet Gleim, who looked very comfortable and stately in the circle of powdered perukes. His admiration for Frederick the Great had inspired him to write some beautiful military songs, and his love of poetry and literature made him an enthusiastic admirer of all those devoted themselves to literary pursuits. Besides, he was rich and liberal, and it was very natural that the poets, and authors exerted themselves with marked assiduity to please Father Gleim. They were gratified to have him print their works for a small remuneration in an annual which he entitled the "Almanach of the Muses." He was just reading aloud at the duchess's soiree from the late edition of the almanach, and the society listened with earnest and kind attention, occasionally interrupted with an enthusiastic "Bravo!" or "Excellent!" from the duchess, followed by a murmur of assent around the table, which caused the poet's face to brighten with joy and satisfaction, and him to read on with increased energy.

The entrance of the duke and Goethe was unobserved, as it was understood that the former wished no notice to be taken of his going or coming, and the duchess had also waved her hand, not to interrupt Father

Gleim. The poet has just finished the new poem of melodious rhythm of imprisoned Shubart. As he paused to wipe the perspiration from his brow and sip a little raspberry water, a tall, slender young man, in the Werther costume, approached, bowing, and regarding the poet so kindly, that the glance of his fine black eyes fell like a sunbeam on the heart of the old man. "You appear somewhat fatigued, my good sir," said the unknown, in a sweet, sonorous voice. "Will you not permit me to relieve you, and read in your stead from this glorious book of yours?"

"Do so, my dear Gleim," said the Duchess Amelia, smiling, "you seem really exhausted; let the young man continue the agreeable and welcome entertainment."

Father Gleim was very well pleased; he handed the book to the young stranger with a graceful bow, as the latter seated himself opposite to him, and next to Fraulein Gochhausen.

He commenced in a clear, distinct voice. The verses flowed from his lips gracefully, and in a cultivated style. The company listened with devoted attention, and Father Gleim, the protector of all the young poets, sat delighted, nodding consent, with a pleasant smile. It must all be charming—it had come into existence under his fostering care. What beautiful verses to listen to! "Die Zephyre lauschen, Die Balche rauschen, Die Sonus Verbreitet ihr Licht mit Wonne!"

And how charmingly the young man read them! Suddenly Father Gleim startled, and the smile died upon his lips. What was it? What was the young man reading? Verse which were not in the collection, and which were more remarkable than he had ever heard from his young poets. "Those are not in the Annual," cried Gleim, quite forgetting decorum,—"that—"

One glance from the fine black eyes of the young man so confounded Father Gleim, that he ceased in the midst of a sentence, and, staring in breathless astonishment, listened. Glorious thoughts were expressed therein, and the poets of the Muse Almanach might have thanked God if the like had occurred to them. Love was not the burden of the song; neither hearts, griefs, nor bliss, but satire, lashing right and left with graceful dexterity, and dealing a harmless thrust to every one. All were forced to laugh; the happy faces animated and inspired every thing. The brilliant satirical verses rushed like rockets from the lips of the reader—a real illumination of wit and humor, of good-natured jokes and biting sarcasm, and it delighted the old man that every one had received hits and thrusts but himself; he had been spared until now! Every one regarded him, smiling and amused, as the reader exalted the merits of the Maecenas, and praised him highly for the interest he took in the poet's heart, soul, and purse, and shouted victory when one excelled. But suddenly the good father also changed, and, instead of the patron on the right throne, there was a turkey-cock on the round nest, which zealously sought to hatch out the many eggs that he had to take care of for others besides his own; he sat brooding untiringly, and shed many a tear of joy over the fine number of eggs, yet it happened that a poetical viper had put but under him one of chalk, which he cared for with the others.

Herr Gleim could no longer contain himself, and, striking the table, he cried, "That is either Goethe or the devil!" The entire company burst into uncontrollable laughter, and the old man shouted the second time, though inwardly angry, "It is either Goethe or the devil!"

"Both, dear Father Gleim," said Wieland, who was drying his tears from laughter, "it is Goethe, and he has the devil in him to-day. He is like a wild colt, which kicks out behind and before, and it would be well not to approach him too near." *[Footnote: Wieland's own words.—See Lewes' "Life of Goethe," vol. i., p. 432.]*

Goethe alone retained his composure, and continued reading in a louder voice, which hushed all conversation. He lashed with bitter sarcasm "him who assumed to be a god—a wise man—and who counted for nothing better than a pretentious, saucy fellow, who made himself the scorn of the poets by his sweet, Werther-like sighs, and other worthless lamentations, heeding neither God nor the devil!"

And so he stormed and thundered, ridiculed and slandered his own flesh and blood, until Goechhausen, red with anger, rose and snatched the book from his hand, and closed his lips with her hand, crying: "If you do not cease, Goethe, I will write to your beloved mother, Frau Aja, that a satirist, a calumniator has had the impudence to defame and slur her beloved son in a most sinful and shameful manner! I will write to her, indeed, if you do not stop!"

Goethe rose, and bowing offered his hand to Father Gleim in such a friendly, affectionate manner, that the old man, quite delighted, thanked him heartily for the pleasure and surprise which he had afforded him.

The duke, however, seated himself by the little lady of honor. "Thusnelda, you are an incomparable creature, and quite calculated to be the ancestress of all the Germans. I declare myself your cavalier for the evening, and will devote myself to you as your most humble servant, and will not quit your side for a moment."

"Very beautiful it will be, my dear duke, a most charming idyl; in true Watteau style, I will be the sweet shepherdess, and lead your highness by a little ribbon. But where is my present—my surprise?"

"You must not be impatient, Thusnelda, but wait what time will produce. You will have it; if not to-day, to-morrow. Every day brings its own care and sorrow."

"Ah, duke, instead of giving me my surprise, you beat me with doggerels. That comes from having a Goethe for companion and friend. Crazy tricks, like chicken-pox, are contagious, and the latter you have caught, duke. It is a new kind of genius distemper. Very fortunately, our dear Countess Werther has another malady, or she might be infected. Perhaps she has it already, Count Werther—how is it?'

"I do not know, Fraulein," replied the count, startled from reverie. "I really do not know! My wife is quite ill, for that reason has gone to our estate to recover her peace and quiet. It is unfortunately quite impossible for me to visit her there; but my dear, faithful friend, Baron von Einsiedel, will drive over to-morrow at my request, my commission—"

"To set the fox to keep the geese," interrupted Thusnelda in her lively manner.

"No, not that, Fraulein," said Count Werther, quite confused, as the duke burst into a merry laugh, calling Thusnelda a witty Kobold, and as her faithful Celadon offered her his arm to conduct her to his mother, the Duchess Amelia.

The company were all in a very happy frame of mind. Goethe's charming impromptu had kindled wit and humor upon every lip. He himself was the happiest of all, for Charlotte was by his side, gazing upon him with her large, thoughtful eyes, and permitting him to be her cavalier for the evening.

The duke also devoted himself to Fraulein von Goechhausen, who was this evening unsurpassably witty and caustic, delighting him, and making the Duchess Amelia laugh, and the Duchess Louisa sometimes to slightly shrug her shoulders and shake her head with disapproval.

In the midst of a most interesting conversation with Frau von Stein, Goethe was informed that some one awaited him in the anteroom. He went out quickly, and upon returning he whispered to the duke, who nodded, and answered him in a low tone, and then Goethe betook himself to the Duchess Amelia.

"What is it?" the latter asked. "Have important dispatches arrived?"

"No; I come to your highness as courier from your son. The duke begs that you will lock the door of your anteroom when you retire, and that you will upon no condition open it, no matter how much Thusnelda may beg and implore."

"Will you not injure my poor Goechhausen, you wanton fellow?"

"No! it is not very dangerous, duchess. It is only a harmless surprise, which the duke promised Fraulein von Goechhausen."

"Very well, then, it can take place; I promise to be quite deaf to all Thusnelda's knocking and thumping, and I shall be glad to be informed to-morrow what the trick is. I prefer not to inquire to-day, as I might feel obliged to veto it if it were too severe. But look, the Duchess Louisa will break up; does she know any thing about the affair?"

"No, your highness, you know very well that the young duchess—"

"Is much more sensible than the old one, and shakes her head disapprovingly when she hears of your ingenuous tricks. Perhaps it would be well if I were equally sensible, but there is no help for it. I like bright, happy people, and I think when youth vents itself, old age is more sedate and reasonable."

"You are quite right, duchess. Mankind resembles new wine. If the must does not ferment and foam well, no good wine will come of it. But look at our Charles, with the saucy jest upon his lip, and the fire of inspiration in those bright brown eyes. One day a fine, strong wine will clear itself from this glorious fermenting must."

"I hope so, Goethe, and if the gods grant it, the great merit will belong to you, who have proved yourself a good vintager, and we will rejoice together in your glorious success."

CHAPTER XXIII
WITCHCRAFT

An hour later the palace Belvedere was silent and deserted; the guests had taken their departure. The duchess had her suite and commanded them to retire. Fraulein von Gochhausen alone remained with her mistress, chatting by the bedside, and recapitulating in her amusing style all important and unimportant events of the soiree, The duchess smiled at the mischievous remarks with which she ornamented her relation, and at her keen, individualizing of persons.

"Fraulein Gochhausen, you are the most wicked and the merriest mocking-bird God ever created," cried the duchess, "Have done with your scandals, go up to your room, piously say your evening prayers, and stretch yourself upon your maiden bed."

"Soon, duchess; only one thing more have I to call your attention to. There is a gossip afloat about the Werthers. I perceive it in the air, as the dove scents the vulture."

"You alarm me, Gochhausen; what good is it? You do not mean that the lovely Countess Werther—"

"Is not only very weary of her husband, but looks about for a substitute—a friend, as the ingenious ladies now call him. That is what I mean, and I know the so-called friend which the sweet sentimental countess has chosen."

"It is the Baron von Einsiedel, is it not?" asked the duchess. "That is to say, his younger brother, the gay lieutenant, not our good friend par excellence.

"Yes, I mean the brother, and I have warned and taunted the count this week past, but it is impossible to awake him from his stupidity and thoughtlessness."

"Again you are giving loose reins to your naughty tongue, Thusnelda. Count Werther is a thoroughly scholarly person, whom I often envy his knowledge of the languages. He has studied Sanscrit and the cuneated letters, among other ancient tongues."

"It may be that he understands the dead languages, but the living ones not in the least. The language of the eyes and inspiration he is blind to, with seeing eyes! My dear duchess, if you are not watchful, and prevent the affair with timely interference, a scandal will grow out of it, and you know well that it would be a welcome opportunity for our Weimar Philistines (as the Jena students call commonplace gossips) to cry 'Murder,' and howl about the immoral example of geniuses, which Wolfgang Goethe has introduced at court."

"You are right," said the duchess, musingly; "your apt tongue and keen eye are ever carefully watching, like a good shepherd-dog, that none of the sheep go astray and are lost. And you do not mind attacking this or that one in the leg with your sharp teeth!"

"Let those scream who are unjustly bitten, your highness! Believe me, the countess will not cry out; she will much more likely take care not to receive a well-merited rebuke. I beg your grace to prevent the gossip! Not on account of this silly, sentimental young woman, or her pedantic husband, but that our young duke and Goethe may not be exposed to scandal, as well as your highness."

"You are right—we must take care to prevent it. Has not the countess been absent at her estate four days?"

"Yes, your highness, it is just this that troubles me. She went away as sound as a fish, and has suddenly fallen very ill. No physician has been called, but, to-morrow, the count will commission his dear friend the baron to drive to his country-seat, and bring him tidings of his better-half."

"We must circumvent this. In the morning we will arrange a pleasure-drive, of the whole court, to the country-seat of Count Werther. It shall be a surprise. Let Fourier give out the invitations early to-morrow, for a country party, destination unknown. The distribution of the couples in the carriages shall be decided by lot. Take care that Lieutenant Einsiedel is your cavalier, so that when we arrive at the little Werther, he will already be appropriated, and then we will induce her to return with us and spend some time at Belvedere. Now, good-night, Thusnelda; I am very tired and need repose. Sleep already weighs upon my eyelids, and will close them as soon as you are gone. Good-night, my child—sleep well!"

The little deformed court lady kissed the extended hand, the candlestick, with only a stump of a taper in it, and withdrew from the princely sleeping-room, courtesying, and wishing her mistress good-night, with pleasant dreams.

The anteroom was dark and deserted. The lights were all extinguished, and Fraulein Goechhausen was, in truth, the only person who had not long since retired in the ducal palace. She was accustomed to be the last, accustomed to traverse the long, lonely corridors, and mount two flights of stairs to her bedroom upon the third story. The gay duchess, being very fond of society, had had the second story arranged guest-chambers and drawing-rooms.

Why should the little court lady be afraid to-night? She had not thought of it, but stepped forward briskly to mount the stairs. It was surely very disagreeable for the wind to extinguish her lamp at that instant, just at the turning of stairs, and she could not account for it, as none of the windows were open, and there was no trace of a draft. However, it was an undeniable fact, the light was out and she was in total darkness—not even a star was to be seen in the clouded sky. It was, indeed, true that Thusnelda was so accustomed to the way that it mattered little whether she had a light or not. Now she had reached the corridor and she could not fail to find the door, as there was but one, that of her own room. She stretched out her hand to open it, but, strange to say, she missed the knob! Then she was sure that it was farther on; she felt along the wall, but still it eluded her grasp. It was unheard of—no handle and not a door even to be found! The wall was bare and smooth, and papered the entire length. A slight shudder crept over the courageous little woman's heart, and she could not explain to herself what it all meant. She called her maid, but no answer—not a sound interrupted the stillness! "I will go down to the duchess," murmured Thusnelda; "perhaps she is awake, and then I can re-light my taper!"

The door was fastened; the duchess had locked the ante-room to-night for the first time.

Thusnelda tapped lightly, and begged an entrance humbly and imploringly. No answer, every thing was quiet. She recalled that the duchess had told her that she was very weary, and would sleep as soon as she was alone, which she undoubtedly had done.

Thusnelda did not presume to awake her by knocking louder. She would be patient, and mount again to her room. Surely she must have made a mistake, and turned to the left of the corridor, where there was no door, instead of the right, as she ought to have done. It must be that it was her fault. She groped along the dark flights of stairs to the upper gallery, carefully seeking the right this time, but in vain. Again she felt only the smooth wall. Terrified, she knew not whether she was awake or dreaming, or whether she might not be in an enchanted castle, or walking in her sleep in a strange house. Just here she ought to find her room and the maid awaiting her, but it was lonely, deserted, and strange—no door, no maid. Thusnelda, with trembling hands smoothed her face, pulled first her nose, and then her hair, to identify herself. "Is it I?" she said. "Am I, indeed, myself? Am I awake? I know that I am lady of honor to the Duchess Amelia, and that upon the upper story is my room. Do not be foolish, and imagine that witchcraft comes to pass; the door is there, and it can be found." Thusnelda renewed her search with out-spread arms and wide-spread fingers, feeling first this side of the wall and then the other.

By daylight the deformed little lady of honor must have been a very droll figure, in full toilet, dancing along the wall as if suspended by her outstretched hands. Oh, it was quite vain to seek any longer. It must be enchantment, and the door had disappeared. An indefinable dream crept over Thusnelda, and she was cast down. For the first time a jest failed her trembling lips, and she wept with anguish. Yes, she, the keen, mordant, jesting little woman, prayed and implored her Maker to unloose her from the enchantment, and permit her to find the long-sought-for entrance. But praying was in vain, the door was not to be found, it was witch craft, and she must submit to it. The rustling and moving her arms frightened her now, and when she walked the darkness prevented her seeing if any one followed her; so she crouched upon the floor, yielding to the unavoidable necessity passing the night there—the night of enchantment and witchery. *[Footnote: See Lewes' "Life and Writings of Goethe," vol. 1., p. 408.]*

Not alone for Fraulein Goechhausen was this beautiful May-night of sad experience with witches. There were other places at Weimar. In the neighborhood of the ducal park, in the midst of green-meadows, stood a simple little cottage. Near it flowed the Ilm, spanned by three bridges, all closed by gates, so that no one could reach the cottage without the occupant's consent. It was as secure as a fortress or an island of the sea, and distinctly visible even in the night, its white walls rising against the dark perspective of the park. This is the poet's Eldorado, his paradise, presented to Wolfgang Goethe by his friend the Duke Charles Augustus. It was late as the possessor wound his way toward his Tusculum, as he familiarly called it, and, more attracted by the aspect of the heavens than by sleep, sought the balcony, to gaze at the dark mass of clouds chasing each other like armies in retreat and pursuit; one moment veiling the moon, at another revealing her full disk, and soon again covering the earth with dark shadows, until the lightning flashed down in snaky windings, making the darkness momentarily visible with her lurid glare. It was a glorious spectacle for the intuitive, sympathetic soul of the poet, and he yielded to its influence with delight. He heard the voice of God in the rolling of the thunder, and sought to comprehend the unutterable, and understand it in this poetical sense. Voices spake to him in the rushing of the storm, the sighing of the trees, and the rustling of the foliage. The storm passed quickly, a profound quiet and solemnity spread out over the nightly world, and it lay as if in repose, smiling in blissful dreams. The air was filled with perfumes, wafted to the balcony upon which dreamed the poet with unclosed eyelids and waking thoughts. The clouds were all dispersed; full and clear was suspended the moon in the deep, blue vault, where twinkled thousands of stars, whispering of unknown worlds, and the mysteries of Nature, and the greatness of Him who created them all.

> *"Oh, beloved, golden moon, how calmly you look down upon me, sublime and lovely at the same time! When I gaze at you, moving so quietly, floating in infinity, and contemplating reflect thyself in finiteness, I think of you, oh Charlotte, who stands above me like the moon so bright and mild, and I envelop myself in your rays, and my spirit becomes heavenly in your light.*
>
> *Mir ist es, denk ich nur an Dich,*
> *Als in den Mond zu seh'n,*
> *Ein suesser Friede weht um mich,*
> *Weiss nicht, wie mir gescheh'n!*

"Yes, like sweet peace, and quiet, sacred moonlight, my thoughts shall be of you, Charlotte; not like the glowing rays of the sun, or the cold light of the stars. Bright and beaming like the moon you are to me, spreading around me your soft light. Oh, beautiful golden moon, mirrored in the water, you lie as in a silvery bath, and would entice me to seek you in the murmuring depths. Hark! how the ruffled waves of the Ilm with repeated gentle caresses kiss the shore, rush from thence in golden links down the river! Sweet of the Ilm, I come, I come!"

Goethe hastened from the balcony, threw aside his apparel, plunged into the silvery flood, shouting with joy.

What heavenly pleasure to float there, rocked by the murmuring waves, gazing at the silvery stars and the golden moon, a lovely May night, listening to the voices of Nature! Add to that the perfume-laden breeze rising from the rain-refreshed meadows. How glorious to plunge into the cool stream, splashing and dashing the water, and then to shoot like a fish through the drops falling like golden rain! Suddenly, while swimming, Goethe raised his head to listen. He thought he heard footsteps on the poet's forbidden bridge. The moon distinctly revealed a peasant from Oberweimar, who would be early to the weekly market, and so serve himself to the shortest route while no one could see him.

"Such presumption deserves punishment, my good peasant, and if there is no one else to do it the ghosts must."

Listen, what a savage yell from under the bridge, and then another more unearthly!

The peasant, frightened, stopped suddenly, and looked down into the river. "Oh, what can it be?"

A glistening white arm is raised menacingly toward the bridge. A white figure, with a black head and long black hair, is seen plunging and splashing, while fearful yells are heard from the deep. Then it disappeared, to return, and menace, and yell, and plunge again.

The peasant shrieked with terror, and was answered with a cruel laugh. The white figure sank and rose from the river screeching and yelling, and the peasant shrieked also with terror.

"A ghost! a ghost! oh, have mercy upon us! Amen! amen!"

Fright lent him wings, and he fled, followed by the savage yells of the white figure, and never stopped until he reached Oberweimar, where he related to the astonished and terrified neighbors that there was a river-ghost just by the bridge which led to the cottage of the mad secretary of legation, Goethe, and which howled in the moonlight.*[Footnote: This tradition of the ghost of the Ilm has been preserved in Weimar, since Goethe's nocturnal bath, until our time.—See Lewes, vol. i., p. 451.]*

With the peasant also disappeared the ghost of the Ilm.

Like a happy child of Nature, refreshed, Goethe went to his room and then again sought the balcony, to throw himself upon the carpet and gaze at the blue starry vault, and enjoy the glories of heaven with thoughtful devotion, and think of Charlotte—only of her, not once of the poor Thusnelda von Goechhausen, who passed the night upon the stairs of the Palace Belvedere, and who, at last weary with fright and exhaustion, fell asleep, and was awakened by the Duchess Amelia in the morning, laughingly demanding why she preferred the landing of the stairs for a place of repose.

"Because I am bewitched, duchess, and my sleeping-room has disappeared from earth—because some cursed demon or wizard has enchanted me, this wicked—"

"Beware what you say!" interrupted the duchess; "it is most probably the duke that you are inveighing against, and calling a demon and wizard."

At this Thusnelda sprang up as if struck by an electric shock—"The surprise, this is what the duke promised me."

"Very likely," laughed the duchess. "The courier just arrived with a letter from my son to you, and I came to bring it myself, and found you, to my surprise, sleeping here. Read it, and tell me what he says!"

"Oh, listen, your highness!" cried Thusnelda, after having hastily perused the contents of the ducal missive.

"'I hope I have succeeded to surprise you! Demons and wizards have closed your doors, And weeping you slept on the stairway alone. All witchcraft has now disappeared. Go seek The surprise that from Berlin I brought you, Which I now offer for an atonement.'"

"An insolent fellow, indeed, is my son," said the duchess, "but you see, Thusnelda, he says, pater peccavi, and I am convinced that you will find something very pretty and acceptable in your room."

"I will not take it—indeed I will not," pouted the lady of honor. "He so fearfully tormented me last night. I assure your highness I was half dead with terror and—"

"And yet you will forgive him, Thusnelda, for the duke is your declared favorite; you dare not reproach him were he never so insolent, for you are just as much so, and not a hair's-breadth better. Come, go up and see what it is."

She went, and found four masons, who had been at work since daybreak to remove the wall and replace the door. Thusnelda was obliged to laugh in spite of the unhappy night she had passed, as she climbed over rubbish and ruins into her room, and met her maid dissolved in tears, who related to her that "the duke had had her walled in, for fear she would tell the trick to her mistress."

"And so you were really hermetically sealed?" said the duchess.

"Yes, your highness," whimpered the maid, "I thought I never should see daylight again. I wept and prayed all night. The only thing that consoled me was the duke's command, which Philip brought to me, to give this little box to Fraulein so soon as the wall should be taken away in the morning."

"Give it to me, Lieschen," cried Thusnelda, impatiently, her face beaming with satisfaction, however, when she opened the box. "Now, duchess, that is what I call a surprise, and the duke shall be, as he ever has been, my favorite. If he does sometimes play rude tricks, he makes it all right again, in a very generous and princely manner. See what a beautiful watch his highness has brought me, ornamented with diamonds!"

"Yes, it is very pretty; give it to me that I may return it to the duke, and not mortify him too much, as you will not wear it."

"I will accept it, duchess," cried Thusnelda, laughing—"and all is forgiven and forgotten."

CHAPTER XXIV
THE PURSE-PROUD MAN

"Trude, is there no news from him yet? Have you never seen him since? Did he not tell you about it?"

"No, my dearest Marie," sighed old Trude. "There is no word, no message from him. I have been twenty times to the baker's in eight days, and waited at the corner of the street, where we agreed to meet, but no Moritz was there, and I have not been able to hear any thing about him."

"Something must have happened to him," sighed Marie. "He is very ill, perhaps dying, and—"

"No, no, my child, he is not ill, I will tell you all about it, if you will not worry. I have been to Herr Moritz's lodgings to-day. I could not wait any longer, and—"

"Did you see him, and speak with him, Trude?"

"No Marie, he was not there; and the people in the house told me that he had been gone for a week."

"Gone!" repeated Marie, thoughtfully. "What does it mean? What could persuade him to abandon me in this hour of need? Tell me, Trude, what do you think? Console me if you can. You really know nothing further than that he is gone?"

"A little bit more, but not much, my heart's child. When the people told me that he had disappeared eight days ago, it seemed as if one of the Alps had fallen on my heart, and my limbs trembled so I could go no farther, and I was obliged to sit down upon the stairs and cry bitterly, picturing all sorts of dreadful things to myself."

"Dreadful things?" asked Marie. "Oh, Trude, you do not believe that my good, brave Moritz could do any thing sinful and cowardly, like wicked men? You do not think that my beloved—oh, no, no—I know that he is more noble; he will bear the burden of life as I will, so long as it pleases God."

The old woman hung down her head, and humbly folded her hands. "Forgive me, my child, that I have such weak and sinful thoughts. I will apologize for them in my heart to you and your beloved so long as I live. After I had cried enough, I determined to go to the Gray Cloister, and beg the director to see me!"

"Did you see him to speak with him, dear good Trude?"

"Yes, dear child. I told him I was an aged aunt of Herr Moritz, who had come to Berlin to visit him; and finding that he was absent, I would like to know where he had gone, and, how long he would remain away."

"Oh, Trude, how clever you are, and how kindly you think of every thing!" cried Marie, embracing her old nurse, and kissing affectionately her sunburnt, wrinkled cheek. "What did he say?"

"He told me that Herr Moritz had begged permission to be absent fourteen days to take an urgent, unavoidable journey; that ten days had already expired, and he would soon return."

"Then he will be here in four days, and perhaps will bring hope and aid! He has gone to seek it; I know and I feel it, though I cannot divine where the assistance will come from. Oh, Trude, if I could only gain a favorable delay until Moritz returns!"

"Every thing is arranged," murmured Trude. "The marriage license is already made out, and Parson Dietrich has promised to be ready at any hour. Herr Ebenstreit has sent the money, doubling the amount required to the 'Invalids' Hospital' at Berlin, so that when the papers of nobility arrive, there—"

"Hush!" interrupted Marie, "do not speak of it. It is fearful to think of, and it crazes me to hear it. I will resort to every extreme. Since my father and mother are deaf to my entreaties, I will try to move him to pity. I have never been able to see him alone; my mother is watchful that an explanation should be impossible between us. I will implore this man to have pity upon me, and confide in him to whom they would sell me."

Trude shook her head mournfully. "I fear it will be in vain, dear child. This man has no heart. I have proved him, and I know it.—Hark the bell rings! Who can it be?"

Both stepped out of the little garret-room to peep over the banister. Since Marie had been betrothed to the rich banker Ebenstreit, the general had received from his kind wife a servant in pompous livery for his own service. This servant had already opened the door, and Marie heard him announce in a loud voice, "Herr Ebenstreit!"

"He!" Marie started back with horror. "He, so early in the morning! this is no accident, Trude. What does it mean? Hush! the servant is coming!"

"I will go down," whispered Trude; "perhaps I can hear something."

Trude hurried away as her young lady glided back into her room, and never glanced at the servant who sprang past her upon the stairs.

"He is a hypocrite and a spy; he has been hired to watch and observe my child, and he will betray her if he discovers any thing."

The servant announced, with respectful, humble mien, that Herr Ebenstreit had arrived, and Frau von Werrig desired her daughter to descend to the parlor.

"Very well—say that I will come directly."

The servant remained rubbing his hands in an undecided, embarrassed manner.

"Why do you not go down?" asked Marie. "Have you any thing further to tell me?"

"I would say," said he, spying about the room, as if he were afraid some one were listening, "that if a poor, simple man like myself could be useful to you, and you could confide in me your commissions, I should be too happy to prove to you that Carl Leberecht is an honest fellow, and has a heart, and it hurts his feelings to see the miss suffer so much."

"I thank you," said Marie, gently. "I am glad to feel that you have sympathy for me."

"If I can be of the least service to you, have the goodness to call me, and give me your commissions."

"Indeed I will, although I do not believe it practicable."

"I hope miss will not betray me to Frau von Werrig or old Trude."

"No, I promise you that, and here is my hand upon it."

The servant kissed the extended hand respectfully. "I will enter into the service of my young lady at once, and tell her she must prepare for the worst: Herr Ebenstreit just said, 'The diploma of nobility has arrived.'"

Marie turned deadly pale, and for an instant it seemed as if she would sink down from fright, but she recovered herself and conquered her weakness.

"Thank you, it is very well that I should know that; I will go down directly," said she.

With calm, proud bearing Marie entered the sitting-room of her parents, and returned the salutations of her betrothed, who hastened toward her with tender assiduity.

"My dear Marie," cried her mother, "I have the honor to present to you Herr Ebenstreit von Leuthen. The certificate of nobility arrived this morning."

"I congratulate you, mother—you have at last found the long-desired heir to your name."

"Congratulate me above all, my beautiful betrothed," said Herr Ebenstreit, in a hoarse, scarcely intelligible voice. "This title crowns all my wishes, as it makes me your husband. I came to beg, dear Marie, that our marriage should take place to-morrow, as there is nothing now to prevent."

"Sir," she proudly interrupted him, "have I ever permitted this familiar appellation?"

"I have allowed it," blurted out the general, packed in cushions in his roiling chair. "Proceed, my dear son."

The latter bowed with a grateful smile, and continued: "I would beg, my dear Marie, to choose whether our wedding-journey shall be in the direction of Italy, Spain, France, or wherever else it may please her."

"Is it thus arranged?" asked Marie. "Is the marriage to take place early to-morrow, and then the happy pair take a journey?"

"Yes," answered her mother, hastily, "it is so decided upon, and it will be carried out. You may naturally, my dear daughter, have some preference; so make it known—I am sure your betrothed will joyfully accord it."

"I will avail myself of this permission," she quietly answered. "I wish to have a private conversation with this gentleman immediately, and without witnesses."

"Oh, how unfortunate I am!" sighed Herr Ebenstreit. "My dear Marie asks just that which I unfortunately cannot grant her."

"What should prevent your fulfilling my wish?" asked Marie.

"My promise," he whined. "On the very day of my betrothal, I was obliged to promise my dear mother-in-law never to speak with you alone or correspond with my sweet lady-love."

"These are the rules of decency and of etiquette, which I hope my daughter will respect," said Frau von Werrig, in a severe tone. "No virtuous young girl would presume to receive her betrothed alone or exchange love-letters with him before marriage!"

"After the wedding there will be opportunities enough for such follies," grumbled the general.

"You may be sure that I shall use them, dear father," laughed Ebenstreit. "I would beg my respected mother to release me a half-hour from my oath to-day, that I may indulge the first expressed wish that my future wife favors me with."

"It is impossible, my son. I never deviate from my principles. You will not speak with my daughter before marriage, except in the presence of her parents."

"Mother, do you insist upon it?" cried Marie, terrified. "Will you not indulge this slight wish?"

"'This slight wish!'" sneered her mother. "As if I did not know why you ask this private conversation. You wish to persuade our son-in-law to what you in vain have tried to implore your parents to do. A modest maiden has nothing to say to her future husband, which her parents, and above all her mother, could not hear. So tell your betrothed what you desire."

"Well, mother, you must then take the consequences.—Herr Ebenstreit, they will force me to become your wife, they will sell me as merchandise to you, and you have accepted the bargain in good faith, believing that I agree to sacrifice my freedom and human rights for riches. They have deceived you, sir! I am not ready to give myself up to the highest bidder. I am a woman, with a heart to love and hate, who esteems affection superior to wealth. I cannot marry you, and I beg you not to teach me to hate you."

A savage curse broke forth from the general, who, forgetting his gout, rose furious, shaking his clinched fist at his daughter.

His wife was immediately by his side, and pushed him into his armchair, commanding him, in her harsh, cold to remain quiet and take care of his health, and listen to what his son-in-law had to say to his unfeeling and unnatural daughter. "He alone has to decide.—Speak, my dear son," said she, turning to the young man, who, with a malicious smile, had listened to the baroness, fixing his dull-blue eyes upon the young girl, who never seemed so desirable to him, as she now stood before him with glowing cheeks.

"Again I say, speak, my dear son, and tell my daughter the truth; do you hear, the truth?"

"If you will permit me, my dearest mother, I will," answered Ebenstreit, with submissive kindness, again regarding the daughter. "You have made me a sad confession, Marie," said he, sighing, "but I will acknowledge that I am not surprised, for your mother told me when I asked for your hand, that she feared I should never gain your consent, for you did not love me, although she herself, and the general, would grant theirs."

"Was that all that I told you?" asked the mother, coldly.

"No, not all," continued Ebenstreit, slightly inclining; "you added, 'My daughter loves a beggar, a poor school-master, and she entertains the romantic idea of marrying him.'"

"And what did you reply?" asked Marie, almost breathless.

"My dear Marie, I laughed, repeating my proposal of marriage to your mother, saying, that I was ready to take up the combat with the poor pedagogue, and that you seemed all the more interesting and amiable for this romantic love. Life is so tedious and wretched, that one is glad to have some change and distraction. I assure you, I have not been so entertained for long years, as in the last fourteen days in this silent war with you. It amuses me infinitely to see you so stubborn and prudish, and increases my love for you. How could it be otherwise? The rich banker, Ebenstreit, has never seen a woman who was not ready to accept his hand, and why should he not love the first one who resists it? You have excited my self-love and vanity. You have made the marriage a matter of ambition, and you will comprehend that my answer is: 'Fraulein von Leuthen must and shall be my wife, no matter what it costs me. She defies my riches and despises money, so I will force her to respect my wealth and recognize its power. Besides, she is a cruel, egotistical daughter; who has no pity for her poor parents, and is capable of seeing them perish for her foolish attachment. I will make her a good child, and force her to make her parents, and thereby herself, happy.' All this I said to myself, and I have acted and shall act accordingly. I have only to add that the ceremony will take place to-morrow, at eleven. We will leave immediately after. Have the goodness therefore to choose in which direction, that I may at once make the necessary arrangements."

"Lost—lost without hope!" cried Marie, in anguish, covering her face with her hands.

"Rather say rescued from misfortune," answered Ebenstreit, quietly. "Believe me, there is but one sorrow that may not be borne, may not be conquered, and that is poverty, which is a corroding, consuming malady, annihilating body, and soul, swifter and surer than the most subtle poison. It stifles all noble feelings, all poetical thoughts and great deeds, and, believe me, love even cannot resist its terrible power. One day you will understand this. I will be patient and indulgent, and await it with hope."

"Oh, what a noble and high-minded man!" cried the mother, with emphasis.—"Marie should kneel and thank her Maker for such a magnanimous savior and lover, who will shield her from all evil and misfortune."

Sobbing and sighing, the daughter had stood with her face concealed; now she regarded the cold-hearted, smiling woman, with flashing eyes and keen contempt.

"Thank him!" she cried; "no, I accuse, I curse him. He is an atheist, and denies love. He is not capable of a noble thought or action, scorning and defaming all that is beautiful and elevated, worshipping only mammon. I will never marry him. You may force me to the altar, and there I will denounce him."

"She will kill me," cried the general; "she will murder her aged parents, leaving them to starve and perish, and—"

"Silence!" commanded his wife. "Leave off your complaints, she is not worth the tears or remonstrances of her parents. She would try to be our murderess, but she shall not.—My son, inform her of your decision. Answer her."

"The response to your romantic language is simple and natural, my dear Marie. I have already entered into your feelings, and am prepared for this idea of refusing your lover at the altar, which is found in novels, and I supposed that it might occur to you. Money compasses all things and according to our wishes. My fortune procures for me a dispensation from public authorities to be married here in the house of our dear parents. The law demands four witnesses, who will be represented by your parents, my servant Philip, and the sacristan whom the clergyman will bring."

"And they will hear me abjure you."

"It is very possible, dearest, but the witnesses will not listen to you. Money makes the deaf to hear, and the hearing ones deaf. Old parson Dietrich knows the story of your love, and believes, with us, that it is a malady that you must be cured of. Therefore, in pity to you, he will not listen, and the others are paid to keep silent."

"Is there no hope, O Heaven?" cried Marie, imploringly. "O God, Thou hast permitted it—hast Thou no pity in my need, and sendest me no aid?" Rushing to her father, and kneeling at his feet, she continued: "Have mercy upon your poor child! You are an old man, and may live but a few years; do not burden your conscience with the fearful reproaches of your only child, whom you will condemn to an inconsolably long and unhappy life."

"Have you no pity yourself? Do you not know that I, your father, am so poor, that I have not even the necessary care? You wish your parents to sacrifice themselves for you, and suffer want! No, the daughter should sacrifice herself for her parents."

"A beautiful sacrifice, a fine sorrow!" sneered her mother. "She will be a rich woman, and have the most splendid house and furniture and most costly equipage in Berlin!"

"And a husband who adores her," cried Ebenstreit, "and who will feel it his duty to make her and her parents happy. Resolve bravely to bury the past, and look the immutable future joyfully in the face. Eleven will be the happy hour; fear not that the altar will not be worthy the charming bride of such a rich family. Money will procure every thing, and I will send a florist who will change this room into a blooming temple, fit to receive the goddess of love. In your room you will find the gift of my affection, a simple wedding-dress, which I trust you will approve of. Oh, do not shake your head, do not say that you will never wear it; you must believe that all resistance is in vain. You will become my wife, I and my money will it."

"And I," cried Marie, standing before him pale and defiant, regarding him with unspeakable contempt, "I and my love will it not. May God judge between us! May He forgive those who have brought this misfortune upon me! I can only say, 'Woe to them!'"

"Woe to you!" cried her mother. "Woe to the seducer who has persuaded our child to sin and crime, and—"

"Hush mother! I will not permit you to slander him whom I love, and ever shall, so long—"

"Until you forget him, and love me, Marie," said Ebenstreit. Approaching her, he seized her hand, and pressed a kiss upon it.

She drew it away with disgust, and turned slowly to the door, tossing back her head proudly. "Where are you going?" demanded her mother.

With her hand upon the knob, she replied, turning her pale, wan face to her mother, "To my own room, which I suppose is permitted to me, as there is nothing more to be said."

Her mother would reply, and retain her, but her son-in-law held her gently back. "Let her go," said he; "she needs rest for composure and to accustom herself to the thought that her fate is unavoidable."

"But what if she should resort to desperate means in her mad infatuation and foolish passion? Some one must watch her continually, for she may try to elope."

"You are right, dearest mother, some one must be with her, in whom she will confide. Would it not be possible to win old Trude?"

"No, nothing would gain her; she is a silly fool, who thinks only Marie is of consequence."

Ebenstreit shrugged his shoulders. "That means that she would sell herself at a high price. I beg that you will send for her."

"You will see," said she, calling the old woman, who entered from the opposite door.

Trude looked about, scowling and grumbling. "Leberecht told me my mistress called me."

"Why do you then look so furious, and what are you seeking on the table?" asked Frau von Werrig.

"My money," cried Trude, vehemently. "I thought that you called me to pay me, and that my wages were all counted out on the table. But I see there is nothing there, and I fear I shall get none, and be poor as a church-mouse all my life long. Your honor promised me positively that, as soon as the wedding was decided upon, you would pay me every farthing, with interest, and I depended upon it."

"You shall have all, and much more than the general's wife promised you, if you will be a true and faithful servant to us," said Ebenstreit.

"That I always have been, and ever shall be," snarled Trude. "No person can say aught against me. Now, I want my money."

"And obstinate enough you have been too," said her mistress. "Can you deny that you have not always taken my daughter's part?"

"I do not deny it. I have nursed her from childhood, and I love her as my own child, and would do any thing to make her happy!"

"Do you believe, Trude," cried the general, "that Marie could be happy with that poor, starving wretch of a school-master? Has she not experienced in her own home the misfortune and shame of poverty?"

"I know it well," sighed the old one, sadly, "and it has converted me to believe that it would be a great misfortune for Marie to marry the poor school-master."

"Well, will you then faithfully help us to prevent it?" quickly asked Ebenstreit.

"How can I do it?" she sighed, shrugging her shoulder.

"You can persuade my daughter to be reasonable, and yield to that which she cannot prevent. You are the only one who can make any impression upon Marie, as she confides in you. Watch her, that in a moment of passionate desperation she does not commit some rash act. You can tell us, further, what she says, and warn us of any crazy plan she might form to carry out her own will."

"That is to say, I must betray my Marie?" cried Trude, angrily.

"No, not betray, but rescue her. Will you do it?" asked Ebenstreit.

"I wish to be paid my wages, my two hundred thalers, that I have honestly earned, and I will have them."

Ebenstreit took a piece of paper from his pocket. Writing a few lines with a pencil, he laid it upon the table. "If you will take this to my cashier after the ceremony to-morrow, he will pay you four hundred thalers."

"Four hundred thalers in cash," cried Trude, joyfully clapping her hands. "Shall all that beautiful money be mine, and—No, I do not believe you," she cried, her face reassuming its gloomy, suspicious look. "You promise it to me to-day, that I may assist you, and persuade Marie to the marriage, but to-morrow, when old Trude is of no more use, you will send me away penniless. Oh, I know how it is. I have lived long enough to understand the tricks of rich people. I will see the cash first—only for that will I sell myself."

"The old woman pleases me," said Ebenstreit. "She is practical, and she is right.—If I promise you the money in an hour, will you persuade Marie to cease her foolish resistance, and be my wife? Will you watch over her, and tell us if any thing unusual occurs?"

"Four hundred thalers is a pretty sum," repeated Trude, in a low voice to herself. "I might buy myself a place in the hospital, and have enough left to get me a new bed and neat furniture and—"

Here her voice was lost in unintelligible mumbling, and, much excited, she appeared to count eagerly. With her bony forefinger she numbered over the fingers of her left hand, as if each were a fortune that she must verify and examine.

The mother and the banker regarded each other with mocking looks; the general looked at the money, grumbling: "If I had had four hundred thalers the last time I played, I could have won back my money in playing again."

"Old woman," said Ebenstreit, "have you not finished with your reckoning?"

"Yes," she said, with an exultant laugh, "I have done! Four hundred thalers are not sufficient. I must have five, and if you will give them to me in cash in an hour, then I will do every thing that you wish, and persuade Marie to the marriage. I will watch her day and night, and tell you every thing that she says and does. But I must have five hundred in cash!"

Ebenstreit turned his dull-blue eyes to Frau von Werrig with a triumphant smile. "Did you not tell me the old woman could not be bought? I knew that I was right. You did not offer her money enough; she will sell herself dear as possible."

"Yes, as dear as she can," laughed Trude—"five hundred is my price."

"You shall have it in cash in an hour," said Ebenstreit, in a friendly manner.

"So much money," whined the general; "it would have saved me if I had had it that last time."

"My son-in-law, I must confess you are exceedingly generous," remarked the mother.

"No sum would be too great to assure me my bride. Go now, Trude, you shall have the money in time.—Will you allow me, father, to send your servant to my office for it?"

"Send Leberecht here, Trude!"

The old woman hurried out of the room, but the door once closed, her manner changed. One might have supposed a sudden cramp had seized her, from her distorted face, and twitching and panting, and beating the air with her clinched fists, and her quivering lips uttering broken words.

Approaching footsteps warned her to assume her general manner and expression, and cease her manipulations. "The ladies and gentlemen wish you in the parlor," mumbled Trude to the servant descending the stairs. "But where have you been, and what have you to do up there?"

"I was looking for you, lovely one—nothing more!"

"Well, now you have found me, tell me what you want? I know you were sneaking about, listening, because you thought I was with Marie. I understand you better than you think I do. I have found many a viper, and I am familiar with their aspect. Go! they are waiting for you, and let me find you again spying about, and I will throw a pail of water on you!"

With this friendly assurance Trude dismissed Leberecht, and hastened with youthful activity to the little garret-room, when Marie fell upon her neck, weeping bitterly.

"Calm yourself—do not weep so—it breaks my heart, my dear child."

"And mine cannot break. I must endure all this anguish and survive this shame. Help me, my good mother, stand by me! It is impossible for me to marry that dreadful man. I have sworn constancy to my beloved Moritz, and I must be firm, or die!"

"Die? then you will kill me!" murmured the old one, "for, if you go, I must go also. But we will not give up yet, as we are both living; we will not despair for life. I am going once more to Moritz's lodgings; it may be he has returned, and will rescue you."

"Oh, do, good Trude; tell him that I have courage and determination to risk and bear every thing—that I will await him; that nothing would be too difficult or dangerous to serve to unite me to him! Tell him that I prefer a life of poverty and want by his side, to abundance and riches in a splendid palace with that detested creature—but no, say nothing about it, he knows it well! If he has returned, tell him all that has happened, and that I am resolved to brave the utmost, to save myself!"

"I will go, dear child, but I have first my work to do, and enough of it too—but listen to what they have made me become." Hastily, in a low voice, she related to Marie the story of her corruption, excited as before, her limbs shaking and her fists clinched. "They say we old women resemble cats, but from to-day forth I know that is a shameful lie! If I had possessed their nature and claws, I should have sprung at the throat of this rascal, and torn out his windpipe; but, instead of that, I stood as if delighted with his degrading proposal! Oh, fie! the good-for-nothing kidnapper would tempt a poor creature! Let us wait, they will get their reward. He shall pay me the five hundred thalers, and then this trader of hearts shall recognize that, however much ill-earned money he may throw away, love and constancy are hot to be bought. We will teach him a lesson," and with this, the old servant ceased, gasping for breath.

"Go now, Trude, and learn if he has returned; upon him depends my happiness, and life even—he is my last hope!"

"I am going, but first I would get the wages of my sin, and play the hypocrite, and tell a few untruths; then I will go to Moritz's lodgings, and the baker also. Do not despair; I have a joyful presentiment that God will have pity upon us and send us aid." Trude kissed and embraced her child, and scarcely waited an hour, when she was demanded in the parlor to receive her money.

Herr Ebenstreit was heartily delighted with her zealous impatience, and handed her ten rolls of gold, reminding her of the conditions.

"I have already consoled her a little, and she begins to change. I hope every thing will turn for good. Just leave her alone with me."

"But first, I must go and see my aged brother, who will take care of my money," replied Trude. "He is a safe man and will not spend it."

"Trude," cried the general, "what an old fool! to seek at distance what is so near you. I will take your money, and give you interest. Do you hear? I will take care of it!"

"Thank you, general, I'd rather give it to my brother, on account of the relationship." She slipped out of the room, hid the money in her bed, and hurriedly left the house.

Scarcely an hour passed ere Trude returned as fleetly as she went. She cast only a look into the kitchen, and hastened up to Marie's room. Her success was evident in her happy, smiling face, and coming home she had repeated to herself, "How happy Marie will be!" almost the entire way.

She had but closed the door, when the mean little Leberecht glided from behind the chimney, and crept to listen at the door.

Within was a lively conversation, and twice a shout of joy was heard and Marie, exultant, cried, "Oh, Trude! dear Trude! all goes well, I fear nothing now. God has sent me the savior which I implored!"

Leberecht stood, bent over, applying his ear to the keyhole, listening to every word.

Oh, Trude! if you could only have seen the traitor, glued to the door, with open eyes and mouth! Could you have seen the eavesdropper rubbing his hands together, grinning, and listening in breathless suspense!

Why cannot you surprise him, Trude, and fulfil your threat to deluge him and chase him away from your child's door? They forgot the necessity of prudence, and the possibility of being overheard. At last it occurred to the old servant, and she tore open the door, but no one was there—it was deserted and still.

"God be thanked, no one has listened," whispered Trude. "I will go down and tell them that I hope, if we can stay alone all day, you will be calmer and more reasonable."

"Do it, Trude; I do not dare to see any one for fear my face will betray me, and my mother has very sharp eyes. Return soon."

She opened the door, and saw not the eavesdropper and spy, who had but just time to conceal himself, and stand maliciously grinning at the retreating figure of the faithful servant.

He slipped lightly from his hiding-place down to his sleeping-room, in a niche under the stairs. For a long time he reflected, upon his bedside—his watery blue eyes staring at nothing. "This must be well considered," he mumbled. "There is, at last, a capital to be won. Which shall I do first, to grasp a good deal? Shall I wait, or go at once to Herr Ebenstreit? Very naturally they would both deny it, and say that I had made up the whole story to gain money. I had better let the affair go on: they can take a short drive, and when they are about an hour absent, I will sell my secret at a higher price. Now I will pretend to be quite harmless, and after supper let the bomb burst!"

CHAPTER XXV
THE ELOPEMENT

Evening had set in. The card-table had been arranged, and Leberecht had rolled his master to it, taking his place behind his chair. The hour of whist the general impatiently awaited the entire day, and it was regularly observed. Even in the contract with his adopted son it had been expressly mentioned as a duty, that he should not only secure to them yearly income, but also devote an hour to cards every evening.

Herr Ebenstreit regarded it as a tax, which he must observe until married. The general was much his superior at cards, and, moreover, played the dummy, and the stake being high, it was quite an income for the future father-in-law, and regarded by him as the one bright spot in his daily life.

The cards had been dealt, and Leberecht had assorted the general's, and placed them in his gouty hand, when Trude entered, exultingly.

"What has happened? What makes you interrupt us?" cried the general. "Did you not remember that I have told you always not to disturb us at this hour."

"Yes, general, but I thought good news was never amiss."

"What have you pleasant to tell us?" harshly demanded Frau von Werrig.

"My young lady's compliments," cried Trude, triumphantly; "she begins to see that she must yield to her fate, and that it will do no good to resist any longer. She will be ready for the ceremony at eleven o'clock to-morrow morning."

The general uttered a cry of joy, and struck the table so violently, with his hand, that the cards were thrown together.

His wife bowed dignifiedly, and the happy bridegroom gave old Trude some gold-pieces upon the favorable news.

"Has she, then, been converted by your persuasion?" he asked.

"Through my persuasion and her own good sense. She understands that, if she cannot marry her dear Moritz, Herr Ebenstreit is the most fit husband, because he loves her, and is so generous to her old parents. One thing she would like an answer to—can I accompany her to her new home?"

"Yes, old woman, it will be very agreeable to have so sensible a person," said Ebenstreit. "Tell Marie that it gives me pleasure to fulfil her wish."

"In that case I would repeat that Fraulein begs for indulgence and forbearance until to-morrow, and would like to remain alone to compose herself."

"I do not wish, in the least, to see her," said her mother; "she can do what she likes until then."

"I will tell Marie, and she will rejoice," cried Trude.

"Tell her, from her father, that it is very agreeable to him not to see her pale, wretched-looking face again till morning.—Now, my son, pay attention, and you, Trude, do not presume to interrupt us again. Leberecht, play out my ace of hearts."

The latter, with his eyes cast down, and with a perfectly indifferent manner, played the card indicated, and Trude left the room quietly and unobserved.

"Every thing is arranged, my child," said Trude, as she re-entered Marie's room. "They are playing cards, which always lasts two hours, then Herr Ebenstreit goes away, and the family will go to bed. You have eighteen hours, before you will be discovered. Hark! it strikes seven, and it is already quite dark. When the post-horn sounds, then it is time."

"Oh, Trude! my dear mother, my heart almost ceases to beat, with anxiety, and I quake with fear," sighed Marie. "I am conscious that I have commenced a fearful undertaking!"

"They have driven you to it—it is not your fault," said Trude, consolingly. "Every human being is free to work out his own good or bad fortune, and, as our dear Old Fritz says, 'to be happy in the future world in his own way.' They have sold you for money, and you only prove to them that you are no slave."

"And I prove also that I am a disobedient daughter," added Marie, trembling. "At this hour, it weighs like a heavy burden upon my heart, and the words of Holy Writ burn into my very soul—'Honor thy father and thy mother, that it may be well with thee.'"

"You have honored them all your life," said Trude, solemnly; "I can witness it before God and man. You have worked for them without thanks or love, receiving only contempt. It is also written, 'Thou shalt leave father and mother, and cleave unto thy husband.' You still follow the commands of God, and may it bring you happiness and blessing. My prayers and thoughts go with you, my child! a mother could not love her offspring more tenderly than I do you."

"No mother could more tenderly and faithfully care for her than you have for me, Trude," cried Marie, pressing her lovingly to her breast. "Through you alone is my rescue possible, for you give us the money to undertake the long journey."

"Not I," she laughed; "it is Herr Ebenstreit, and that makes it the more amusing; the wicked always set the traps into which they fall themselves." Suddenly the loud, quivering tones of the post-horn were heard, "Es ritten drei Reiter zum Thore hinaus."

"He has come!" cried Marie, and her face beamed with delight. "He calls me! I am coming!—Farewell, dear, peaceful room, where I have so toiled, wept, and suffered! I shall never see thee again! My beloved calls me, and I go to follow him even unto death! Pardon me, O God! Thou seest that I cannot do otherwise! They would force me to perjury, and I dare not break my oath! I cannot forsake him whom I love!—When they curse me, Trude, kneel, and implor God to bless me, who is the Father of love! My conscience does not reproach me. I have worked for them when they needed it; now their adopted son, to whom they have sold their name, allows them a yearly rent, and I can work for myself."

"Hark! there is the post-horn again, you must go," murmured Trude, struggling to force back her tears.

"Bless me, mother," implored Marie, kneeling.

"God's blessing go with you," she said, laying her hands upon her head, "and may it render of no avail the curses of men, but permit you to walk in love and happiness!"

"Amen, amen!" sighed Marie, "now farewell, dear mother, farewell!"

Marie rose, and kissing Trude again, flitted down the stairs, and out of the house, Trude following, holding her breath and listening in fearful excitement.

Again resounded the post-horn.

"They are gone," murmured Trude, bowing her head and praying long and fervently.

The general was particularly fortunate this evening, which caused him to be unusually cheerful and satisfied. After every rubber he gathered up the thalers, until he had amassed a most satisfactory pile. As the clock struck ten, Frau von Werrig declared that they must finish and go to bed.

The general yielded, with a sigh, to her decision, for he knew, by long years of experience, that it would be in vain to defy her will. He shoved his winnings into a leather bag, which he always carried with him, and gave Leberecht the order to roll away his chair, when the servant, with a solemn bow, stepped closely to him, and begged the general to listen to him a moment.

"Well, what have you to say?" he asked.

"I have only one request—that you will permit me to prove that I am a faithful servant, who looks out for the good of his employers. You have given Trude five hundred thalers that she might watch over your daughter. I can show you how well she deserved it, and how differently your humble servant would have done.—Have the goodness, Frau von Werrig, to call Trude to bid Fraulein come down, for you have something important to communicate to her."

His mistress proudly regarded him and seemed to try to read his meaning in his smiling, humble face. "And if my daughter comes, what have you to say?"

"If she comes, then I am a miserable fool and scoundrel, but I beg you to call Trude."

It was a long time before the old woman appeared, confused and sleepy, asking—"what they wanted at such a late hour?"

"Go and tell my daughter that I wish to see her at once."

Trude trembled, but composed herself, saying, "There is time enough to-morrow. Fraulein has been asleep a long time."

"She lies," sneered Leberecht, taking the precaution to protect himself behind the general's arm-chair. "She knows that she is not in bed."

"Oh, you sneak, you rascal," cried Trude, shaking her fist at him, "how dare you say that I tell a lie? How can such a miserable creature as you impute to others what you do yourself every time that you open your mouth?"

"Frau von Werrig, she is only quarrelling, in order to gain time—every moment is precious. I beg you to go up-stairs, and see for yourself, if your daughter is there."

"Fraulein has locked the door so as not to be disturbed."

"Ah," said Leberecht, "Trude has locked it, and has the key in her pocket."

"Give up the key," shrieked the general, who in vain tried to rise, "or I will call the police, and send you to prison."

"Do it, but I will not give it to you."

"Do you not see she has it?" cried Leberecht.

"Oh, you wretch, I will pay you—I will scratch your eyes out, you miserable creature!"

"Trude, be quiet," commanded Ebenstreit; "the general orders to give up the key—do it!"

"Yes, do it at once," shrieked Frau von Werrig, "or I will dismiss you from my service."

"That you will not have to do, as I shall go myself. I will not give up the key."

"The door is old, and with a good push one could open it," said Leberecht.

"Come, my son, let us see," said the mother.

They hastened up to the room, while the general scolded, furiously that he must sit still. Leberecht and Trude cast furious, menacing glances at each other.

Suddenly a loud crash was heard.

"They have broken open the door!" cried the general.

"I said that it was old and frail—what do you say now, beautiful Trude?"

The old woman wiped with her hand the drops of perspiration from her forehead, caused by her anguish. "You are a bad fellow, and God will punish you for your treason, that you have tormented a noble, unhappy girl. I saw that you were an eavesdropper, and you know all."

"She is gone!" shrieked the mother, rushing into the room.

"The room is empty," cried Ebenstreit. "Marie is not there. Tell us, Leberecht, what you know about it."

"I will, if we can agree about the pay—the old woman bothers me, and beg the young gentleman to go into the next room with me."

"O Almighty God, have compassion upon my poor little Marie," murmured Trude, kneeling, and covering her face.

Ebenstreit in the mean time withdrew to the other room, followed by the servant.

"Speak!" commanded his master, "and tell me what you have to say."

Leberecht shrugged his shoulders. "We are two men who have urgent business with each other. I am not at present a servant and you the master. I am a man who has an important secret to sell, and you are the man who would buy it."

"What strange, unheard-of language is this?" said Ebenstreit, astonished.

"The language of a man who cannot only deprive the rich banker Ebenstreit of a lovely wife, but of his title also. You said yourself, sir, this morning, that it was only valid if you succeeded in marrying the daughter of General von Leuthen. No none knows where you can find your bride but me."

"And Trude," said Ebenstreit, quickly.

"You know she will not betray Fraulein, and you have not even tried to make her."

"You are mistaken; Trude is as easily bought as any one."

"You say that because she has taken five hundred thalers from you. She has not helped you, and it is useless to ask for your money, as she has not got it."

"How so? Has she given it away?"

"You provided the money for your bride to run away and marry elsewhere, as Trude gave it to them."

Ebenstreit stamped his foot with rage, striding backward and forward in furious excitement, while Leberecht watched him, sardonically smiling. "Let us come to an end with this business," said Ebenstreit, stopping before his servant. "You know where Fraulein can be found, and you wish to sell the secret—tell me your price."

"Three thousand thalers, and a clerkship in your bank, which you intend to continue under another name."

"You are beside yourself. I am not so foolish as to grant such senseless demands."

"Every hour that you wait I demand a thousand thalers more, and if you stop to reflect long your betrothed and your title both are lost."

"You are a miserable scamp!" cried Ebenstreit, enraged; "I will inform the police. There are means enough to force you to give the information."

"I do not believe it. Trude will not tell you, and I should like to know what can force me if I will not. The king has done away with torture, and I have informed you how to make me speak. Three thousand thalers and a clerkship in your office. Take care! it is almost eleven o'clock—at midnight I shall demand four thousand."

CHAPTER XXVI
UNDER THE STARRY HEAVENS

It was a beautiful, clear, moonlight night. The world reposed in silence. Mankind with their cares and sorrows, their joys and hopes, had gone to rest. Over town and village, over highway and forest had flitted the sweet, consoling angel—Sleep. The sad were soothed, the heavy-laden were lightened of their burdens, to the despairing were brought golden dreams, to the weary rest. Sighing and sorrowful, he turned from those with a sad face whose conscience banished repose, and, ah! their number was legion. To the wakeful and blissful he smilingly glanced, breathing a prayer and a blessing; but these were few and far between—for happiness is a rare guest, and tarries with mortals but fitfully. As he glided past the joyful couple who, with watchful love and grateful hearts, sat in the carriage rolling over the silent, deserted highway, two tears fell from his eyes, and his starry wings were wider outspread to rush more quickly past.

"Look, my dear Marie, two stars just fell from heaven. They are a greeting to you, loved one, and they would say they guide us on our way."

"Oh, Philip, it is a sign of ill-luck! Falling stars betoken misfortune!"

She clung closer to his side, and laid her head upon his shoulder. He pressed her more lovingly to his heart. "Do not fear, dear Marie; separation only could cause us unhappiness—we have long borne it, and now it is forever past. You have given yourself to me for my own, and I am yours, heart and soul; we speed on through the night to the morning of the bright, sunny future, never more to be parted."

"Never!" she fervently murmured. "Oh, may God hear our prayer. Never, never to part! Yet, while the word falls from my lips, a shudder creeps through my soul."

"Wherefore this despair, dearest? Reflect, no one will be apprised of our flight till early morning, and then they will not know whither we have fled. Meanwhile we rush on to Hamburg, where a packet-ship sails every Wednesday for England; arriving there, we will first go to Suffolk, to my old friend the vicar of Tunningham. I was his guest many weeks last year, and he often related to me the privilege which had been conferred on the parish church for a long time to perform valid marriages for those to whose union there were obstacles interposed elsewhere. He will bless the union of our love, and will accord me the lawful right to call you my own before God and man. We will not return at once to Germany. I have many connections and literary friends in London, who will assist me to worthy occupation. Besides, I closed an agreement some weeks since with the publisher Nicolai in Berlin for a new work. I will write it in London; it will be none the less favored coming from a distance."

"My flowers and paintings will also be as well received in as in Berlin," added Marie, smilingly.

"No, Marie, you shall not work. I shall have the precious care of providing for you, which will be my pride and happiness. Oh, my beloved, what a crowning bliss to possess a sweet, dear wife, who is only rich in imperishable treasures, and poor in external riches! What delight to toil for her, and feel that there lives in my intellect the power to grant her every wish, and to compensate her in the slightest degree the boundless wealth of her affection! To a loving mind there is no prouder, happier feeling than to be the only source of support to the wife of his love—to know that she looks to him for the fulfilment of her slightest wish in life. I thank my Maker that you are poor, Marie, and that I am permitted to toil for you. How else could I reward you for all you have sacrificed for me?"

"You cannot suppose, dear Philip, that the riches of my obtrusive lover would have been any attraction to me. Money could never compensate for the loss of your love. You are my life, and from you alone can I receive happiness or unhappiness. At your side I am rich and joyous, though we may outwardly need; without you I should be poor with superfluity. I am proud that we in spirit have freed ourselves from those fictitious externals with which the foolish burden themselves. Oh, my beloved Philip, my whole soul is exultant that we are never more to part—no, not even in eternity, for I believe that love is an undying sentiment, and the soul can never be darkened by death which is beaming with affection."

"You are right, Marie, love is the immortality of the soul; through it man is regenerated and soars to the regions of eternal light. When I recall how desolate and gloomy was my life, how joyless the days dragged on before I loved you, I almost menaced Heaven that it created me to wander alone through this desert. The brightest sun's rays now gild my future, and it seems as if we were alone in paradise, and that the creation entire glorified my happiness, and all the voices of Nature shouted a greeting to you, dearest. Oh, Marie, if I lived a thousand years, my heart would retain its youthful love and adoration for you, who have saved me from myself, have freed my soul from the constraining fetters of a sad, joyless existence. Repose your head upon my heart, and may it rest there many happy years, and receive in this hour my oath to love, esteem, and honor you as my most precious treasure! You shall be wife, child, sister, and friend. My soul shall be frank and open to you; for you I will strive and toil, and will cherish and foster the happiness received from you as my most treasured gift. Give me your hand, Marie."

She laid it within his own strong, manly hand, gently pressing it.

The large full moon, high above them, lighted up these noble faces, making the eyes, which were bent upon each other, more radiant. Swiftly the carriage rolled on, the night-breeze fanning their cheeks and waving back their raven curls.

Moritz raised their clasped hands, and gazed at the starry heaven.

"We lift them up unto Thee, O God. Thou hast heard my oath, O Eternal Spirit, who dwellest among the stars; receive it, and bless the woman I love!"

"Receive also my oath, O my Maker. Regard the man to whom I have sworn eternal fidelity, bless him, and bless me. Let us live in love and die in constancy."

Moritz responded, "Amen, my beloved, amen!"

They embraced each other fervently. Onward rolled the carriage through the tranquil, blissful night. Oh why cannot these steeds borrow wings from the night-wind? Why cannot the soaring spirit bear aloft its earthly tenement? With divine joy and heavenly confidence you gaze at the stars. You smilingly interchange thoughts of the blissful future, whilst dire misfortune approaches, and will soon seize you in its poisonous grasp! Do you not hear it? Does not the echo of swift-prancing steeds ring in your ears? Do you not hear the shrieking and calling after you?

They listen only to the voice of tenderness speaking in their hearts, and would that the solemn quiet of this dialogue might not be broken by a loud word from their lips.

The post-horn sounded! They halted at a lonely house near the highway. It is the station. Change horses! There is not a light to be seen. Three times the postilion blew a pealing blast ere they could awake the inmates. The window was at last opened, and a sleepy, complaining voice questioned the number of horses and the distance of the next post.

Slowly they were brought forward, and still more slowly were they attached to the carriage, and all arranged. What matters it? The night is lovely, and like a dream it seems to remain under the starry heavens, spread out like a canopy above them.

Does not your heart tell you that sorrow strides on like the storm? Do you not hear the voices still shrieking after you?

The postilion mounted his horse, and again the trumpet pealed forth its merry air, and was answered with a shout of triumph from the swift pursuers.

Marie raised her head from Philip's shoulder. "What was it? Did you not hear it?"

"What, my beloved, what should I hear? Do the stars salute you? Do the angels greet their sister upon earth?"

"Hark! there it is again! Do you not hear it? Listen! does it not seem as if one called 'Halt! halt!'"

"Yes, truly, I hear it now also! What can happen, love? Why trouble ourselves about the outer world and the existence of other beings?"

"I know not, but I am so anxious, my heart almost ceases to beat, with terror!"

"Halt! halt!" the wind carries forward the shriek, and above their heads it sounds like the screeching of ravens.

"Strange! For whom are they calling?" Moritz looked back along the highway. White and clear it lay in the moonlight, but, far in the distance was a black mass, taking form and shape at every moment!

Horsemen! horsemen! in full speed they come!

"Postilion! drive on! quick! Let the horses gallop! There is a forest near—drive us to that, that we may hide ourselves in the thicket! Onward, postilion! we are not thieves or murderers. A hundred thalers are yours, if you save us!"

The postilion beat his horses! In full chase they followed—more and more distinctly were heard the curses and yells.

"Oh, God in heaven, have mercy upon us in our need!"

"Faster, postilion!—in mercy, faster!"

"Halt! halt!—in the name of the king, halt!"

This startled the postilion, and he turned to listen, and again a furious voice yelled, "In the name of the king, halt!"

The postilion drew up. "Forgive me, sir, but I must respect the name of the king."

Forward galloped the horsemen.

"Philip," whispered Marie, "why do we live—why do we not die?"

He folded her in his arms, and passionately kissed her, perhaps for the last time. "Marie, be mindful of our oath—constant unto death!"

"Constant unto death!" she repeated.

"Be firm and defy all the storms of life!"

Marie repeated it, with heightened courage.

The horsemen surrounded the carriage, the riders upon panting steeds! Two officers in uniform sprang to the side, laying their hands upon Moritz's shoulder. "Conrector Philip Moritz, we arrest you in the name of the king! You are accused of eloping with a minor, and we are commanded to transport you to Spandau until further orders!" Upon the other side two other horsemen halted. The foremost was Herr Ebenstreit, who laid his hand upon Marie, and saw not or cared not that she shudderingly shrank away.

"My dear Marie, I come as the ambassador of your parents, and am fully empowered to lead your back to your father's house."

She answered not, but sat immovable and benumbed with terror, the tears rolling down her cheeks.

"You arrest me in the name of the king," cried Moritz; "I bow to the law. I beg only to speak to that man," pointing to Ebenstreit, with contempt. "Sir, dismount, I have important business with you!"

"We have nothing to say to each other," answered Ebenstreit, calmly.

"But I!" cried Moritz, springing forward, furious as a lion, "I have something to say to you, you rascal, and I will treat you accordingly!"

He savagely tore the whip from the postilion's hand, and struck Ebenstreit in the face. "Now," cried he, triumphantly, "I have forced you to give me satisfaction!"

The police swung themselves from their saddles, and Leberecht quickly dismounted. They clinched Moritz by the feet and hands. It was a desperate struggle, and Marie gazed at them with folded hands, praying without words. They seized him and held him fast with manacles. A shriek, and Marie sank fainting. Moritz's head sank upon his breast, almost in the agony of death.

"Take him to the next station, my friends," commanded Ebenstreit, "the carriage is already ordered to remove him to Spandau." He dismounted, and now took the place by Marie, who still lay in a dead faint. "Postilion, mount and turn your carriage, I retain you until the next station. If you drive quickly, there is a louis d'or for you."

"I will drive as if the devil were after me, sir!" shouted the postilion, and turned to gallop off, when Ebenstreit ordered him to halt, and Leberecht to get up on the box. Then turning to the officers, "Gentlemen," said he, proudly, "you are witnesses to the ill-treatment and insults of this woman-stealer. You will certify that the blood flowed down my face."

"I will myself make it known before all men," cried Moritz, with a contemptuous laugh. "I have insulted you and branded you."

"We will give our evidence," respectfully replied the officers. "As soon as we have delivered our prisoner at Spandau, we will announce ourselves to you."

"Then you will receive from me the promised reward of a hundred thalers. If you hush up the entire adventure, so that it is not noised about, after three months, still another hundred."

"We will be silent, Herr Ebenstreit."

"I believe you; a hundred thalers is a pretty sum. Forward, Leberecht, make the postilion push on, that we may arrive in Berlin before daybreak, and no one know of this abominable affair."

The postilion laughed with delight, at the thought of the louis d'or. Upon the box sat Leberecht, a smile of malicious triumph upon his face. "This has been a lucky night," said he; "we have all done a good business, but I am the most fortunate, with my three thousand thalers and a fine place. I wish he had waited an hour later, and then I should have had another thousand!"

Ebenstreit sat with triumphant smile also, by his betrothed. "Money is the king of the world—with it one can accomplish all things," said he to himself; "if I had been a poor fellow, the general would not have chosen me, nor the king have given me a title, nor could I have won back my beautiful bride. Money gives position, and I hope will give me the power to revenge myself for the pain in my face." He turned menacingly toward Moritz, who saw it not.

With bowed head, speechless, as if numb with the horror of his misfortune, he rode with fettered hands between the two officers, incapable of fleeing, as they had even bound a cord around his arms, each end held fast by one of the riders.

The stars and the moon shone down upon him as brightly beautiful as an hour previous. Oh, Marie, you were right, falling stars betoken misfortune! Your star has fallen!

CHAPTER XXVII
THE SACRIFICE

Since that painful night, four weeks had passed, four long ones to poor old Trude. To her beloved child they had fled in happy unconsciousness. In the delirium of fever, her thoughts wandered to her lover, always dwelling upon her hopes and happiness. In the intervals of reason she asked for him with fearful excitement and anxiety, then again her mind was clouded, and the cry of anguish was changed into a smile.

Then came the days of convalescence and the return to consciousness, and with it thc mourning over crushed hopes. Slowly had Trude, the faithful nurse, who watched by her bedside day and night, answered her excited questions, and to her little by little the circumstances of the elopement—how Leberecht had played the eavesdropper and sold Marie's secret for gold; how he had previously arranged to pursue them, informing the police, ordering the horses, and sending forward a courier to provide fresh relays at every station.

Trude depicted the anger of her father and the threats of her mother to send her to prison. But before she could execute her purpose, Ebenstreit had brought home the unconscious child, and she herself had lifted her from the carriage and borne her, with the aid of her mistress, to her own little attic room.

Marie listened to these relations with a gloomy calmness and a defiant sorrow. Illness had wrought a peculiar change in her mind, and hardened the gentle, tender feelings of the young girl. Grief had steeled her soul, benumbed her heart, and she had risen from her couch as one born anew to grief and torture. Her present situation and lost happiness had changed the young, loving, tenderly-sensitive maiden to the courageous, energetic, and defiant woman, who recognized a future of self-renunciation, combat, and resignation.

Trude observed these changes with disquietude and care. She wished Marie would only once complain, or burst into tears. After the first storm of despair had passed, the tears refused to flow, and her eyes were bright and undimmed. Only once had profound emotion been awakened, as Trude asked her if she had forgotten her unhappy lover, and cared no more to learn his fate. It had the desired effect.

A deathly paleness overspread her delicate, transparent cheek. "I know how he is," she said, turning away her face, "I realize his sufferings by my own. We are miserable, lost—and no hope but in death. Ere this comes, there is a desert to traverse in heat, and dust, and storm, and frost, alone, without consolation or support. Hush, Trude! do not seek to revive miserable hopes. I know my fate, and I will endure it. Tell me what you know about him? Where is he? Have they accused him? Speak! do not fear to tell me every thing!" But fearing herself, she threw her handkerchief quickly over her face, and sat with it covered whilst Trude spoke.

"I know but little of poor, dear Moritz. He has never returned to his lodgings. A day or two after that night, two officers sealed his effects, and took away his clothes. His hostess has not the least suspicion of the mysterious disappearance of her otherwise quiet, regular lodger. The secret of the elopement has been carefully guarded, as no one of the neighbors know it, and there is no gossip about you and Moritz. Those who think he is travelling are not surprised at his having left without taking leave, as they say he was accustomed to do so. But," continued Trude, in a lower tone, "Herr Gedicke looked very sad and grave, as I asked for the Conrector Moritz. 'He has disappeared,' he sighed, 'and I know not if we shall ever see him again.' 'Oh, Jemima!' I screamed, 'you do not think that he has committed a self-injury!' 'No,' said the director, 'not he himself, he is too honorable a man. Others have ill-treated him and made him unhappy for life.' It was in vain to ask further; he knew not or he would not say any thing. I believe your family know where poor Moritz is, for your mother speaks of him as one in the penitentiary, and quite triumphantly she told me yesterday that the king, in his new book of laws, had expressly condemned the person who elopes with a minor to be sent to the house of correction for ten years, and then she laughed so cruelly, that I trembled to hear her."

As Trude related this, she searchingly glanced at Marie to observe the effect of her words, hoping to see her weep or complain and that, at last, grief would melt the icy crust around her heart.

But Marie sat motionless and without uttering a sound—not a sigh or a moan escaped her. After a long silence, when her grief was too deep for tears, she drew the handkerchief from her face, the pallor and rigidity of which startled Trude.

She sprang forward, folding her in her arms. "Marie, child of my heart, do weep, do complain! I know that he loved you dearly, and deserves that you should mourn for him. Have you no more confidence, though, in your old Trude? Is she no longer worthy to share your grief?"

Marie laid her languid head upon the bosom of her faithful nurse; a long-drawn, piercing cry of anguish was her response, she trembled violently, and the tears ran down her cheeks.

Trude raised her eyes to heaven, murmuring, "I thank thee, O Lord! Her heart is not dead! It lives, for it suffers!"

"It suffers," groaned Marie, "the anguish of death."

This passionate outburst of feeling was of but short duration. Her tears were dried, and her quivering face assumed its usually calm expression.

"Trude," said she, gently, continuing to repose upon her bosom, "I am so wretched that words cannot express it or tears soothe it. If I should give myself up to sorrow and mourning I should die, and that cannot be, for I must live to wait for him—to rescue him. How I know not yet; my thoughts and resolutions are so confused that they flicker like the ignes fatui. I will force my mind to be calm, and these wandering lights shall unite in one glowing flame to destroy the walls and obstructions which confine him. He is a prisoner; I feel it in my heart, and I must live to free him. This is my task, and I will accomplish it; therefore I would be composed, and strong in myself. Wonder not that I weep or complain no more, and do not refer to my misfortune. I should die if I did not suppress this anguish, and I would become strong and active. Seek not to enfeeble me, but aid me to harden myself; refrain from complaint, that I may be silent. I think only of him, and I ask nothing further than to yield my life to free him. Let us never speak of it again, for I feel that all the firmness which I had gained has been swept from me in this giving way, and that I must begin anew."

From this hour she commenced to build, and rose upon her grief as on a column which projects toward heaven; leaned upon it, and received, as Brisaeus from the earth, the power of life and action. She had already so conquered herself as to be able to leave her own quiet room, and descend to that of her parents. There she would sit calmly for hours, listening attentively to the conversation, hoping to catch some word that might give her a clew.

They avoided every exciting topic, and were milder and more thoughtful for her. Even her mother made no reproaches, and never alluded to the past, because she feared to delay her recovery, and remove the longed-for goal in hindering the marriage with Ebenstreit. The latter carefully avoided troubling her by his presence; when he heard Marie's step in the anteroom, who descended at a certain hour every day, he withdrew by the other entrance.

"Who goes out every time I come in?" asked Marie, one day as she appeared in the sitting-room.

The general coughed with embarrassment, and glanced anxiously at his wife, whose eyes rested upon her daughter with a cold, searching expression. Their eyes met, and were riveted upon each other. A cold, cruel smile played around the thin, bloodless lips of the mother as she recognized the defiance and firmness in her child, and felt that she had recovered.

"It is your betrothed," she answered, "our dear Ebenstreit—a good, generous, and self-sacrificing son, for whom we thank God every day, who wishes to spare you the annoyance of seeing him."

"He need not inconvenience himself on my account. Nothing excites or wounds my feelings now. It would be a pity for your heartless, thankless daughter to deprive you of the society of your dear son. Let him remain; it is not necessary for us to notice one another."

Her parents regarded each other astonished, and, as she ceased, they still listened to the dying tones of her voice, which sounded so strangely to them. "She is much changed," mumbled the general to himself. "She does not seem the same person, she is so haughty and majestic. She might well inspire fear."

The following day, as Marie entered the room, Ebenstreit was there. He approached her, extending both hands smiling, and greeting her with tender words, rejoicing at her recovery.

She took no notice of his friendly demonstrations, but coldly and harshly regarded his smiling face, and particularly the broad, blood-red scar which ran from forehead to chin. Then suddenly her face lighted up, and an expression of savage triumph shot from her eyes. "How disfigured you look," she cried exultingly. "Where did you get that scar?"

"You know well, Marie," he murmured, gloomily.

"Yes," she cried, triumphantly. "I know it. He branded you, and you will wear this mark before God and man as long as you live."

"You are very cruel to remind me of it, Marie," he softly whispered.

She laughed aloud so wild and savagely, that even her mother was startled. "Cruel—I cruel!" she cried. "Ah, sir, it becomes you indeed to accuse me of it!"

Trude entered at this instant, pale and excited.

"What is the matter?"

"There is some one here who wishes to speak with you, Marie; he has something very important to tell you."

"How dare you announce any one without my permission?" cried Frau von Werrig.

"Silence, mother!—if I may be allowed, let us hear who it is.—Speak, dear Trude, who is it?"

"It is the Director Gedicke from the Gray Cloister," said Trude, with quivering voice.

Marie was startled—a glowing red overspread her cheeks, and she was obliged to lean against a chair for support.

"I forbid you to receive him," said her mother.

She suddenly ceased, and stared at the door, which opened at that moment, the tall, dignified form of a venerable old man appearing.

"Pardon me, sir," said he, with a cold, reserved manner, "if I enter before I receive permission. The command of the king, to which I believe we all yield without resistance, empowers me to do so."

"How, sir, you come by the king's order?" asked the general, who rose with difficulty. "Has his majesty given you a message for General von Leuthen?"

"No, general, I come with a communication from his majesty to Fraulein von Leuthen, the betrothed of Herr Ebenstreit, and the order runs to deliver the same personally and without witnesses."

"Professor," cried the mother, shrugging her shoulders, "you mistake us for very innocent people, if you suppose we believe this silly invention, and that you can gain a secret conversation by a ruse with our daughter. You are the director of the gymnasium, and naturally the friend of Conrector Moritz. In his name you will speak, and bring a secret message. Very sly, indeed, very sly, but it will not succeed."

For response, the director drew two large folded documents from his pocket, approaching the general. "Do you recognize this seal?" he asked.

"Yes," solemnly answered the general; "it is the royal seal from the king's private cabinet."

"Read the address upon this, and the unopened letter."

"Truly, the latter is directed to my daughter, and the other to Professor Gedicke."

Herr Gedicke opened the letter, asking the general if he could recognize the king's handwriting.

"Yes," he answered, "I know it well."

"Have the goodness to read the lines upon the margin," mid the professor, unfolding the letter, so that he could only read those referred to.

The general read: "Professor Gedicke shall go himself to Fraulein von Leuthen, and bring her to reason, reading the document to her without witnesses. I wish this affair to come to an end. Teach Mamselle mores! mores! mores! FREDERICK."

"You have heard the royal command, ladies and gentlemen; will you respect it?" said the professor, turning around with an air of proud satisfaction.

"My dear son-in-law," said the general, solemnly, "it is a royal command; give me your arm, as you know I am feeble; and you, my wife, take my other arm, and we will go into the next room. Hush! not a word—we have only to obey, and not reason."

He seized his wife's hand hastily and firmly, that she should not slip away, and winked to Ebenstreit, upon whose support he crossed the room, drawing his wife with him, and pushing open the door of the next with his foot.

Marie had stood during the whole transaction pale and rigid in the centre of the room, looking haughty and defiant as long as her parents and Herr Ebenstreit were present. Now, as the door closed, life and action were visible in this marble form; she rushed to the old gentleman, scarce respiring, and looking up at his dignified, sad face, asked: "Is he living? Tell me only this, or is he ill?"

"Yes, he lives, he does not suffer from bodily ills, but the sickness of the soul."

"And do not I also?" asked she, with quivering voice. "Oh! I know what he suffers, as we are wretched from the same cause. But tell me, have you seen him?"

"Yes, Fraulein, I have."

"Where is he? Where did you see him?"

"In prison!"

Marie grew paler, and retreated, shuddering. The director continued: "In a dark, damp prison at Spandau. The poor fellow has been there for two months without air, light, or occupation, and his only society is his own revengeful thoughts and angry love-complaints."

Marie gave one hollow moan, covering her corpse-like face with her hands.

"In this abode of torture, in this dwelling of the damned, he must remain ten long years, if death does not release him?"

"What did you say?" she groaned. "Ten long years? Have they condemned him?"

"Yes, he was guilty of a great crime—eloping with a minor—who, with the king's consent, and that of her parents, was betrothed to another. Read the sentence of the court, which was forwarded to me as the head of the college where Moritz was employed. See, here is the king's signature, which affirms the sentence, rendering it legal, and here upon the margin are the lines your father read."

Trembling, Marie perused the contents. "Ten years in the house of correction!" she murmured. "On my account condemned to a living death! No, no, it is impossible! It cannot be! Ten years of the best part of life! He condemned as a criminal! I will go to the king. I will throw myself at his feet, imploring for mercy. I am the guilty one—I alone! They should judge me, and send me to the penitentiary! I will go to the king! He must and will hear me!"

"He will not," sighed the director. "Listen to me, poor child! As I heard the sentence, I felt it my duty to summon all my powers to rescue Moritz, for I love him as a son, and had set my hopes upon him."

"I thank you for this kind word," said Marie, seizing the hand of the old man, and pressing it to her lips.

"I went immediately to Minister von Herzberg, and, upon his advice, as he explained to me the king might lighten his punishment, I betook myself to Frederick's winter-quarters at Breslau."

"You noble, generous man, I shall love you for it as long as I live. Did you speak with the king?"

"Yes, and every thing that my heart or mind could inspire, to excuse and justify my unhappy friend, I have said—but all in vain. The king was much embittered, because he had had the grace to grant him an audience, and explain the impossibility of the fulfilment of his petition. I did not cease begging and imploring, until I softened the generous heart of the king."

"Has he pardoned Moritz?" Marie asked, with brightening hopes.

"Under certain conditions he will allow that he should escape secretly from prison. They are formally written, and if Moritz consents and binds himself by oath, he will not only be freed, but provided with means to go to England, and receive immediately an appointment as translator to the Prussian embassy at London."

"What are the conditions, sir?"

"They are, first, that Moritz shall by oath renounce every wish and thought of uniting himself with Fraulein von Leuthen; secondly, that before he leaves the prison, he shall write to the young lady, in which he shall solemnly release her, and enjoin it upon her as a duty to accept the hand of the man to whom her parents have betrothed her. These were the conditions, and the king commanded me to go to Spandau, and with sensible representations, to confer with Moritz, and persuade him to accept them, and assure himself of freedom, and an honorable future, free from care."

"You saw Moritz?"

"Yes."

"Did you communicate the conditions?"

"Yes."

"And he?"

"He refused, with rage and indignation!"

"He refused?" cried Marie, joyfully. "Oh, my dear Philip, I thank you. You love me truly and faithfully. Your glorious example shall inspire me to be as firm as you."

"Unhappy child, you know not what you are saying!" cried the director, sadly. "If you really love him, you could not follow his example. Read what the king has written."

She took, in breathless silence, the document, and broke the seal, unfolding the paper, but her hand shook it so violently, that she could not distinguish the words.

She returned it to the director. "Read it, I cannot," she said, and sank kneeling, looking up to the old man with unspeakable anguish, and listening to every word that fell from his lips. It ran thus:

"His majesty announces to Mademoiselle Marie von Leuthen that he is exceedingly indignant at her improper and undutiful conduct, which does not at all become a maiden loving of honor, and particularly a noble one. His majesty ennobled her father for a brave deed, and he is angry that the daughter should bring shame upon the title, in giving way, not only to a passion which is beneath her, but is so little mindful of morality as to flee from the paternal house, at night, in an improper manner, with a man whose wife, according to the command of the king and the will of her father, she could never be. If his majesty did not respect the former service of her father, and the new title, he would send the daughter to the house of correction, and punish her according to the law. But he will leave her to the reproaches of conscience, and let the weight of the law fall upon her partner in guilt, Philip Moritz. He is rightly sentenced to ten years in the house of correction, and he will not be released one year or one day from the same, as he is guilty of a great crime, and his sentence is just."

"Just!" shrieked Marie, in anguish—"ten years just?"

The director continued to read: "His majesty will propose a last opportunity to the obstinate and inconsiderate young lady to reinstate her own honor, and release at the same time Conrector Moritz. His majesty has personal knowledge of the latter, and respects his scholarly attainments and capability and would bring an end to this affair for the general good. If mademoiselle, as becomes an honorable young woman, and an obedient daughter, follows the wishes of her father, and without delay marries Herr Ebenstreit, and leads a respectable life with him, the same hour of the ceremony Conrector Moritz shall be released, and a fit position be created for him. This is the final decision of the king. If the daughter does not submit in perfect obedience, she will burden her conscience with a great crime, and thank herself for Moritz's unfortunate fate. His majesty will be immediately informed of her decision. If she listens to reason, to morality, and affection, she will submit to the proposition which Director Gedicke is commissioned to make known to her, and announce to her parents in his presence that she will obediently follow their commands, Conrector Moritz will be at once set at liberty; otherwise he will be sent to Brandenburg to the house of correction. This is the unalterable will of the king. Signed, in the name of the king, FREDERICK."

"Now decide, my child," continued the director, after a solemn pause. "I know nothing to add to this royal writing. If it has not itself spoken to your heart, your reason and your honor, words are useless."

"O God, it is cruel—it is terrible!" cried Marie. "Shall I break my oath of constancy, becoming faithless, and suffer him to curse me, for he will never pardon me, but despise me!"

She sprang up like a tigress, with her eyes flashing. "Oh," cried she, "he may even believe that I have been enticed by riches, by a brilliant future! No—no! I cannot consent! May God have mercy on me if the king will not! I will not break my oath! No one but Moritz shall ever be my husband!"

"Unhappy girl," cried the old man, sadly, "I will give you one last inducement. I know not whether you have any knowledge of Moritz's past life, so tried and painful, which has made him easily excited and eccentric. A danger menaces him worse than imprisonment or death. His unaccustomed life, and the solitude of his dark, damp prison, is causing a fearful excitement in him. He is habituated to intellectual occupation. When he is obliged to put on the prisoner's jacket in the house of correction and spin wool, it will not kill him—it will make him mad!"

A piercing cry was Marie's answer. "That is not true—it is impossible. He crazy!—you only say that to compel me to do what you will. His bright mind could not be obscured through the severest proofs."

"You do not believe me? You think that an old man, with gray hair, and one foot in the grave, and who loves Moritz, could tell you a shameful untruth! I swear to you by the heads of my children, by all that is holy, that Moritz already suffers from an excitement of the brain; and if he does not soon have liberty and mental occupation, it is almost certain that he will become insane."

Almost convulsed with anguish, Marie seized the old man's hand with fierce passion. "He shall not be crazed," she shrieked. "He shall not suffer—he shall not be imprisoned and buried in the house of correction on my account. I will rescue him—I and my love! I am prepared to do what the king commands! I will—marry the man—which—my parents have chosen. But—tell me, will he then be free?"

"To-day even—in three hours, my poor child!"

"Free! And I shall have saved him! Tell me what I have to do. What is the king's will?"

"First sign this document," said the director, as he drew a second paper. "It runs thus: 'I, Marie von Leuthen, that of my own free will and consent I will renounce every other engagement, and will marry Herr Ebenstreit von Leuthen, and be a faithful wife to him. I witness with my signature the same.'"

"Give it to me quickly," she gasped. "I will sign it! He must be free! He shall not go mad!"

She rapidly signed the paper. "Here is my sentence of death! But he will live! Take it!"

"My child," cried the old man, deeply agitated, "God will be mindful of this sacrifice, and in the hour of death it will beam brightly upon you. You have by this act rescued a noble and excellent being, and when he wins fame from science and art he will owe to you alone the gratitude."

"He shall not thank me!" she whispered. "He shall live and—if he can be happy!—this is all that I ask for! What is there further to be done?"

"To announce to your parents in my presence that you will marry Herr Ebenstreit, and let the ceremony take place as soon as possible."

"You swear that he shall then be released? You are an old man—reflect well; you swear to me that as soon as the marriage takes place, Philip Moritz will be free this very day and that he will be reinstated in an honorable, active occupation?"

"I swear it to you upon my word of honor, by my hope of reward from above."

"I believe you. Call my parents. But first—you are a father, and love your children well. I have never had a father who loved me, or ever laid his hand upon my head to bless me. You say that you love Moritz as a son! Oh, love me for a moment as your daughter, and bless me!"

The old man folded her in his arms, tears streaming down his cheeks. "God bless you, my daughter, as I bless you!"

"I dare not tarry," she shuddered. "Let my parents enter."

Slowly the venerable man traversed the room. Marie pressed her hands to her heart, looking to heaven. As the door opened, and the general entered, leaning upon Ebenstreit's arm, followed by his wife, Marie approached them with a haughty, determined manner, who regarded her with astonishment.

"Father," she said, slowly and calmly, "I am ready to follow your wishes. Send for the clergyman: I consent to marry this man to-day, upon one condition."

"Make it known, my dear Marie. Name your condition. I will joyfully fulfil it," said Ebenstreit.

"I demand that we leave to-day for the East, to go to Egypt—Palestine—and remain away from this place for years. Are you agreed to it?"

"To all that which my dear Marie wishes."

"You can now weave the bridal-wreath in my hair, mother. I consent to the marriage."

Three hours later the preparations were completed. Every thing had awaited this for three months.

In the sitting-room, the decorators had quickly built a marriage-altar, and ornamented the walls with garlands of flowers, with festoons of gauze and silk, with flags and standards. The mother wore the costly silk which her rich son-in-law had honored her with for the occasion, and also adorned herself with the gold ornaments which were equally his gift. The father wore his gold-embroidered uniform, and imagined himself a stately figure, as the gout left him the use of his limbs this day.

The invited witnesses began to assemble. Just then Ebenstreit von Leuthen drove up in the handsome travelling-carriage, which was a wedding-gift to his wife, and excited the admiration of the numerous street public.

Old Trude, in her simple dark Sunday dress, had awaited the appearance of the bridegroom, and went to announce his arrival to the bride.

Marie was in her little garret-room, so unlike in its present appearance to its former simplicity and comfort—as unlike as the occupant to the rosy, smiling young girl, who, yonder by the little brown table in the window-niche, taught her pupils, or with busy, skilful hands made the loveliest flowers, the income of which she gave to her parents, joyfully and although she never received thanks or recognition for the same. Now the same little table was covered with morocco cases, whose half-open covers revealed brilliant ornaments, laces, and sweet perfumes; superb silk dresses, cloaks, and shawls, ornamented with lace, lay about upon the bed and chairs.

Herr Ebenstreit von Leuthen had truly given his bride a princely dowry, and her mother had spread the things around room.

Since Marie gave her consent to the marriage, she had followed out their wishes without opposition. She wore a white satin dress, covered with gold lace, her arms, neck, and ears, adorned with diamonds. The coiffeur had powdered and arranged her hair, without her ever casting a glance into the Psyche-mirror which her betrothed had had the gallantry to send to her room. She let him arrange the costly bridal veil; but when he would place the crown of myrtle, she waved him back.

"Your work is finished," she said; "my mother will place that, I thank you."

As Trude entered, Marie was standing in the centre of the room, regarding it with sinister, angry looks.

"There you are, Trude," she said, "I am glad to see you a moment alone, for I have something to tell you. I have spoken with my future husband, demanding that you live with me as long as I live. Immediately after the ceremony you will go to my future home and remain there as house-keeper during my absence."

Sadly the old woman shook her head. "No, that is too important a place for me. I will not lead a lazy life, and play the fine woman. I was made to work with my hands."

"Do what you will in the house," answered Marie. "Only promise me that you will not leave me, and when I return that I shall find you there. If you leave me, I will never come back. Promise me!"

"Then I will promise you, my poor child," sighed Trude.

Marie laughed scornfully. "You call me poor—do you not see I am rich? I carry a fortune about my neck. Go, do not bewail me—I am rich!"

"Marie, do not laugh so, it makes me feel badly," whispered the old woman. "I came to tell you the bridegroom and the clergyman are there."

"The time has arrived for the marriage of the rich and happy bride. Go, Trude, beg my mother to come up and adorn me with the myrtle-wreath."

"Dear Marie, can I not do it?" asked Trude, with quivering voice.

"No, not you; touch not the fatal wreath! You have no part in that! Call my mother—it is time!"

Trude turned sadly toward the door, Marie glancing after her, and calling her back with gentle tone.

"Trude, my dear, faithful mother, kiss me once more." She threw her arms around Marie's neck and imprinted a loving kiss upon her forehead, weeping. "Now go, Trude—we must not give way; you know me; you well understand my feelings, and see into my heart."

The old woman went out, drying her eyes. Marie uttered her last farewell. "With you the past goes forth, with you my youth and hope! When the door again opens, my future enters a strange, fearful life. Woe to those who have prepared it for me—woe to those who have so cruelly treated me! They will yet see what they have done. The good angel is extinct within me. Wicked demons will now assume their over me. I will have no pity—I will revenge myself; that I swear to Moritz!"

Her mother rustled in, clothed in her splendid wedding-garments. "Did you send for me, dear Marie?" she whispered.

"Yes, mother—I beg you to put on my myrtle-wreath."

"How! have you no endearment for me?" she asked, smilingly. "Why do you say 'you' instead of 'thou?'"

"It is better so, mother," she coldly answered. "Will you adorn me with the bridal-wreath?"

"Willingly, my dear child; it is very beautiful and becoming."

"Do you realize, mother, what you are doing? You place the wreath to consecrate me to an inconsolably unhappy life with the man that I hate and despise!"

"My dear child, I know that you think so to-day; but you will soon change, and find that wealth is a supportable misfortune."

"Mother, one day you will recall these words. Crown me for the hated bridal. The sacrifice is prepared!"

BOOK IV
THE VISIBLES AND THE INVISIBLES

CHAPTER XXVIII
OLD FRITZ

The war terminated, the hostile armies returned to their different German countries. Frederick the Great had gained his point, forcing Austria to renounce the possession of Bavaria. The Prince of Zweibruecken had been solemnly recognized by him as the rightful heir to the electorate, and the lawful ruler and possessor of Bavaria. The Emperor Joseph had submitted with profound regret and bitter animosity to the will of his mother, the reigning empress, and consented to the peace negotiations of Baron von Thugut. Having signed the document of the same, in his quality of co-regent, he angrily threw aside the pen, casting a furious glance at the hard, impenetrable face of Thugut, saying: "Tell her majesty that I have accomplished my last act as co-regent, and I now abdicate. From henceforth I will still lie her obedient son, but no submissive joint ruler, to only follow devotedly her imperial will. Therefore I resign, and never will trouble myself in future about the acts of the government." The emperor kept his word. He retired, piqued, into solitude, wounded in the depths of his soul, and afterward travelled, leaving the government entirely to the empress and her pious confessors.

Bavaria was rescued! It owed its existence to the watchfulness, sagacity, and disinterested aid of Prussia's great king. The Elector Maximilian vowed in his delight that he, as well as his successors and heirs, would never forget that Bavaria must ascribe its continuance to Prussia alone, and therefore the gratitude of the princes of this electorate could not and never would be extinguished toward the royal house of Prussia. Frederick received these overflowing acknowledgments with the calmness of a philosopher and the smile of a skeptic. He understood mankind sufficiently to know what to expect from their oaths; to know that in the course of time there is nothing more oppressive and intolerable than gratitude, that it soon becomes a burden which they would gladly throw off their bent shoulders at any price, and become the enemy of him to whom they had sworn eternal thankfulness. Frederick regarded these oaths of Bavaria not as a security for the future, but as a payment on account of the past.

"I did not go forth to render the Bavarian princes indebted to me," said he, to his only confidante, Count Herzberg, as he brought to him, at Sans-Souci, the renewed expression of thanks of the prince elector. "I would only protect Germany against Austria's grasp, and preserve the equilibrium of the German empire. Believe me, the house of Hapsburg is a dangerous enemy for the little German principalities, and if my successor does not bear it in mind, and guard himself against their flatteries and cat's-paws, Austria will fleece him as the cat the mouse who is enticed by the odor of the bacon. Prussia shall be neither a mouse in the German empire, nor serve as a roast for Austria. But she shall be a well-trained shepherd's dog for the dear, patient herd, and take care that none go astray and are lost."

"Your majesty has drawn an unfortunate character for the future of our country," sighed Herzberg, thoughtfully, "and I must grant that it is sketched with severe but correct outlines so it follows that poor Germany has many combats and hardships in store."

"What do you mean?" asked the king. "What characteristic did I name?"

"Your majesty pointed out Austria as the cat watching for prey in Germany. Prussia, on the contrary, as the shepherd's dog, which should watch the native herd, and occasionally bite those who wander from the flock. The comparison is apt, and clearly exposes the natural hostility of the two nations. Nature has placed the cat and the dog in eternal enmity, and there is no compromise to be thought of, to say nothing of friendship. There may, now and then, be a truce; the cat may draw in her claws, and the dog may cease to howl and growl, but the combat will renew itself, and never end, but in the death of one party, and the victorious triumph of the other."

"You are right," said the king, nodding slightly. "From this natural hostility will proceed many combats and storms for our land, and much blood will be shed on its account. Let us look to the future, and try to ward off the coming evil, in erecting high barriers against the cat-like springs of the enemy. I will think out a security for Germany. But first, mon cher ami, we have to care for our own country and people. The war has greatly injured my poor subjects. Industry is prostrated and prosperity disturbed. We must seek new sources of acquisition, and sustain those which are exhausted. For this, we must think of fresh taxes, and other sources of income."

"Sire," said Herzberg, shrugging his shoulders, "the taxes are already so heavy that it will be difficult to increase them."

"You are greatly mistaken," cried the king, with increased animation. "I will impose a tax upon those things which are now exempt, and establish a capable administration for the purpose. Bread, flour, meat, and beer, the sustenance of the poor, shall remain as they are, for I will not that they shall pay more. But tobacco, coffee, and tea, are superfluous things, which the prosperous and rich consume. Whoever will smoke, and drink tea or coffee, can and shall pay for being a gourmand!"

"I beg pardon, but it is just these taxes which will create the greatest discontent," answered Herzberg. "Your majesty will remember that the duty on coffee was complained of and criticised by every one, and the poor people grumbled more than all. In spite of the resistance of government, coffee has become, more and more, a means of nourishment and refreshment for the lower class."

"I will teach them to renounce it," cried the king, striking the table violently with his staff "I will not suffer so much money to go out of the country for this abominable beverage! My people shall re-learn to drink their beer, instead of this infamous stuff, as I had to do when a young man. What was good enough for the crown prince of Prussia, will to-day suffice for his subjects. I tell you, Herzberg, I will teach them to drink their beer, or pay dearly for this bad, foreign stuff. Then we will see which will conquer, Prussian beer or foreign coffee."

"It is possible that the former will be victorious on account of their poverty and the high duties; but in any case the people will be discontented, and grumble against your majesty."

"Do you suppose that I care for that?" asked the king, with a quick, fiery glance at the calm, earnest face of his confidant. "Do you think that I care for the applause of the people, or trouble myself about their complaints? I regard their shouting or their grumbling about as much as the humming or buzzing of a fly upon the wall. If it dares to light upon my nose, I brush it off; and if I can, I catch it. Beyond that, it is its nature to hum and buzz. Herzberg, you understand that if a ruler should listen to the praises or discontent of his subjects, he would soon be a lost man, and would not know his own mind. The people are changeable as the weather; to-morrow they crush under their feet what to-day they bore aloft, and praise one day what they stone the next. Do not talk to me about the people! I know this childish, foolish mass, and he is lost who counts upon their favor. It is all the same to me whether they like or hate me. I shall always do my duty to my subjects according to the best of my knowledge and ability, as it becomes an honorable and faithful officer. As the chief and most responsible servant of my kingdom, I should be mindful to increase her income and diminish her expenses—to lay taxes upon the rich, and lighten them for the poor. This is my task, and I will fulfil it so long as I live!"

"Oh," cried Herzberg, with enthusiasm, "would that the entire nation might hear these words, and engrave them upon their hearts!"

"Why that, mon cher?" asked Frederick, shrugging his shoulders. "I do not ask to be deified; my subjects are perfectly welcome to discuss my acts, so long as they pay me punctually, and order and quiet are respected and preserved."

"All that is done," said Herzberg, joyfully. "The machine of state is so well arranged, that she has fulfilled her duty during the war, and will soon reestablish prosperity."

"Particularly," cried the king, "if we rightly understand the art of agriculture. In the end every thing depends upon him who best cultivates his field. This is the highest art, for without it there would be no merchants, courtiers, kings, poets, or philosophers. The productions of the earth are the truest riches. He who improves his ground, brings waste land under the plough, drains the swamps, makes the most glorious conquests over barbarism."

"And those are also conquerors, sire," said Herzberg, smiling, "who drain the mental swamps, and improve the waste mental ground. Such are those who increase the schools and instruct the people. I have caused the school authorities to report to me, according to your majesty's command. A happy progress has been noticed everywhere. Cultivation and education are advancing; and since our teachers have adopted the principles of Rousseau, a more humane spirit is perceptible throughout our schools."

"What principle do we owe to Jean Jacques?" asked the king.

"Sire, the principle that man is good by nature!"

"Ah, mon cher, who says that knows but little of the abominable race to which we belong!" *[Footnote: The king's words.—See "Prussia." vol. iv., p. 221.]*

"Do you not believe in this doctrine?" asked Herzberg.

The king raised his large blue eyes musingly to the busts placed upon the bookcases, and around the walls. They lingered long upon those of Homer, Plato, and D'Alembert; then turned to that of Voltaire, with its satyr-like face. "No, I do not believe it," he sadly responded. "Mankind is an ignoble race; still one must love them, for among the wicked are always some worthy ones, whose light beams so brightly clear, that they change night into day. During my life I have learned to know many base, miserable creatures, but I have become reconciled to them, as I have also found some who were virtuous and excellent—some who were noble and beautiful, as the grains of wheat among the chaff. You belong to the latter, my Herzberg; and as in heaven many unjust will be forgiven for one just person, so will I upon earth forgive on your account the Trencks, Schaffgotschs, Goernes, Voltaires, Wallraves, Glasows, Dahsens, and all the traitors, poisoners, and perfidious ones, as they may be called. Remain by my side and sustain me, to prevent many a wicked thing and bring to pass much that is good. I shall always be grateful to you in my heart for it; that you can depend upon even if my weather-beaten face looks ill-humored, and my voice is peevish. Remember that I am a fretful old man, who is daily wasting away, approaching that bourne from which no traveller has ever returned."

"God grant that your majesty may be far removed from this bourne!" said Herzberg, with emotion. "And He may grant it on account of your subjects, who are so much in need of your care and government."

"There is no one upon earth who could not be replaced," said the king, shaking his head. "When I am gone, they will shout to my successor. I trust my subjects will exchange a good ruler for their fretful old king. I have been very well satisfied with him during the campaign, and he has shown ability in the diplomatic mission to St. Petersburg. He has proved himself a soldier and a diplomat, and I hope he will become a great king. Herzberg, why do you not answer me, but cast down your eyes? What does your silence mean?"

"Nothing at all—truly nothing! The crown prince has a noble, generous heart, a good understanding; only—"

"Why hesitate, Herzberg? Go on—what is your 'only?'"

"I would only say that the crown prince must beware and not be governed by others."

"Oh, you mean that he will be ruled by mistresses and favorites?"

"I do fear it, your majesty! You well know that the crown princes are generally the antipodes of those ascendant to the throne. If the ruler has only an enlightened mind, and is free from prejudices, so—"

"Is his crown prince an obscurer," added quickly the king, "having the more prejudices, and is capable of being ruled by mystics and exorcists. Is not that your meaning?"

Count Herzberg nodded. The king continued with animation: "Some one has told me of a new friend who returned from the war with the prince, and who belongs to the Rosicrucians and exhorters, and hopes to find many adherents here for such deceptions. Is it true?"

"Yes, sire. It is Colonel Bischofswerder, a Rosicrucian and necromancer and of course of very pleasant address. He has indeed already gained much power over the impressible mind of Frederick William, and his importance is greatly on the increase."

"What does the crown prince's mistress say to it? Is she not jealous?"

"Of which one does your majesty speak?"

The king started, and his eyes flashed. "What!" he cried with vehemence, "is there a question of several? Has the crown prince others besides Wilhelmine Enke, whom I have tolerated?"

"Sire, unfortunately, the prince has not a very faithful heart. Besides, it is Bischofswerder's plan, as I suppose, to separate him from Wilhelmine, who will not subordinate herself to him, and who even dares to mock the necromancers and visionaries, and oppose them to the crown prince."

"Does Enke do that?" asked the king.

"Yes, sire," answered Herzberg, as the king rose and slowly paced the room. "And one must acknowledge that in that she does well and nobly. Otherwise one cannot reproach her. She leads a quiet, retired life, very seldom leaving her beautiful villa at Charlottenburg, but devotes herself to the education of her children. She is surrounded with highly-educated men, savants, poets, and artists, who indeed all belong to the enlightened, the so-called Illuminati, and which are a thorn in the eye to Colonel Bischofswerder. Your majesty will perceive that I have some good informants in this circle, and the latest news they bring me is that the bad influence is upon the increase. The Rosicrucians reproach the prince for his immoral connection with Wilhelmine Enke, as they would replace her by one who gives herself up to them."

"That shall not take place," cried the king. "No, we will not suffer that; and particularly when we are forced to recognize such abominable connections, we should endeavor to choose the most desirable. I cannot permit that this person, who has at least heart and understanding, should be pushed aside by Bischofswerder. My nephew shall retain her, and she shall drive away the Rosicrucians with all their deviltries. Herzberg, go and tell the crown prince, from me, that I order—"

His majesty suddenly stopped, and looked at Herzberg with surprise, who was smiling.

"Why do you laugh, Herzberg?"

"I was not laughing, sire. If my lip quivered against my will, it was because I stupidly and foolishly dared to finish the broken sentence."

"Well, how did you manage to conclude it?"

"Sire, your majesty said, 'Tell the crown prince that I order him'—and there you ceased. I added 'order him to love Wilhelmine Enke, and be faithful to her.' I beg pardon for my mistake. I should have known that your majesty could never command the execution of that which is not to be forced; that my great king recognizes, as well as I, that love is not compulsory, or fidelity either. Pardon me for my impertinence, and tell me the order which I shall take to the crown prince from my beloved king and master."

The king stepped close up to the minister, and gazed with a half-sad, half-tender expression in the noble and gentle face of Herzberg, and in the sensible brown eyes, which sank not beneath the fiery glance of Frederick. Then, slowly raising his hand from the staff, he menaced him with his long, bony forefinger.

"Herzberg, you are a rogue, and will teach me morals. Indeed, you are right—love is not compulsory, but one can sometimes aid it. Say nothing to the prince. The interior of his house must, indeed, be left to himself, but we will keep our eyes open and be watchful. Do so also, Herzberg, and if you discover any thing, tell me; and if Wilhelmine Enke needs assistance against the infamous Rosicrucians, and with her aid this mystic rabble can be suppressed, inform me, and I am ready to send her succor. Ah! Herzberg, is it not a melancholy fact that one must fight his way through so much wickedness to obtain so little that is good? My whole life has passed in toil and trouble; I have grown old before my time, and would rest from my labors, and harvest in the last few years, what I have sown in a lifetime. Is it not sad that I hope for no fruit, and that the seed that I have scattered will be trodden under foot by my successor? I must gaze at the future without joy, without consolation!"

The king turned to the window, perhaps to hide the tears which stood in his eyes. Herzberg did not presume to interrupt the sad silence, but gazed with an expression of the deepest sympathy at the little bent form, in the threadbare coat. Grief filled his heart at the thought that this head was not only bowed down by the weight of years and well-deserved laurels, but also from its many cares and griefs, and hopeless peering into the future.

The king turned again, and his eyes were bright and un-dimmed. "We must never lose courage," said he, "and we must have a reserve corps in life as well as upon the field of battle. For the world resembles the latter, and the former is a continual war, in which we must not be discouraged nor cast down, if there is not hope in our souls. I will cling to As you have said, and I have also found it true, that crown prince is a good and brave man, and possesses a keen understanding, we may succeed in bringing him from the erroneous ways in which his youth, levity, and the counsels of wicked friends have led him. We will try with kindness and friendliness, as I believe these have more effect upon him. Let us not even scorn to aid Wilhelmine in so far as is compatible with honor. If a mistress is necessary to the happiness of the prince, this one seems the most worthy of all to encourage. Beyond the clouds the stars are still shining, and it appears to me as if I see in perspective in the heaven of Prussia's future, a star which promises a bright light with years. Do you not think with me, the little Prince Frederick William is a rising star?"

"Yes, your majesty," answered Herzberg, joyfully, "He is a splendid little boy, of simple and innocent heart, and bright, vigorous mind, modest and unpretending."

"You see," cried the king, evidently cheered, "there is one star and we will watch over it, that it is not obscured. I must see the prince oftener. He shall visit me every month and his governors and teachers shall report to me every quarter. We will watch over his education, and train him to be a good king for the future, and guard ourselves against being pusillanimous, foolish, and fretful, and not be discouraged in life. I have entered my last lustrum, or five years. Hush! do not dispute it, but believe me! My physique is worn out, and the mental grows dull, and although I live and move about, I am half in the grave. There are two coffins in this room, which contain the greater part of my past. Look around, do you not see them?"

"No," said Herzberg, as he glanced at the different articles of furniture, "I see none."

"Look upon the table by the window—what do you there see?"

"Your majesty, there is an instrument-case and a sword-sheath."

"They are the ones I refer to. In the case lies my flute, that is to say, my youth, love, poesy, and art, are encoffined there. In the sheath is my sword, which is my manhood, energy, laurels, and fame. I will never play the flute or draw the sword again. All that is past!"

"But there still remains for the great king a noble work to perfect," cried Herzberg. "Youth has flown, and the war-songs are hushed. The poet and hero will change to the lawgiver. Sire, you have made Prussia great and powerful externally; there remains a greater work, to make her the same within. You have added new provinces, give them now a new code of laws. You will no longer unsheath the sword of the hero; then raise that of justice high above your subjects!"

"I will," cried the king, with beaming eyes. "You have rightly seized and comprehended what alone seems to me worthy of will and execution. There shall be but one law for the high and the low, the poor and the rich. The distinguished Chancellor Carmer shall immediately go to work upon it, and you shall aid him. The necessity of such a reform we have lately felt in the Arnold process, where the judge decided in favor of the rich, and wronged the poor man. How could the judge sustain Count Schmettau against the miller Arnold, who had been deprived of the water for his mill, when it was so evident that it was unjust?"

"I beg pardon, majesty, but I believe the judge obeyed the very letter of the law, and—"

"Then this law must be annulled," interrupted the king. "This is why I revoked the judge's sentence, and sent the obstinate fellows to the fortress, sustaining the miller in his right deposing the arrogant Chancellor Furst. I had long resolved upon it, for I knew that he was a haughty fellow, who let the poor crowd his anteroom, and listened to the flattery of the high-born rabble who courted him. I only waited an occasion to bow his haughty head. This offered, and I availed myself of it, voila tout. It is to be hoped that it will be good example for all courts of justice. They will remember that the least peasant and beggar is a human being as much as the king, and that justice should be accorded to if they do not, they will have to deal with me. If a college of justice practises injustice, it is more dangerous than a band of robbers; for one can protect himself from the latter but the former are rascals wearing the mantle of justice, to exercise their own evil passions, from whom no man can protect himself, and they are the greatest scoundrels in the world and deserve a double punishment. I therefore deposed the unjust judge, and sent him to the fortress at Spandau, that all might take warning by his fate." *[Footnote: The king's own words.—Seo "Prussia, Frederick the Great," vol. iv.]*

"This Arnold trial belongs to history," said Herzberg. "The lawyers will refer to it after the lapse of centuries, and the poor and the oppressed will recall and bless the thoughtfulness of the great king, who would open just as wide a gate for them to enter the heaven of justice as to the rich and noble. This new code of laws will beam above the crown of gold and of laurels, with the splendor of the civil crown, whose brilliants are the tears of gratitude of your people."

"May it be so," said Frederick, with earnestness. "Now tell me, do you know what day of the month it is?"

"Sire, it is the 30th of May.'"

"Yes, you will remember it is the anniversary of Voltaire's death, and after I have quarrelled for two years with the priests and so-called holy fathers at Rome, I have gained my point, and the honor shall be shown him here in Berlin which the priests and friars have refused to the immortal poet in his own country. To-day, exactly at the hour which Voltaire died, the mass for the dead will be read in the Catholic church, to free his immortal soul from purgatory. I have, indeed, no idea of an immortal soul. If there are any, and if it has to endure the threefold heat of which Father Tobias, of Silesia, related to me, I do not believe that the priests, for a few thalers, can loose the unhappy spirit from the bake-oven. But as they refuse burial to the spirit of Voltaire, in order to insult him after death, so must I avail myself of this occasion to offer a last homage to the great poet, which will take place at four o'clock. Go to the mass, Herzberg, and tell me to-morrow how it went off—whether the priests make right pious faces and burn much incense. Adieu. Au revoir, demain."

As the king dismissed, with a friendly wave of the hand, his confidential minister, he passed into his cabinet, remaining an hour with his counsellors. At dinner appeared some of the generals, weather-worn and bent, with wrinkled faces and dull eyes. Souvenirs of the glorious years of fame and victory. The king nodded kindly to them, but during the entire meal, he only let some indifferent questions fall from his lips, which were devotedly and tediously answered by some one of the old generals. As their dry, peevish voices resounded through the high, vaulted room, it seemed to reawaken in Frederick's heart the souvenirs of memory and become the echo of vanished days. He gazed up at the little Cupids, in the varied play of bright colors, looking down from the clouds, and the goddesses trumpeting through their long tubes the fame of the immortal, the same as formerly, when they smiled from the clouds upon the beaming face of the young king, dining in the distinguished circle of his friends Voltaire, D'Argens, Algarotti, La Melbrie, and Keith.

The Cupids were fresh as ever, and the goddesses had not removed the trumpets from their lips. But where were the of the merry round-table? Returned to dust. The jests and poesy have died away—all have sunken to decay and darkness. The king silently raised his glass of Tokay, gazing up to the clouds and Cupids, draining it slowly in sacrifice for the dead. Then with a vehement, contemptuous movement, he threw the glass over his shoulder, shivering it into a thousand pieces. The old generals, after dessert, had gently sunk into their afternoon nap, and now started, frightened, looking wildly around, as if they expected the enemy were approaching. Alkmene crept from under the king's chair muffing with her long, delicate nose, the glistening pieces of glass, and the footman bent himself to carefully pick them up.

The king rose silently, saluting the old generals, pointing with his staff to the large folding-doors which led to the garden.

The footmen hastened forward to open them, and stand in stiff, military order upon each side. Frederick walked slowly out, mounting the two steps which led to the upper terrace, signing to the attendants to close the doors.

He was alone. Only Windspiel was there to spring about joyfully, barking, and turning to meet him, who wandered on the border of the terrace, where he had formerly walked with his friends. Now he stopped to gaze up the broad, deserted steps which led from terrace to terrace, as if he could re-people them with the well-known forms, and could see them approach and greet him with the look of endless love and constancy. Then he raised his eyes to heaven, as if to seek there those he in vain sought upon earth.

"Do you not see me, my friends?" he asked, in a gentle but sad voice. "Do you not look down wonderingly where you saw a cheerful, smiling king, upon the now bent, shrunken old man, cold and phlegmatic, who seldom speaks, and then causes every one to yawn? Oh, where have you fled, beautiful spring-time of life—wherein once we used to enliven our conversations with the wit of the Athenians, and the jest fluttered upon our lips as we glided through life in the bold enjoyment of youth? Banished is the dance, and I creep about, leaning upon my staff, enfeebled in body, and with saddened heart! Oh, awful change, unhappy old age! What does it aid me that I am a king? I have won many a battle, but now I am vanquished by age and death and am alone!" *[Footnote: The king's words.—See "Posthumous Works," vol. x., p. 100.]*

A slight breeze rustled through the trees, fanning, caressingly, the cheeks of the king. The perfume of sweet flowers rose from the terrace, and below rushed the cascade. The marble groups around the fountain glistened in the golden rays of the sun, and in the dark foliage fluttered and sang the merry birds of summer.

Suddenly the wind wafted from the church at Potsdam the clear tones of a bell, announcing to the king the hour of four, the death of Voltaire.

The king walked along to the rose-arbor, to the temple of friendship, where the bust of his sister Frederika was placed. He seated himself near the entrance, listening to the ringing voice of the bell, and recalling that the death-mass had now commenced in Berlin.

The service sacred to memory! The prayer for the immortal soul! As the lonely king sat there, calm and bowed down, a solemn prayer and holy mass rose from his own soul. He bowed lower his head, and, without realizing it himself, traced letters in the sand at his feet, with no witness but the blue heavens above him, and Windspiel who curiously eyed the lines. Thinking of the prayer for Voltaire's undying soul, the king had written the word of profoundest mystery and revelation, of hope and prophecy—"Immortality."

The wind gently rustled in the trees, wafting the perfume of flowers. Sweet stillness reigned around, and lowly sang the birds as if not to waken the king, who slept by the marble form of his beloved sister—Windspiel upon his knees, and in the sand at his feet the word traced by his own hand, "Immortality."

CHAPTER XXIX
CAGLIOSTRO'S RETURN

Wilhelmine Enke was still living at her villa at Charlottenburg. She was, as formerly, the "unmarried" daughter of the hautboy-player, the favorite and friend of the crown prince; the same as two years previous, when he presented her before the Bavarian campaign, with this house and There was no change in her outward circumstances; her life passed regularly and calmly. The once fresh and beautiful cheek had lost somewhat of its youthful, roseate hue, and the smile of the ruby lips was less haughty, and the warmth of those brilliant eyes was subdued. This was the only perceptible difference wrought by the little vexations and troubles incident to her position. She had found some bitter drops in the golden goblet which the prince in his love pressed to her lips—drops which were uncongenial to lips accustomed to the sweets of life.

To-day she had awaited him at dinner, and had just received a very friendly but laconic letter, excusing himself until the following morning. This was an unpalatable drop. Wilhlemine paced back and forth the solitary, gloomy path, at the foot of the garden, re-reading this letter, and examining every word to search out its hidden meaning.

"They have brought this about," she murmured, tearing the letter into little pieces, which lighted upon the shrubbery like butterflies. "Yes, it is their work. They have sought by all possible means to draw him into their power, and away from me. And they will succeed, as there are two of them, and the princess sustains them; and I am alone, unsupported. I am entirely alone—alone!"

"If you are alone, then, it is surely your own fault," said an earnest, solemn voice, and at the same instant a tall form approached from the shrubbery which bordered the side of the garden.

"Cagliostro!" shrieked Wilhelmine, shrinking terrified away. "Oh, mercy upon me, it is Cagliostro!"

"Why are you so frightened, my daughter?" he asked, gently. "Why do you withdraw from me, and cast down your eyes?"

"I thought you were in Courland," she stammered, confused.

"And whilst you thought me afar, you forgot your sacred oath and holy duty," he replied, in a harsh, severe tone. "Oh my daughter, the Invisibles weep and lament bitterly over you."

"I am curious to see these tears," said Wilhelmine, who had now recovered her self-composure. "Do you think, Herr Magus, any of them could be found in the eyes of Colonel Bischofswerder and his intimate friend Woellner? Do you pretend that they also weep over me?"

"They do not belong to the Invisibles, but the Visibles. But their souls are true and faithful, and would have to mourn over the unhappy one who could forget her vows."

"Then allow me to say that I abjure these tears, and laugh at the idea that these hypocrites and necromancers weep over me."

"My daughter, what words are these, and how strangely altered you are! I have come from the far north, and but just alighted from the travelling-carriage. I came at once to see you, and hoped to be greeted joyfully with a kiss of love, and what do I hear instead? Harsh words filled with scorn and mockery, and disobedience against the Invisible Fathers, to whom you have sworn fidelity and submission!"

"You have forced me to it!" she cried, impetuously. "In my own house you came upon me and compelled me to take part in your mystic assembly."

"If one loves humanity, he must insist upon its accepting happiness," said Cagliostro, solemnly. "We recognized in you one of the elect, one of the great souls which are worthy to see the light, and sun themselves in the rays of knowledge. Therefore we accepted you among the spirits of the alliance, and—"

"And made great promises, of which not one has been fulfilled. Where is the title of countess, the influence, position, honor, and dignity, which you prophesied to me?"

"Where are the deeds you promised to perform, the witnesses of your fidelity and devotion?" he thunderingly demanded. "You have dared to rebel against the holy alliance! Your short-sighted spirit presumes to mock those eyes which perceive that you are straying away! Beware—Wilhemine, beware! I came to-day to warn you, when I return it will be to punish you. Turn, oh turn while there is yet time! Submit your will to the Fathers, as you have sworn to do! The promised reward will not fail, and Wilhelmine Enke will become a countess, a princess, and the most distinguished and powerful will bow before her. The Fathers demand of you repentance, and renunciation of the worst enemies of the Rosicrucians. Members, and even chiefs and pioneers of the Illuminati and Freemasons are welcomed at your house."

"Why should they not be?" asked she, smiling. "They are happy, cheerful spirits, void of mysteries, and do not torture people with mysticisms. They have but one aim, a great and glorious one, to free the mind from superstition and hypocrisy. They encounter with open countenance the false devotees who would force men into spiritual servitude, that they may become the slaves of their will. You call them 'Illuminati,' while they have undertaken to illuminate the minds with the beams of knowledge which the Rosicrucians obscure in a mystical fog."

"Unhappy one, do you dare to say that to me?" cried Cagliostro, menacingly.

"Yes," she responded, keeping her large, brown eyes firmly fixed upon Cagliostro's angry face. "That I dare to repeat to you, and I would also remark that we are not in the mystical assembly of the Rosicrucians, and your familiar 'Du' is out of place. I belong to the Illuminati, and mingle with the freethinkers. They have not, indeed, promised me titles, honors, or dignities, but they have amused me, have driven ennui from the house, and instead of mysticisms, brought me poesy, and instead of the invisible holy church, the Greek temple. It is possible my life may not be a godly one, but it is as happy as the gods, and that is something in this tedious world."

"I regard you with astonishment," said Cagliostro, "for I recognize in your countenance that the devil has won you over to his power, and in you he speaks with the bold insolence of the sinful. Subdue, unhappy child, your rash speech, that the Fathers may not hear of it, and crush you in their wrath."

"I do not fear their thunderbolts, permit me to tell you. We are in Prussia; the great king watches over all his subjects; neither the Romish Church nor the Rosicrucians can obscure the light of knowledge. He will not suffer a ghost, sneaking in the dark, to exercise power here, and he will not refuse the protection to me which is accorded to the least of his subjects. I do not fear you, and I will tell you the truth entire, I believe you to be a hypocrite and a charlatan, who—"

"Miserable one!" interrupted Cagliostro, as he furiously rushed to her, seizing her by the arm—"cease, unhappy one, or your life is forfeited to the invisible avengers!"

Wilhelmine shook her head, and encountered his flaming eyes with a proud glance. "I repeat your own words—cease, or your life will be forfeited! Perhaps you think I do not know what happened to you in Mittau, where you were recognized as a charlatan, who fooled the poor creatures into the belief of his miraculous acts, which consisted in lightening their purses to the benefit of his own. You were obliged to flee from Mitlau in the night, to save yourself, your treasures, and wonderful man-traps, and the beautiful Lorenza Feliciana. Beware! The Empress of Russia had a certain Joseph Balsamo pursued, who had practised great deception, and people pretend that he resembles Count Cagliostro. The Empress Catherine is a good friend and ally of the King of Prussia, and if the happy idea should occur to me to propose seeking the necromancer here, the Great Kophta might come a miserable end."

"On the contrary, it would only be a welcome occasion for the Great Kophta to reveal himself, and hurl his despicable, malicious enemy into the dust at his feet," replied Cagliostro, calmly. "Try it, you faithless, fallen daughter of the Invisibles—try to unloose the pack of my enemies, to recognize that all their yelling and barking does not trouble the noble stag to whom God has given the whole world for His forestward that He should rule therein. I have listened to you unto the end, and I regard your invectives and accusations as not worthy of a reply or justification, and I laugh at your menaces. But I warn you, Wilhelmine Enke, defy not the Invisibles, and offend not the Holy Fathers, by your continued resistance. Turn, misguided child of sin—turn while there is yet time! In their name I offer you a last chance, their forbearance is without bounds, and their mercy long enduring."

"I neither desire your forbearance nor mercy," cried she, proudly. "I will have no companionship with my enemies, and the Rosicrucians are such, for Bischofswerder and Woellner both hate me, and would put me aside. There is no reconciliation where only hostility is possible."

"The heavenly listen not to the voices of the earthly, and prove themselves, the most noble when the least deserved. They will protect and watch over you, even against your will, and never will they be deaf to your cry for aid in the hour of Here is a token of their grace toward you. Take this ring—do you recognize it?"

Wilhelmine regarded it attentively. "This is the ring which I gave at the tribute-altar instead of gold, which you desired."

"The Invisibles sent it to you to-day as the precious pledge of their favor. You shall keep it, and wear it as a token of their heavenly forbearance, and when you turn back from the erroneous ways into which the Illuminati have led you, send it to the circle of Berlin directors, either Bischofswerder or Wollner, and they will come to your rescue. Farewell! I forgive you all your wicked words, which fall like spent arrows from the helmet of my righteousness."

Cagliostro turned proudly away, and disappeared in the bushes.

Wilhelmine placed the ring upon her finger, turning it to watch the play of colors. "I do not know why," said she, "but it has not the same brilliancy as formerly. I will take it to the jeweller Wagner, and ask him if it is the same stone. Perhaps the Great Kophta has tried some of his miracles upon it. I will at once send the servant to Minister von Herzberg, and inform him that Cagliostro is here. He has promised me protection in the name of the king, and I feel that I shall now have need of it."

She hurried to the house, and devoted herself to the writing of the said letter—a task she was but little accustomed to. She had learned to speak French very prettily, and to express herself skilfully and wittily in German, and under her royal master, the crown prince Frederick William, gained much valuable scientific knowledge. But to write fluently was quite another thing, and it was a long time before the epistle was finished. However, happily accomplished, she commanded the servant to take it to Berlin.

He bowed with silent submission; but once having quitted the house, a cunning smile was visible upon his face, and he availed himself of a stage-coach which was going in the same direction. "I can afford this expense," said he, arranging himself comfortably. "When I have money in my pocket why should I walk the long distance? I was very clever to tell Bischofswerder that the Minister von Herzberg had secretly visited my mistress, and it was equally clever of him to give me a louis d'or, and promise me the same every time that I should bring him important news. Indeed, I think to-day he may well thank me, and I believe, if I often inform him, he will advance me a degree, and at last I shall be admitted to the circle of the elect, while I now belong to the outside circle, who know nothing and hope every thing."

CHAPTER XXX
THE TRIUMVIRATE

While Wilhelmine's servant gave himself up to his hopes, slowly down the broad avenue, an elegant four-in-hand carriage rolled past him, and stopped at the house where lived Colonel Bischofswerder, long before he had reached the Brandenburg Gate. A gentleman sprang out, hastening past the footman into the house, where a servant evidently awaited his arrival, and preceded him with devout mien, throwing open the wide folding-doors and announcing, in a solemn voice—"His excellency, Count Cagliostro." He then respectfully withdrew, bowing profoundly as the count passed, and closed quickly and noiselessly the doors behind him.

The two gentlemen within hastened to meet the count, who nodded smilingly, and extended to them with a gracious condescension his white hand sparkling with diamonds. "My dear brothers," said he, "you have unfortunately announced me the truth—Wilhelmine Enke is faithless—is an apostate."

"A courtesan, ensnared by the devil of unchastity," murmured the elder of the two—a man of long, lank figure, pale, pock-marked face, the broad high forehead shaded with but little hair, the watery blue eyes turned upward, as if in pious ecstasy, and the large, bony hands either folded as if in prayer, or as if in quiet contemplation, twirling his thumbs around each other. "I have always said so," said he, with a long-drawn sigh; "she is a temptress, whom Satan, in bodily repetition of himself, has placed by the prince's side, and his salvation cannot be counted upon until this person is removed."

"And you, my beloved brother, think otherwise—do you not?" asked Cagliostro, gently.

"Yes," answered Bischofswerder, "you know well, sublime master and ruler, how much I esteem and love the worthy and honorable Wollner, and how much weight his opinion has with me. In all my reports to the Invisible Fathers I have always particularly mentioned him, and it was upon my wish and proposal that they appointed him director of one of the three Berlin circles. He is occupied near me in the confederacy, and is also in the service of the crown prince, for it was by my especial, earnest recommendation that his highness called him to Berlin from the exchequer of Prince Henry at Rheinsberg, that he might give him lectures in politics and other branches of administration, I do not say it to boast, although I have always regarded it as an honor to have opened the way to a distinguished man, to have his great talents properly valued. I only say it to prove my high appreciation of dear brother Wollner, and to defend myself, master, in your eyes, that I differ in opinion from him, and do not advise a violent removal of this person, to whom the prince is more attached than he himself knows of."

"It is not necessary to excuse yourself to me, my son," said Cagliostro, pompously. "The eyes which the Invisibles have lighted up with a beam of revelation, see into the depths of things, and reveal the most hidden. I have glanced into your hearts, and I will tell you that which I have therein read. You, Hans Rudolph von Bischofswerder, belong to the world; its joys and sorrows agitate you. You have a longing for science and the knowledge of the Invisibles, and you would also enjoy the Visibles, and take part in the pleasures of life. What you would allow yourself, that you would also grant to your royal master, whose friend and leader you are, and who, one day, will be the future king and ruler of the visible world, and a faithful son and servant of the Invisibles. Is it not thus?"

"It is so," answered Bischofswerder, who, with wondering astonishment, drank in every word that fell from Cagliostro's lips as a revelation. "You have read the inmost thoughts of my heart, and what I scarcely suspected myself, you are knowing of, lord and master."

"Toil and strive, my son, and you shall rise to the highest grade, in which presentiment and recognition, thinking and knowing, are one."

He extended to Bischofswerder his hand, who fervently pressed it to his lips; then turned to Wollner, who, with upturned gaze and folded hands, might have been praying, for his thumbs were not turning around, but rested, quietly crossed.

"You, my son and brother," continued Cagliostro, with his lofty, haughty reserve, "your thoughts are diverted from earth, and the joys of this world have no charm for you!" "I have laid the oath of virtue and chastity upon the altar of the Invisibles," replied Wollner, with a severe tone of voice. "I have given myself to a pious life of abstinence, and sworn to employ every means to lead those that I can attain to upon the narrow path which leads to the paradise of science, of knowledge, and heavenly joys. How could I forget my oath, which is to win the prince, who is to become a light and shield in the holy order, from the broad course of vice, to the pathway of the blest? How can I bear to see him lost in sin who is elected to virtue, and who longs for the light of knowledge?"

"But, in order to bear the light in its brightness, he must have passed through the darkness and gloom of sin," said Cagliostro. "After the days of error follow those of knowledge. This is what causes the mildness of our brother Theophilus, whom the earthly world calls Bischofswerder, whilst you, brother Chrysophorus, demand from the prince the severest virtue, which is the first great vow of the brothers advancing in the holy order of the Rosicrucians. You are both wrong and both right. It is well to be lenient as brother Theophilus, but that must have its limit, and the night wanderer who stands upon the brink of a precipice must be awakened, but not with violent words, or calling loudly his name, because a sudden awakening would only hasten his fall. Slowly and carefully must he be roused; as one would by degrees accustom the invalid eyes to the mid-day, so must the light of virtue and knowledge dawn upon the eyes, ill from vice, with prudent foresight. Hear my proposal. Summon the three circles of the brothers of the highest degree to a sitting to-night. You have told me that the prince desires to belong to the seeing ones, and be in communion with the spiritual world. This night his wish shall be fulfilled, to see the spirits, and a new future shall rise before him. My time is limited; let us arrange every thing, for the voices of the Invisibles already call me home."

At this instant a modest knocking was heard at the door, which was repeated at different intervals.

"It is my servant," said Bischofswerder, "and he has undoubtedly an important communication for me."

He opened the door, speaking with the person outside in a low tone, and returned with a sealed note.

Cagliostro, apparently, was lest in deep thought and indifferent to the conversation without, directing quietly and calmly, in the mean time, a few questions to Wollner, and, as it seemed, listening only to his answers. Yet as Bischofswerder approached him, saying, "it is, indeed, important news; I have proof in hand that—" he interrupted him with a commanding motion, and finished the broken sentence: "—that Wilhelmine Enke is a powerful adversary, having connection with the court, as this letter from her is directed to Minister Herzberg. Is it not this that you would say, Theophilus?"

Astonished, he replied in the affirmative, begging his master to read it.

"It is unnecessary," replied Cagliostro, waving back the letter; "to the seeing eyes every thing is revealed. This person announces to Minister von Herzberg that the deceiver and necromancer, Cagliostro, in his flight from Mittau, has visited her to menace her. She begs protection for herself and an arrest for me; that I am known as Count Julien, at the hotel King of Portugal, at Berlin, and that haste is necessary."

Both gentlemen glanced astonished and enraptured, first at the sealed epistle and then at the great Magus.

"Open the letter and convince yourselves of the contents!" commanded Cagliostro.

"It is unnecessary," cried Bischofswerder, with enthusiasm. "We recognize in you truth and knowledge; you have revealed to us the contents."

"Nay, there is a lingering doubt in the mind of brother Chrysophorus!" said Cagliostro, regarding Woellner fixedly, who stood with downcast eyes before him.

"My ruler and master," stammered Woellner, in confusion, "I dare not doubt, only—"

"You would only be convinced, open then the letter," interrupted Cagliostro, sarcastically.

With a sharp knife, Bischofswerder cut the end of the envelope, and handed the letter to him.

"Give it to Chrysophorus," commanded the count. "He shall read it, and may the incredulous become a believer!"

Woellner perused the epistle with a slightly tremulous voice, stopping now and then, at an illegible word, which his master quickly supplied to him, finishing the sentence as correctly as if he held the writing in his hand.

The contents were exactly as Cagliostro had given them, and the farther Wollner read, the more his voice quivered and Bischofswerder's enthusiasm increased.

As the reading was finished, the former sank, with uplifted hands, before his master, as if imploring mercy from a mighty, crushing power.

"I have been unbelieving as Tobias, doubting as Paul; have mercy on me, O master! for in this hour the divine light of belief and knowledge banishes doubt from my sinful heart. I acknowledge thy supernatural power and heavenly wisdom! My whole being bows in humility before you and your sublimity, and henceforth I will only be your humble scholar and servant, the tool of your will. Forgive me, all-knowing one, if my heart doubted. Breathe upon me the breath of knowledge, and lay thy august right hand upon my head, and penetrate me with thy heavenly power."

"Have mercy upon me also," cried Bischofswerder, as he kneeled beside Woellner, and, like him, raised his hands imploringly to Cagliostro.

"Breathe upon me the breath of thy grace, and regard me, the repentant and unworthy, with thy heavenly glance!"

Cagliostro looked to heaven, and from his lips there fell disconnected words of exhortation; suddenly he drew forth his hands, which he had pushed into his gown and crossed upon his breast, stretching them out with wide-spread fingers.

"Come to me, ye spirits!" he cried, in a loud, thundering voice. "Ye spirits of fire and air, come to me! Ye shall flame and burn upon the heads of these two persons and announce to them that the Invisibles are with us. Come to me, ye spirits of fire!"

He clinched his fingers, extending them again, and upon the points there danced and flickered a blue light. A heavenly smile shone upon the beautiful face of the Magus, his hands slowly sank upon the heads of the kneeling ones, the flames gliding upon their heads, resting there a moment, and then dying away.

"The Invisibles have proclaimed themselves to you through the sign of fire," cried Cagliostro. "The sacred flame has glowed upon your heads, and I now press upon your brow the solemn kiss of consecration and knowledge!"

He bowed down to the kneeling ones. It seemed as if a cloud of perfume had passed over their glowing faces, or as if an odorous lily had been pressed upon their foreheads, and their hearts quivered with delight. He passed his hand lightly over their faces, and a feeling of rapture spread through their whole being. Then as he commanded them to rise, they obeyed, without realizing that they had limbs or body, but regarded the miracle-worker, entranced with his smile.

Cagliostro, with hasty decision and earnest, commanding air, made a few opposite strokes in the air, and immediately the faces of the magnetized looked as if they had awakened from a dream of splendor and delight to insipid, flat reality.

"I have permitted you to behold, for an instant, the mysteries and miracles which are serviceable to the knowing ones," said Cagliostro, with calm earnestness. "Your souls were in communion with the Invisibles, and from the source of knowledge a spark of illumination fell upon your heads. Guard it as a heavenly secret that no one should know of, and now let us continue our conversation."

"Permit me once more to lay my head at your feet, and receive power from the touch thereof," implored Bischofswerder.

"Let me embrace your knees, and entreat pardon and grace," begged Woellner, as he sank down to clasp them, and the former threw himself at the feet of his master, passionately kissing them.

Smilingly he received their homage, and assisted them to rise.

"Now let us speak in a human, reasonable manner, my friends. Brother Theophilus, you, first of all, return the letter to the envelope and seal it."

Bischofswerder obeyed; taking from the table a little bottle and a small brush, he carefully applied an adhesive substance to the edges, pressing them firmly together.

"Master, no one could discover that it had been opened. Command what shall be done with it."

"Give it to your servant, that he may return it to him who brought it, and the latter can now deliver it at its address."

"To the Minister Herzberg!" they both cried, amazed. "It is impossible; he is a sworn enemy of the holy order and your own heavenly person. He could take the most violent measures, and cause your excellency to be arrested."

"I believe it," smiled Cagliostro. "The great Frederick would announce triumphantly that he had had the great Semiramis of the North taken, which the Russian police had failed to accomplish. It would be a welcome triumph for unbelievers and fools, and they would trumpet it joyfully through the world! It must not be; although my spirit in its power and might would soon release my body, yet I will not grant this momentary triumph to my enemies. My time is limited; I must forth to Egypt, where the Brothers of the Millennium will assemble in the course of a week in the pyramids, to announce to me their will for the coming century. I am the Spirit of God, which the Invisibles have willed to enter a human form, therefore it must be regarded as sacred and protected."

"Allow me to guard, with my life, your sublime person!" cried Bischofswerder.

"And I also implore you to grant me the happiness to watch over the security of your heavenly self, and defend it to the last drop of my blood!" cried Woellner; "only tell us what we have to do."

"Above all things obey my command concerning the letter," replied the count, smiling.

Bischofswerder submissively went out with the epistle, returning in a few moments. "It is as you have ordered: in a quarter of an hour it will be in the hands of Minister Herzberg."

"No," replied the count, fixing his eyes upon empty space, "it will not be there, for Herzberg is not at home. I now see him driving in a carriage with four black steeds to the country. At this instant he is crossing a bridge, now he enters a town, turning down one of the streets, where the noise of the wheels is lost. Again I hear him, leaving by the gate, ascending a broad avenue."

"It is the route to Sans-Souci," murmured Bischofswerder, in a low voice, but the count must have understood him, as he repeated aloud:

"Yes, that is the route to Sans-Souci, and the lonely, fretful old king will keep his minister the entire day, and will not receive the missive from his secret female accomplice until his return in the evening, and then he will dispatch his bailiffs in all haste to the hotel to arrest Count St. Julien, and forward an order to every gate to forbid his departure. It will be too late, however—he will have already departed."

"Departed!" cried the two gentlemen, frightened. "Will you, then, forsake us?"

"Hush, my brothers, be quiet!" answered Cagliostro. "I shall have departed for the profane, but I will remain here for the consecrated until to-morrow morning. It oft happens that the lofty even must come down, and the brilliant obscure themselves. To-day I must descend from my spiritual height, and humble myself in the dust of lowliness. When the unholy and unconsecrated essay to behold that which they should not with their earthly eyes; they must be blinded with earthly dust, and for those which are not worthy of miracles, we must sometimes condescend to jugglers' tricks. By the latter I will mislead my enemies to-day. How many gates are there to the city of Berlin?"

"There are nine, master."

"Send immediately messengers around in your circles to order eight travelling-carriages and sixteen large black trunks. Further, send me eight confidential discreet men of my height and size, with eight perukes, exactly the cut of mine. Command four post-horses, with two postilions for eight different addresses. This is all that is necessary for the moment."

"All shall be faithfully and quickly accomplished," said Bischofswerder, humbly. "We will divide the execution of your orders, and there only remains to appoint the time and place when and where to direct the postilions."

"All this will follow; forget not, in trifling, earthly things, the great heavenly circumstances. Summon the consecrated of the highest degree of your circle to go to-night to the palace of Prince Frederick William at Potsdam, and under the very eyes of the old freethinking king we will open to the crown prince the doors of the spiritual world, and consecrate him to the highest degree. But first the Invisibles shall speak with him, and announce the heavenly region of the unapproachable. Finish the preparations, my brothers—fulfil exactly and punctually my orders, and then come to the hotel to receive my last commands."

CHAPTER XXXI
FUTURE PLANS

Cagliostro quitted the two confidants, entered his carriage awaiting him before the door, and drove to the hotel. The host and chief waiter received him with extreme deference, both accompanying him up the stairs—the latter throwing wide open the large doors of his room. The count turned, and, in addressing some indifferent question to the host, opened his gold-embroidered blue satin vest.

The host turned pale, and shrank back, as if seized with a sudden fright. Cagliostro passed on, motioning him to follow, which he humbly obeyed, sinking upon his knees as the door closed.

"Have you recognized the sign which I wear upon my breast?"

"Yes, master," he stammered, bowing down with the greatest reverence.

"Then you belong to the elect of the Inner Temple, for the sign of knowledge is only made known to them."

"I do, indeed, understand its mysteries, master, and I know that one of the Invisibles, in infinite condescension, appears in a visible form before me. Immeasurable as the happiness, is my obedience! Command me, master; my life and riches belong to the holy alliance!"

"Rise and receive my orders," replied Cagliostro, with great dignity. In a brief, dictatorial manner he communicated the necessary arrangements; then dismissed him with a haughty nod, and entered the adjoining room of his wife, Lorenza Feliciana.

She had thrown herself upon the divan, in charming neglige. Her head was encircled with black ringlets, which she wore unpowdered, despite the fashion. Her eyes were closed, and her beautiful shoulders were but half concealed by a black lace veil.

She slept so quietly and soundly that the count did not awaken her upon entering. He approached her lightly upon the soft carpet, and stood regarding her attentively. A pleasant smile spread over his face, softening its expression, and his eyes beamed with passionate tenderness.

"She is indeed beautiful," he murmured, softly. "No one could withstand the charm of this wonderful woman. Ah, would that I could crush these wicked spirits within me, silence all these seductive, sinful voices, and fly to some secluded valley of our dear fatherland, and there, reposing on her love, let life glide calmly on and smile at the past without regret, as a fading dream! Would that I could forget, and become again pure and innocent, blest in my affection, simple in my tastes, and without wants! But no, it is too late! I cannot retreat, the demons will not be driven out; to them my soul belongs, and I must fulfil my destiny!—Awake, Lorenza, awake!" Her beautiful form shook with fright; she started, opened her eyes, demanding, "What is the matter? Who is here?"

"It is I, Lorenza," he said, sadly; "I was obliged to awaken you, to tell you something important."

"Are the pursuers here? Have they discovered us? Are they coming to take us to prison?"

"No, no; be quiet, Lorenza, no one has discovered us!"

"Quiet!" she repeated, with a scornful laugh. "We have travelled day and night the last ten days, hiding ourselves in miserable holes and dens, under assumed names, believing our pursuers were at our hacks; and now that we are showing ourselves publicly, you ask me to be quiet! I have slept for the first time since that fearful night in Mittau, and it is very cruel and thoughtless of you to wake me, if the bailiffs are not here, and danger does not menace us."

"For the moment we are safe, but I have something important to tell you."

"Important?" she cried, shrugging her shoulders. "What is of consequence to me, since that night? Oh, when I think of it, I could shriek with rage, I could annihilate myself in despair!"

"It was indeed a dreadful experience, and my heart quakes when I think of it," said Cagliostro, gloomily. "The secret assembly consisted of the highest and most influential of the Courland nobility. Suspecting no wrong, not even that there could be traitors among the believers who would falsify my spirit apparatus, I gave myself up to conjuring the departed."

"And I upon my fairy throne," added Lorenza, "couched in the innocent costume of the celestial, only veiled with a silvery cloud, heard a sudden shriek. The room was quite dark; I saw, upon opening my eyes, that no spirits enlivened it."

"Every thing failed—that is to say, my assistants let it fail," said the count, "and the assembly began to murmur. Suddenly, instead of the departed princes and heroes, what fearful forms arose!"

"Apes, cats, and other animals," cried Lorenza, with a loud laugh. "Oh, what an irresistible sight! In spite of my anger I had to laugh, and laugh I did upon the fairy throne, like—"

"Like a foolish child who neither knows nor understands danger," interrupted the count. "Your laughing soon ceased in the fearful tumult and uproar. They shrieked for light, the ladies fled, and the men menaced me with loud curses, calling me a charlatan, and threatening my life!"

"Mine also," cried Lorenza; "oh, what insults and ill-treatment I was forced to listen to! They rushed upon me, shrieking for the brilliants and money which they had brought me as an offering. How they scolded and called me a deceiver! I was only very beautiful and coquettish, and that was no deception! I charmed them with my coyness, and they brought me the most costly presents, because I was a virtuous woman. Now they reproached me, demanding a return of them all, which they had forced upon me of their own free will. I was obliged to bear it silently in my costume of innocence, and as goddess I could not defend myself and speak with human beings—who pushed up to the throne. It was a very ridiculous position; happily I did not quite lose my senses, but let the apparatus play, and disappeared into my dressing-room below, which fortunately closed above me. I dressed, and rushed to your room to rescue my treasures."

"Even in this extreme danger you only thought of your riches, not of me," said Cagliostro, with a bitter smile.

"Have you not taught me yourself that money was the only thing worth striving to possess? Have you not revealed to in wisdom that riches alone make us happy, and procure for us honor, power, love, and constancy? Ah! Joseph, have you not made me the miserable, heartless creature that I am? Can you reproach me that your teaching has borne such good fruit? I am happy to be the priestess of wealth, and grateful for what you have made known to me."

"It is true," sighed Cagliostro, "I have taught you the truth of things; I have disclosed to you the world's motive power. Riches are indeed the god upon earth, toward whom all are pressing, rushing on. We must all follow and serve him as slaves, or be crushed under the wheels of his triumphal car. Men talk and reason about the storm and pressure which is spreading through the world, and finally will reduce every thing to storm the eternal and undying bliss of wealth, and press on for gold."

"To think that we have lost every thing!" cried Lorenza, springing up and stamping with her silken-shod foot; "every thing is lost that I have been years gaining, by hypocrisy, deception, and coquetry. They have robbed me! The shameful barbarians have seized all our effects. The police surrounded the house, guarding every entrance, and we were obliged to escape by the roof into the house of one of the brothers, leaving all our treasures behind."

"You exaggerate, Lorenza, and represent it worse than it is. Look around; you are surrounded with luxury and comfort. Our great undertakings in Courland and St. Petersburg have failed, it is true, and the Russian empress has ordered me to be driven away and pursued. But the Invisible Fathers have not forsaken me, as they know that I am a useful tool in their hands. They have carefully provided me with money, passports, and instructions. We have lost thousands, but we will regain them, for the future is ours. I am protected by the order, and called to a new and important mission in Paris, to strive for the sacred aim of the Church."

"And have they no mission for me?" asked Lorenza. "Is there nothing further for me to do in that city than to be a beautiful woman, and play tricks for my dear husband?"

"Great events await you in Paris, which we will aid you to prepare. The Invisible Fathers send you before me to the Cardinal de Rohan. You are going to Paris in the service of the revolution of minds. The carriage is ordered, and you are to set off this very hour."

"And when are you going, Joseph?" Lorenza asked, with a touch of melancholy.

"I shall officially depart in an hour, but in reality at the same time that the Baroness von Balmore leaves the hotel in her travelling-carriage. Near the waiting-maid will a servant sit upon the box. I shall be he."

"Officially you depart in an hour; what does that mean?" Cagliostro smiled. "It is a long story and a comical one. Come, seat yourself by me upon the sofa; repose your head upon me, and listen to what I will relate to you."

CHAPTER XXXII
MIRACLES AND SPIRITS

Late in the afternoon of the same day a travelling-carriage drove up before the hotel "King of Portugal," in the Burgstrasse, with two large black trunks strapped upon it behind the footman's box, and the postilion, sitting by the coachman, playing the beautiful and popular air, "Es ritten drei Reuter cum Thore hinaus!"

Count St. Julien descended the stairs, followed by the host, and nodded in a lofty manner to the two waiters and hostler awaiting him at the entrance, who returned it by a profound bow, at the same time not failing to see the white hand extended with the trinkgeld.

The host himself closed the carriage door, and the count departed amid the merry peals of the postilion, the former gazing after him with the satisfaction of one who has made a good bargain. The servants watched it, too, until it had disappeared around the corner of the next street.

At this instant the quivering tones of a post-horn were heard, and an open caleche appeared and stopped before the hotel with two large black travelling-trunks upon it, and the postilion upon the box blowing the popular air, "Es ritten drei Reuter zum Thore hinaus!"

The host observed the empty carriage with a smile, but the servants asked themselves astonished what it meant, and as they turned and saw Count St. Julien descending the stairs, they were startled. He offered them the usual trinkgeld, entered the carriage, and rolled away with a commanding nod.

The host seemed speechless with astonishment, and stood as if rooted to the spot. The servants stared after the carriage until it turned the corner; when just then a post-horn was heard playing the agreeable melody of "Drei Reuter," and a travelling-carriage with two large black trunks drove up to the door.

The servants turned pale, looking shyly toward the stairs. Slowly and with great dignity Count St. Julien descended, greeting them with a gentlemanly nod as he passed, and, extending his white hand with a trinkgeld, mounted his carriage, and drove away.

The host stood as if stunned, outside the door, looking right and left with unspeakable terror. The servants tremblingly fixed their eyes upon the stairs, no longer possessing the power to move, but heard the post-horn, and the carriage which drove up to the door the third time. Slowly and proudly Count St. Julien advanced. It was the same cold, grave face, with the thick black beard, and the powdered peruke, the curls of which overshadowed the brow and cheeks. He wore exactly the same dark-brown cloak over the black velvet dress. The white hand, with broad lace wrist-ruffles, reached them also a trinkgeld.

This time the fellows had scarcely self-possession sufficient to take the present, for every thing swam before their eyes, and their hearts one moment almost ceased to beat, and then palpitated with the feverish rapidity of terror.

"I would run away," murmured the chief waiter, as Count St. Julien for the fourth time drove away, "if my feet were not riveted to the floor."

"If I could move mine I would have gone long ago," groaned the second waiter, the clear drops standing upon his forehead. "It is witchcraft! Oh, Heaven! they are coming again, playing the 'Drei Reuter.'"

The count descended the stairs for the fifth time, whispered to the hostler, who was quite engrossed counting his money, handed the trinkgeld to the pale fellows by the door, and mounted his carriage, driving away amid the merry peals of the post-horn.

"Julius," murmured the steward, softly, "give my hair a good pulling, that I may awake from this horrible dream."

"I cannot," he whimpered, "my hands and feet are lame. I cannot move."

"I will," said the hostler, courageously stretching forth his hand, and pulling it so vigorously that the steward was fully convinced of the reality of things.

Again the post-horn sounded the "Drei Reuter;" again the carriage stopped before the door, and the count descended, giving to every one a gift like the "Maedchen aus der Fremde," and for the sixth time rolled away.

"We are bewitched; it is a ghost from the infernal regions!" groaned the steward.

"I cannot abide it any longer—I shall die!" said the second waiter.

"I do not mind it," said the hostler, as he jingled the money; "if they are ghosts from hell, the eight groschen do not come from there, for they are quite cool. See how—Ah, there comes the count again!"

For the seventh time he passed down the stairway, by the servants, who wore no longer standing but kneeling, which the count received as a proof of their profound respect, and slipped the money into their hands.

"Praise God, all good spirits!" murmured the head waiter; but neither the count nor the money seemed to be moved by the pious exhortation, for he quietly entered his carriage, and the eight groschen lay in the servant's hand, at which the hostler remarked that he would stand there all night if the count would only continually pass by with groschen. It pleased the count to descend the stairs yet twice more, divide the trinkgeld, and mount his carriage. As he drove away the ninth time, it appeared as if the Drei Reuter were determined to drive out of the gate and forsake the hotel "King of Portugal." The host waited awhile, and talked with the neighbors, who, roused by the continual blast of the post-horn, were curious to know how it happened that so many guests were departing by extra posts. Whereupon the host, in a hollow, sepulchral voice, his eyes glaring, and shrugging his shoulders, declared that there had been but one gentleman at the hotel, but nine times he had seen him drive away, and the devil must have a hand in the matter!

Shaking his head, he returned to the hotel, and found the servants busily counting their money, occasionally casting covetous looks toward the stairs, as if they hoped the count would again descend.

Exactly as Cagliostro had foretold, Minister Herzberg did not return from Sans-Souci until late in the evening, and then found Wilhelmine's letter in his cabinet.

Immediately the police were instructed to arrest Count St. Julien at the hotel "King of Portugal."

An hour later the chief of the police came to say that the count had already been gone two hours. He repeated the account of the host, corroborated by the servants, of nine different counts having driven away from the hotel.

Herzberg smiled. "We have to deal with a very clever scoundrel," said he, "and it is no other than the so-called Count Cagliostro, who was lately exposed as a bold trickster in Mittau and St. Petersburg, and about whose arrest the Empress Catharine is very much exercised. It would be very agreeable to the king to show this little attention to her imperial highness, and trap the adroit pickpocket."

"We might succeed in catching him in his flight," remarked the chief. "For the last six months the king has given orders that every passport should be examined at the gates, and the route of the travellers noted down, which is all registered and sent to the king. It would be very easy to discover by which gate he departed, and his route, and then have him pursued."

"That is well thought of, director; hasten to put it into execution, and inform us of the result." He returned in an hour to the minister's cabinet, shaking his head gravely. "Your excellency, it is very strange, but he is a wizard. This man has driven out of the nine gates at the same hour and minute."

Herzberg laughed. "This is one of his tricks, and by it I recognize the great necromancer."

"Your excellency, this is no trickery, but witchery. It is impossible for any one man to drive out of the nine gates at the same hour, in the same carriage, with two large black trunks and a postilion blowing the same melody, and provided with a correct passport, which he shows and is recognized as Count St. Julien, who is going to Paris by Hamburg. Here are the nine registers from the different gates, all the same, if I am not bewitched and do not read straight."

"This trick does honor to the count," said Herzberg, smiling. "To-morrow you shall accompany me to Sans-Souci and read aloud the registers to the king. Do you think it will be impossible to pursue the count now?"

"I should be very happy to follow your excellency's judgment in this matter, and arrest the rascal in any way that you could point out," said the director.

"I am convinced that he is in the city; and driving put of the nine gates at the same time was the best manner to escape being discovered," said Herzberg. "He is concealed in some one of the houses of the brothers, and we shall be obliged to let him escape this time."

In order the more securely to carry out the initiation of Prince Frederick William, in company with Bischofswerder and Woellner, Cagliostro had arranged his pretended departure. For a long time the prince had expressed an extreme desire to be received into the mysteries of the miraculous and holy order, of which he had heard his friends speak with so much reverence. But he had been put off from time to time with regrets and shrugs of the shoulders, and expressions of the impossibility of granting the request.

"The spirits do not always appear even to the consecrated," said Bischofswerder. "They make themselves known after many fervent prayers and imploringss, and when we have withdrawn from every one who could entice us to doubt or disbelief. I fear that it would be impossible to conjure the spirits of the departed, so long as your highness honors a certain lady with your particular favor, who ridicules the sublime order and mingles with its enemies. How can they appear to those who have just been in the company of a friend of the Illuminati and unbelievers?"

"The spirit-world only reveals itself to the virtuous and pure," said Woellner, in a harsh, dry voice. "Its inhabitants cannot approach those who are not chaste and innocent, for sin and vice surround them with a thick fog, which keeps them at a distance from the clear atmosphere of the sublime. If you would call up the spirits, you must remove this woman who entices you from the path of virtue, and renders the sphere impure around you."

Despite the warnings and the great wish the prince had to be received into the spirit-world, and become a member of the highest grade of the Rosicrucians, he could not resolve to forsake her who had been his friend for ten years, and who had borne shame and degradation on his account, refusing eligible and rich men rather than leave him and become a legitimate wife. Wilhelmine was the beloved of his youth, the mother of his two dear children, and she alone knew how to drive away the ennui which pursued the prince, with her amiable, subtle wit. Nay, he could not be so ungrateful, so heartless, as to reject her who had so tenderly loved him when young and beautiful, now that the first bloom of youth and beauty had faded!

Bischofswerder and Woellner recognized this difficulty, and applied themselves the more energetically for its removal. They supposed that the unexpected arrival of Cagliostro would very naturally appear to the prince as a special messenger, sent, without doubt, from the fathers, to accomplish his conversion. They announced to the prince that the Invisibles had taken pity upon his desire for knowledge, and had consented to permit him to gaze into the regions of the blest, although he wandered in the path of vice, and that he must hold himself in readiness to accompany the messenger whenever he should be sent to call him.

For this reason the crown prince had written to Wilhelmine that she should not expect him until the following morning, and he did not quit his room the entire day, with excited expectation awaiting the summons. As evening set in the prince was cast down, and quite of the opinion that the Invisibles did not deem him worthy to enter their pure presence, and thought that Wilhelmine must be the hinderance. Whilst he was reflecting whether to sacrifice his beloved to the salvation of his soul, the secret door gently opened, and two men, masked and wrapped in black cloaks, entered and placed themselves near the door. The prince did not remark their entrance, and was quite frightened as he chanced to turn, and saw these two immovable figures.

With quivering voice he demanded their mission.

In the same tone, as if one were an echo of the other, they answered, "We desire nothing, but you demand knowledge of the spirit-world, and would have its mysteries revealed to you, which the Invisibles will now grant you. Follow us, therefore!" They reopened the secret door; one of the masked preceded the prince, and the other followed him.

The prince shuddered at the thought that he might be rushing into some unknown danger, and intrusting himself to those who would misuse his confidence. He demanded to see their faces, declaring himself prepared to follow, when acquainted with his guides.

"It would then be better to remain," replied one of the masked. "He who lacks confidence is not worthy of it, and he who trusts only the Visibles, the Invisibles flee."

The prince recognized the voice of Bischofswerder, and smiled, but he knew not that it was permitted him to hear it to inspire him with courage.

"Well, so let it be; the fathers shall see that I am a believer," cried the prince.

Immediately one of the brothers put his own cloak, three-cornered hat, and mask upon his highness, still remaining cloaked and masked himself, much to the astonishment of the passive prince. "Come, now, the Invisibles await you," said one of the masked. The prince stepped courageously into the little corridor which led to the secret stairway, one brother preceding him, causing a soft light to illumine their path, the other following him.

In silence they reached the side-door of the palace, where a close carriage awaited them.

"Where are you taking me?" asked Frederick William, as he entered, followed by the two brothers.

"To the Invisibles," answered a strange voice.

Again the prince essayed to begin a conversation, his only response being, "Purify your heart and pray." Silently they galloped over paved and unpaved streets, the prince heartily repenting having been drawn into this adventure. He thought of his charming and beloved Wilhelmine, and half determined to give the command to drive to Charlottenburg. The fact of Bischofswerder being with him, and fearful of appearing weak and wanting in courage in the eyes of his friend and favorite, prevented him.

After several hours' drive, they stopped at the marble palace of Potsdam, near the one which the prince was accustomed to occupy. His highness looked cautiously around, and breathed more freely, as he felt that he was now surely among friends.

The white palace stood silent and deserted in the darkness, this palace at Potsdam being only used for the guests of the king. The carriage stopped at the side-door, where there was no sentinel, and they alighted, entering the palace, winding along the corridors in the same order as before, guided by the glimmering light of the one preceding. Solemn music, strange ringing sounds, fell upon the ear as they advanced. Sometimes they were sharp and cutting as glass, then threatening and penetrating as the wind, shrieking and moaning, causing one to be very nervous if not terrified.

The farther they proceeded the louder grew the sounds, and at intervals groans, moans and wailings were heard, as of those waiting and imploring for mercy.

One of the brothers now opened a door, and then placing themselves upon each side, the unknown voice announced to the prince that they had arrived at the long-sought-for goal.

"What have we come here for?" asked the prince.

"To behold that which you have many times petitioned to be permitted to see," replied Bischofswerder, gently encouraging and inspiring Frederick William. "The Invisibles have at last yielded to your wishes, and the spirits which you summon will appear. If your courage fails you, and you dread the presence of the departed, command to be reconducted to your palace, and we will obey; but renounce forever the sublime happiness of beholding the Invisibles and of holding communion with the spirit-world!"

"I fear not, but wish to be in the company of the spirits," answered the prince, proudly.

"Kneel," they commanded, permitting him to enter, "and thrice summon in a loud voice the names of three departed, who will answer your questions. Beware of approaching them, for their glance is death and their breath destruction! Therefore remain kneeling, as it becomes a mortal in the presence of an immortal. Hope and pray, brother!"

As the door closed upon the prince, and he found himself in such impenetrable darkness, he sank upon his knees, for he dared not advance, and retreat was impossible, in spite of heart-quakings.

The shrill, penetrating music ceased, and a voice from a distance called: "Summon thrice those that thou desirest to see."

"Marcus Aurelius, Leibnitz, and the distinguished elector," called the prince in a loud voice.

"Who summoned me?" was responded in hollow, sepulchral tones, and directly over the crown prince a blue, vaporous light was visible—at first only a cloud, then by degrees increasing and condensing itself into a human shape, until it took the form of a Roman warrior of the olden time; no other than Marcus Aurelius, in helmet and coat-of-mail, with a pale, earth-colored face and glaring eyes.

"Who summoned me?" repeated the figure. The prince's lips refused to respond, and shuddering he gazed upon the corpse-like face, so exact in feature to the old Roman emperor.

"You answer me not!" thundered the voice, "but I will tell you who you are—one lost in sin and an apostate!—the crown prince of Prussia, a future king, who will be called to govern a people, and knows not self-government! Turn from the path of vice while it is yet time; rise from the dust, that the ashes of retribution do not bury you in a living tomb, like the sinful Pompeians. No monument marks the place of the sinful; he sinks into the night of oblivion, or he is cursed by succeeding generations. Therefore turn from the errors of sin. Rise to virtue, that the blessed may approach you. I shudder in your presence. Woe to you! woe! woe!"

The cloud-portrait vanished, and darkness reigned for a moment. The prince cried in anguish: "I will hear no more; this air oppresses me—open the door—I renounce communion with the spirits; I will go out!"

The light reappeared in the dark room and another form hovered over the prince—of grave, obscure face, with a great peruke, staring at him. He recognized the distinguished philosopher Leibnitz, whom he had desired to see, but who now filled him with unspeakable terror. Like the former spirit, he also, when unanswered, reproached the erring prince, conjuring him to return to virtue.

As the menacing ghost disappeared, the prince felt for the door, and shook it with the power which terror lends, crying, "Open, open!" It opened not, and the third summoned, the great elector, Frederick William, appeared, with high, up-lifted arm, glittering eyes, advancing with angry mien, shaking his lion's mane against the erring son of his house, whom he menaced with curses and revenge, if he did not renounce the courtesan who had seduced him to vice and unchastity.

"I will become better," groaned the prince. "I will perform the wish of the spirits. Only have mercy on me—free me. Help! help! Open the door, Bischofswerder, I will do better. Open the door!"

This time it really opened, and a long train of dark, masked forms entered the dusky room surrounding the prince, wringing their hands, imploring him to turn from sin, and forsake the unholy woman.

They whimpered, they implored, sinking upon their knees, beating their clinched hands, and weeping: "Turn, beloved elect! Renounce Wilhelmine Enke; renounce vice! Repulse the seductress, and turn your countenance to Virtue which you have seen in all her beauty!"

"I will perform that which you demand," wept the prince, as the deathly terror and nervous excitement made him yielding.

"Swear!" cried the chorus of masks.

"I swear that Wilhelmine Enke shall no longer be my mistress. I swear by all that is holy that I will renounce her! I—"

Voice failed him; there was a ringing and buzzing in his ears; every thing swam before his eyes, and he sank fainting. The prince awoke after long unconsciousness, and found himself upon his bed in the new palace at Potsdam, Bischofswerder at his side, watching him with the tenderest sympathy. He bent over him and pressed his hand to his lips with a cry of delight. "Heaven be praised; my dear prince, you have awaked to commence a new life! You now belong to the virtuous and honorable, whom the Invisible Fathers bless!"

"Is it true, Bischofswerder," said the prince, languidly, "that I have sworn to renounce Wilhelmine Enke, and never to love her more?"

"You have sworn it by all that is holy, and all in heaven and on earth have heard your oath, and there is joy thereat."

The prince turned his head, that Bischofswerder might not see the tears streaming down his cheeks.

CHAPTER XXXIII
THE RETURN HOME

The beautiful house which Herr Ebenstreit von Leuthen possessed upon the finest street in Berlin, "Unter den Linden," had been newly arranged and splendidly ornamented since his marriage and elevation to a title, and now awaited his arrival. For many weeks mechanics and artists had been busily employed; and the good housekeeper, old Trude, saw with bewildering astonishment the daily increasing splendor of gilded furniture, costly mirrors and chandeliers, soft carpets, tapestries, and gold-embroidered curtains, exquisite paintings and statuary, which the possessor had forwarded from Italy, and many other objects of art standing upon gilt and marble tables.

Every thing was completed. The bustle of the busy workmen had ceased, and Trude slowly wandered through the solitary rooms, examining every article. Her face bespoke dissatisfaction, and a smile of contempt was visible there.

"Miserable trash, for which they have sold my poor child!" murmured the old woman. "For these worthless, glittering toys have they ruined the happiness of the dear innocent heart, and on them the guilt will fall if her soul is lost! I remark how she is changed in her letters since her shameful, mercenary marriage. She writes of nothing but the arrangement of her house, and speaks as if the beauty and costliness of things were only to be thought of, and there is not even a confidential, heart-felt word for her old Trude. It would seem as if she had forgotten all former objects of interest. Oh, what trouble and sorrows the rich have! That good-for-nothing money hardens their hearts and makes them evil and selfish."

The loud ringing of a bell sounded through the solitary drawing-rooms.

"That is, undoubtedly, the general's wife," said Trude, shaking her head. "She rings as if she would announce the king, with her nose turned up so high, or as if she were the money-sacks of her son-in-law!"

Trude was right; her shrill voice was heard ordering the steward, who had but just arrived. "It is abominable, it is unheard of!" she cried, as with a heavy push she burst open the door; "this man presumes to contradict me, and—ah, there you are, Trude!"

"Here I am," she answered; "were you looking for me?"

"Yes, and I would ask you if my orders are not the same as if given by Herr Ebenstreit von Leuthen or his wife, or have you instructed the new steward otherwise, which, it is laughable to say, you have engaged?"

"No, I have not instructed him thus. Dear Marie has not ordered it in her letter."

"Dear Marie," repeated Frau von Werrig. "How can you permit yourself to speak so intimately of the rich Baroness von Ebenstreit?"

"Very true, it is not right," sighed Trude; "I beg pardon."

"I came here to see if every thing was in readiness, and ordered the steward to ornament the doors and corridors with garlands of flowers; he has had the boldness to tell me he dares not do it!"

"He is right, Frau von Leuthen. Baroness Ebenstreit von Leuthen (have I got the title right?) wrote and expressly forbade any festivity to greet her arrival. Here is the letter—I carry it around with me; I will read it to you: 'I expressly forbid any manifestation whatever to be made at our return, whether of garlands or flowers, as they are only hypocrisy and falsehood. I wish no one there to receive me—remember, Trude, no one! Inform my family that, as soon as I have recovered from the fatigue of the journey, I will make them the visit of duty with the baron.'"

"What cold, heartless words are these! One could hardly believe that a daughter was writing of her parents."

"On her wedding-day she perhaps forgot that she had any," said Trude, shrugging her shoulders, "and she should not be at once reminded of that trying occasion on her return. I expect her every moment, as the courier has already arrived an hour ago, and it would be better—"

"You cannot be so impudent as to tell me to leave? Indeed, I will not be prevented from waiting to receive my only child that I have not seen for three years. One can well believe that a mother would be impatient to embrace her dear daughter! I have no other happiness but my beloved child, and I long, unspeakably, to press her to my heart and tell her my sorrow."

"Sorrow! is it possible that Frau von Werrig has any griefs? I supposed there was nothing in the world troubled her."

"And yet I am very much tormented. I can well tell you, Trude, as you are familiar with our circumstances," sighed the countess. "You know the general is tolerably well; the journeys to Wiesbaden and Teplitz have cured him of the gout unfortunately, so that he can go about."

"Are you sorry for that, Frau von Werrig?"

"Certainly I am, Trude, as he has returned to his former habits, frequenting the society of drinking-houses and gamblers. Imagine the general played yesterday, lost all his ready money, and that was not enough, but signed away the year's pension from Herr von Ebenstreit, during which time we have nothing but the miserable army annuity to live upon."

"Then your income will be less to live upon than formerly, for dear Marie earned something with her flowers and lessons which she gave to you, although she was never thanked for it. She was then my dear good Marie, so industrious and patient, and worked untiringly for her parents! Then she forgot them not, and toiled early and late, and, oh, it breaks my heart to think of it, and I must cry in your presence!"

She raised the corner of her dark-blue apron and dried her eyes, holding it there as she continued to weep.

"What an ugly apron!" cried the countess, "and how meanly you are dressed altogether! Is that the way you intend to go looking as the housekeeper of a rich and genteel family? Go, Trude, quickly, and put something better on, that you may receive your master and mistress in a suitable dress."

"I shall remain as I am, for I am very properly dressed. It may not be suitable for a housekeeper, but it becomes old Trude, and it is my Sunday frock, which I always wore when I was maid-of-all-work to you. You may not remember it, but dear Marie (I should say Baroness von Ebenstreit) will, perhaps, and it may recall her little room in the garret, and then—"

"And then she will at last think, Trude, how we took care of her, and how thankful she ought to be to her parents that they married her to a rich man. If Marie sees it at last—"

"You forget with whom you speak, Frau von Werrig," Trude interrupted her, scornfully, "and that it does not become you to speak of Marie to old Trude, but you should remember her title."

"Well, then, when Baroness von Ebenstreit enters this costly house, she must understand that her mother was mindful of her best interests, and that she owes all this to her; and you, Trude, must remind her of it, and tell her about my dreadful trial with her father, and that it is my daughter's duty to release me from it, and beg her husband not to deduct the gambling-debt from the pension, but pay it this once. For it would be a dreadful injustice to make me suffer for the general's rage for play, and show but little gratitude for the riches which I brought her. You will tell my daughter all this, Trude, and—"

"I will not tell her any thing at all, Frau von Werrig," interrupted. Trude, warmly. "May my good genius keep me from that, and burdening my conscience with such falsehoods.—Hark! A carriage is coming, and a post-horn sounded. They have arrived!"

Old Trude hurried out just as they drove up to the door. The steward and two servants in livery rushed down the steps to assist them to alight, and Trude also to greet her favorite, who was now so pale, grave, and chilling in her appearance.

The large eyes of the lady rested with cold indifference upon the old woman, whose eyes were turned to her with the tenderest expression. "I thank you," she said, coldly. "Husband! I beg you to give me your arm." Proudly she passed the statuary, and over the soft carpets without comment, or even a word for old Trude.

The steward and housekeeper followed the silent couple.

"Shall I take you to your room first?" asked Ebenstreit, "or will you do me the pleasure to look at the newly-arranged drawing-rooms?"

"Certainly," she replied, with indifference. "We will first look at the drawing-rooms, as we shall probably receive much company this winter, and they are of the first importance. You know that I dislike solitude."

"Indeed, I recall that we are very seldom alone!" sighed her husband.

"It would be fearful if we were," replied his wife, with marked indifference.

The steward just now opened the little door of the ante-room, sparkling with chandeliers and mirrors. "Ah! this is really beautiful, and well chosen," cried Ebenstreit, looking about with an air of great pride and satisfaction. "Tell me, Marie, is it not worthy of you?"

Glancing coldly around, she replied: "It does not please at all. The furniture is very costly, and reminds one of the parvenu. Every thing recalls the riches of the newly-titled banker."

Her husband's brow contracted, but he did not trust himself to contest his dissatisfaction with his cold, proud wife, but sought another vent for it.

"You are very unkind, Marie. Have the goodness to tell me how you, with these severe ideas, can suffer that Trude for a moment should appear before us in this poor-looking dress which, indeed, does not recall any wealth!"

Frau von Ebenstreit's eyes glanced quickly over the old who, she said, was the only object which did not bespeak the gaudiness of newly-acquired wealth, but she appeared as the respectable servant of an old and noble family in fitting dress. "Remain as you are, Trude, and do not let yourself be misled by our follies! I—but what is that I see?" she cried as the steward opened the next door at the silent nod of her husband.

"Oh, my beloved children, there you are at last; after three years' absence I have the happiness to embrace you, my only daughter," cried Frau von Werrig, as she approached them with outstretched arms and an affectionate smile, essaying to throw her arms around Marie's neck, who waved her back.

"My child, my child," whimpered the mother, "is it possible that my daughter can receive me thus after so long a separation?"

Turning to Trude, Marie asked her, with a reproving look and tone, if she had received her letter, or if she had forgotten her express commands that no one but the servants should be in the house to receive them.

"I did not forget it, my lady, and I have read the orders to Frau von Werrig, but she—"

"Knew that this wish had no reference to her, as she is her mother—Tell me, my beloved son, is it not very natural and fitting that I should be here to receive you?'

"I find it a matter of course," answered Von Ebenstreit, to whom it appeared a relief to find an ally in the mother against his proud and beautiful wife. "I rejoice to see our dear mother here, and I beg Marie will join me."

Marie cast an angry glance toward her husband, which so confused and perplexed him, that he looked down. Then advancing toward the drawing-room, with her usual cold demeanor, without further comment upon the ostentatious furniture, she commanded her husband to follow, who obeyed, giving his arm to his mother-in-law.

"Oh, this is glorious!" he cried, smiling. "What splendor, what luxury! Tell me, my dear mother, is not this beautiful reception-room very aristocratically and appropriately fitted up?"

"I should think a princess or a queen might be satisfied with it," she cried, with enthusiasm. "Even in royal palaces there is nothing of the kind to compare to this gold-embroidered tapestry."

"Baron," said Marie, commandingly, "have the kindness to dismiss the steward. I wish to speak with you and Frau von Werrig."

The steward slipped out without waiting to be sent, and Trude stood near the door, turning to the young baroness, as if to ask if she might remain.

"Did you not hear, Trude?" cried the mother, impatiently. "Tell her to go!"

"Remain, Trude," said Marie, quietly. "You are familiar with the past. I have nothing to deny to you; shut the door and stay here.—And now," she continued, as her voice lost its gentleness, when she addressed her mother, "if it is agreeable to you, I should like to have an understanding with you!"

"But, my child," sighed the mother, "how strangely altered you are! You address me, your mother, as Frau von Werrig, and you speak to Ebenstreit in a very formal manner, who has been your dear, faithful husband for three years. Oh, my darling son, what does this ceremonious manner mean?"

"The very first hour, after our marriage, that we were alone my dear Marie severely reproved me for having addressed her in an intimate, affectionate manner, like the common class, as she called it, and I have never done so since."

"You must be convinced that I am right," said Marie, calmly, "and that it does not become two beings, who neither love nor esteem each other, and who live in the most ceremonious manner, to address one another with endearing epithets. At any rate we are not accountable to any one, and Frau von Leuthen must know the relations we bear to each other in the so-called marriage, as it is her arrangement for the most part."

"And I pride myself upon it," she cried, with animation. "I have brought about this marriage, which is good fortune to us, and I hope my daughter will prove her gratitude, and my son will show me the affection he has so often sworn to me."

"I do not know what my husband may have sworn to you, but permit me to say, I do not understand whom you, Frau von Werrig, address as daughter here; if you accidentally refer to me, you are in error; I have never possessed a mother to love me, although formerly, during long years I endeavored with tender assiduity to win a parent's heart. That is long past, however. The very day that I married Herr von Ebenstreit I renounced all family ties, and resolved to be self-reliant. My husband will witness that he has never known me to yield, and that I have always been firm and resolute in my decision."

"No one would doubt it," replied Ebenstreit, timidly. "We had a very strange marriage, which scarce deserves the name. We resemble more two companions who have joined in business, the one side reluctantly, and the other joyfully. I long for a happy married life, which has been quite impossible thus far."

"And will be to the end, which you will yet learn; and Fran von Werrig should understand it, as she brought about the union, and should not be in doubt as to the conclusion."

"I acknowledge that I am almost speechless and quite paralyzed with that which I see and hear. I should doubt that this cold, proud woman before me were my daughter, if it were not for the name she bears, and her features."

"That which you and my husband have caused me to become. He knew that I neither loved nor esteemed him, and that a union with him seemed so unendurable that I would have sought refuge in death, if I had not vowed to support life to attain the aim which I imposed upon myself. That is all past; it is the future which we must arrange. I am glad that you are here, Frau von Werrig, that we may understand each other once for all; but you came against my wishes."

"You must excuse it, dear Marie. It was the longing of mother's heart which led me hither; the love—"

A cold, contemptuous glance of the large eyes caused the mother to cease, and quail before her daughter.

After a short pause Marie continued: "I wish to exercise alone and unhindered the executive rights of a lady in her own house. Do you acknowledge the justice of this, my husband?"

"Perfectly and unconditionally, dear Marie. You know that I have no other will but yours, which is my highest happiness to submit myself to in all things, always hoping to gain your love and win your heart; that—"

"That this woman has changed to stone," said Marie, coldly, pointing to her mother. "As you then recognize me as the mistress of this house, I shall avail myself of my just right, and no one can prevent me, for I stand alone, absolved from all family ties. By my birth and your riches, I shall occupy the position of a woman of the world, and as such I shall live."

"I am delighted to hear it, Marie," cried her husband. "For this reason I have had the drawing-rooms furnished in the most costly manner, and I shall be proud to receive the aristocratic society who will come to render homage to my wife, as they have done everywhere in Paris, London, Rome, Madrid, and St. Petersburg. We have frequented the highest circle in all these cities, and they have crowded our drawing-rooms, charmed with the beauty, distinguished manners, tone of the world, of your daughter."

"I beg of you to make but one subject the sole object of conversation," said Marie, harshly. "I have said that I will avail myself of the privilege, as mistress of this house, of receiving no one whom I do not wish to see, and no one can enter without consent. Is it clearly understood, husband?"

"Yes," he answered, somewhat agitated; "it is the right of every housekeeper—I understand you."

"It is also clear to me," cried Frau von Werrig, with difficulty suppressing her wrath. "But I will await the decisive word, and see whether it is possible for a daughter to have the insolent presumption to drive he mother from her house!"

"I have already informed you that I have no mother, and that no one has the right to call me daughter. If you await my decision, you shall now hear it; you are not included among those that I wish to receive in my house!"

"Ah, dear Marie, you are cruel!" cried her husband, quite frightened.

"She is a degenerate, good-for-nothing creature!" cried the mother.

"If I am so, who has caused it but you, both of you? Who broke my heart, and crushed it under foot until it ceased to feel, and turned to stone? Bear the consequences of your cruelty and heartlessness! I cannot change it, and I repeat, Frau von Werrig has not the right to enter this house, or to remain here any longer!"

Scalding tears fell from the mother's eyes as she shrieked, "She drives me from her house!"

"I am only treating you as you behaved to one of the noblest and best of men," replied Marie, voice and look betraying her deep feeling. "You thrust from your door, with scorn and contempt, a man worthy of your esteem and recognition, although you knew that my heart was breaking. I am only following your example and exercising my just rights, and am less guilty than you are, as neither of us has need of the respect or esteem of the other."

"Can you suffer this, my son? Do you allow any one in your presence to treat me so shamefully? After all, it is your house; do speak and exercise your right as master here: tell your wife that I am her mother, and you, my adopted son, who bears my name, and that I have the just right to come here as often as it pleases me."

"Speak your mind to Frau von Werrig," said Marie, as Ebenstreit remained silent. "Decide which shall remain, as one or the other of us must leave; you are perfectly free to choose."

"Then, naturally, there is no choice left me," replied Ebenstreit, despondingly. "I declare myself for my wife, of course, who is the noblest and proudest beauty in Berlin, and will make my house the centre of attraction to the aristocracy, nobility, and wealth. This is my greatest pride, and to secure this I wooed my beautiful bride, and have submitted to all the sorrow and humiliation which have been my portion. If I must choose between the mother and daughter, I naturally prefer the latter."

"He abandons me also!" cried the mother. "You are an ungrateful, wretched man! You forget that you owe every thing to me, and that without me you were a miserable mercenary, whose stupidity and tediousness were the ridicule of every one, and you had never gained the entrance to a genteel house. What have you now become? A high-born man, whose house every one will crowd, and who could even appear at court, as he bears our noble and distinguished name. To whom do you owe all this, but to me alone?"

"God in heaven, Thou hearest it!" cried Marie, solemnly, with uplifted arms. "She acknowledges that she alone has brought this misfortune upon me, and in this hour I stand justified."

"Pardon, Frau von Werrig," said Ebenstreit, haughtily; "you are going too far. After my fortune, I thank you for my position. I am certainly of insignificant birth, but I am ambitious and rich. I said to myself, 'Money can bring about all that I wish,' and you see it has accomplished it. My wealth procured me a title, a splendid house, a beautiful wife, and a position in society. I acknowledge that you aided me in the carrying out of my plans, but you would not have done it, if I had not been in a position to pay you. You receive a very considerable annuity from me, therefore you cannot accuse me of ingratitude, but must confess that you have driven a very good bargain. You must forgive me if I beg of you to end this painful scene."

"That means that I must leave," said Frau von Werrig, mildly, remembering the gambling debt and the annuity. "Very well, I will go, and promise you never to return, upon two conditions."

"Have the goodness to communicate them," said Ebenstreit.

"The first is, pay the gambling-debt of my husband, who has played away the entire sum you allow us yearly, and do not deduct it from our income. The second is, increase your allowance five hundred thalers, without letting the general know it, and pay it to me."

"It is impossible," cried Ebenstreit, terrified. "You mistake me for a Croesus, whose wealth is inexhaustible. If this expenditure and demand increase, my colossal fortune will be entirely wasted, and—"

"You exaggerate," interrupted Marie, with a peculiar brilliancy in her eyes. "Such wealth as yours is never-ending, and the banking business, which you are still engaged in under another name, is an inexhaustible source of wealth. I beg you to accept these conditions, that we may at last be at peace."

"Very well," said Ebenstreit, to whom the words of Marie sounded as the sweetest music. "I will then accord your wishes, and you shall have the five hundred thalers for yourself."

"For me alone?"

"Yes, for yourself alone, Frau von Werrig."

"Who vouches for the fulfilment of your promise?"

"My word, Frau von Werrig."

"I have no confidence but in a written promise."

"Then I will have it made out, and bring you the document to-morrow morning."

"Then our business is finished, and I can go.—Farewell, baroness; this is my last word to you. I cursed you from the moment you came into being. If you had been a son, the rich estate in trust of my family would have passed to you, of which I was the natural heir. As it was, it went to a distant relative, and we received nothing. Therefore your parents could not rejoice at your birth, and we only pardoned you when you married a rich man, who could free us from want, and now the separation is no grief to us. You have always been a disagreeable burden, and I am only quit of a discomfort, and renounce forever the sight of you.—Give me your arm, my son, and accompany me at least to the threshold of your house, that you may be able to say to this cold-hearted viper, that she is forever rid of the sight of her mother, who will never think of her but with chilling contempt." She seized Ebenstreit by the arm, who had not the courage to resist her, and drew him along with her, casting a look of supreme disgust at old Trude, who stood pale and sad near the door.

CHAPTER XXXIV
BEHIND THE MASK

As the door closed, and Marie found herself alone with her old friend and nurse, a peculiar change was visible in her sad face; something of its former sunny radiance brightened its usually sorrowful expression, and she turned to greet Trude with the smile of earlier, happier days, though it was tinged with sadness and grief. Impulsively she threw her arms around her faithful nurse, kissing her, and, with quivering lip, whispering: "A greeting and a blessing for you, dear mother! Take me to your kind, disinterested heart, and let me there find repose from all this torture and love the poor lost one, who—"

She drew suddenly back, her face assuming its usually cold, look as she heard her husband enter.

"She is gone, dear Marie. I hope that you are gratified with my decision, and perceive therein a proof of my excessive love and esteem for you," said Ebenstreit, drawing a long breath.

"I did not desire this polite evidence of it," she coldly responded. "We have solemnized our entrance into this house in a fitting manner, and the important matter remaining for us is to make known our arrival to the society of Berlin. The horses purchased in Alexandria, and the new carriage from London, have already arrived—have they not?"

"My book-keeper so informed me a fortnight since, when we were in Paris, and complained of the enormous sum which he had to disburse."

"You must forbid him such a liberty once for all," said she, and the strange blending of joy and scorn was visible in her face. "It is inadmissible for a subordinate to presume to complain to his master, or advise him. He has only to listen and obey. This all your inferiors must understand, and know that they will be dismissed who murmur or advise!"

"I will instruct them accordingly," he sighed, "though I must confess my head-man well understands financial operations, and during the many years that he has been with me has won the right to be consulted and advised with."

"Then prove your gratitude as it becomes a true cavalier and a nobleman," dictated Marie. "Settle his salary as an annuity upon him, and replace him."

"But he receives very great wages, and is still very active, though advanced."

"The more the reason to pension him, that he may repose his remaining years and enjoy the fruit of his labors. But do as you like. I have only told you how a noble cavalier would act; if you choose to bargain and haggle, it is your own affair."

"Heaven keep me from acting otherwise than as a nobleman!" cried Ebenstreit.

Marie nodded assent, desiring that the carriage might be ordered, with the Arab horses. "We will make our visits at once, as I will, for the first time, open our large house for a soiree to-morrow evening," she added.

"Ah, that is charming!" said Ebenstreit, delighted. "I shall at last have the opportunity of seeing the aristocratic Berlin society, and enter upon the rank of my new title."

"Yes," she replied, with an expression of irrepressible scorn, "you will have this enjoyment. Send me the steward, I wish to give him a list of the invited guests. You can add to it at your pleasure."

"I have no one to invite," cried her husband.

"No matter! Make the necessary preparations. I will go to my room to make my toilet."

"Will you not allow me to accompany you? You are not yet familiar with the house."

"Trude will show it to me, and you can at the same time give the orders."

Nodding proudly to Ebenstreit, she told Trude to precede her, following the old woman through the suite of brilliant rooms.

"Here is my lady's dressing-room," said Trude, entering one ornamented with mirrors, laces, and gauzes.

The French waiting-maid was busy within, unpacking the large trunks filled with silk and satin dresses which had been purchased by the dozens in Paris.

"Lay out an elegant visiting toilet; I will return directly, after Trude has shown me the house," They entered the adjoining chamber, Marie's sleeping-room and found the German maid arranging the lace and silk coverings for her mistress to repose herself after the long journey. Marie betrayed no inclination for repose, but questioned Trude as to whither the other door led to.

"Into the little corridor, baroness."

"Did I not order that there should be but one entrance to my sleeping-room, and that from the dressing-room?"

"Your commands have been strictly obeyed," replied Trude. "The only door from the corridor leads to my two rooms, and there is but one entrance to them upon the other side, which can be securely fastened."

Into the simple, quiet room, at the baroness's request, Trude opened the door, saying, "Here we can be alone."

Marie pointed silently to the second door, and the old woman nodded: "That is it," said she. "I have done every thing as you directed. After you left, they sent me the furniture of your little garret-room, which I have arranged exactly as it stood there."

As Marie opened the door and found herself in the small room, so like the one where she had made flowers, given lessons, consoled by her only friend, Trude, her pride and reserve vanished. Sinking upon her knees, as if crushed, she gave way to her long-pent-up grief in one cry of anguish, clinging to Trude, and weeping bitterly.

"Here I am, my faithful nurse, returned to you more wretched and miserable than when I left: then, I felt that I could scorn the world, and now I despise myself. Oh, Trude, they have caused my wretchedness, they have made me selfish and unkind. I was contented until now, and rejoiced in my misery, and triumphantly thought of the time when I was wont to bewail my broken heart and lost soul. Once more with you, and surrounded with the souvenirs of my girlhood, I feel a horror of myself, and could sink in shame and contrition. I have become as bad as they are. Can you forgive the hard-hearted daughter who banished her own mother from her house? I felt that I could not endure her presence, and feared that an inveterate rancor and hate would overpower me, and that I should curse her."

"She deserves it, my poor child," whispered Trude, the tears streaming down her cheeks. "She has just told you that she never loved you, and in this painful scene she thought only of bargaining and making money. God has heard her and forgiven you as I do, and I beg and implore Him to punish those who have made you so wretched, and that He will have no mercy upon them, as they have shown none to you. It breaks my heart to see you so changed, and I can hardly believe this cold, haughty lady is my Marie. In your tears I recognize you, and I bless God that you can weep; your grief proves to me that you are yet the child of my heart."

"Oh Trude, you know not how I have longed to see you; it was my only consolation in these painful years. When I doubted every human being, then I thought of you, and was comforted and sustained."

"And was there no one else to think of, my child?"

"Yes," she gently murmured, "I thought of him. Tell me all you know about him, and hide nothing from me in this hour."

"I thought you would ask me, and I went to Director Gedicke yesterday, to inform myself."

"What did you hear? Tell me the most important. Does he live? Is he restored to health?"

"He lives, but, for one year, he was so wretched that he could not teach; now he is better. Herr Gedicke went himself to Spandau, immediately after the wedding, and brought him back with him, relating as forbearingly and carefully as possible the circumstances of your marriage, and of your sacrificing yourself for him alone."

"How did he receive it? What did he say?"

"Nothing. His eyes were fixed, and his lips uttered not a sound. This lasted for weeks, and suddenly he became excited, enraged, and they were obliged to bind him to keep him from injuring himself."

"Tell me no more," cried Marie, shuddering. "I thought myself stronger, nay, heartless, and yet it seems as if a hand of iron were tearing, rending my soul!"

"That is well," said Trude, gently; "you must awaken from this hardened indifference; giving way to your grief in tears will soften your heart, and it will again be penetrated with the love of God and mankind. I will tell you every thing; you ought to know how poor, dear Moritz suffered. After he vented his rage he became melancholy, and withdrew to Halle in solitude, living in a hay-loft. His favorite books and an old piano were his only companions; no one presumed to intrude him, and they even conveyed his food secretly to him, shoving it through a door. He talked aloud to himself for hours long, and at night sang so touchingly, accompanying himself upon the piano, that those who listened wept."

Marie wept also—scalding tears trickled through her fingers as she lay upon the floor.

Trude continued: "Moritz lived in this way one year; his friends knew how he was suffering, and they proved in their deeds how much they loved and esteemed him. The teachers at the Gymnasium divided his hours of instruction among them, that he should not forfeit his place and lose his salary. Even the king showed great sympathy for him, sending to inquire for him. Herr Gedicke visited him frequently at Halle; and once when about to mount the ladder to the hay-loft he met Moritz descending, carefully dressed, in a reasonable, gentle mood, and then he returned with him to Berlin. There was great rejoicing in the college over his return, and they feted him, witnessing so much love for him that it was really touching. He has been promoted to professor, and at the express command of the king he teaches the young Prince Frederick William in Latin and Greek. Oh, he is so much esteemed and—"

"And is married I hope," murmured Marie. "Is he not happily married, Trude?"

"No. Herr Gedicke says he could marry a wealthy girl, for he is a great favorite, and is invited into the most distinguished society. He repels every one, and has become a woman-hater."

"He hates them—does that mean that he hates me?"

"Yes, he thoroughly scorns and despises you; so much so that Herr Gedicke says you should know of it, and keep out of his way. He has sworn to publicly show his contempt for you, and therefore his friends wish you to be apprised of it, and not encounter him in society."

"It is well, I thank you," said Marie, rising; "I will act accordingly. Kiss me once more, my dear mother, and let me repose my weary head upon your bosom. Ah, Trude, what a sorrow life is!"

"You will yet learn to love it again, Marie."

"If I thought that I could sink so low, I would kill myself this very hour. I know myself better, and only for revenge do I live. Hush! say nothing more. Look at me! I am cursed, and there in those gaudy rooms in my purgatory; here is my paradise, and here the wicked demon may dare to change into the sad, wretched wife, who mourns the happy days already flown, and weeps the inconsolable future. Oft will I come here in the night when those sleep who think me so proud and happy, and you alone shall behold me as I am. Now I must back to purgatory.—Farewell!"

A half hour later a splendid carriage drove from the house of Herr Ebenstreit von Leuthen. The people upon the street stood in wondering admiration of the beautiful Arab horses with the costly silver-mounted harness, and sought to catch a glimpse of the occupants of the carriage, an insignificant, meagre, blond-haired man, who appeared like a servant beside the lovely pale wife, though proud and indifferent, who kept her eyes fixed steadily before her.

The chasseur, with his waving plumes, sat upon the box beside the rich-liveried coachman.

As the married couple returned from their drive, having left their cards at the most distinguished houses in Berlin, the baroness handed the list of guests to be invited to the baron to examine. He glanced hastily over it, assuring her that every thing should be directed as she desired, deferring all to her superior knowledge. Suddenly he seemed confused, even frightened. "What is the matter? What were you about to remark?" asked Marie, indifferently.

"I was in error. I have, without doubt, read it wrong. I beg pardon for a foolish blunder, but will you tell me this name?"

Marie bent forward to look at the paper which her husband handed her, and, pointing with her finger, read "Professor Philip Moritz."

"Do you intend to invite him?" asked Ebenstreit, quite alarmed.

"Why should I not? He belongs to the circle of friends and acquaintances, and it is natural that I should include him. Moreover, there is not a little gossip, and it is necessary to silence it. If you are not of my opinion, strike out the name."

"Not at all, dearest. On the contrary, you are perfectly right, and I admire you for it."

"Then give the list to the butler, for it is quite time that the invitations were given out."

CHAPTER XXXV
THE CURSE

The evening of the soiree had arrived. In quick succession drove the carriages up the broad entrance to the mansion of Herr Ebenstreit, The curious street public pressed in compact masses near the gate to peep in, or at least catch a fugitive glance of the ladies alighting from their carriages, who were received by the butler at the foot of the carpeted steps. A host of gold-bespangled footmen lined the entrance upon each side, which was ornamented with the most exquisite hot-house plants, filling the air with perfume.

Two tall, stately footmen, with broad gold shoulder-bands and large gilt batons, stood at the door of the anteroom, which was brilliantly illuminated with chandeliers and side-lights, reflected in the numerous mirrors. The anteroom led into the reception-room by wide folding-doors, where the names were given to the usher, who announced them in a stentorian voice in the drawing-room. There stood the Baron von Ebenstreit to receive the guests, all smiles, and with bustling assiduity accompany them to the adjoining drawing-room to present them to the baroness.

Among the select company were conspicuous the most distinguished names of the aristocracy. Generals and staff-officers, countesses and baronesses were crowded together, with the ladies of the financial world, near ministers and counsellors in this gorgeous saloon, which was the delight and admiration of the envious, and excited the tongues of the slanderous. Those acquainted gathered in the window-niches and cosy corners, maliciously criticising the motley crowd, and eminently consoled with the sure prospect of the ruin of the late banker, surrounding himself with such unbecoming splendor and luxury, the bad taste of his arrogant, overdressed, and extravagant wife.

"Have you noticed her parure of diamonds?" whispered the Countess Moltke to Fran von Morien. "If they are real, then she wears an estate upon her shoulders."

"The family estate of Von Leuthen," laughingly replied Frau von Morien. "You know, I suppose, that the father of General von Leuthen was a brick-burner, and he may have succeeded in changing a few bricks into diamonds."

"You are wicked, sweet one," replied the countess, smiling. "One must acknowledge that her toilet is charming. I have never seen its equal. The gold lace over the rose-colored satin is superb."

"Yes, and the mingling of straw feathers, diamonds, flowers, lace, and birds is truly ridiculous in her head-dress."

"It must have been copied exactly from the one which the Queen Marie Antoinette wore at the ball at Versailles a fortnight since. The baroness was present at this court ball with her greyhound of a husband, and created quite a sensation with her costly recherchee toilet, as the French ambassador told us yesterday."

"Certainly not by her manner," said Frau von Morien. "She is insupportably arrogant and self-sufficient. What do you think of this pretentious manner of announcing our names as if we were at an auction where they sold titles?"

"It is a very good French custom," remarked the countess. "But it does not become a lady of doubtful nobility and uncertain position, to introduce foreign customs here. She should leave this to others, and modestly accept those already in use by us."

"One remarks the puffed-up parvenue," whispered Frau von Morien. "Every thing smells of the varnish upon the newly-painted coat-of-arms."

"Hush, my friend! I there comes the baroness leaning upon the arm of the French ambassador. She is indeed imposing in appearance, and one could mistake her for a queen."

"Could any one ever suppose that this queen once made flowers to sell? Come, countess, I have just thought of a charming scene to revenge myself upon this arrogant personage."

Giving her arm to the countess, she approached her hostess leaning upon the arm of the Marquis de Treves, the French ambassador, as they were standing beneath the immense chandelier of rock crystal, which sparkled above them like a crown of stars, causing her diamonds to look as if in one blaze of different hues.

"Oh, permit us to sun ourselves in your rays, ma toute belle," said the Countess Moltke. "One could well fancy themselves in a fairy palace, so enchanting is everything here."

"And the baroness's appearance confirms this impression," remarked the gallant Frenchman. "Fancy could not well paint a more lovely fairy in one's happiest dreams."

"Yes, truly I wander around as if in an enchanted scene. I feel as if I must seize myself by the head and be well shaken, to convince myself that I am really awake and not dreaming a chapter from Aladdin. I made the effort, but felt the wreath of roses in my hair, and—"

"And that convinced you of your wakefulness," said the baroness, a little haughtily. Turning to the ambassador, she added: "Do you observe, monsieur le marquis, what a delicate attention this lady shows me in wearing a wreath of flowers which I manufactured?"

"Comment! The baroness is truly a fairy! She causes flowers to grow at her pleasure, and vies with Nature. It seems impossible. I can scarcely believe it."

"And yet it is true," said Frau von Morien. "The baroness, indeed, fabricated these roses three years since, when she had the kindness to work for me. You will acknowledge that I have kept them well?"

"It was no kindness of mine, but a necessity," said the baroness, "and I must confess that I would not have undertaken so troublesome a piece of work from pure goodness or pleasure. You will remember that I was very poor before my marriage, and as Frau von Morien was one of my customers, it is very natural that she possesses my flowers. She gave me many orders, and paid me a very small price, for she is very practical and prudent, and understands bargaining and cheapening, and when one is poor they are obliged to yield to the shameless parsimony of the rich. I thank you, my dear benefactress, for the honor you have shown me in wearing my flowers, for it has been a pleasant occasion to explain ourselves and recognize each other. Have the kindness to recall other remembrances of the past."

"I do not remember possessing any other souvenirs," replied the countess, confused.

"Have you forgotten that I gave French lessons to your niece, the present Frau von Hohenthal? She came to me three times weekly, because the lessons were a few groschen cheaper at the house."

At this instant the usher announced in a loud voice, "Professor Philip Moritz."

A gentleman of slight proportions, in an elegant fashionable dress, appeared and remained standing in the doorway, his large black eyes wandering searchingly through the drawing-room. Herr von Ebenstreit approached, extending him his hand, uttering a few unintelligible words, which his guest appeared not to notice, but, slightly inclining, asked if he would present him to the lady of the house.

"Have the kindness to follow me," said Ebenstreit, leading Moritz through the circle of jesting, slandering ladies and gentlemen, to the centre of the room, where Marie was still standing with the French ambassador and the two ladies.

"My dear," said her husband, "I have brought you an old acquaintance, Professor Moritz."

As Ebenstreit would retreat, Moritz commanded him to remain, placing his white-gloved hand upon his arm, and holding him fast. "I would ask you one question before I speak with the baroness."

Moritz spoke so loud, and in such a strange, harsh, and repulsive manner, that every one turned astonished, asking himself what it meant. Conversation was hushed, and the curious pressed toward the peculiar group in the centre to the baroness, who regarded her husband perfectly composed, and the pale man, with the flashing eyes, the glance of which pierced her like daggers.

A breathless silence reigned, broken only by Ebenstreit's trembling voice. "What is it, professor? How can I serve you?"

"Tell me who you are?" replied Moritz, with a gruff laugh.

"I am the Baron Ebenstreit von Leuthen!"

"And the scar which you bear upon your face, is it not the mark of a whip, with which I lashed a certain Herr Ebenstreit three years since, who prevented my eloping with my betrothed? I challenged him to fight a duel, but the coward refused me satisfaction, and then I struck him in the face, causing the blood to flow. Answer me—are you this gentleman?"

Not a sound interrupted the fearfully long pause which followed. Every one turned astonished to Ebenstreit, who, pale as death, was powerless to utter a word, but stood staring at his opponent.

"Why do you not answer me?" cried Moritz, stamping his foot. "Are you the coward? Was this red scar caused by the whip-lash?"

Another long pause ensued, and a distinctly audible voice was heard, saying, "Yes, it is he!"

"Who replied to me?" asked Moritz, turning his angry glance away from Ebenstreit.

"I," said Marie. "I reply for my husband!"

"You? Are you the wife of this man?" thundered Moritz.

"I am," Marie answered.

"Is this invitation directed to me from you?" he continued, drawing a paper from his pocket. "Did you permit yourself to invite me to your house?"

"Yes, I did," she calmly answered.

"And by what right, madame? This is the question I wish answered, and I came here for that purpose."

"I invited you because I desired to see you."

"Shameless one!" cried Moritz, furious.

"Sir," cried the ambassador, placing himself before Moritz, defying his anger, "you forget that you are speaking to a lady. As her husband is silent, I declare myself her knight, and I will not suffer her to be injured by word or look.

"How can you hinder me?" cried Moritz, with scorn. "What will you do if I dash this paper at her feet, and forbid her to ever write my name again?" Making a ball of it, he suited the action to the word, casting a defiant look at the marquis.

"I shall order the footmen to thrust you out of the house. Here, servants, remove this man; he is an escaped lunatic, undoubtedly."

Two footmen pressed forward through the circle which crowded around Moritz.

"Whoever touches me, death to him!" thundered Moritz, laying his hand upon a small sword at his side.

"Let no one dare lay a hand on this gentleman," cried Marie, with a commanding wave of her hand to the lackeys. "I beseech you, marquis, and you, honored guests, to quietly await the conclusion of this scene, and to permit Herr Moritz to finish speaking."

"Do you mean to defy me, madame?" muttered Moritz, gnashing his teeth. "You perhaps count upon my magnanimity to keep silent, and not disclose the secrets of the past to this aristocratic assembly. I stand here as its accusing spirit, and condemn you as a shameless perjurer.—I will ask you who are here rendering homage to this woman, if you know who she is, and of what she has been guilty? As a young girl she was as sweet and innocent as an angel, and seemed more like a divine revelation. To think of her, inspired and elevated one's thoughts, and heaven was mirrored in her eyes. She was poor, and yet so infinitely rich, that if a king had laid all his treasures at her feet, as the gift of his love, he would receive more than he gave, for in her heart reposed the wealth of the whole human race. Oh! I could weep tears of blood in reflecting upon what she was, and what she has become. Smile and mock, ladies and gentlemen; my brain is crazed, and I weep for my lost angel."

Moritz dashed his hands to his face, and stood swaying backward and forward, sobbing.

Sighs and regrets were heard in the room. The ladies pressed their handkerchiefs to their eyes; others regarded with lively sympathy the handsome young man, who deeply interested them, and gazed reproachfully at the young baroness, expecting her to be crushed with these reproaches and tears, but who, on the contrary, stood with proud composure, her face beaming with joy, gazing at Moritz.

"It is past—my last tear is shed, and my last wail has been uttered," cried Philip, uncovering his face. "My angel has changed into a despicable woman. I loved her as the wretched, disconsolate being adores the one who reveals paradise to him; and she fooled me into the belief that she loved me. We exchanged vows of eternal constancy and affection, and promised each other to bear joyfully every ill in life, and never separate until death. I should have doubted myself, rather than she who stood above me, like a divine revelation. I wished to win her by toil and industry, by my intellect, and the fame by which I could render my name illustrious. It was, indeed, nothing in the eyes of her grasping parents; they repulsed me with scorn and pride, but Marie encouraged me to perfect confidence in her affection. Whilst I wandered on foot to Silesia, like a poor pilgrim toward happiness, to humble myself before the king, to beg and combat for my angel, there came temptation, sin, and vulgarity, in the form of this pale, cowed-down man, who stands beside my betrothed gasping with rage. The temptation of riches changed my angel into a demon, a miserable woman bartered for gold! She betrayed her love, yielding it up for filthy lucre, crushing her nobler nature in the dust, and driving over it, as did Tullia the dead body of her father. She sold herself for riches, before which you all kneel, as if worshipping the golden calf! After selling her soul to a man whom she despised, even if he were not rich, she has had the boldness to summon me, the down-trodden and half-crazed victim, to her gilded palace, as if I were a slave to be attached to her triumphal car. I am a free man, and have come here only to hurl contempt in her face, to brand her before you all as a perjurer and a traitress, whom I never will pardon, but will curse with my latest breath! Now I have relieved my heart of its burden, I command this woman to deny what I have said, if she can."

With a dictatorial wave of the hand, he pointed excitedly Marie. A deathlike stillness reigned. Even the lights seemed to grow dim, and every one was oppressed as if by excessive sultriness.

Again Moritz commanded Marie to acknowledge the truth of his accusations before the honored assembly.

She encountered his angry glance with calmness, and a smile was perceptible upon her lip. "Yes, said she, I acknowledge that I am a perjurer and a traitor. I have sold myself for riches, and yielded my peace of soul and my love for mammon. I might justify myself, but I refrain from it, and will only say that you have told the truth! One day you will cease to curse me, and, perhaps a tear of pity will glisten in the eye now flashing with scorn and anger. The poor wife who lies in the dust implores for the last blessing of your love!"

"Marie!" he cried, with heart-rending anguish, "oh, Marie!" and rushed toward her, kneeling before her, and clinging to her, pressing a kiss upon her hand and weeping aloud. Only for a moment did he give way, and then sprang up wildly, rushing through the crowd, out of the room.

A fearful silence ensued. No one had the courage to break it. Every one hoped that Marie, through a simulated fainting, would end the painful scene, and give the guests an opportunity to withdraw. No such thoughtfulness for her friends occurred to her.

She turned to the Marquis de Treves, who stood pale and deeply agitated behind her, and burst into a loud laugh.

"How pale you are! Have you taken this comedy for truth? Did you think this theatrical performance was a reality? You have forgotten what I told you a month since in Paris, that I had a native talent for acting. You would contest the matter with me, and I bet you that I could introduce an impromptu scene in my house, with such artistic skill, that you would be quite deceived."

"Indeed I do recall it; how could I have forgotten it?" replied the marquis, with the ready tact of the diplomat.

"Have I won?" asked Marie, smiling.

"You have played your role, baroness, like an artiste of consummate talent, and to-morrow I shall have the honor to cancel the debt in your favor."

"Now, then, give me your arm, marquis, and conduct me to the dancing-room, and you, worthy guests, follow us," said. Marie, leading the way.

The merry music even was not sufficient to dissipate the awkward oppression, and by midnight the guests had taken leave, and Marie stood under the chandelier, pale and rigid, opposite her husband. He had summoned courage to bewail the terrible scene, weeping and mourning over her cruelty and his shame. Marie, with chilling indifference, regarded him without one visible trace of pity.

"You realized what you were doing when you imposed the scorn of this marriage upon me," she said. "I have never deceived you with vain hopes! You have sown dragons' teeth, and warriors have sprung up to revenge me upon you. Serve yourself of your riches to fight the combatants. See if you can bargain for a quiet conscience as easily as you purchased me! My soul is free though, and it hovers over you as the spirit of revenge.—Beware!"

She slowly turned and quitted the room. Her diamonds sparkled and blazed in the myriads of lights. The large mirrors reflected the image of a haughty woman, who swept proudly past like a goddess of revenge!

Ebenstreit stood gazing after her. He had a horror of the lonely still room, so gorgeous and brilliantly illuminated—a shudder crept over him, and he sank, weeping bitterly.

In the little room, the buried happiness of the past, Marie knelt, with outstretched arms, imploring heaven for mercy. "I thank Thee, Heavenly Father, that I have been permitted to see him again! My sacrifice was not in vain—he lives! He is free, and his mind is clear and bright. I thank Thee that he still loves me. His anger is but love!"

CHAPTER XXXVI
THE KING AND THE ROSICRUCIANS

The joy which Bischofswerder said, reigned in heaven and upon earth over the return of the crown prince to the path of virtue, in having forsaken Wilhelmine Enke, was of but short duration.

The Invisibles and the pious Rosicrucians soon learned that sagacious and cunning woman defied the spirits and abjured the oaths.

Since the night of his communion with the departed, Frederick William had never visited Charlottenburg—never seen the house which contained all that he held most dear; he had returned Wilhelmine's letters unopened, and had even had the courage to refuse himself to the children, who came to see him.

If he had been left to consult his own heart, he would not probably have had sufficient resolution to have done this; Bischofswerder and Woellner never left him for a moment, as they said the Invisible Fathers had commanded them to tarry with the much-loved brother in these first days of trial and temptation, and to elevate and gladden him with edifying conversations and scientific investigations.

The prayers and exhortations were the duty of Woellner, who, besides this, continued his daily discourses upon the administration of government, preparing the prince for the important command of the royal regiments, which they hoped favorable destiny would soon grant him.

The scientific researches were the part of Bischofswerder, and he entered upon his duties with the zeal and pleasure of an inquiring mind, itself hopeful and believing.

In the cabinet arranged in the new palace at Potsdam, the prince and his dear Bischofswerder worked daily, many hours, to discover the great hope of the alchemist—the philosopher's stone. Not finding it, unfortunately, they brewed all sorts of miraculous drinks, which were welcome to the prince as the elixir of eternal youth and constant love. In the evenings they communed with the spirits of the distinguished departed, which, moved at the earnest prayers of Woellner, and the fervent exhortation of the crown prince, always had the goodness to appear, and witness their satisfaction for their much-loved son, as they called him, for continuing brave and faithful, and not falling into the unholy snares of the seductress.

The crown prince, however, experienced not the least self-contentment. Each day renewed the yearning for the beloved of his youth and for his children, for which those of his wife were no compensation—neither the silent, awkward Prince Frederick William, nor his crying little brother. In his dreams he saw Wilhelmine dissolved in tears, calling upon him in most tender accents, and when he awoke, it was to an inconsolable grief. He wept with heart-felt sorrow; his oath alone kept him from hastening to her; it bound him, and fettered his earnest wish to see her, making him sad and melancholy.

The spirits had no pity nor mercy upon him. His two confidants encouraged his virtue and piety from morning till night, exalting his excited fancy with their marvellous relations and apparitions.

One day as they were on the point of commencing the morning prayers to the Invisibles, a royal footman appeared, with the command to betake themselves to Sans-Souci, where the king awaited them.

A royal carriage was in attendance to convey them. There was no alternative but obedience.

"Perhaps Fate destines us to become martyrs to the holy cause," said Woellner, devoutly folding his hands.

"We may never enjoy the happiness of seeing our dear brothers of the confederacy again," sighed Bischofswerder. "Our spirits will always be with you, my prince, and the Invisible Fathers will protect you in all your ways."

The crown prince, deeply moved, separated from his friends with tears in his eyes; but as the carriage rolled away he felt relieved as of an oppressive burden, and breathed more freely.

At the same time a footman entered, bearing upon a golden salver a letter for the prince. Unobserved and free to act, he read it, and as he sat musingly thinking over its contents, so tender and affectionate, he re-read it, and rising, made a bold resolve, his face beaming with happiness, to order his carriage, which he did, and in a few moments more drove at full speed away from the palace.

Bischofswerder and Woellner, in the mean time, arrived at Sans-Souci. The footman awaiting them conducted them at once through the picture-gallery, into the little corridor leading to the king's cabinet, and there left them to announce them to his majesty. Both gentlemen heard their names called in a loud voice, and the response of the king: "Let them wait in the little corridor until I permit them to enter."

The footman returned and with subdued voice made known the royal command, and departed, carefully closing the door.

There was no seat in the narrow, little corridor, and the air was close and oppressive.

They could hear voices in mingled conversation; sometimes it seemed as if the king were communicating commands; again, as if he dictated in a suppressed voice. The Rosicrucians knew very well it was the hour of the cabinet council, and they waited patiently and steadfastly, but as their watches revealed the fact that three hours had passed, and every noise was hushed, they concluded they were forgotten, and resolved to remind the lackey of their presence.

"Indeed, this standing is quite insupportable," whispered Woellner.

They both slipped to the entrance and tried the bronze knob, but although it turned, the door opened not, and was evidently fastened upon the outside. They looked alarmed at each other, asking what it could mean. "Can it be intentional? Are we imprisoned here? We must be resigned, although it is a severe experience." At last, patience exhausted, they resolved to bear it no longer, and tapped gently at the door of the king. The loud bark of a dog was their only response, and again all was still.

"Evidently there is no one there," sighed Bischofswerder. "It is the hour of dining of the king."

"I wish it were ours also," whined Woellner. "I confess I yearn for bodily nourishment, and my legs sink under me."

"I am fearfully hungry," groaned Bischofswerder; "besides, the air is suffocating. I am resolved to go to extremes, and make a noise."

He rushed like a caged boar from one door to the other, shrieking for the lackey to open the door; but as before, a loud bark was the only response.

"The Lord has forsaken us," whimpered Woellner. "The sublime Fathers have turned their faces away from us. We will pray for mercy and beg for a release!" and he sank upon his knees.

"What will that avail us here, where neither prayers nor devotion are heeded? Only energy and determination will aid us at Sans-Souci. Come, let us thump and bang until they set us free!" cried Bischofswerder, peevishly.

Their hands were lame, and their voices hoarse with their exertions; and no longer able to stand, they sank down upon the floor hungry and exhausted, almost weeping with rage and despair.

At last, after long hours of misery, they heard a noise in the adjoining room. The king had again entered his cabinet. The door opened, and the lackey motioned to the two gentlemen to enter. They rose with difficulty and staggered into the room, the door being closed behind them.

His majesty was seated in his arm-chair, with his three-cornered hat on, leaning his chin upon his hands, crossed upon his staff. He fixed his great blue eyes, with a searching glance, upon the two Rosicrucians; then turned to his minister, Herzberg, who was seated at the table covered with documents.

"These are, then, the two great props of the Rosicrucians?" asked Frederick—"the two charlatans whom they have told me make hell hot for the crown prince, continually lighting it up with their prayers and litanies."

"Your majesty," answered Herzberg, smiling, "these gentlemen are Colonel Bischofswerder and the councillor of the exchequer, Woellner, whom your majesty has commanded to appear before you."

"You are the two gentlemen who work miracles, and have the effrontery to summon the spirit of our ancestor, the great elector, and the Emperor Marcus Aurelius?"

"Sire," stammered Bischofswerder, "we have tried to summon spirits."

"And I too," cried the king, "only they will not come; therefore I wished to see the enchanters, and would like to purchase the secret."

"Pardon me, most gracious sire," said Woellner, humbly, "you must first be received in the holy order of the Rosicrucians."

"Thanks," cried the king, "I am not ready for the like follies, and whilst I live the Invisibles must take heed not to become too visible, or they will be taken care of. I will not permit Prussia to retrograde. It has cost too much trouble to enlighten the people, bring them to reason, and banish hypocrisy. Say to the Rosicrucians that they shall leave the crown prince in peace, or I will chase them to the devil, who will receive them with open arms! It could do no harm to appeal to the prince's conscience to lead an honorable life, and direct his thoughts more to study than to love, but you shall not make a hypocrite of him and misuse his natural good-nature. If the Rosicrucians try to force the prince and rule him, I will show them that I am master, and will no longer suffer their absurdities, but will break up the whole nest of them! I have been much, annoyed at the deep despondency of the crown prince. You shall not represent to him that baseness and virtue are the same, and that he is the latter when he betrays those to whom he has sworn fidelity and affection. An honorable man must, above all, he cognizant of benefits, and not forsake those who have sacrificed their honor and love to him, and have proved their fidelity. Have you understood me, gentlemen?"

"It will be my holy duty to follow strictly your majesty's commands," said Bischofswerder.

"And I also will strive to promote the will of my king," asserted Woellner.

"It will be necessary to do so, or you two gentlemen may find yourselves at Spandau. I would say to you once for all, I will not suffer any sects; every one can worship God in his own way. No one shall have the arrogant presumption to declare himself one of the elect. We are all sinners. The Rosicrucians are not better than the Illuminati or Freemasons, and none are more worthy than the tailor and cobbler who does his duty. Adieu!"

The king nodded quickly and pointed to the door out of which the two brothers were about to disappear, when he called them back.

"If the prince is not at the palace on your return, I advise you not to pursue him, but reflect that the Invisibles may have summoned him to a communion of spirits; I believe, too, that I kept you waiting; but without doubt you were comforted by the Fathers, who bore you away upon their wings, and gave you food and drink! Those who are protected by the spirits, and can summon them at pleasure, can never want. If you are hungry, call up the departed Lucullus, that he may provide for you to eat; and if you have no earthly seat, summon Semiramis that she may send you her hanging gardens for the quiet repose of the elect! I am rejoiced that you have enjoyed such celestial refreshments in the corridor. Adieu!"

The king gazed sadly after them. Approaching Herzberg, he said: "I felt, as I looked at the two rogues, that it was a pity to grow old. Did you think that I would let them off so easily?"

"Sire, I really do not understand you," replied Herzberg, shrugging his shoulders. "I know not, in your most active youthful days, how you could have done otherwise."

"I will tell you that, if I were not an old man, void of decision and energy, I would have had these fellows taken to Spandau for life!" said the king, striking the table with his staff.

"Your majesty does yourself injustice," said Herzberg, smiling. "You were ever a just monarch in your most ardent youth, and never set aside the law. These men were not guilty of any positive crime."

"They are daily and hourly guilty of enticing away from me the crown prince, and making the future ruler of my country an obscurer, a necromancer, and at the same time a libertine! I was obliged to overlook his youthful preference for Wilhelmine Enke, and wink at this amour, for I know that crown prince is human, and his affections are to be consulted. If he cannot love the wife which diplomacy chooses for him, then he must be permitted the chosen one of his heart to console him for the forced marriage. At the same time this person was passable, and without the usual fault of such creatures, a desire to rule and mingle in politics. She seems to be unambitious and unpretentious. These Rosicrucians would banish her by increasing the number of favorites, that they may rule him, and make the future King of Prussia a complete tool in their hands. They excite his mind, which is not too well balanced, and rob him by their witchcraft of the intellect that he has. They promise him to find the philosopher's stone, and make a fool of him. Am I not right?"

"I must acknowledge that you are," sighed Herzberg.

"And admit also that it would be just to send these in, famous fellows as criminals to Spandau."

"Sire, unfortunately, there are crimes and offences which the law does not reach, and which cannot be judged."

"When I was young," said the king, "I tore up and stamped upon every weed that I found in my garden. Shall I now let these two grow and infect the air, because the law gives me no right to crush them? Formerly I would have torn them leaf from leaf, but now I am old and useless, my hand is weak, and lacks the strength to uproot them, therefore I suffer them to stand, and all the other abominable things which these rogues bring to pass. A cloud is rising, from which a storm will one day burst over Prussia; but I cannot dissipate it, for the little strength and breath that remains I have need of for the government; and, moreover, I have no superfluous time for the future, but must live and work only for the present."

"But the blessing of your exertions will be felt in the future. The deeds of a great man are not extinguished with his death, but shine like a star, disseminating light beyond his grave!"

"This light is just what the Rosicrucians will take care to extinguish like a tallow candle with too long a wick, and it is good fortune that the astronomers have awarded me a little glorification in the heavens, and accorded me a star, for the Rosicrucians would not let it shine here below. I must console myself with this, and recall that when it is dark and lowering here, I have a star above in the sky!"

"This star is Frederick's honor," cried Herzberg. "It will beam upon future generations, and become the guiding light of the sons and nephews of your house, and they will learn to be as sagacious and wise as the Great Frederick."

"There you have made a great error, Herzberg," replied the king, quickly. "Future generations are newer taught by the past—grandchildren think themselves wiser than their grandparents. The greatest of heroes is forgotten, and his deeds buried in the dust of ages. You have given me a glorious title of honor, and I know how little I deserve it."

"A title which will be confirmed in centuries to come, for every history will speak of Frederick the Second as Frederick Great."

"In history it may be, but the people will speak of me as 'Old Fritz'—that will be on the lips of those who love me, and expression of endearment; on the lips of those who hate me, one of disaffection. I am, indeed, 'Old Fritz,' which the Bischofswerders and Woellners also call me, and try to make the crown prince believe that I have outlived my period, and do not understand or esteem the modern time. In their eyes I am a dismantled ship of state, which the storms of life have rendered unseaworthy. They would refit the vessel, and give it a new flag, sending Old Fritz, the helmsman, to the devil! The day of my death they will hoist this flag, with 'Modern Time' inscribed upon it in large letters. I shall then be united in Elysium with Voltaire, Jordan, Suhm, and all my other friends, as we were wont to be at Sans-Souci, and look down with a pitying smile upon the Modern Time and Old Folly!—Vale!"

CHAPTER XXXVII
THE ESPOUSALS

Both Bischofswerder and Woellner hastened to avail themselves of the commanding "adieu," and quit the royal presence. Without, the carriage was ready to reconvey them to the new palace. They were so exhausted that neither of them uttered a word, the last injunctions of the king ringing in their ears.

Silently they alighted upon arriving, but as the footman came out to meet them they asked, simultaneously, if his royal highness had dined.

"His highness is not here, having departed immediately after the two gentlemen, and is not yet returned," he answered.

"You may serve us something to eat as quickly as possible in the little dining-room. Let it be ready in a quarter of an hour," commanded Bischofswerder.

"Now that we are alone, what do you think of this affair?" asked Woellner.

"I cannot vouchsafe a reply until I have eaten a pheasant's wing, and drunken my champagne," replied Bischofswerder.

He kept his word, preserving a solemn silence until a good half of the bird had disappeared, and many glasses of iced champagne.

Then Bischofswerder leaned back in his comfortable armchair with infinite ease, whilst his friend occupied himself with the most pious zeal with the pheasant, rejoicing at this revelation of the Invisibles. Bischofswerder let him enjoy it, and ordered the footman to serve the dessert and withdraw.

"Now I am prepared to reply to you, my dear friend, that we are alone. I believe the king would have sent us to Spandau at once if we had opposed his free-thinking opinions."

"I am convinced of it," sighed Woellner, eyeing the remains of the bird with a melancholy glance. "We shall have much to endure for the holy cause which we serve."

"That is to say, we will have much to suffer if we, in fanatical indiscretion, do not submit to circumstances," said Bischofswerder.

"You cannot traduce the sublime Fathers!" cried Woellner;—"for the body's security, we cannot endanger the salvation of our souls, and, like Peter, deny our master."

"No, my much-loved and noble friend. But we must be wise as serpents, and our duty to the holy order is to preserve its useful tools that they may not be lost. You will agree with me in this?"

"Indeed, I do admit it," replied Wollner, pathetically.

"Further, you will acknowledge that we are very useful, and I might say indispensable tools of the Sublime Order of the Rosicrucians and the Invisible Fathers of the Order of Jesus? It is our task to secure an abiding-place to the proscribed and, cursed, to plough and sow the field, which will yield good fruit for humanity entire, and particularly our order, when the crown prince ascends the throne. We will here erect a kingdom of the future, and it is all-important to lay so secure a corner-stone in the heart of his highness that nothing can shake or dislodge it. Who could perfect this work if we were not here? Who would dare to undertake the difficult task if we should fail? Who would carry on a secret and continued warfare with this artful and powerful seductress if we were conquered?"

"No one would do it," sighed Woellner, "no one would sacrifice themselves like Samson for this Delilah."

"We will together be the Samson," replied Bischofswerder, drawing a glass of sparkling champagne. "We will be the Samson which the Philistines drove out, but this woman shall not practise the arts of Delilah upon us in putting our eyes out or cutting off our hair. Against two Samsons the most artful and beautiful Delilah is not wary enough; and if we cannot conquer her, we must resort to other means."

"What may they be, dear brother?"

"We must compromise the matter."

Woellner sprang up, and a flush of anger or from champagne overspread his face "Compromise with the sinful creature!" he cried, impetuously. "Make peace with the seductress, who leads the prince from the path of virtue!"

"Yes, we must be on friendly terms with this woman, who could greatly injure us as an enemy, and aid us infinitely as a friend. This is my intention, and I am the more convinced that we must accept this middle course, as she is protected by the king."

"Because he knows from his spies that she mingles with the Illuminati and the Freemasons, and that she is our opponent," said Woellner.

"The more the reason, my noble zealot, to win her friendship, who will have validity and power until the crown prince reigns, and this old godless freethinker of a king is in his gravel Then Prussia will commence a new era, and we shall be lords, and guide the machine of state. For such lofty aims one ought to be ready to compromise with his Satanic majesty even. Then why not with this little she-devil, whose power is fading every year with her youth and beauty?"

"It is quite true, we should be mindful of the device of our Invisible Fathers. The end sanctifies the means," sighed Woellner.

"I believe it to be indispensable, and you will grant that I am right. Do you not see that the prince has availed himself of our absence to go there, and has not yet returned?"

"What!" shrieked Woellner, clasping his hands—"you do not mean that—"

"That Rinaldo has returned to the enchanted garden of Armida."

"Oh, let us hasten to release him at once, and revue his soul from perdition!" cried Woellner, springing up.

"On the contrary, let us await him here without a word of reproach upon his return. This will touch his tender heart which we must work upon, if we would get him into our power, for to us he must belong. Fill our glasses with the sparkling wine, and drink to the contract with Wilhelmine Enke."

Just as merrily they quaffed the champagne in the little cosy dining-room at Charlottenburg, where the prince and Wilhelmine were rejoicing over a reconciliation, no one being present but the two children. Their joyous laugh and innocent jests delighted the father, and the beaming eyes, sweet smile, and witty conversation of his favorite, filled his heart with pleasure.

Not a word of reproach escaped her, but exultant and joyous she hastened with outstretched arms to meet him, kissing away all his attempts to implore pardon, and thanking him that he had returned to her.

At first the prince gave himself up to the joy of the reunion with his beloved Wilhelmine sad children; but now, as the first outburst had passed, the quiet, happy dinner being finished, and they had returned to the sitting-room, a tinge of melancholy earnestness overshadowed his amiable face.

Wilhelmine threw her arms gently around his neck as she sat beside him upon the divan, and looked up to him with a tender questioning glance. "Your thoughts are veiled, dearest; will you not confide to me that which lies concealed there?"

"Ah, Wilhelmine, it is a mourning veil, and hides the sorrow of renunciation."

"I do not understand you, Frederick," she smilingly replied. "Who could compel you to an abnegation which would cause you grief?"

"Listen to me, Wilhelmine, and understand that I am suffering from circumstances—an oath taken in the pressure of the moment. Try to comprehend me, my dear child."

Drawing her closer to him, he faithfully related to her the night of the communion of the spirits, and his consequent oath.

"Is that all, my dear?" she replied, smiling, as he finished.

"What do you mean?" he asked, astonished.

"Nothing more than I would know if you have only sworn to renounce Wilhelmine Enke!"

"What could I have done more prejudicial to you?" he cried, not a little irritated.

"Surely you could not injure or grieve me more, and therefore I am not a little surprised that the pious Fathers could so carelessly word their oaths. You have sworn to renounce your affection to and separate from Wilhelmine Enke; so it follows that the Invisibles only demand that you give up my name, not myself, and that is easily changed, and my dear prince will not become a perjurer."

"I do not quite understand you; but I perceive by the arch expression of your face that you have conceived a lucky escape for your unhappy Frederick William. Explain to me, dearest, your meaning."

"I must change my name by marrying some one!" she whispered.

"Marry! and I give you to another? I will never consent to that," he cried, alarmed.

"Not to a husband, only a name," said she. "These Rosicrucians are such extraordinarily virtuous and pure beings, loving you so infinitely and disinterestedly, that it grieves them that my love for you does not shun the light, and throw over itself the mantle of hypocritical virtue! We will yield to the zealous purity of the Rosicrucians," continued Wilhelmine, her eyes sparkling, "and wrap this Wilhelmine Enke in a mantle of virtue by giving her a husband; and then, when she walks out with her children the passers-by will not have to blush with shame, and cry, 'There goes the miss with her children!' I have conceived and planned during this long and painful separation, and I am resolved to submit humbly to the pious Fathers, who are so zealously watchful for the salvation of your soul and my good fame."

"That is to say, you are determined to snap your fingers at them! Your plan is a good one, but you will find no one to aid you in a sham marriage!"

"I have already found one," whispered Wilhelmine, smiling. "Your valet de chambre Rietz is willing to stand with me in a sham marriage."

"My body-servant!"

"Yes, Frederick William! You will confess that I am not ambitious, and only consent to it to secure our happiness from the persecution of these virtuous men. Here is the contract," said she, drawing from her dress-pocket a paper, which she unfolded. "He promises to give me his name, and regard me as a stranger always, for the sum of four hundred thalers annually, with the promise of promotion to confidential servant when the noble crown prince shall ascend the throne. *[Footnote: Historical.—See F. Forster, "Latest Prussian History," vol. 1., p. 74.]* Will you sign it?"

"I will do any thing that will grant me your affection, in spite of my unhappy oath. Give me the paper. I will sign it. When is the wedding?"

"The moment that you, my dear lord and master, have inscribed your name," said Wilhelmine, handing him the pen, and pointing to the paper.

The prince wrote the desired signature, quickly throwing the pen across the room, shouting, "Long live Wilhelmine Rietz, who has rescued me from perjury and sin! Come to my arms, outstretched to press to my heart the most beautiful, most intelligent, and most diplomatic of women!"

Two days later it was related in Berlin that Wilhelmine Enke had married the princely valet de chambre Rietz, the crown prince being present at the ceremony, which took place at a small village near Potsdam.

Under the head of marriages, the Berlin newspapers announced "Wilhelmine Enke to Carl Rietz."

"Ah, my Rosicrucians," cried Wilhelmine, laughingly, as she read this notice, a mischievous triumph sparkling in her eyes; "ah, my heroes in virtue, for once you are outwitted, and I am victorious! I would like to witness their surprise. How they will laugh and swear over it! The favorite of a prince married to a valet de chambre! Wait until the prince becomes a king, then Wilhelmine Rietz will develop into a beautiful butterfly, and the wife of the valet de chambre will become a countess—nay, a princess. The Great Kophta has promised it, and he shall keep his word. I wear his ring, which sparkles and glistens, although the jeweller declares the diamond has been exchanged for a false stone. No matter, if it only shines like the real one. Every thing earthly is deception, falsehood, and glitter. Every one is storming and pressing on in savage eagerness toward fortune, honor, and fame! I will have my part in it. The storm and pressure of the world rage in my own heart. The fire of ambition is lighted in my soul, and the insatiable thirst for fortune consumes me. Blaze and burn until the day that Frederick William ascends the throne; then the low-born daughter of the trumpeter will become the high-born countess. The false stone will change to the sparkling diamond and Cagliostro shall then serve me."

CHAPTER XXXVIII
REVENGE FULFILLED

Since the soiree at the house of the rich banker, Ebenstreit, an entire winter had passed in pleasures and fetes. The position of Baron Ebenstreit von Leuthen had been recognized in aristocratic society, thanks to his dinners, soirees, balls, fetes, and particularly to his lovely, spirited, and proud wife. Herr Ebenstreit von Leuthen had reached the acme of his ambition; his house was the resort of the most distinguished society; the extravagance and superb arrangements of his dinners and fetes were the theme of every tongue. This excessive admiration flattered the vain, ambitious parvenu extremely, and it was the happiest day of his life when Prince Henry of Prussia, brother of Frederick the Great, did him the unspeakable honor to dine with him. This gratifying day he owed to his wife, and, as he said, it ought to be kept as the greatest triumph of money over prejudice and etiquette—the day upon which a royal prince recognized the rich and newly-created noble as his equal. Ebenstreit's entrance into the highest circle of aristocracy was due to the management and tone of the world of his wife, who understood the elegancies of life, passing as an example and ideal of an elegant woman, of which her husband was very proud. He lauded his original and crafty idea of devoting his money to such a satisfactory purchase as a sensible and ladylike wife, although the union was not a happy one, and, in the proper acceptation of the word, no marriage at all.

Whilst all were entertained at the fetes, and envied the splendor and wealth of Baron von Ebenstreit, there were many sinister remarks as to the possibility of sustaining this expenditure upon such a grand scale. It was whispered about that the banking-house, conducted under another name, had lost in extensive speculations, and that the baron lived upon his principal instead of his interest. The business community declared that the firm entered into the most daring and senseless undertakings, and that it must go to ruin. The old book-keeper, Splittgerber, who had for many years conducted the business, had been pensioned by the baron, and commenced for himself. His successor had once ventured to warn the nobleman, and represent to him the danger which threatened him, for which he was immediately dismissed, and the fact communicated to the entire house, at a special assemblage of the clerks for the purpose, with the warning of a like fate for every subordinate who should presume to criticise the acts of the principals, or proffer advice to them. Since this no one had ventured to repeat the offence, but every member of the house occupied himself in drawing a profit from the general and daily increasing confusion, and save something from the wreck which would inevitably ensue. The baron, with pretentious unconcern, dazzled by his unusual honors, permitted his business affairs to take their course with smiling unconcern, and when unsuccessful, to hide the mistakes of the banker under the pomp of the baron.

Marie, indulging in the style of a great lady, appeared not to notice or trouble herself at all about these things. She entertained most luxuriantly, and spent enormous sums upon her toilet, changed the costly livery of her numerous retinue of servants every month, as well as the furniture of the drawing-rooms; and presented with generous liberality her superfluous ornaments, dresses, and furniture to her dear high-born friends, who greedily accepted them, and were overflowing in their tender protestations and gratitude, whilst they in secret revolted at the presumption of the arrogant woman, who permitted herself to send them her cast-off things.

They rejoiced to receive them, however, and reappeared in her splendid drawing-rooms, enduring the pride and neglect of the baroness, and calling her their dear friend, whom they in secret envied and hated.

Did Marie know this, or did she let herself be deceived by these friendly protestations? Occasionally, when her friends embraced and kissed her, a languid smile flitted over her haughty face; and once as she wandered through the suite of rooms, awaiting her guests, she caught the reflection of a beautiful woman in the costly Venetian mirrors, sparkling with diamonds and wearing a silver-embroidered dress with a train. She gazed at this woman with an expression of ineffable scorn, and whispered to her: "Suffer yet awhile, you shall soon be released. This miserable trash will disappear. Only be firm—I hear already the cracking of the house which will soon fall a wreck at your feet!"

Others heard it also. As preparations were being made for a grand dinner, with which the Baron and Baroness von Ebenstreit would close the season, the former head bookkeeper of the baron appeared at the palace, demanding, with anxious mien, to see the principal.

Just at the moment the baron and his wife were in the large reception-room, which the decorator was splendidly arranging, under the direction of the baroness, with flowers, festoons, columns, and statues. Ebenstreit was watching admiringly the tasteful and costly display as the footman announced the former book-keeper and present banker, Splittgerber.

"He must come at another time," cried Ebenstreit, impatiently, "I am busy now; I—"

"Excuse me, baron," replied an earnest, gentle voice behind him, "that I have followed the lackey and entered unbidden. I come on urgent business, and I must indeed speak with you instantly!"

"Be brief then, at least," cried Ebenstreit, peevishly. "You see that my wife is here, and we are very busy arranging for a grand dinner to-day."

Herr Splittgerber, instead of replying, cast a peculiarly sad, searching glance through the beautifully-adorned room, and at the two lackeys, who stood on each side of the wide folding-doors.

"Permit that these servants withdraw, and order them to close the doors," said the book-keeper, almost commandingly. Ebenstreit, overruled by the solemn earnestness, obeyed against his will.

"Would you like me to leave also, sir?" said Marie, with a calm, haughty manner. "You have only to ask it and the baron will, undoubtedly, accord your request."

"On the contrary, I beg you to remain," quietly replied Splittgerber, "for what I have to say concerns you and your husband equally."

"Now, then, I beg you to say it quickly," cried Ebenstreit, impatiently; "I repeat, that we are very busy with preparing for to-day's festival."

"You will not give any fete to-day," said Splittgerber, solemnly.

Ebenstreit, cringing and frightened, gazed at the old man who looked sadly at him.

The baroness laughed aloud, sneeringly. "My dear sir, your tone and manner remind me of the wicked spirit at the horrible moment in the story when he comes to demand the bartered soul, and the enchanted castle falls a wreck!"

"Your comparison is an apt one, baroness," sighed the old man.—"I came to you, baron, because I loved your father. I have served your house thirty years, and amassed the little I had to commence business with in your service. Moreover, when you so suddenly dismissed me, you not only gave me my salary as a pension, but you funded the annuity with a considerable sum, which makes me, through your house, independent in means."

"You may thank my wife for that. She demanded, when I dismissed you, that I should compensate you with the liberality of a true nobleman."

"Oh, would that you had not done it, baroness!" cried Splittgerber—"would that you had permitted the old faithful pioneer in the business to remain by your husband! He might have warded off this misfortune and saved you by his experience and advice."

"For this very reason I demanded your removal. You permitted yourself to proffer advice which I felt did not become you," replied Marie, with a strange smile of triumph.

"And, I repeat, would that you had not done it!" sighed the old man. "I came to warn you, to conjure you, to save yourselves—to flee while there is yet time."

"Oh, mercy! what has happened?" cried Ebenstreit, terrified.

"The banking-house of Ebenstreit, founded under the name of Ludwig, associated with Ehlert of Amsterdam, four months since, to buy and load ships for the Calcutta market. Herr Ebenstreit gathered together the last wrecks of his fortune remaining from his ruinous speculations, to win enormously in this investment. Besides, he indorsed the notes of the Amsterdam house for the sum of eighty thousand dollars, which has been drawn, so that their notes are protested there. Herr Ebenstreit will have to pay this sum!"

"What else?" asked Ebenstreit, almost breathless.

"The house of Ehlert, in Amsterdam, has failed; the principal has fled with the coffers; the notes for eighty thousand dollars were protested, and you, baron, must pay this sum to-day, or declare yourself a bankrupt, and go to prison for debt."

Instantaneously a suppressed cry and a laugh were heard. Ebenstreit sank upon a seat, concealing his pallid face with his hands, while Marie stood at his side, her face beaming with joy.

"I am lost, I do not possess the eighth part of that sum! I cannot pay it. I must submit, for there are no further means to prevent it."

"No," replied Marie, with haughty tranquillity, "you have no further means to prevent it. The rich banker Ebenstreit will leave this house, no longer his own, to enter the debtor's prison poor as a beggar—nay, worse, a defrauder!"

"Oh, how cruel you are!" groaned Ebenstreit.

"Did you say, baroness, that this house is no longer his?" asked Splittgerber, alarmed.

"No," she triumphantly cried. "It belongs to me, and all that is in it—the pictures, statues, silver, diamonds, and pearls. Oh, I am still a rich woman!"

"And do you mean to retain this wealth if your husband becomes bankrupt? Do you not possess a common interest?" asked Splittgerber.

"No, thank Heaven, the community of interest was given up a year since," cried Ebenstreit, joyfully. "Baroness von Ebenstreit is the lawful possessor of this house and furniture. I was not so indiscreet as you supposed. I have at least secured this to my wife, and she will be a rich woman even if I fail, and will not let me starve. I shall divide about ten per cent with my creditors, but my wife will be rich enough for us both."

"This gives me to understand that you intend to make a fraudulent bankruptcy. You have settled every thing upon your wife to save yourself from the unhappy consequences of your failure. You will still be a rich man if your wife should sell her house, works of art, diamonds, gold and silver service, and equipages."

"Yes, indeed, a very rich man," said Marie. "In the last few weeks I have had my property estimated, and it would at least bring three hundred thousand dollars."

"If the baron only possessed this, he could pay his creditors, and have a small amount over, sufficient to live upon economically and genteelly. But you would rather enjoy splendor, and are not particular about living honorably. You will undoubtedly sell your property, and go to Paris, to revel in luxury and pleasure, while your defrauded creditors may, through you come to poverty and want.—Baron, I now see that your wife did well to bring about my removal. I should have, above all things, given you the unwelcome advice to sustain your honor unblemished, and dispose of your costly surroundings for the benefit of your creditors, that when you die it may be with a clear conscience. You prefer a life of luxury and ease, rocking your conscience to sleep until God will rouse it to a fearful awaking. But do as you like. I came here to offer you assistance, thinking that you would dispose of this property, and after paying your creditors have sufficient to live upon. Then I could be permitted to prove my fidelity to you. I now see that I was a fool. Yet in parting I will still beg of you to avoid the unfavorable impression of this dinner. The bill of exchange will be presented at four o'clock, and the bearer will not be satisfied with the excuse of your non-payment on account of dinner-company. You will be obliged to settle at once or be arrested. I have learned this from your chief creditor, and I begged him to have forbearance for you. I shall now justify him in showing you none, as you do not deserve it!—Farewell!"

The old book-keeper turned with a slight nod, and strode away through the drawing-room.

"Have you nothing to say to him? Will you let him go thus?" asked Marie, impetuously.

"Nothing at all. What should I say?" he replied, shrugging his shoulders.

"Then I will speak with him." Marie called loudly after Splittgerber, saying, "I have a word to speak to you."

The book-keeper remained standing near the door, and turning with downcast face, demanded of Marie what she wished.

"I have something to tell you," she replied, with her usual tranquil, proud demeanor, approaching Splittgerber, who regarded her with severity and contempt, which she met with a gentle, friendly expression, a sweet smile hovering on her lips.

Marie came close up to the old man, who awaited her with haughty defiance, and never advanced one step to meet her—a lady splendidly bedecked with diamonds and gold-embroidered satin. She whispered a few words in his ear. He started, and, astonished, looked into her face, as if questioning what he heard. She nodded, smiling, and bent again to say a few words.

Suddenly Splittgerber seemed metamorphosed. His gloomy face brightened a little, and his insolent glance was changed to one of deep emotion, Bowing profoundly as he held the baroness's proffered hand to take leave, he pressed it most respectfully to his lips.

"You will return in an hour?" Marie asked.

"Yes; I shall seek the gentlemen, and bring them with me," he graciously replied.

"Thanks; I will then await you."

Splittgerber departed, and Marie returned to Ebenstreit who, amazed, muttered some unintelligible words, having listened to her mysterious conversation with the old book-keeper.

"Now to you, sir!" said she, her whole tone and manner changing to harsh command; "the hour for settling our accounts has arrived—the hour that I have awaited, purchasing it by four years of torture, self-contempt, and despair. This comedy is at an end. I will buy of you my freedom. Do you hear me? I will cast off these galley-chains. I will be free!"

"Oh, Marie!" he cried, retreating in terror, "with what fearful detestation you regard me!"

"Do you wonder at it? Have I ever concealed this hate from you, or ever given you hope to believe that a reconciliation would be possible between us?"

"No, truly you have not, but now you will forgive me, for you know how I love you, and have provided for your future. You will remain rich, and I shall be poor."

Marie regarded him with unspeakable contempt. "You are more despicable than I thought you were. You do not deserve forbearance or pity, for you are a dishonorable bankrupt, who cares not how much others may suffer, provided his future is secured. I will not, however, suffer the name which I have borne against my will, to be defamed and become a mark for scorn. I will compel you to remain an honest man, and be just to your creditors. I propose to pay the bills of exchange, which will be presented to you to-day, provided you will consent to my conditions."

"Oh, Marie, you are an angel!" he cried, rushing toward her and kneeling at her feet, "I will do all that you wish, and consent to every thing you propose."

"Will you swear it?" she coldly replied.

"I swear that I accept your conditions."

"Bring the writing-materials from the window-niche, and seat yourself by this table."

Ebenstreit brought them, and seated himself by the Florentine mosaic table, near which Marie was standing.

She drew from her pocket a paper, which she unfolded and placed before him to sign. "Sign this with your full name, and add, 'With my own free will and consent,'" she commandingly ordered him.

"But you will first make known to me the contents?"

"You have sworn to sign it," she said, "and unless you accept my conditions, you are welcome to be incarcerated for life in the debtor's prison. You have only to choose. If you decide in the negative, I will exert myself that your creditors do not free you. I should trust in the justice of God having sent you there, and that man in miserable pity should not act against His will in freeing you. Now decide; will you sign the paper, or go to prison as a dishonorable bankrupt?"

He hastily seized the pen and wrote his name, handing the paper to Marie, sighing.

"You have forgotten to add the clause, 'With my own free will and consent,'" she replied, hastily glancing at it, letting the paper drop like a wilted leaf, and her eyes flashing with scorn.

Ebenstreit saw it, and as he again handed her the paper, he exclaimed, "I read in your eyes the intense hate you bear me."

"Yes," she replied, composedly, "not only hate, but scorn. Hush! no response. You knew it long before I was forced to stand at the altar with you. I warned you not to unite yourself to me, and you had the impious audacity to defy me with your riches. The seed of hate which you then sowed, you may to-day reap the fruits of. You shall recognize now that money is miserable trash, and that when deprived of it you will never win sympathy from your so-called friends, but they will turn from you with contempt, when you crave their pity or aid."

"I think that you exaggerate, dearest," said Ebenstreit, fawningly. "You have many devoted friends among the ladies, and I can well say that I have found, among the distinguished gentlemen who visit our house, many noble, excellent ones who have met me with a warmth of friendship—"

"Because they would borrow money of the rich man," interrupted Marie.

"Of course my coffers have always been accessible to my dear friends, and I prized the honor of proving my friendship by my deeds."

"You will realize to-day how they prove their gratitude to you for it. Go, receive the good friends whom you have invited. It is time that they were here, and I perceive the carriages are approaching."

Marie motioned to the door, with a dictatorial wave of her hand, and Ebenstreit betook himself to the reception-room. Just as he crossed the threshold, the usher announced "Herr Gedicke! Ebenstreit greeted him hastily in passing, and the old man went on to meet the baroness, who was hastening toward him.

"You have most graciously invited me to your house to-day, and you will excuse me that my earnest wish to see you has brought me earlier than any other guest."

"I begged you to come a quarter of an hour sooner, for I would gladly speak with you alone a few moments."

"I thought so, and hastened up here."

"Did not my old Trude go to see you some days since?" asked Marie, timidly.

"She did, and you can well understand that I was much affected and surprised at her visit. I thought that you had forgotten me, baroness, and that every souvenir of the past had fled from your memory. I now see that your noble, faithful heart can never forget, and therefore has never ceased to suffer, which I ought to regret, for your sake, but for my own it pleased me to receive your kind greeting."

Marie pressed her hand to her eyes and sighed audibly. "Pray do not speak so gently to me—it enervates me, and I would force myself to endure to-day. Only tell me, did Trude communicate to you my wishes, and will it be possible for you to fulfil them?"

"Your brave, good friend brought me a thousand dollars, praying me to convey this to Herr Moritz in order to defray the expenses of a journey to Italy."

"Have you accomplished it, and in such a manner that he does not suspect the source from whence it came? He would not receive it if he had the least suspicion of it. I have seen him secretly several times as he passed to and fro from the Gymnasium, and he appeared to me to grow paler and more languid every day."

"It is true that since you have come back he has changed. The old melancholy seems to have returned."

"He needs distraction; he must go away and forget me. It has always been his earnest wish to travel in Italy. You must tell him that you have succeeded in getting the money for him."

"I bethought myself of Moritz's publisher, represented to him how necessary it was for the health of Professor Moritz to travel, begged of him to order a work upon Italy, and particularly the works of art of Rome, and propose to Moritz the acceptance of the money for that object, as he was quite too proud to receive it as a present."

"That was an excellent idea," cried Marie. "Has it been accomplished?"

"Yes, as Herr Maurer made the proposal, and Moritz replied, sighing, that he had not the means for such a journey, the publisher immediately offered him half of the remuneration in advance; consequently he starts to-morrow for Italy, unknowing of the thousand dollars being your gift."

[Footnote: This work, which was published after his return, still excites the highest interest, and is entitled "Travels of a German in Italy during 1786 and 1787.—Letters of Philip Carl Moritz," 8 vols., Berlin, published by Frederick Maurer.]

"How much I thank you!" she joyfully cried. "Moritz is saved; he will now recover, and forget all his grief in studying the objects of interest in the Eternal City."

"Do you really believe that?" asked Herr Gedicke. "Were you not also in Italy?"

"I was indeed there two years, but it was very different with me. It is difficult to forget you are a slave, when listening all the while to the clanking of your chains."

"My poor child, I read with sorrow the history of the past years in your grief-stricken face. It is the first time we have met since your marriage."

"See what these years have made of me!—a miserable wife, whom the world esteems, but who recoils from herself. My heart has changed to stone, and I feel metamorphosed. The sight of you recalls that fearful hour, melting my heart and causing the tears to flow. At that time you blessed me, my friend and father. Oh, grant me your blessing again in this hour of sorrow! I implore you for it, before an important decision! I long for the sympathy of a noble soul!"

"I know not, my child, with what grief this hour may be laden for you; but I lay my hand again upon your head, imploring God in His divine mercy to sustain you!"

"Countess von Moltke and Frau von Morien!" announced the usher. In brilliant toilets the ladies rustled in, hastening toward the baroness, who had now regained her wonted composure, and received them in her usual stately manner.

"How perfectly charming you look to-night!" cried Countess Moltke. "To me you are ever the impersonation of the goddess of wealth and beauty strewing everywhere with lavish generosity your gifts, and turning every thing to gold with your touch."

"But whose heart has remained tender and gentle," added Frau von Morien.—"You are indeed a goddess, always enhancing the pleasures of others. To-day I wear the beautiful bracelet which you sent me because I admired it."

"And I, ma toute belle," cried the countess, "have adorned myself with this superb gold brocade which you so kindly had sent from Paris for me."

"You have forgotten, countess, that you begged of me to give the order for you."

"Ah, that is true! Then I am your debtor."

"If you are not too proud to receive it as a present?"

"Oh, most certainly not; on the contrary, I thank you, my dear.—Tell me, my dear Morien, is not this woman an angel?"

At this instant the French ambassador, Marquis Treves, appeared among the numerous guests, whom the baroness stepped quickly forward to welcome, withdrawing with him into the window-niche.

"Welcome, marquis," she said, quickly, in a low voice, "Have you brought me the promised papers?"

Drawing a sealed packet from his coat-pocket, he handed it to the baroness with a low bow, saying: "I would draw your attention to the fact once more, dear madam, that I have abided by the price named by yourself, in making this sale, although I am still of the opinion that it is below its value."

"The sum is sufficient for my wants, and I rated its value according as it is taxed."

"There are a hundred thousand dollars in bills of exchange, payable at the French embassy at any moment," said the marquis.

"I thank you, sir, for this proof of friendly attention; and as it may be the last time we meet, I would assure you that I shall always remember your many and thoughtful kindnesses."

"You speak, baroness, as if you would forsake the circle of which you are the brightest ornament."

"No, the friends will forsake me," she replied, with a peculiar smile. "Ere an hour shall pass not one of all these numerous guests will remain here.—Ah, there comes the decision! See there, marquis!"

The usher announced "Banker Splittgerber." The old man entered followed by two men of not very presentable appearance, and whose toilet was but little in keeping with the brilliantly-decorated room and the aristocratic guests.

Never heeding the sneers nor contemptuous smiles, the faithful bookkeeper wound his way, through the crowd of elegantly dressed ladies and gentlemen, accompanied by the two men, up to Ebenstreit, who, with instinctive politeness, had placed himself near Marie.

"Gentlemen," said Splittgerber, in a loud voice, "this is Baron Ebenstreit von Leuthen, principal of the banking-house Ludwig."

The two gentlemen approached, one of them saying, "They sent us here from your office."

"This is not the place for business," replied Ebenstreit. "Follow me!"

"No, gentlemen, remain here," cried Marie. "Our guests present are such intimate, devoted friends that we have nothing to conceal from them; but on the contrary, I am convinced they will only be too happy of the occasion to prove their friendship, of which they have so often assured us.—These gentlemen demand the payment of a bill of exchange for eighty thousand dollars. Take my portfolio, Ebenstreit; there is a pencil in it. Go around and make a collection; undoubtedly the entire sum will be soon noted down."

Ebenstreit approached the Baron von Frankenstein, saying: "Pardon me if I recall to your memory the sum of one thousand louis d'ors, due for four black horses three months since."

"My dear sir," cried the baron, "this is a strange manner to collect one's debts. We were invited to a feast, and a pistol is pointed at us, demanding our debts to be cancelled!"

"How strange! How ridiculous!" heard one here and there among the guests, as they, with one accord, pressed toward the door to make their exit, which they found fastened.

"Remain," cried Marie, with stately dignity. "I wish you honored guests to be witness of this scene in the hour of justification, as you were also present at the one when one of the noblest and best of men cursed me.—Banker Splittgerber, take these bills of exchange for one hundred thousand dollars. Pay these gentlemen, and devote the remainder to the other debts as far as it will go."

As the three men withdrew by a side-drier, Marie exclaimed: "I will now explain to you that Baron von Leuthen is ruined—poor as a beggar when he will not work."

"Marie," cried Ebenstreit, terrified, rushing toward her, and seizing her by the arm. "Marie—"

She threw off his hand from her in anger. "Do not touch me, sir, and do not presume either to address me with any endearments. You have yourself said that our marriage was not a veritable one, but was like the union of associates in business, and now I would inform you it is dissolved: the one is a bankrupt; the other a woman whom you cursed, and who reclaims of you four years of shame and degradation. You wonder at my speaking thus, but you do not know this man, my friends."

As she spoke, a door opened at the farther end of the room, and Trude entered in her simple dress, followed by Philip Moritz. Unobserved the two glided behind the charming grotto which had been arranged with flowers and wreaths in one of the niches. Every eye was turned upon the pale, stately beauty, erect in the centre of the room.

"Stay here, for no one can see us," whispered Trude. "I could not bear to have you leave Berlin without hearing the justification of my dear Marie, and may God pardon me for letting you come here unbeknown to her! Listen, and pray to Him to forgive you the great injustice that you have done her. Be quiet, that no one may see you, and Marie be angry with her old Trude."

"Yes," continued Marie, with chilling contempt, "you should know this man before whom you have all bowed, pressed the hand, and called your friend, because he was rich, and, thanks to his wealth alone, became a titled man—a baron, buying the hand of a poor but noble maiden, whom he knew despised him, and passionately loved another, having sworn eternal constancy to him. I am that young girl. I begged, nay implored him, not to pursue me, but he was void of pity, mocked my tears, and said he could buy my love, and my heart would at last be touched by the influence of his wealth. I should have preferred to die, but Fate ordered that the one I loved, by my fault, should by imprisonment atone our brief dream of bliss. I could only save him by accepting this man; these were the conditions. I became his wife before the world, and took my oath in his presence to revenge myself, and after four years I shall accomplish it. I have spent his money, and of the rich man made a beggar. God be praised, I can now revenge myself in freeing myself!"

"Free yourself? It is not true! You are my wife still," replied Ebenstreit, alarmed.

A radiant smile flitted over Marie's face as she defied Ebenstreit with the law of the Great Frederick, who had decided that every unhappy couple without offspring could separate by their own free will and consent, having signed a paper to that effect.

"Is that the paper which you have made me sign?" cried Ebenstreit, alarmed.

"Yes, drawn up by my notary, and both of our names are signed to it."

"It is a fraud!" cried Ebenstreit. "I will protest against it."

"Do it, and you will find it a vain effort. I promised to pay your debt if you would put your name to the document then placed before you, which you did. Ask the Marquis Treves how I paid your debts: he will answer you that he has given me the money."

"I had the honor to pay to the baroness one hundred thousand dollars, as she rightly informs you."

"Yes," continued Marie, "the marquis is the present possessor of this house and all that it contains—furniture, statues, and pictures; also the equipages and silver. To my mother I sent my diamonds, costly laces, and dresses, to indemnify her for the annuity which Herr von Ebenstreit settled upon her as purchase-money which he cannot pay, now that he is ruined."

"Marquis," cried Ebenstreit, pale with anger, "have you really bought this house and its contents?"

"I have done so, and the one hundred thousand dollars the baroness has paid over to Herr Splittgerber."

"Oh! I am ruined," groaned Ebenstreit—"I am lost!" and, covering his face with his hands, he rushed from the room.

Marie gazed at him with a sad expression, saying: "Ladies and gentlemen, you now know to whom this house belongs. You can no longer say that I am the daughter whom the late General von Leuthen sold to a rich man. I am free!"

At this moment a side-door opened, and Frau von Leuthen was heard saying to old Trude: "Let me in! it is in vain to hold me back. I will have an explanation from my daughter, and learn what all this means." As she pushed herself into the room, she exclaimed: "Ah, it is a fete day! There is the baroness in all her glory and splendor. She is not crazed, as I feared this morning, when she sent me all her ornaments and fine dresses and laces, with a note, sealed with black, inscribed upon it, 'Will Of the Baroness Ebenstreit von Leuthen.' I opened it, and read: 'I give to my mother my precious ornaments, laces, and dresses, to secure to her the pension which she has lost.—Marie. 'I came here to learn if my daughter were dead, and what the conclusion of this lost pension may be, and I find—"

"You find the confirmation of all that I wrote to you," replied Marie, coldly. "Baron Ebenstreit von Leuthen is ruined. I have secured to you, in the sum which my jewels and laces will bring you, the annuity, so that you have not lost the money promised you for your daughter, and the marriage you have arranged has at least borne good fruit to you."

"You are a cruel, ungrateful child," cried the mother. "I have long known it, and rejected you from my heart, and from all shame I will yet protect the name you bear. I have just seen a sign in the Friedrich-strasse, 'Flower manufactory of Marie von Leuthen.' What does this mean? Terrified, I stared speechless at these fearful words, and at the busy workmen preparing the house."

"I will explain it to you," cried Marie, with radiant mien. "I have again become the flower-maker, and beg your favor, Countess von Moltke, Frau von Morien, and all the other ladies. I am free, and no longer the wife of a hated husband—no longer the distinguished and wealthy woman. All delusion and mockery have vanished. The costly dress and jewels that I now wear I will cast of from me as the last souvenir of the past."

Unclasping the diamond necklace and bracelets, she handed them to her mother, saying: "Take them, and also this dress, the last finery I possess." She unloosed the band, and the long white satin train fell at her feet. Emerging from it as from a silvery cloud, she stood before them in a simple white dress, as she was clothed in her girlhood. "Take them all," she joyfully cried. "Take them, mother, it is all past. I am now myself again. Farewell, witnesses of this scene! I now quit your circle; and you, my mother, I forgive you; may the thoughts of your unhappy child never trouble you, waking or sleeping; may you forget that your daughter lives, and is wretched. Revenge has not softened my grief, or removed your curse from my head!"

"I will lift it off your brow, Marie!" cried Moritz, suddenly appearing from the window-niche, with beaming face and outstretched arms, approaching Marie, whom surprised and alarmed, retreated. "Oh, noble, courageous woman, forgive me that I have been an unbidden witness to this scene, though by this means I now clearly recognize your strength of mind, and elevation of soul, and the wrong that I have committed in doubting and cursing you during these four years of gloom and despair. I bow before you, Marie, and implore you, upon my knees, to forgive me all the cruel, harsh words that I have uttered—that I have dared as a wretched fool to doubt you in this long night of despair. The day is dawning again upon us; a new sun will yet cheer us with its rays. Do not turn from me, but look at me, and grant me forgiveness.—My dear friend and father, speak for me, for you know what I have suffered. Beg of her to forgive me."

"Marie," said the venerable old man, approaching her, gently putting his arm around her, "God has willed that you, my poor, long-tried child, should pass through a season of extreme sorrow. You are now released, and all that belonged to you has vanished!"

As he spoke, he signed to the guests to withdraw. Many had already escaped the painful scene by the side-door. Marie was now alone in the magnificent apartment, with Herr Gedicke and Moritz. She still stood, with concealed face, in the centre of the room.

"Oh, Marie," implored Moritz, "hide not your dear face from me! Read in mine the deep grief of the past and the bliss of the future. I thank God that this unnatural union is severed, and that you are free. Be courageous to the end!" Moritz impetuously drew her hand away, revealing her tearful countenance, as her head sank upon his shoulder. "Can you not forgive me, Marie?" he cried, with deep emotion. "We have both wandered through a waste of grief, and now approach life radiant with happiness. Oh, speak to me, Marie; can you not love me and forgive me?"

She gazed into his eyes, and in their depths read that which gradually softened her hardened features, and caused a smile to play upon her lip. "I love you dearly, devotedly; let this be our parting word. Go forth into the world, Moritz; my affection will follow you whithersoever you wander, and my soul will be true to you through all eternity, though we are forever separated. The poor wife, with her dismal retrospections, must not cast a shadow upon your future. Go, my beloved—Italy awaits you, and art will console you!"

"Follow me, dear Marie; only by your side am I happy. You are free and independent," cried Moritz.

"Oh, father," cried Marie, leaning upon the venerable old man, "explain to him that I am still the wife of that hated man!"

"She is right, Philip; do not urge her further. She must first be legally separated, and this weary heart must have time to recover its wonted calm. Go to Italy, and confide your future and happiness to my care. Marie has lost a mother, but she shall find a father in me. I will watch over her until your return."

Just then the door opened, and Trude entered. "Every thing is ready; all the things which used to stand in the little garret-room are packed and sent to the manufactory. Shall we go, too, dear child?"

"Yes," she cried, embracing the faithful old woman. "Farewell, Philip—Italy calls you!"

"I will go, but when I return will you not be my wife?"

Marie gazed at Moritz, radiant with happiness, saying: "The answer is engraven upon my heart. Return, and then I will joyfully respond to your love before God and man!"